BOOK ONE OF THE NIGERIAN COWBOY SERIES

NIGERIAN COWBOY

A NOVEL

BY

DR. EMMANUEL X. OKORO

Published by Hemingway Publishers

Cover design by Hemingway Publishers

ISBN: Printed in the United States

DEDICATION

First and foremost, I am grateful to God, whose grace, favor, and courage enabled me to overcome procrastination and take determined steps. To God be the glory.

Special thanks to Freddie Tatum and family, Margaret's Hardwick, Ray and Louann Larson and their family, and the McCullough family—thank you.

To my lovely wife and children, your unwavering love, support, and encouragement have been my anchor throughout this journey. Your belief in me, even in moments of doubt, continues to inspire every word of this book. This one is for you.

Author's Note

Writing *Nigerian Cowboy* has been a deeply personal journey for me. As a U.S. citizen of Nigerian origin, I've often wrestled with themes of identity and belonging. This story became a way of exploring those struggles through the lens of a cowboy's journey.

Jacob's story is not just about survival; it's about embracing who you are, where you come from, and the faith that carries you through the darkest times.

—Dr. Emmanuel X. Okoro

AUTHOR'S REFLECTIONS

Selected Quotes from the Published Works of Dr. Emmanuel X. Okoro

Nigerian Cowboy

Theme: Identity, Redemption, Courage, Culture

"I am a cowboy—a Nigerian cowboy. And I don't ride just for rodeos. I ride for redemption."

"You don't need to erase your roots to stand tall in new soil. Sometimes, it's your roots that give you the strength to ride."

"Even when the world told him he didn't belong, he carved out a space with faith, grit, and an untamed dream."

"Stories can heal, awaken, and empower. I write for the soul."

"Courage is when you write anyway—even when the world tells you not to."

Acknowledgments

First, I thank God, whose strength and wisdom guided me through every step of this journey. Without His grace, this book would not have been possible.

To my family—your love, patience, and belief in me have been my rock. To my wife and children: thank you for your constant encouragement and for being my foundation.

I am deeply grateful to Freddie Tatum and his family for their generosity and support. Your kindness has meant the world to me.

Special thanks to Margaret Hardwick, Ray and Louann Larson and their family, and the McCullough family—thank you for believing in both me and this project from the beginning.

To my editor, Hemingway Publisher and Michael Kirby—your expertise and care shaped this book into what it is today. I appreciate your dedication.

And finally, to everyone who walked beside me, offered feedback, and lifted me in prayer—your support carried me through every challenge. This book belongs as much to you as it does to me.

Table of Contents

Page left blank intentionally

Chapter 1
The Dreamer's Beginning

The Boy with Big Dreams

Jacob Obi stared up at the sky, his heart racing as if it were chasing wild stallions he had only seen on TV. He wasn't merely dreaming—he was *yearning*. Beneath the shade of a sprawling mango tree, he lay quietly on the cool earth, lost in a world he imagined—one where cowboys ruled the land, wore wide-brimmed hats, and rode across endless plains. The wind brushed his face, a faint echo of the freedom he longed for.

The world around him was far from the one in his mind. His family's house, nestled in the heart of their Nigerian village, carried the scent of freshly plowed soil, smoke drifting from his father's small chapel, and the constant bustle of his mother selling produce at the local market. But none of it matched the vision Jacob carried in his heart. To him, the sound of galloping hooves and the sight of cowboys lassoing wild cattle was more than fantasy—it was truth.

The Laughing Village

Jacob had shared his dream with anyone who would listen, but no one took him seriously. To them, his desire to become a cowboy was just a boyhood fantasy—a source of amusement to be quickly dismissed.

"Jacob," his cousin Bayo would tease, his voice thick with mockery, "you're going to ride what? A donkey? We don't even have horses here!"

The other boys in the village would burst into laughter, mimicking his every move. They swaggered with exaggerated steps, pretending to hold imaginary ropes, imitating what they thought a cowboy should look like.

"Is this how you look on horseback? Too bad your dream is stuck on the ground, boy!"

Jacob would laugh along, but inside, it stung. The dream was real to him, even if it seemed like a joke to everyone else. Was he crazy? At times, he wondered if his dream would fade, like the childhood toys and comic books he had already outgrown. But deep down, he knew better.

I'll show them one day, he thought, clenching his fist. *I'll show them what a Nigerian cowboy can do.*

The Pastor's Son

Jacob's father, Pastor Obi, was a stern man—a pillar of the village. Every Sunday, his voice boomed from the pulpit, filling the small church across the dirt road from their house. His mother, Rhoda, was equally hardworking. She ran a small farm and sold vegetables at the market, supporting the family with grit and grace. Their lives were rooted in faith, community, and the values of hard work.

But Jacob felt torn between his family's expectations and his own dreams. His father hoped he would follow in his footsteps to take over the church. His mother wanted him to help with the farm. But Jacob's heart wasn't in farming or preaching. He wanted more. He wanted to be a cowboy.

One evening, after dinner, Pastor Obi sat Jacob down on the porch.

"Jacob," he said, his voice soft but firm, "you are the eldest son. You will help me with the church. This is the family calling."

Jacob nodded stiffly, his thoughts drifting far away. Cowboys riding across vast, open fields blurred the stern gaze of his father.

"Yes, Papa," he muttered. The words felt foreign on his tongue.

Rhoda, watching from the doorway, gave Jacob a gentle, knowing smile.

"One day, you'll find your own path, Jacob. But remember—it's not about chasing dreams that don't feed the family. You must help your father provide."

Jacob looked away, his heart wild and untamed, like the horses he had only seen on television. It was already far from home, galloping toward a world where cowboys reigned.

The Spark of a Dream

At thirteen, Jacob's dream suddenly felt closer than ever. The school bulletin board posted an announcement that made his pulse race: a scholarship opportunity to study abroad in America. In Texas. The land of cowboys.

"Studying abroad? In America?" Jacob whispered, his breath catching in his throat. His heart pounded like hooves thundering across open plains.

He read the fine print again, barely believing his eyes. *Texas*— where cowboys roamed free, and every sunset stretched across endless skies.

This was it. His chance.

Excitement burned within him. The dream, once a distant fantasy, was now within reach. He could almost feel the sun on his face, reins gripped in his hands, the wind sweeping across wide-open spaces.

This was no longer just a dream. It was a possibility.

The Countdown Begins

The days crawled by—too slow and too fast—like time caught between two worlds. Jacob counted down the weeks, the hours, and the minutes until the interview. He hoped. He prayed. He dreamed.

Two months. It felt like a lifetime.

Soon, everything he had ever known—the village, his family, the life they had planned for him—might be left behind. Ahead lay a world he could only imagine.

Texas.

The land of cowboys.

Each evening, Jacob walked the dusty dirt roads, his thoughts miles away. His eyes shone with quiet determination.

"I'll finally be there," he whispered, the words barely audible. "I'll finally be where cowboys belong."

CHAPTER 2
A SUNDAY SERVICE AT THE OBI FAMILY CHURCH

The Final Praise Before the Journey

Jacob stood by his window, watching the early morning light spill across the horizon like watercolor. His heart fluttered—uneasy, expectant. Texas was just days away. But today was sacred: his final Sunday service with the people who raised him.

The Obi family compound stirred with life. Roosters crowed in the distance. The crisp air carried the earthy scent of dew, charcoal smoke, and simmering tomato stew. The promise of a new day, wrapped in the rhythm of tradition.

From the church hall came the vibrant pulse of pre-service praise— drums rolling, hands clapping, voices soaring like birds into the sky. The music wrapped around Jacob like a warm, familiar shawl. The church hadn't even started, yet worship had already ignited. That was Nigeria: loud, alive, and steeped in spirit.

He stepped into the courtyard, and the wave of community energy met him like a current. It pulsed through him—the laughter, the colors, the joy. Every step toward the church hall felt like a step away from the world he knew and toward one unknown.

Inside the Church

The sanctuary pulsed with life. Music pounded. Arms lifted. Voices harmonized in unrestrained celebration. It was sacred chaos—reverent, raw, and electric. The scent of incense mingled with the tantalizing aroma of jollof rice and fried plantains wafting from the church kitchen, where preparations for the after-service feast were already underway.

"Jacob!" his mother called sharply, her voice cutting through the noise like a bell.

She stood near the front, regal in a shimmering red lace dress. Her hands were raised, her eyes shut in worship, but still—she saw him. She always did.

Jacob chuckled under his breath. Mama could be lost in the Spirit and still notice if your shoes were not polished.

He eased into the crowd. Mama Chigozie, the praise leader, stood at the altar like a firebrand. Her silver headwrap sparkled as she belted worship with a voice that could shake mountains. Her presence drew people in, urging them to dance harder, sing louder, and believe deeper.

"Lift your hands to the Lord!" she commanded.

The room obeyed. Arms rose. Hearts opened. Even Jacob's foot tapped without permission. In the front row, Uncle Tunde looked moments away from levitating. Hands stretched so high. Auntie Ngozi danced with such fervor her shawl flew off, smacking a startled usher in the face.

Jacob grinned. "There goes Auntie Ngozi. She hasn't breathed in five minutes."

Around him, the room shimmered with life—Ankara prints swirling, agbadas fluttering, children spinning in dizzy joy. His younger sister, Ifeoma, twirled beside him, radiant in a yellow dress.

"Jacob, you're not dancing!" she teased, tugging his sleeve.

He hesitated. Texas tugged at his thoughts, the unknown world whispering at the edge of his spirit.

"Not today, Ifeoma," he replied with a soft grin. "I'll be dancing in Texas soon enough."

She rolled her eyes and kept dancing; the symphony of joy swallowed her laughter.

The music climbed higher, crescendoing into something beyond sound—something spiritual. It held all of it: joy, longing, pride, fear, faith. Jacob closed his eyes, breathing it in. At that moment, he wasn't the boy leaving. He was just *Jacob*—a son, a brother, a worshipper.

Then, the music softened like the tide receding.

Mama Chigozie lifted her hand. Stillness followed.

Pastor Isaac, Jacob's father, stepped forward. Tall, composed, his voice deep and sure.

"My dear family," he began, eyes sweeping the room, "Today we give thanks not just for another Sunday but for a new beginning. Our son, Jacob, is preparing to journey abroad for further studies. Let us bless him."

Silence settled. Jacob bowed his head. As his father prayed, he felt the weight of everything—love, hope, unspoken fears. Hands reached toward him. Voices whispered blessings. "Amen." "God, go with you." "We cover you in Jesus' name."

And yet, even as the prayer echoed, Jacob's mind wandered. Would Texas accept him? Would he be enough?

When the music returned, something had shifted.

This time, Jacob didn't resist. His feet moved. His body swayed. He raised his hands.

He laughed. He danced. He worshipped without holding back.

For the first time that day, he wasn't the boy saying goodbye.

He was the boy becoming.

The Countdown: The Night Before the Journey

Evening settled with gentle grace. Laughter echoed from the dinner table as the Obi family shared stories, advice, and more than one helping of fried fish.

But by midnight, the house had gone quiet.

Jacob lay awake, staring at the ceiling. His suitcase stood zipped. Passport ready. Sleep had long fled.

He sat up and dressed in white T-shirt, snug jeans. Then, the crown: a brand-new cowboy hat.

He placed it on his head, adjusting the angle in the mirror.

"Yeah," he whispered, smiling. "Texas, here I come."

In his mind, the plains stretched wide—ranch gates, dusty roads, and southern drawls.

But doubts lingered. Would they laugh at his accent? Would they call him a joke?

A soft creak in the hallway broke his thoughts.

His mother appeared, wrapped in her night wrapper, her hair tied back. She froze in the doorway.

"Jacob," she whispered, half-asleep. "What... what are you wearing?"

He turned slowly, the hat still perched with pride.

"I'm going to Texas, Mama. Figured I should look the part."

Her eyes widened.

"Look what part? You look like a Nollywood cowboy auditioning for *Who Wants to Be a Texan!*"

He shrugged. "I'm just blending in early."

Footsteps approached. His younger brother peeked in, chuckling. Their father followed, raising an eyebrow like a disapproving judge.

His mother folded her arms.

"Jacob. Go and change. *Now.*"

He sighed and disappeared into the closet. Moments later, he returned with a button-down shirt, khakis, and no hat.

His mother adjusted his collar gently. "Now, that's my son."

Jacob nodded, stealing one last glance at the hat lying on the bed.

Soon.

As they gathered their things and made their way toward the airport, Jacob carried the hat under his arm.

His next chapter waited—wide skies, wild dreams, and a path that would test everything he thought he knew.

But for now, he walked forward with his family, heart full of praise, and a cowboy hat in hand.

CHAPTER 3
WELCOME TO TEXAS

A Sky Full of Promise

Jacob squinted out the airplane window, his heart racing with excitement. Below, Texas unfolded like a grand painting—vast plains, patches of green, and golden fields stretching to the horizon. In his mind, the scene looked straight out of a Western movie: a lone cowboy galloping across open land, tumbleweeds rolling past, dramatic music swelling in the background.

Then the wheels hit the tarmac—and so did reality.

The Texas Airport That Wasn't a Western Movie

As the plane taxied to the gate, Jacob half-hoped for a glimpse of cowboy life. Maybe a few boots, wide-brimmed hats—something to set the tone for his big arrival.

But no such luck.

The terminal buzzed with modern travelers—phones glued to their hands, earbuds in, no cowboy hats in sight. Not even a pair of spurred boots.

"Where's the cowboy vibe?" Jacob muttered, scanning the crowd.

Chuka, his training buddy, already had his bag slung over one shoulder. "What, you thought we were landing in *Tombstone*? There are cowboys here, man... just mostly standing in line at Starbucks."

Jacob squinted again, hoping for a John Wayne lookalike. All he saw was a man in a suit, briefcase in one hand, scrolling through his phone with the other.

Disappointment settled in like a flat tire.

Chuka nudged him. "Relax. We're in Texas. Just not the Hollywood version. Wait till you meet Hank—he'll bring your cowboy dreams to life."

"I thought I signed up for the Wild West," Jacob muttered, "not overpriced coffee and people in yoga pants."

The Ride That Wasn't a Horse

They moved toward the baggage claim. With every step, the situation felt more real. No saloons. No shootouts. Just luggage, neon signs, and the faint hum of escalators.

Chuka clapped him on the back. "Let me guess—you thought you'd be riding horseback by now?"

Jacob sighed. "I was hoping for at least a horse-drawn carriage. Or a cowboy with a lasso."

Chuka laughed. "Keep dreaming. Right now, we've got an old truck, a dusty ranch, and a whole lot of work ahead. Come on, cowboy. Let's get you broken in before you start expecting a showdown at sundown."

Outside, the Texas sun hit Jacob like a wall of heat. He squinted, adjusting his imaginary spurs, trying to summon his inner Clint Eastwood.

The truck they climbed into was as old as the jokes Chuka told. It groaned with every bump in the road. Chuka cranked up the AC as they rumbled toward the ranch.

Jacob stared out the window, hoping for cacti—maybe even a ghost town. Instead, there were fields, fence posts, and the occasional windmill spinning lazily in the hot breeze.

The Cowpoke's First Lesson: Shovel Duty

"So," Jacob ventured, adjusting the cowboy hat he'd bought at the airport gift shop, "do we, like... rope cattle or wrestle bulls or something?"

Chuka chuckled. "Maybe later, partner. First, you've got to prove you can shovel manure without complaining. Then we'll talk about bulls. Welcome to the glamorous life of a real cowboy."

Jacob groaned. "Nothing says 'dream job' like shoveling poop."

"Hey," Chuka teased, "this is just your initiation. After that, we move on to the real stuff. And by 'real,' I mean 'still involves poop.'"

They pulled up to a tired-looking barn surrounded by even more tired-looking horses. Hank, the ranch owner, leaned on a shovel, grinning like he'd seen every wannabe cowboy in the book.

Jacob stepped out into the heat and extended a hand. "Hey, I'm Jacob. I guess I'm here to learn what it means to be a cowboy."

Hank sized him up—boots to hat, city-boy charm and all.

"You're gonna need more than a handshake, son," Hank said, voice gruff but not unkind. "You'll need boots, a shovel, and a whole lot of patience."

Jacob nodded, still unsure what he'd gotten himself into.

Manure Mountain: Jacob's Rite of Passage

Hank tossed him a shovel and pointed to a mountain of manure that looked like it had been growing since the Alamo.

"First lesson: chores. If you can't handle this, you're not cut out for the cowboy life."

Jacob stared, horrified. "You want me to shovel *that*?"

"Yup," Hank said with a grin. "All cowboys start here. Shovel first. Ride later. You earn your saddle, son."

Chuka lounged on the porch, trying not to laugh. "Don't worry, man. We all start somewhere. You've got to shovel the dream before you can ride into it."

With a sigh worthy of an Oscar nomination, Jacob grabbed the shovel and got to work. His movements were stiff and exaggerated—part slow-motion montage, part slapstick comedy.

A Cowboy's First Victory

Sweat dripped down his back. The sun beat down with unforgiving intensity. This wasn't the fantasy. It wasn't even the bootleg version of the fantasy.

After what felt like hours, Hank wandered over and clapped a calloused hand on Jacob's back.

"Not bad, city boy. I bet you didn't know the first thing about horse manure when you landed."

Jacob wiped his brow. "You got that right. I thought cowboy life meant hats, horses, and dramatic standoffs—not... this."

Hank laughed. "That's Hollywood. This here? This is the real deal. And every real cowboy starts in the dirt."

Jacob nodded, a small grin creeping up his face. "I guess I can't argue with that."

From the porch, Chuka cupped his hands and shouted, "Hey, look at that! The new guy's making friends with the manure! At this rate, you'll be a ranch hand by next week!"

Jacob grinned, shovel in hand. "Don't get too comfortable. I'm coming for that saddle."

CHAPTER 4
THE WILD RIDE

City Feet, Country Roads

The sun crept over the horizon, spilling golden light across the sprawling ranch like honey on toast. A new day had arrived, and Jacob was already struggling to find his balance, quite literally. He stood next to a large brown horse named Sally, trying to ignore the anxiety gnawing at his stomach.

Jacob wasn't exactly what you'd call "country." He'd grown up in the city, where life revolved around late-night study sessions, cafeteria food, and cramming for exams. He was a college student, not a cowboy. Still, here he was, staring down a horse the size of a small building with a ridiculous sense of determination.

He reached up, brushed the hair out of his eyes, and shot a sideways glance at Chuka, who was already striding toward his horse with the ease of someone born with a saddle attached to their back.

"Ready for the ride, college boy?" Chuka grinned, the mischievous glint in his eyes making Jacob's stomach churn a little more.

Jacob tried to smile back, but it probably looked more like a grimace. "Yeah. I mean, it's just like riding a bike, right?" His voice wavered a little too much for someone trying to act cool. *Just like a bike. Except it's alive. And potentially a little pissed off.*

"Uh-huh," Chuka said, clearly enjoying the inner turmoil Jacob was battling. "Except your bike has a mind of its own and doesn't care if you fall off."

Jacob couldn't help but laugh nervously. "Oh, great."

The Calm Before the Tumble

Chuka had already mounted his horse and was glancing over at Jacob with a look that seemed to say, *You're gonna regret this.* But Jacob was determined. He had survived finals, 3 a.m. coffee binges, and group projects with people who didn't do their fair share. Surely, this couldn't be that bad.

Sally snorted and pawed at the ground, her gaze fixed on Jacob with a look that seemed to say, *I dare you.*

Jacob let out a deep breath and swung a leg over the saddle. His foot barely made it into the stirrup, but after some awkward flailing, he finally managed to get seated. The horse's movements were smooth at first—almost as if she were waiting for him to make the first mistake.

"Look at you, all official and stuff," Chuka said, a smirk playing on his lips. "You're practically a cowboy already."

"Yeah, just need a hat and some boots, and I'm good to go." Jacob grinned, though his mind raced. *Please don't fall. Not in front of Chuka. Not in front of Sally. Not in front of God and the cows.*

"Keep the reins steady," Chuka added, chuckling. "And try not to look like you've never seen a horse before."

"I mean, I've seen them in books," Jacob shot back. "Does that count?"

"You're gonna need more than that," Chuka said, and with a quick click of his tongue, his horse trotted off.

Jacob, who hadn't yet figured out how to get Sally to move, gave a little kick to her side.

Sally stared at him for a moment as if contemplating whether it was worth it to move. Then, with a sudden burst of speed, she shot forward.

Jacob wasn't ready for it.

The Great Fall

"Whoa, whoa, WHOA!" Jacob yelped, gripping the reins for dear life. But Sally was already in full motion, her hooves pounding the earth beneath her, her mane flying behind like a banner. Jacob had tried to prepare by memorizing horse-riding techniques from Wikipedia, but now he realized none of it had prepared him for the sheer power of an animal that could run faster than his brain could process.

In the next instant, he was airborne.

In slow motion, Jacob's life flashed before his eyes—not the meaningful parts, but the awkward ones: college classes, midnight pizza runs, and that one spectacular faceplant in front of the entire freshman class.

And then, with all the grace of a fallen leaf, Jacob landed in a massive pile of hay.

He groaned, face down in the soft bedding. The smell of straw filled his nose, and he couldn't decide if he was relieved or embarrassed.

Chuka's laughter echoed across the ranch. "Nice dismount, cowboy!"

Jacob picked himself up, brushing hay from his clothes. His pride was more battered than his body, but he wasn't about to let Chuka have the last laugh. "I meant to do that," he said, dusting off his jeans with exaggerated effort. "Just testing the landing technique."

"Yeah, looks like you're a natural at falling," Chuka teased, still holding his stomach from laughing.

Jacob shot him a look. "Alright, alright. I'll admit that didn't go exactly according to plan."

Sally, who had been quietly watching the spectacle, snorted as if she were some judgmental aunt. She probably had more dignity in her hoof than Jacob had in his entire body.

Getting Back in the Saddle

But Jacob wasn't done. He stood up, wiping the dust off his pants, and gave Sally an exaggerated pat on the side. "Alright, let's try this again. You and me, kid. We're a team now."

Chuka raised an eyebrow. "Yeah? Because the horse didn't seem too impressed with you as its partner."

"I think we just need some bonding time," Jacob said, grabbing the reins again. "It's cool. We'll work through our issues." He sounded like he was trying to convince himself more than anyone else.

With a deep breath, he swung back into the saddle, this time with a little more focus. Sally snorted but didn't try to buck him off again. Instead, they started trotting at a slower pace, with Jacob keeping his grip steady on the reins. For a few moments, he thought he might just pull this off.

And then, out of nowhere, Sally suddenly turned left without warning.

"Whoa! What the—!" Jacob yelped, gripping the reins with both hands, his whole body leaning to the right to compensate for the unexpected move.

"Looks like Sally's got her idea of fun," Chuka called back, riding ahead with ease. "Don't worry, you're doing great!"

Jacob's voice was a mixture of disbelief and sarcasm. "Great? I'm basically a glorified crash test dummy right now. Look at me—I'm a wreck."

But, somehow, he was starting to get the hang of it. Slowly but surely, he began to feel the rhythm of the horse's movements. It wasn't the smooth, effortless ride he had imagined, but it was progress. And that, at least, was something.

Sally's pace began to settle, and Jacob let out a breath of relief. He wasn't entirely sure he had control yet, but for now, he was staying upright. Maybe this cowboy thing wasn't going to be so impossible after all.

A Cowboy in the Making

As they rode through the fields, with Chuka offering a few more pointers, Jacob couldn't help but smile. The wind was in his face, the sun warming his back, and the world felt oddly peaceful. Sure, he had a few bruises, and his pride had taken a hit, but there was something undeniably thrilling about this.

"Not bad for a city boy," Chuka said, throwing him a thumbs-up. "You'll be riding like a pro in no time."

Jacob shot him a grin. "Just wait 'til I start roping cattle."

Chuka's eyes widened with mock horror. "You can rope cattle when you can stay on a horse for more than ten minutes without falling off!"

Jacob gave Sally a little pat. "I'm getting there," he said, straightening in the saddle. "One very bumpy, slightly heroic step at a time."

CHAPTER 5
"A HORSE IS A HORSE, OF COURSE"

The Dawn of a New Day on the Ranch

The sun was just beginning to peek over the horizon, casting a soft golden glow across the sprawling ranch. Jacob squinted, his eyes adjusting to the vastness of it all. Morning dew clung to the grass, and a light breeze carried the fresh scent of wildflowers, blending with the earthy aroma of hay and horses. The air was rich with the smell of damp earth, freshly cut hay, and the faint trace of leather saddles. The gentle sound of horse hooves clicking on hard-packed dirt reached Jacob's ears as the serenity of the morning settled over the ranch.

He'd never considered the smell of hay as "fresh" before, but here it was—one of those small things slowly becoming familiar.

Standing at the edge of the stable, Jacob let the wind brush against his face. The world he had left behind—the comfort of his books and the hum of his university dorm—felt miles away. Yet, in this wide, open space, there was a pull he hadn't expected. It was as if the ranch was calling him to slow down, to let go of the rush and find purpose in the simplicity of each moment.

There was something oddly peaceful about it—the slow rhythm of life here, far removed from city traffic and the glow of fluorescent lights. Still, he couldn't shake the feeling that ranching was a million miles from his world of textbooks and caffeine-fueled all-nighters. He smiled to himself, thinking maybe his new life could use a little less caffeine... and a lot more horse sense.

Chuka's Challenge

"Ready to get back to it, city boy?"

Chuka's voice pulled Jacob from his thoughts. He turned to see his friend leaning against the fence, arms crossed, a grin tugging at his lips.

Jacob sighed dramatically. "If you mean 'ready to fail miserably again,' then yeah, I'm totally ready."

Chuka chuckled, pushing off the fence. "Don't worry. You'll get it. Eventually, but first, we're taking it easy today. No lassoing cattle, no jumping on wild horses. Today's about getting back on the horse. Literally."

Jacob raised an eyebrow. "You mean the horse that tried to throw me into the fence yesterday?"

Chuka's grin widened. "Exactly. That's the one. She's got character."

The horse in question—a sleek brown mare with a sassy air—tossed her mane as if in response. Jacob took a cautious step forward, eyeing the animal with a mix of wariness and resolve.

Chuka noticed and shook his head. "You're staring at her like she's got a giant 'kick me' sign on her back."

"You'd be surprised what happens when you try to ride a horse for the first time, and it decides you're better off on the ground."

"Oh, come on." Chuka walked over and patted the horse's side. "You just need to make peace with her. Talk to her. Get to know her. Like this."

He turned to the horse and, in a tone that was both absurd and somehow convincing, said, "Listen, Midnight. We're gonna have a good day, alright? No bucking, no kicking, no spitting. You be good, and I'll bring you a carrot later."

Jacob stared at him. "Did you just name-drop carrots to a horse?"

Chuka shrugged. "You'd be surprised. They like that kind of stuff."

Jacob gave him a skeptical look but said nothing. If Chuka could talk to horses, maybe he could learn to keep his legs in one piece.

The Great Horse Ride (Or Not)

The morning passed slowly, with Chuka offering occasional critiques that Jacob mostly ignored. But then came the inevitable.

"Alright, let's see what you've got," Chuka said, handing him the reins with a grin. "Time to ride Midnight."

Jacob swung his leg over the mare, trying to remember everything Chuka had told him. His first mistake? Thinking he could actually do this. Midnight snorted beneath him as if to say, *Nice try.* He clutched the reins like a lifeline, legs stiff with fear. As the horse jolted forward, he gripped tighter, praying the saddle wouldn't toss him off like a rag doll.

"Whoa!" Jacob yelped, reins slipping from his hands as the mare bolted. His legs flailed as she galloped forward, and he could hear Chuka laughing behind him.

"See? That's what happens when you talk too big!" Chuka called out.

Still half on the horse and half off, Jacob tried to steady himself. "It's not my fault! She's... she's got a mind of her own!" He couldn't help but laugh at how ridiculous he must have looked.

Eventually, Midnight slowed and came to a stop in front of Chuka, who was doubled over in laughter. Jacob, now a heap on the ground, looked up with a rueful grin.

"You really should stop laughing at me," he muttered, brushing dirt from his cheek. "I'm starting to think this whole ranching thing is just a big prank."

Chuka extended a hand to help him up. "Nope. Just the first day. And the second. And the third. Maybe the fourth. We'll see."

"Great," Jacob grumbled, taking the hand and letting Chuka pull him to his feet.

"That's the spirit!" Chuka slapped him on the back—hard enough to nearly knock him over again.

The Long Road Ahead

The rest of the day was filled with more attempts at improving Jacob's riding. Chuka was relentless, offering advice that often sounded more like teasing. But despite the bruises to his ego (and backside), Jacob was starting to get the hang of it—sort of. He was beginning to realize that maybe, just maybe, the secret to riding a horse wasn't about conquering the animal but learning to work with it. Not that he'd fully accepted that idea yet.

As the day drew to a close, the two stood once more at the edge of the stable, looking out over the horizon as the last light of day faded. The wind had picked up, and Jacob felt a deep calm settle over him. It wasn't perfect, and it sure wasn't easy, but something about this life was beginning to make sense.

"You know," Jacob said, breaking the silence, "I never thought I'd end up here. I always imagined I'd be in a library, buried in books, maybe chasing a PhD in something obscure no one cared about."

Chuka glanced at him, expression softening. "You still could. No one's stopping you. But you might find something here you never expected."

Jacob looked out across the ranch. Horses grazed in the distance. A small flock of birds took flight in the fading light.

"I think... I think I might be starting to. Just takes some getting used to."

"Trust me," Chuka said, nudging him with his elbow. "You'll fit in just fine. I'm pretty sure the horses are already getting attached to you."

Jacob snorted. "Oh, great. First, the horses, then the cows. Maybe I'll start a club."

Chuka laughed. "You're already halfway there."

As the sun dipped below the horizon, Jacob felt a quiet peace settle in his chest. Maybe this *was* where he was supposed to be—awkward moments, mishaps, and all. And as for Midnight, well... they'd get along eventually. He was sure of it.

CHAPTER 6
THE CITY SLICKER MEETS THE TOWN

Arriving in the Hustle and Bustle

The sun barely peeked over the horizon as Jacob and Chuka rolled into the heart of the bustling town. The truck rumbled to a halt outside a local shop, its engine fading into the symphony of street noises—a stark contrast to the peaceful quiet of the ranch they had just left. Jacob took a moment to process the shift. The streets were alive with movement and color; it was a different world entirely.

"Well, this is... busy," Jacob muttered, wide-eyed.

Chuka, already making his way toward the shop, flashed a grin. "You ain't seen nothin' yet, cowboy."

Jacob, adjusting his hat awkwardly, felt it was less a fashion statement and more a target for every possible mistake he was about to make.

A Shopkeeper with an Attitude

Inside the small shop, the bell above the door gave a loud, melodious *ding* as the temperature seemed to dip slightly. The camera panned over shelves crammed with trinkets, from dusty jars of pickles to a wild array of cowboy hats in every possible style.

Behind the counter, the shopkeeper stood, her gaze sharp as a hawk, sizing up Jacob and Chuka with an air of suspicion.

"Well, well, well," she drawled, raising an eyebrow. "Looks like we've got ourselves a new cowboy in town. You lost, or just lookin' for somethin' that fits?"

Jacob cleared his throat and gave a hesitant smile. "Uh, no, ma'am. Just... looking around."

She glanced at his cowboy hat, a smirk tugging at her lips. "That hat? It costs more than half my stock, hon. I'm guessing you have no idea what it's for, huh?"

Jacob, taken off guard, blinked. "Well, it keeps the sun off my face, ma'am."

The shopkeeper laughed—a surprising and contagious sound. "Sun protection? *Cowboy 101*, huh? I bet you can't even tie a decent knot."

Jacob rubbed the back of his neck nervously. "Well... I'm good at picking up hay bales, ma'am."

She stared at him, unblinking, then gave a small, knowing smile. "Sure. But let's see if you can handle a real cowboy skill. First things first—you gotta get some cans."

The Cans of Chaos

Jacob, determined to show he wasn't a complete city slicker, reached for a can of beans on the top shelf. The moment his fingers brushed the can, everything went sideways. The shelf wobbled, and in a chain reaction of disaster, cans began to tumble down in a clattering mess.

Slow-motion shot: The cans fell one by one—Jacob's face twisted in panic as he tried, futilely, to catch them. Each can bounced off the shelves and clattered to the floor in an endless cascade of metal.

"Oh no!" Jacob muttered, dodging the rolling cans. *Crash!* Another can bounced off his shoulder.

"Need some help there, cowboy?" The shopkeeper's voice oozed amusement from behind the counter.

Jacob froze, sweat dripping down his forehead as a large can of tomatoes came hurtling toward his face. "I reckon I'm lassoing the wrong things today," he said with a sheepish grin.

Chuka, standing in the doorway, couldn't hold back his laughter. "Guess those cans didn't sign up for the rodeo!"

Just as things were about to spiral out of control, a mischievous child ran in, laughing at Jacob's mishap.

"Hey! Are you the cowboy they were talking about?" the child asked with a cheeky grin. Then, turning to the shopkeeper: "Bet you five bucks he can't rope a goat!"

Caught off guard, Jacob straightened up, a grin spreading across his face. "Well, little one, you're about to get a show today!"

The child flashed a toothy grin. "I'll hold you to that."

Jacob's Struggle: A Cowboy Lost in the Crowd

After the disaster, Jacob found himself standing outside the shop, staring at the bustling town, his cowboy hat perched awkwardly on his head. The events of the day weighed on him, and he sighed, trying to regain some sense of calm.

Internal monologue: This isn't how I pictured my cowboy life going. I've spent all my life on the ranch... but here? I feel like I'm fumbling through everything. I know how to work with cattle and ride bulls, but the town's got a rhythm all its own, and I'm... just out of sync.

He let out a deep breath and glanced at Chuka, who had a knowing, teasing grin on his face.

"You alright, cowboy?" Chuka asked, his voice soft but filled with understanding.

Jacob hesitated. "I feel... out of place. I've always known what to do back home, but here, I'm just... me."

Chuka clapped him on the back. "You'll get used to it. Just gotta look at the world through different eyes. You're not a town guy yet, but you've got the spirit of a cowboy. And that's what matters."

Jacob smiled faintly, the tension easing a little. He glanced at the road ahead of him.

Cinematic shot: The camera panned out, showing the wide-open road stretching ahead, symbolizing the journey still to come.

Local Color: Small-Town Interactions and Humor

Inside the shop, the townsfolk began to gather, their curious eyes following Jacob as they exchanged amused whispers. A local teenager, who had been leaning casually against the counter, looked Jacob up and down.

"You really a cowboy?" she asked, raising an eyebrow.

Jacob grinned. "Well, I sure look the part, don't I?"

She snorted. "You look like you're about to break out into a country song. Can you actually... cowboy?"

Jacob tilted his head, giving her a sly smile. "Give me a minute. I'll show you what I've got."

Nearby, an older man leaned in with a chuckle. "Son, I've been around long enough to see real cowboys. And I'll tell you this: if you can't rope a cow, you're not foolin' anyone."

Chuka shot Jacob a teasing wink. "Careful, Jacob. The town's issuing a challenge."

Jacob straightened, rolling up his sleeves. "Alright, I'm game."

The Road Ahead: Embracing the Challenge

As the sun dipped lower, signaling the end of the day, Jacob and Chuka made their way back to the truck. The day's chaos still hung in the air.

"Well," Jacob said with a grin, "I didn't exactly charm the town with my skills."

Chuka laughed heartily. "You didn't do too badly. You survived the disaster and came out smilin'. Ain't nothin' wrong with that."

Jacob settled into the truck, his cowboy hat now resting comfortably on his head. "I reckon I'm learning," he said softly, more to himself than to Chuka. "Still got a long way to go... but I'm getting the hang of it."

Cinematic shot: The camera pulls back, following the truck as it drives down the road, Jacob's silhouette against the colorful twilight sky—a visual metaphor for the journey ahead.

The Cowboy Journey: Humor and Growth

As the town faded into the rearview mirror, Jacob reflected on the day—the cans, the shopkeeper's playful challenge, and the interactions with the locals. He wasn't just a ranch boy anymore; he was starting to understand that being a cowboy wasn't about fitting into a mold but embracing who you were, no matter where you came from.

"Well," Jacob said with a chuckle, "maybe I'm more of a city-slicker cowboy than I thought."

Chuka smiled, his eyes twinkling with that ever-present knowing gleam. "You're getting there. Just keep that hat on."

For the first time, Jacob felt a little less out of place—and a little more like the cowboy he was always meant to be.

40

CHAPTER 7
A NIGERIAN CELEBRATION –
COWBOYS AT THE WEDDING

"Wherever you go, dance with joy and bring your rhythm with you."

The Wedding Begins

The vibrant sounds of pounding drums echoed through the air, filling every corner of the wedding hall with a joyous rhythm that pulsed like the heartbeat of the celebration. The air was thick with the rich, smoky scent of roasted meat and spices, mingling with bursts of laughter and the hum of animated conversation. The room was a sea of color—brightly patterned fabrics, dazzling *gele* headwraps, *agbadas*, and lace that shimmered under the golden lights. Every movement seemed to sparkle with energy.

Jacob adjusted his cowboy hat, feeling the weight of his boots sink into the floor. He tried to blend in, though his sturdy denim shirt and boots stood out like a sore thumb amidst the intricate embroidery and flowing attire.

He leaned toward Chuka.

"I feel like I've wandered into a completely different rodeo."

Chuka chuckled, his eyes twinkling with mischief.

"Well, partner, this is the Wild West of weddings. Welcome to a *Naija*-style celebration."

Jacob grinned.

"Let's ride it out."

Guests Spray Money: The Nigerian Way

The music swelled as the MC announced the entrance of the bride and groom. Applause erupted, and the crowd parted like a wave, revealing the couple in regal attire—shimmering gold and deep wine-red hues—gliding down the aisle with radiant smiles. Their joy was contagious, and the crowd cheered, their hands fluttering with excitement.

Suddenly, the air filled with fluttering paper. Guests began "spraying" money—dollars and *naira* floating like confetti, catching the light as they rained down around the couple. The fluttering bills sparkled in the air as if caught in a moment of magic.

Jacob blinked, wide-eyed.

"Are they really throwing money?"

"Spraying," Chuka corrected with a laugh. "It's how we show love, honor, and good fortune. It's not just giving—it's celebrating with flair!"

Cowboys and cowgirls alike stared—some clutching their hats in confusion, others laughing nervously.

Erick leaned in, clutching a handful of dollar bills with an expression of awe.

"Oh, my goodness. This is the most fun I've had in a long time. I want to do this every year!"

Jacob nudged him forward.

"Then go on, Erick. Show 'em how a cowboy does it."

With a whoop, Erick stepped into the line, tossing bills high like lassos at a rodeo. The money swirled in the air, landing softly on the bride's *gele* and the groom's shoulder. Some guests ducked, laughing, while others clapped in delight.

"Easy there, partner!" Jacob called out, stifling a laugh.

Erick spun around, a grin on his face.

"Y'all didn't tell me weddings could be this fun!"

The Traditional Dance and Music

As the money-spraying excitement settled, traditional drummers took the spotlight. The deep thump of the talking drum, the rhythm of the *shekere*, and the pulse of the *bàtá* drums filled the hall, creating a sound that seemed to rise from the very earth. Dancers emerged in full regalia, their costumes swirling with color. Their movements were seamless—their waistlines swaying, shoulders rolling with effortless precision. The entire hall seemed to move as one.

Jacob and the other cowboys watched in awe, their jaws nearly hitting the floor.

"Well, this is gonna be a challenge," Erick muttered, adjusting his hat.

Jacob chuckled.

"Feels like breaking a wild stallion—except we're the stallions."

The cowboys and cowgirls stepped forward cautiously, testing the rhythm with awkward stomps and shuffling feet. But the joy was undeniable. Some Nigerian women, noticing their struggle, smiled warmly and jumped in to help.

"Come, sister!" one woman said, taking a cowgirl's hand. "We'll show you how to shake that waist!"

The cowgirls giggled, following along with growing confidence. Jacob attempted to mimic the dancers but ended up looking like he was wrestling an invisible bull.

A Nigerian dancer called out playfully,

"Cowboy, don't fight the rhythm. Just surrender!"

He tried again—loser this time, letting the beat carry him. Though he wasn't graceful, he was having the time of his life. The music had taken hold of him.

Erick, too, gave in completely—clapping his hands, stomping his feet, and spinning in circles like a joyful tornado.

"Now *this* is what I call a party!" he yelled, his hat flying off and landing on a passing guest.

The Cowboys Find Their Groove

By now, the cowboys and cowgirls were all in. They'd found their groove—not perfectly, but with heart. The music had seeped into their bones, and the rhythm wrapped around them like a familiar saddle. Their boots stomped in time with the music, their laughter filling the gaps in the beat.

The hall had transformed into a kaleidoscope of motion—boots and heels, *agbadas* and chaps, *geles* and cowboy hats. Nigerian guests danced alongside their Western visitors, forming a glorious cultural collage. The divide between cultures had blurred, leaving only one common thread—joy.

"This feels just like home, doesn't it?" Jacob asked Chuka, catching his breath as he danced.

Chuka, sweat beading on his forehead, nodded.

"Yeah. Different drum, same heartbeat."

The Final Moments: A Sense of Belonging

As the evening wound down, the bride and groom were surrounded by a wide circle of guests. Everyone—cowboys and Nigerians alike—joined hands in one final dance. The rhythm grew slower, but the energy was no less intense. Jacob found himself twirling with a smiling Nigerian woman, her laughter ringing out like a bell, filling the room with warmth. Around them, voices rose in song, bodies swayed in unison, and the barriers between worlds dissolved into the night.

Jacob looked around, his heart full, his boots worn from dancing, and a sense of belonging washing over him. He was no longer an outsider. He wasn't just a cowboy from a distant land—he was part of this circle, stitched into the joy, bonded by laughter, rhythm, and shared humanity.

As the music slowed and the dancers began to tire, the warmth of the evening lingered. Cowboys tipped their hats. Nigerians raised their hands in blessing. The rhythm had woven them all together.

In that moment, Jacob knew joy didn't speak just one language. It danced in every culture, in every soul brave enough to join the circle.

CHAPTER 8
THE ROAD AHEAD

Post-Wedding Reflection

The morning after the wedding, Jacob sat by the campfire, the warmth of the flames contrasting with the cool air of early morning. The sounds of music, dancing, and laughter from the night before still echoed in his mind. The wedding had been a whirlwind of joy— a beautiful celebration of life, culture, and family. He had expected a quiet event but found himself caught up in something far bigger than anticipated. It was an experience that left him feeling deeply connected.

Chuka sat beside him, leaning back comfortably with his arms resting behind him as he gazed at the horizon. The first rays of sunlight bathed the earth, the soft light painting the scene in hues of gold. A peaceful calm had settled over them after the night's festivities.

"I'll be honest, Chuka," Jacob said, breaking the silence. "I didn't expect to have so much fun. I thought I was just going to be standing there, awkward as hell. But, man, I felt like I was part of something... bigger than just me. I haven't felt that alive in a long time."

Chuka smiled, understanding in his eyes. "That's the power of family and tradition. It pulls you in. When you let it, you become part of something far beyond yourself. No one's just a guest at a Nigerian wedding—you're family, even if it's only for the day."

Jacob nodded, a light smile crossing his face. "Yeah, and the money-throwing thing… what was that all about? I've never seen anything like it."

Chuka chuckled, settling back with a contented sigh. "Ah, the 'money spray.' It's a way of showing respect, appreciation, and love. We throw money as a blessing—it's a gesture of honoring the moment and the people around us. It's not about flaunting wealth; it's about sharing joy."

Jacob shook his head, amused. "It felt like a free-for-all at the end. But honestly, I got caught up in it. I was tossing money around like I had an endless supply."

"You fit right in," Chuka laughed. "You might as well have been born with a naira note in your hand. Everyone loved seeing you join in."

Jacob chuckled, his thoughts drifting. "If anyone had told me I'd be dancing and throwing money in the air at a wedding, I would've laughed at them. But man… I'm glad I did."

His gaze wandered across the expansive landscape as the fire flickered, casting shadows. "You know, Chuka... it was more than just a wedding. It felt like... I don't know, like I was connected to something I didn't even know was missing. My family's not around. Hell, I don't even know what kind of culture I'm part of anymore. But last night... it was like something clicked inside me."

Chuka's eyes softened. He took a deep breath before speaking. "Jacob, it's okay to feel that way. You're not alone. I left Nigeria years ago, but home is always close, always within reach. It's the little things—music, food, laughter—that bring us back to what's familiar."

Jacob nodded, a sense of understanding settling in. "Yeah. I think I get that now."

As the sun rose higher, Jacob felt something inside him shift. It wasn't about fitting into a specific mold—it was about embracing those moments that made him feel whole.

The journey was just beginning.

A New Cowboy Skill

Later that morning, Jacob was back at the ranch, sore from the previous night's dancing but determined to get back to work. He stood by the pen, staring at a cow who seemed unimpressed by his repeated attempts at roping. The sun beat down, and the familiar scent of hay and earth filled the air. Despite the peaceful scene, his frustration mounted.

Swinging the lasso, he missed again. And again. And again.

"Dang it!" Jacob muttered, wiping sweat from his brow. The cow wandered away, completely unfazed by his struggle.

"Jacob!" Erick called out from the side, grinning. "You gotta give it more swing. Get into it!"

Jacob turned, hands on his hips. "More swing? At this rate, I'm gonna rope myself. The cows are probably laughing at me."

Erick chuckled, giving him a thumbs-up. "You're getting closer. Keep going!"

Jacob swung the lasso once more, this time with more confidence. As the rope flew, it landed perfectly around the cow's neck. He froze, staring at the rope, then at the cow.

"I DID IT!" he shouted, his grin wide and proud. "I actually did it!"

Erick whooped, clapping his hands. "That's what I'm talking about, cowboy! You just needed a little faith in yourself."

Jacob exhaled deeply, a smile stretching across his face. "This is just the beginning. Next, I'll rope in the world."

"One cow at a time, partner," Erick laughed.

Integrating Cowboy and Nigerian Culture

Later that day, Jacob and Chuka hosted a casual meal with the other cowboys and cowgirls. The atmosphere was light and full of laughter, and the food—spicy enough to make them sweat—was the star of the show. Jollof rice, pepper soup, and grilled meats sat proudly on the table. Jacob had warned them about the heat, but once they tasted the food, they were hooked.

"This Jollof rice… what's in this stuff?" Erick exclaimed, wide-eyed. "It's amazing. You're telling me this is just rice?"

Jacob grinned, savoring his own bite. "Oh, it's more than just rice. It's all about the spices. You won't know what hit you."

Another cowboy, slightly sweating but smiling, added, "I thought I'd eaten spicy food before, but this... this is on a whole new level."

"Well, now you've officially had Nigerian food," Jacob said, chuckling. "Trust me, you'll want more once you start. Just don't drink too much water, or you'll regret it."

The cowboys laughed; their faces flushed with heat but lit with camaraderie. They exchanged jokes, shared stories, and playfully challenged each other to eat more as Nigerian music and rhythmic clapping filled the background.

"Now that's what I'm talking about," Chuka said, looking over at the cowboys slowly getting the hang of the cuisine. "You can take the cowboy out of the ranch, but you can't take the ranch out of the cowboy."

Laughter rang out. Jacob felt a sense of unity. The fusion of cultures was undeniable, and they were building something deeper than just a team.

The Rodeo Challenge

As the week passed, the tension surrounding the upcoming rodeo competition grew. Jacob had heard of rodeos before, but now, standing on the edge of one, the challenge felt real. It wasn't just about winning—it was about proving something to himself.

"You ready for this?" Chuka asked one afternoon, watching Jacob prepare.

Jacob stood silently for a moment, staring across the ranch. "I don't know, man. I've learned a lot, but when it comes down to it... I'm still just a guy from a different world trying to fit in."

Chuka's voice softened. "It's not about fitting in, Jacob. It's about showing who you really are. The cowboy way isn't about being perfect—it's about being real. You've got the heart of a cowboy. Now you just need to show it."

Jacob's gaze lingered on the horizon, his heart pounding with nerves. "I don't know. Sometimes, I feel like I'm still pretending to be someone I'm not."

Chuka slapped him gently on the back. "You're not pretending. You're discovering who you are. And that's more important than anything. Now go show the world what you've got."

Jacob took a deep breath, the flicker of confidence slowly building within him.

The rodeo wasn't just a competition—it was another step in his journey to becoming the man he was meant to be.

Light Moments and Humor

In the days leading up to the rodeo, tension was mixed with light-hearted moments. Erick's attempts to learn Nigerian dances had everyone in stitches. His stiff efforts to mimic the fluid movements of the women made him look like a cowboy trying to tango.

"Dude, you're supposed to shake your hips, not your whole body," Jacob teased from across the yard.

Erick straightened up, clearly attempting to correct himself, but only made things worse. "I'm just warming up for the rodeo," he grinned. "You know, gotta have rhythm for the ride."

Jacob burst out laughing. "If that's your rhythm, we might need a new strategy for you out there!"

Chuka, overhearing the banter, added, "Maybe we should add *Nigerian Dance 101* to the next lesson."

The laughter was infectious, adding a lightness to the days before the competition. Jacob felt a warm sense of belonging. Whatever happened at the rodeo, he knew now—he was part of something that mattered.

Something far bigger than himself.

54

CHAPTER 9
THE RODEO CHALLENGE

The ranch buzzed with energy in the days leading up to the rodeo. Anticipation hung thick in the air, woven into the sound of boots pounding on wooden planks, the clinking of saddles, and the restless snorts of bulls pacing in their pens. It all blended into a kind of chaotic music—one that matched the storm brewing inside Jacob's chest.

He felt it—the pressure, the heat, the invisible spotlight. This wasn't just another event. This was his moment to show them all—cowboys, ranch hands, and even himself—that he belonged here. That this Nigerian boy who had dared to dream of the West wasn't just playing dress-up. He was the real deal.

As he strolled toward the pens, he spotted Erick attempting a cowboy two-step beside the fence, his arms flailing like a scarecrow in the wind.

Jacob chuckled. "I swear, Erick, if you don't stop trying to shake your hips like that, you're going to dislocate something important."

Erick straightened with mock dignity, brushing imaginary dust off his jeans. "What? Do you have a problem with my rhythm? This is premium Nigerian cowboy fusion, my guy. I'm just warming up for the big show."

Jacob smirked. "If that's your warm-up, I'm terrified to see your main act."

Erick winked. "You should be. I plan to confuse the bull with my footwork."

They shared a laugh, but even in the joking, the weight of the moment wasn't lost on Jacob. Beneath the humor lurked a quiet question—one none of them dared to speak aloud.

Could Jacob really handle this?

He noticed the way the other cowboys looked at him—not unkindly, but with curiosity. Some were skeptical, others respectful. But all were watching. The newcomer with an accent, a foreign past, and something to prove.

Back at the stables, Jacob brushed his horse in silence. The saddle felt heavier today. The lasso, stiffer. Every inch of his gear was familiar—but tonight, it felt like armor. His mind replayed the months leading up to this: the first time he'd ridden a horse, the first time he'd been thrown from it, and the lessons he'd learned along the way. But now, there was no time to reflect. The rodeo was only hours away, and his body could only react.

In the stillness of the stall, a question whispered into his mind like a cold breeze: *What if I fail?*

He clenched his jaw. The fear wasn't about bruises or broken bones—it was about disappointing those who believed in him. People like Maria. Like Chuka. Like himself. He was no longer just trying to succeed for his own sake. He had become a symbol of the dream he'd carried all the way from Nigeria.

He couldn't let them down.

"Why am I doing this?" he murmured.

As if summoned by the question, Chuka appeared beside him, quiet and calm as ever.

"You okay?"

Jacob hesitated. "Just... nervous."

"That's good," Chuka replied, leaning casually on the wooden beam. "Means you care. Means you're alive."

Jacob gave a half-smile, though his eyes remained shadowed.

Chuka continued, "Jacob, you've trained for this. You've fallen and gotten back up more times than I can count. That's what makes you a cowboy—not how long you stay on the bull, but that you never stop getting back on."

Jacob nodded slowly. The tightness in his chest didn't disappear, but it loosened—just a little.

The Rodeo Begins

By morning, the ranch had transformed into a dusty coliseum. Banners fluttered. The bleachers groaned under the weight of cheering spectators. Children wore toy spurs. Vendors sold hot dogs, sodas, and cowboy hats. The sky stretched wide and blue overhead like it was watching with anticipation.

Jacob stood among the other riders behind the chutes, breathing slowly, steadily. The bulls thrashed in their pens, their hooves stamping the ground in an angry rhythm. The energy crackled like dry lightning. The dust seemed to have its own life, swirling through the air as if warning him of what was to come.

His stomach twisted. His palms were slick with sweat, the leather of his gloves sticking to his hands. He had ridden before, but this was different. This was the rodeo. This was the proving ground.

"You ready?" Chuka asked, his voice calm as ever.

Jacob looked ahead, heart pounding. "Ready as I'll ever be."

One by one, the cowboys took their turns. Some were thrown like ragdolls; others rode like legends. The crowd roared with each new attempt. The sound echoed in Jacob's bones, each cheer or groan making the air vibrate with tension.

Erick stepped up. He winked at Jacob before climbing into position.

"Watch this," he said, flashing a grin.

The bull burst out like a beast from another world, kicking and twisting as Erick held on for dear life. His hands were locked tight around the reins, but the bull's fury was unstoppable. He managed a solid eight seconds before being tossed into the dust. The crowd erupted with applause.

Jacob clapped with the others but couldn't stop his knees from trembling. He couldn't help but wonder if he could even last five seconds, let alone eight.

The Bull Ride

His name was called.

Jacob mounted his bull—an enormous, black-eyed brute named *Thunder Jack*. The beast snorted, steam rising from its nostrils. The animal shifted beneath him like a coiled spring, its muscles taut with impatience. Jacob gripped the reins, the leather biting into his palms, and took a deep breath.

He had to focus. He couldn't let his nerves take over.

The gate opened.

The world exploded.

Thunder Jack lurched forward, kicking dirt into the air. Jacob was slammed against the bull's back, his grip straining as the animal bucked. The world became a blur of dust, adrenaline, and raw power. His body jolted with each twist, his spine aching from every violent leap. His legs locked instinctively, his arms burned, muscles screaming in protest. The pain wasn't just physical—it was mental. The weight of belonging pressed down on him. He had to prove it, not just to them but to himself.

His hat flew off. The world grew silent, save for the pounding of his heart. His vision blurred, but all he could focus on was *staying on*. The bull spun, twisted, and leaped. He held on for dear life.

The ground rushed toward him.

Then—*impact*.

The dirt caught him in unforgiving arms. His shoulder hit first, then his back. Pain shot through him like lightning. He rolled instinctively, scrambling away before the bull could double back. Heart racing. Dust in his mouth. His chest burned, but he fought through it, pushing to his hands and knees. The world spun, but he had made it.

A roar broke through the haze.

Applause.

He had made it—barely.

The Aftermath

Jacob sat up, dazed. His ribs ached. His jeans were caked with mud. Chuka and Maria ran toward him, their faces lit with pride.

"You rode that monster like a storm," Chuka laughed, helping him to his feet.

"You lasted almost ten seconds!" Maria added, her eyes sparkling.

Jacob brushed dirt from his shirt. "Felt like a lifetime."

"You made us proud," Chuka said, clapping him on the back. "You didn't win—but you showed heart. And that matters more."

Jacob looked out across the rodeo grounds. The stands. The dust. The bulls. It all felt different now.

He had faced the fear.

He had leapt.

He was a cowboy.

Humor in the Aftermath

Erick sauntered over, rubbing his neck. "Man, that bull tossed you like joll of rice in a blender."

Jacob grinned. "And you? You looked like you were line dancing on a roller coaster."

Erick placed a hand on his chest. "Please. That was my signature move. It's called *The Survival Shuffle*. Trademark pending."

They laughed, the tension melting into easy joy.

Jacob turned back toward the crowd. Somewhere out there were people who believed in him. Somewhere behind him was a journey that had led him here.

He wasn't finished—not by a long shot.

But today, he had ridden the storm.

And he hadn't let go.

Chapter 10
The Calm Before the Storm

Post-Rodeo Reflections

The rodeo had come and gone, leaving Jacob with a bittersweet blend of exhaustion and exhilaration. The bruises on his body told only part of the story; the real wear came from the emotional ride he'd been on. Competing hadn't just been about earning points or applause—it had been about proving something to himself.

And he had. No question about it.

He might not have been the best rider out there, but he'd held his own. More importantly, he'd earned something far greater than any buckle or ribbon—**respect**. In this land, that meant everything. It meant he **belonged**.

That evening, the ranch buzzed with celebration. The local town hall, usually quiet and sleepy, came alive with music and chatter. Cowboys, cowgirls, ranch hands, and townsfolk gathered in their best boots and denim for the traditional post-rodeo dance. It was a rite of passage—another unspoken test of belonging.

Jacob had seen the dance before—from a distance. This time, though, he knew he had to step into the rhythm.

He'd practiced, of course. Watched YouTube videos. Mimicked Nick and Erick's moves in the bunkhouse. Even asked Chuka to count out steps for him one night. But the truth was, country dancing wasn't built into his bones.

Not yet.

Still, tonight, he was going to try.

The Dance That Didn't Go as Planned

Jacob entered the hall like a soldier marching into unfamiliar territory. The scent of barbecue and wood polish filled the air. Strings of lights crisscrossed overhead, and the sound of fiddles and banjos spilled out with infectious energy.

The dancers glided across the floor like water, graceful and effortless. Jacob stood at the edge, watching the tide, then slowly stepped in.

He began cautiously—**one-two, one-two, spin**—trying to follow the rhythm. But his feet had their own agenda. He zigged when he should've zagged. Turned right instead of left. More than once, he nearly bumped into another couple.

Chuckles bubbled from the sidelines. Not mean-spirited—just amused. Encouraging, even.

Still, Jacob pushed on. He wasn't going to quit. Not tonight.

Then something curious happened. The claps started. A few at first, then more joined in.

"Go, Nigerian Cowboy!" someone hollered.

Jacob misread the moment. He thought the applause was for his flawless moves, not the sheer **heart** he was putting into it. Emboldened, he ramped things up. He spun with dramatic flair.

Kicked his leg higher. Moved with such energy that folks on the sidelines had to back up.

The cheering grew louder, the laughter brighter.

Erick couldn't take it anymore. He strode up, grinning from ear to ear.

"Jacob, my guy," he said between laughs, "are you trying to rope the dance floor? 'Cause it looks like you're about to lasso the ceiling."

Jacob's face flushed. But he kept going. His pride wouldn't let him stop.

Then came Tom and Anna, the elderly couple who had been watching quietly from the corner. Tom walked up with a warm, knowing smile.

"You're doing just fine, son," he said, winking. "But you're making it look like square dancing is a contact sport."

Anna, ever graceful, reached for Jacob's arm.

"Come with us. Let's help you find the rhythm—not just the steps."

Jacob hesitated. He opened his mouth to decline politely, but then he caught Maria's eyes from across the room. She was smiling. Not laughing at him—cheering him on.

Anna gave him an encouraging nod.

"Go with them," she mouthed.

With a deep breath, Jacob nodded and followed the couple to the center of the floor.

The Spirit of a Cowboy: Resilience, Courage, and Determination

Tom and Anna didn't teach with strict instructions—they led with joy. They let the music guide them and brought Jacob along for the ride. Each misstep was gently corrected. Each awkward shuffle was met with patience.

Tom's voice cut through the melody, calm and fatherly.

"Being a cowboy, son, isn't just about what you do. It's who you are. It's resilience. It's getting knocked down and getting back up—again and again. Whether it's a rodeo, a dance, or life."

Jacob felt the words settle into his bones. He'd been thinking of the cowboy life as grit and toughness. But this… this was something deeper.

It was about **grace under pressure. Humility in failure**.

And a quiet, unshakable **determination** to rise no matter how many times you fall.

By the time the dance ended, Jacob wasn't suddenly a great dancer, but he wasn't lost either. And more than anything, he felt **peace**.

He didn't need to master every step. He just needed to keep **showing up**.

After the Dance: The Gratitude of the Cowboys

As the music faded and the crowd began to thin, Jacob stepped off the dance floor, sweat on his brow and a wide grin on his face.

"Jacob!" a burly cowboy called out, slapping him on the back.

"You gave us a show, man. Haven't laughed that hard in a while—and I mean that in the best way."

"Yeah," another added, shaking his hand. "You've got guts, my friend. That counts for more than perfect footwork."

Jacob laughed.

"Well, I'm just glad I didn't break a toe out there."

"You brought energy," the first cowboy said. "And heart. That's what this is all about."

As more folks approached—offering handshakes, claps on the shoulder, and the occasional good-natured teasing—Jacob realized something profound.

He was no longer just an outsider trying to fit in.

He was **part of this story now.**

Part of this **world**.

The rodeo, the dance, the struggles—they had all been preparing him not just to survive but to **belong**.

As he walked out of that hall into the cool night air, boots scuffing the gravel, Jacob whispered to himself:

"I'm not just here. I'm home."

CHAPTER 11
THE RIVALRY GROWS

The Rodeo Showdown

The rodeo arena buzzed with anticipation. The sun blazed overhead, casting a golden haze over the dust-kissed grounds. The crowd swelled with energy, their excitement humming in the air like electricity. Jacob stood at the edge of the arena, his boots planted firmly in the dirt, the moment pressing heavily on his shoulders.

The past few days had been filled with laughter, friendships, and the surprising joy of pushing his limits. But today? Today was different. Today wasn't just about skill—it was about pride, rivalry, and proving he belonged.

In the stands, Jake, Adam, Bob, and Lucas stood shoulder to shoulder, their eyes locked on Jacob. To them, his rising popularity was an irritation that refused to go away.

"Showtime," Jake muttered, adjusting his hat with a slow sneer. "Let's see how long you last, *Nigerian Cowboy.*"

Jake: The Top Dog

Jake, the oldest of the group, had long considered himself the king of this arena. He'd fought tooth and nail for the respect he commanded, and he wasn't ready to hand it over—especially not to a Nigerian newcomer. To Jake, Jacob's presence was more than a nuisance—it was a threat to his carefully curated reputation.

He had earned his name in this town through years of sweat and blood. Now, some stranger from across the world was getting cheers and winning respect? It gnawed at him.

Jacob was an anomaly. Everything Jake had learned in the rodeo had come through brute force and grit. But Jacob? He had a calm about him—an easy confidence that was unnerving. It was the kind of thing you either had to break or outlast.

Jacob's Unlikely Confidence

Jacob wasn't blind to the hostility, but he stood undeterred. He'd worked too hard, come too far, to be chased off by ego and resentment.

"I'm just here to be a good cowboy," he whispered to himself.

The phrase had become his anchor. It wasn't just something he said—it was a promise to himself. To the life he was building.

As the bull-riding event approached, Jacob mounted the beast with steady hands and a focused gaze. The crowd's cheers washed over him, and he caught the sound of *"Nigerian Cowboy!"* echoing through the arena.

A small smile broke on his face. His heartbeat wasn't racing—if anything, it was calm. He wasn't in a battle for approval. He was here to prove he belonged on his own terms. He didn't need validation from Jake or anyone else. He just needed to ride.

The bull burst into motion, wild and unrelenting. Jacob's muscles screamed as he held tight, his body a storm of control and chaos. Eight long seconds later, he dismounted, the crowd erupting around him.

The Rivalry Unfolds

Jake's jaw clenched as he watched from the sidelines. Jacob had lasted longer than Jake had the previous year.

"Seriously?" Jake grumbled. "That guy stayed on longer than me?"

Adam scoffed. "Well, don't just stand there. Do something about it."

Bob smirked. "I've got a few ideas to shake him up."

Lucas, quiet but perceptive, hesitated. He wasn't sure what bothered him more: Jacob's rise or the way his friends were reacting. He wasn't the type to stir the pot, but something about Jacob's quiet strength unsettled him.

It wasn't just his skills—it was his demeanor. Where others saw an outsider, Lucas saw a man who wasn't trying to prove himself to anyone. It wasn't a bad thing. In fact, it was a little inspiring.

But in their world, respect had to be earned the hard way. And that meant Jacob had to prove it in the ring—or risk being seen as an easy target.

Adam rolled his eyes. "You just don't want to get shown up."

Lucas didn't respond. But his mind kept spinning. Was Jacob really that different from the rest of them? Or was this just some lucky streak?

A Little Humor Amidst the Tension

After the ride, Erick threw Jacob a thumbs-up. Nick, standing beside him, grinned.

"Man, you did great. I mean, for someone who looked like they were gonna fly off every two seconds, you really hung in there."

Jacob chuckled. "I'm a good cowboy. I love and like to help people," he said, repeating his now-famous motto.

Erick laughed. "That's probably why they hate you."

Nick nodded. "Yeah. You're doing things the right way—and that's what's got them all riled up."

Jacob smirked. "Well, good cowboys don't do that."

More Than Just Competition

The rivalry deepened with each event. Jake brushed against Jacob every chance he got. Bob muttered under his breath about Jacob, "never making it." Adam, bolder than the rest, made offhand remarks about Jacob's Nigerian roots.

Jacob didn't flinch. He smiled, nodded, and carried on.

During one roping event, Jake tampered with Jacob's saddle. But the prank backfired—Jake's own saddle slipped mid-ride, launching him face-first into the dirt. The crowd roared with laughter.

Jacob stifled a laugh. "That's karma, Jake," he said just loud enough to be heard.

Erick and Nick couldn't contain themselves. Even Lucas cracked a reluctant smile.

An Unexpected Ally: Lucas

Later, Lucas pulled Jacob aside, away from the others.

"Look," he said, adjusting his glasses, "I know things are tense. But what they're doing—it's not right."

Jacob studied him, surprised. "You're the last person I expected to say that."

Lucas shrugged, his gaze lingering on his friends across the arena. "They've been messing with you because you're different. They see that, and they can't handle it. But you've got something they don't, Jacob. You've got heart."

Jacob nodded slowly. "Thanks, Lucas. I never came here looking for trouble. But I won't back down either. Good cowboys don't."

Lucas looked away, conflicted. "Just... keep doing what you're doing. Show them who you are. They'll respect that, even if they won't admit it."

Jacob's mouth twitched into a smile. "Good cowboys don't need to be told they're good."

Lucas gave a small, genuine nod before walking off, his face still betraying his inner conflict. Was he on the right side of this? He'd always followed the pack, but something about Jacob's quiet defiance made him question his loyalties.

The Final Showdown

In the final event, Jacob and Jake were pitted against each other. The arena pulsed with anticipation. It was more than just a showdown between two cowboys—it was personal.

Jacob climbed atop the bull. The beast snarled beneath him, anxious and agitated. For a second, doubt flickered in his chest—but it vanished as quickly as it came.

Good cowboys don't back down.

The gate flung open, and the bull exploded into motion. Jacob rode like a storm—controlled, steady, determined. His body swayed with the rhythm of the bull, every movement calculated, every muscle engaged. The crowd screamed, the sound washing over him.

He was no longer just a stranger in this world. He was part of it.

When he finally dismounted, the crowd's roar was thunderous.

Jake approached, his expression stiff.

"You did good," he muttered, eyes lowered. The words weren't exactly friendly, but they weren't bitter either. There was a shift in his tone. A glimmer of respect.

Jacob smiled. "Thanks, Jake. Good cowboys don't need to be told they're good."

Jake didn't respond. But for the first time, Jacob saw something different in him—less rivalry, more respect.

A Cowboy's Heart

The rivalry wasn't gone. Not completely. But something had changed.

Jake's respect, though reluctant, was real. Lucas now stood beside Jacob, along with Erick and Nick.

Jacob looked around at the same arena that had once tried to push him out. Now, it held space for him—not because he demanded it, but because he'd earned it.

"Good cowboys," Jacob said as they walked away, "treat people nice."

Nick slapped him on the back. "And they sure know how to ride bulls."

As they made their way off the grounds, Jacob felt a peace settle over him. He hadn't just survived the rivalry—he'd earned a place here, one step at a time.

76

CHAPTER 12
THE CHALLENGE

Rodeo Night

It was about 5 p.m. on a summer Friday, and the parking lot of the rodeo stadium was beginning to fill up. The air buzzed with excitement—a swirl of rustic and festive scents mingling in the warm evening breeze. The earthy musk of livestock, the sharp tang of fresh hay, and the smoky aroma of grilled meats blended with the distant calls of rodeo announcers and the murmur of an eager crowd. The sounds of hooves pounding the dirt and the crackle of fireworks being prepared in the distance made it feel like the whole town was pulsing to the rhythm of the night.

Tonight was a rodeo musical show, and the crowd buzzed with anticipation, their energy electric as the sun dipped lower, painting the sky in shades of red and orange. The stars of the show weren't just the riders—they were the animals, the music, and the community itself.

Jacob's Arrival and the Encounter

Jacob pulled into the lot with Erick and Nick in his truck, scanning for a space. He spotted one and quickly maneuvered into it before another vehicle could take it. Rodeo nights weren't just about contests—they were a spectacle, a parade of style, music, and community pride.

As they unbuckled their seat belts, Jacob glanced at Nick in the front passenger seat and Erick in the back. Both were animated, caught in a fit of laughter. Nick clapped his hands with excitement while Erick drummed on the seat, emphasizing a punchline. The truck rocked slightly with their joy, their laughter echoing into the warm air.

But the bubble of laughter burst when they stepped out, only to realize they had parked beside Jake's truck.

Jake, Adam, and Lucas were lounging nearby like wolves on watch, their eyes flicking toward Jacob and his friends with subtle but unmistakable hostility.

Jake straightened, crossing his arms with a smirk.

"So, you parked next to us? That's interesting," he said, sarcasm coating his words. "What's so funny, huh?"

The air between the two groups thickened. Jacob, Nick, and Erick fell silent, the tension spreading as Jake's gaze swept over Jacob's truck like it was a joke that told itself.

"Why so late?" Adam asked sharply, cocking an eyebrow. "Did you get lost on the way here?"

Jake chimed in, pacing slowly toward Jacob's truck.

"Took you this long to arrive in this old lady's truck?" he mocked. "It still moves?"

"Yeah," Adam added, "too slow to even be on the road."

Lucas shifted uncomfortably, glancing at Jacob before speaking. "Guys, we're here to have fun. Let the fun begin."

Adam glared at him. "Shut up, Lucas. Learn how this works."

Lucas fell silent, chastised. Jacob's jaw tightened, and his eyes met Jake's with the same cool resolve he had come to rely on.

"Is there a problem here?" Jacob asked, his voice calm but firm.

Jake chuckled and waved it off. "Relax. Just messing around." He strolled toward the truck and touched the hood with exaggerated drama. "But seriously… this is the problem. You guys showed up in this? It can barely keep up."

Jacob raised an eyebrow, his expression unreadable. "What's wrong with my truck?"

Jake shrugged. "You're slow. That's the problem. So, here's the deal—tomorrow at 10 a.m., we race. From here to Cheyenne Center. Two hours. The first one to reach the pole and raise the white flag wins. Loser tips his hat to the winner."

Nick scoffed. "That's stupid."

Jacob locked eyes with Jake, the challenge hanging heavy in the air. This wasn't just about the truck. It wasn't even about the race. It was about something deeper—something that tugged at Jacob's core. A test of pride and determination.

"Jake, are you trying to get us all killed?" Jacob asked, his voice edged with caution yet firm.

Jake grinned. "Either you're a rodeo champion or just another guy who talks a big game."

The words settled like dust on the wind. Jacob didn't want to do it—his instincts screamed at him to walk away. But pride, that nagging desire to prove himself, wouldn't let him back down. He took a deep breath and extended his hand.

"All right. 10 a.m. tomorrow."

Jake's smirk widened as he shook Jacob's hand. "Good."

As Jake and his crew headed toward the stadium, Lucas shook his head, muttering, "Oh my goodness, he took the challenge."

Nick turned to Jacob. "Don't do it. It's not worth it."

Erick, the eternal optimist, slapped Jacob on the back. "Worst case? You wipe the floor with Jake's smug face."

Jacob said nothing. His mind was already racing. His eyes followed Jake into the crowd, but his thoughts were somewhere far down that highway.

The Rodeo Show

The rest of the evening passed in a haze of lights, music, and energy. The rodeo was in full swing—riders performing impossible feats of balance, musicians sending pulses through the air, and food vendors drawing hungry patrons with sizzling temptations. There was something magical about it—the blend of skill and spirit, the power of tradition alive in every cheer and clap.

Jacob, Nick, and Erick enjoyed the festivities. They laughed, danced, and celebrated with the crowd. For a while, the earlier tension faded into the background like smoke on the wind. The world felt right again—at least for a little while.

But as the night wore on and the music faded into the hum of tired chatter, Jacob's thoughts returned to the challenge. The race. The white flag. Jake's smirk.

And the need to prove something—not to Jake, not even to his friends—but to himself.

Jacob's Dream

That night, as Jacob lay in bed, sleep came slowly, his thoughts a whirlpool of excitement and fear surrounding the race. The adrenaline of the upcoming challenge twisted inside him like a knot. His body craved rest, but his mind refused to settle. Finally, the pull of sleep overtook him, dragging him into a restless dream.

In the dream, Jacob found himself standing at Cheyenne Center, the familiar space now twisted under a thick, unnatural fog that blurred the edges of the horizon. The air was heavy, pressing down on him as if trying to keep him from breathing. Before him stood the pole where the white flag—his symbol of victory, his beacon of hope— fluttered in the wind; he could see it clearly, but it felt distant, unreachable.

He stepped forward, his boots crunching softly on the damp earth, each step echoing loudly in the stillness. But just as his fingers brushed against the flag, something shifted. A low growl rumbled through the fog, deep and unsettling.

From the shadows emerged two Rottweilers, their eyes glowing with a feral hunger. They stood between him and the flag, massive and unyielding, their muscles tense and ready to strike. The intensity in their gaze sent a chill down his spine, and his heart skipped a beat. He knew instinctively that these dogs were no ordinary animals— they were guardians of something far more dangerous.

Panicking, Jacob scanned the ground for a way out, his pulse pounding in his ears. In desperation, he grabbed a piece of meat from his pocket, tossing it toward the dogs. They snapped it up greedily, devouring it in a frenzied rush. But once the last scrap was gone, their attention snapped back to him with terrifying focus.

Before Jacob could react, the dogs lunged forward, their teeth bared and their bodies moving with unnatural speed. He ran, his feet pounding against the ground, but the dogs were faster, relentless in their pursuit. His lungs burned, and his legs screamed for mercy, but the dogs were gaining on him, their hot breath on his heels.

Just when he thought he couldn't run any longer, something strange happened. His back arched, and with a sharp, instinctual movement, wings sprouted from his shoulders—large, powerful wings that beat the air with a sound like thunder. The wind rushed past him as he soared higher, leaving the ground—and the dogs—far behind.

But to his horror, the dogs followed in the air. They weren't bound by gravity. Their massive bodies, defying all logic, took the same flight path, their dark bodies cutting through the thick fog as though they were creatures of the air. Their eyes never left Jacob. Their glowing stare was unwavering, filled with the same primal hunger they'd had on the ground. The feeling of being hunted—a deep, visceral fear—gripped Jacob's chest as he soared higher, his wings beating furiously.

He veered left, desperate to break the dogs' pursuit. He banked sharply to the right, forcing the wind to tear at his face, but the dogs followed, their powerful forms cutting through the air with unnatural precision. They weren't just chasing him; they were hunting him. The sharpness of their growls echoed in the dream, reverberating against the fog, growing louder and more oppressive.

Jacob's wings burned with the effort, and his breath came ragged. He couldn't keep this up forever. The trees he had once seen in the distance were now growing closer, their gnarled branches twisting like fingers stretching toward him. He needed to land. He needed somewhere to hide. He darted toward the tree—a towering, ancient oak that loomed out of the fog like a sentinel.

His heart raced as he neared it, the canopy of the tree's branches reaching up like twisted hands, beckoning saw to safety. With one last powerful beat of his wings, Jacob dove toward the lowest branch, just barely managing to catch hold of it with his hands. His legs swung out as he pulled himself up, the sharp bark scraping against his skin. He folded his wings tightly against his back, hoping the cover of the tree would be enough to hide him.

The dogs, however, were not deterred. They landed below him with terrifying ease, their massive bodies hitting the ground with a heavy thud. Their growls were low and menacing, vibrating the air around him. One of them, the larger of the two, stood on its hind legs, its claws scraping against the bark of the tree as it tried to reach him. Its eyes were fixed on Jacob, locked in a deadly stare.

The other dog, smaller but no less menacing, began to climb the tree, its paws gripping the trunk with terrifying speed. Jacob's breath caught in his throat as the dog neared, its sharp teeth bared, dripping with saliva.

Desperation surged through Jacob. His pulse pounded in his ears, the nightmare's intensity overwhelming him. The ground beneath him felt like it was slipping away as he scrambled higher on the branch, but his hands were slick with sweat, and the sharp bark was a poor grip.

The dog lunged again, this time snapping at his legs. Jacob felt its teeth scrape across his boot as he twisted out of the way, but the dog was faster than he could react. It snarled, its jaws wide open, and Jacob's heart raced—this time, there was no escape.

Just as the dog's teeth sank toward his leg, Jacob let out a desperate scream. The sound broke through the suffocating silence of the dream, echoing in the empty space around him.

The Dream Shatters

But in that moment of pure panic, the world around him seemed to fracture. The dog's jaws were just inches from his flesh, but as it lunged, the dream began to break apart. The terrifying clarity of the chase, the looming danger—it all shattered like glass.

Jacob's eyes snapped open, his chest heaving, his heart hammering in his ribs. He was back in his room, in the stillness of his bed, drenched in cold sweat. The lingering echo of the dogs' growls vibrated in his mind, but everything around him was silent.

His breath came in sharp gasps as he pushed himself up, sitting on the edge of the bed. He felt disoriented, still trapped between the world of the dream and the waking reality. His skin was slick with sweat, and his muscles felt like they were on fire from the strain of the nightmare. The terror from the dream still gripped him like a weight in his chest.

"What does it all mean?" Jacob whispered to the empty room, his voice barely audible. He ran a shaky hand through his damp hair, trying to shake off the lingering unease. His mind raced, searching for answers that seemed just out of reach.

The white flag. The race. The Rottweilers. The wings.

It all felt like some kind of twisted omen—symbols of something much deeper than a simple car race. The dogs, the flight, the pursuit—it was as if his mind was trying to warn him, but he couldn't understand the message. The fear, the sense of danger, wasn't just about the race tomorrow. It was about something far more internal. Something Jacob wasn't sure he was ready to face.

The morning light filtered through the curtains, casting a soft glow across the room. It was early—still dark outside—but the day was starting. The alarm buzzed, signaling the beginning of a new day.

Jacob's hand hovered over the button to turn it off, but he didn't press it immediately. He stayed there for a moment, still trying to make sense of the nightmare that had shaken him to his core. The feeling of being hunted, of being cornered with nowhere to go—it clung to him like a shadow.

The race ahead and the challenge he had accepted—those weren't the only things he needed to prepare for. Something more, something deeper, was calling to him. A challenge not just of speed but of courage. Of what he was willing to sacrifice and face.

He stood up from the bed slowly, his legs feeling unsteady as he made his way to the window. The sun was starting to rise, casting a soft light across the quiet town. The birds were just beginning to chirp, and the world felt still as though holding its breath.

Jacob exhaled, his mind still spinning with the remnants of the dream. But one thing was certain: the race wasn't just about proving something to Jake or even to his friends. It was about proving something to himself.

As he dressed for the day ahead, the nightmare's grip loosened just a little. He didn't understand the meaning of the dogs or the wings or the white flag, but he knew one thing: whatever was coming, he couldn't back down now.

CHAPTER 13
THE RACE BEGINS

Race Day: The Calm Before the Storm

The sun was barely above the horizon, casting a golden hue over the sleepy town. Jacob's alarm pierced the silence of the early morning, dragging him from his restless sleep. His dream still lingered in his mind, a foggy recollection of chaos, racing, and the constant pull to prove himself. He stretched, his muscles aching from the weight of anticipation. He yawned, sitting up in bed, the sheets slipping from his bare torso. For a moment, he simply sat there, the warmth of the room and the pull of his thoughts urging him to sink back into the covers. But today wasn't for resting.

He swung his legs over the side of the bed, his feet hitting the cool floor with a soft thud. As he stood, the stiffness in his body reminded him of the tension mounting from the day before. Today was about more than just a race—it was about proving something bigger, something deeper. He walked toward the bathroom, the coolness of the tiles against his feet sharpening his senses. The bathroom mirror greeted him, his reflection a reminder of the challenge ahead. He brushed his teeth, feeling the minty freshness fill his mouth, then splashed cold water on his face. The water was like a jolt to his system, pulling him into focus.

As the droplets slid down his skin, he stared at his reflection—not the boy he once was, but the man who would stand tall today. Jacob's fingers moved methodically to get dressed. He pulled on his favorite pair of jeans, the ones that fit just right, then slipped into his boots. With each movement, a quiet confidence bloomed within him. He tied his boots with precision, the weight of the day pressing in but not crushing him. He was ready.

The adrenaline of the coming race thrummed beneath his skin, and for a moment, the thought of what was to come filled him with both excitement and a sense of quiet power. He glanced over at his phone, noting the time. It was almost time.

The Pre-Race Standoff: Tensions Rise

Jacob grabbed his keys, giving one last look around his room. Then he headed out. The truck was parked outside, waiting for the challenge that would unfold on the open road. He climbed into the driver's seat, his friends Nick and Erick already in the truck, both dressed and ready to go. They exchanged quiet nods, the energy between them already shifting, the weight of the morning pressing in.

Erick, always the cautious one, leaned over. "You good, man? You sure about this?" he asked, his voice low but laced with concern.

Jacob gave him a small, confident smile. "I'm good. We've got this."

Nick, ever the joker, tossed Jacob a playful look. "Hey, at least if you crash, we can blame it on the old truck, right?" he teased, but the underlying tension in his voice was undeniable.

Jacob laughed, the sound cutting through the tension. "Not happening. We've got this."

As they approached the meeting spot, the air thickened with the weight of the competition. Jake's truck was already parked, the hulking vehicle gleaming in the early morning light, its powerful engine a silent promise of speed. Jake leaned against the truck, his usual cocky smirk plastered on his face, flanked by his crew— Adam, Bob, and Lucas. They were ready for the challenge, but Jake's eyes locked onto Jacob's with an intensity that hinted at something darker.

Jacob parked his truck beside them, the two vehicles facing off. The hum of the engines was the only sound that cut through the tense silence. Jake didn't waste any time.

"Hope you're ready to lose," Jake sneered, the words dripping with arrogance. "There's no way your old truck can keep up with mine."

Jacob's gaze remained steady, his calm demeanor unshaken by Jake's taunts. "We'll see about that," he said, his voice quiet but firm.

Nick and Erick climbed out of the truck, both walking over to Jake's vehicle with a sharp eye. Nick, ever the skeptic, crouched down, inspecting the tires. "No tricks, Jake?" he asked, his tone biting.

Jake just smirked. "Nothing you wouldn't expect from a race. But, hey, if you can't keep up, that's not my problem."

Jacob's attention remained on Jake, his focus sharpening. The challenge was real. And with every second that passed, the stakes grew higher.

The Countdown to the Race: The Tension Builds

The wind picked up, kicking up a cloud of dust between the two trucks. The air crackled with competitive energy as the tension between the two groups reached its peak. Jacob's hands clenched around the steering wheel, his knuckles turning white. The weight of the day pressed heavier against his chest now that the moment had arrived. This wasn't just about winning anymore; it was about proving to himself that he had what it took—that he wasn't the same man who had once run from everything. The echoes of his dreams still lingered, reminding him of the chaos and doubts. But now, he couldn't afford to hesitate. The hum of the engines seemed to pulse in rhythm with his heartbeat, a steady reminder of what was at stake. His breaths were shallow, but he forced himself to breathe deeper, to calm the storm brewing within him. The tension was so thick it felt like the entire world was holding its breath, waiting for the first sign of movement, the first sign of action.

You've got this, he told himself. But the words didn't come easily. There was a storm inside him—nerves, guilt, anger, pride—all swirling together. His hands felt the worn leather of the steering wheel, the rough texture grounding him in the present. This moment would define him, whether he liked it or not.

Nick's voice, low but filled with anticipation, broke through his thoughts. "Ready, Jacob?"

Jacob's eyes locked on the finish line in the distance, the small flag barely visible but pulling him toward it like a magnet. It was still a long way off, but it was there, and that was all that mattered. The calm before the storm was almost over. He gave a sharp nod, his voice steady. "Let's do this."

The official called out from the sidelines. "Alright, gentlemen. This is it. The race to Cheyenne Center. On my mark."

Jacob's chest tightened. He didn't answer. He just stared ahead, focusing on the narrow stretch of road in front of him.

"One…" the official called, his voice echoing through the air.

Jacob's grip tightened on the wheel, his muscles taut and ready.

"Two…"

This is it. This is your moment, he thought, trying to focus all his energy on the road ahead, but his mind was still buzzing. Doubt crept in for a second. What if he wasn't enough? What if Jake's truck was too powerful, too fast?

But then, something inside Jacob clicked into place. He wasn't just racing for victory; he was racing to silence that voice in his head— the one that always told him he wasn't good enough.

Nick's voice broke through the rising tension. "You've got this, Jacob."

Erick, always the calm presence, gave him a reassuring nod, though Jacob could see the uncertainty in his eyes. Even Erick felt it. But that only made Jacob more determined. He couldn't let them down. Not today.

"Three!" The official shouted, and the air seemed to explode in that single moment.

The Race Begins: Full Speed Ahead

The screech of tires tore through the morning stillness as both trucks shot forward, engines roaring. Jake's truck surged ahead, a blur of speed, but Jacob didn't flinch. He kept his eyes locked on the road, the race stretching out before him like a battle he was determined to win.

At first, Jake's truck led, the powerful machine roaring ahead. But Jacob didn't let it shake him. He focused on the road; the truck's every movement was in sync with his instincts. The wind whipped through his hair, the rush of speed a drug that fueled his focus. Nick and Erick were quiet in the back, their eyes glued to the road, but Jacob could feel their energy, their support, driving him forward.

The road twisted, the turns sharp and sudden. Jake's truck began to lose some of its edge, the driver overcompensating on a bend. Jacob saw the opportunity—the moment Jake took a wrong turn, veering off slightly. Without hesitation, Jacob slammed his foot on the accelerator, his truck surging forward as he seized the opening. The roar of the engines and the rush of air filled his ears, but his focus remained on the goal—the flag at Cheyenne Center, standing tall and waiting. Every second counted.

Victory at Cheyenne: The Final Stretch

The finish line was in sight. Jacob's truck was gaining on Jake, inching closer, the speed now almost neck-and-neck. He could see the flag in the distance, fluttering in the breeze. His heart raced, adrenaline coursing through his veins as he pushed his truck harder. It was the final stretch, and Jacob wasn't about to back down.

With one last burst of power, Jacob surged ahead. His truck shot past Jake's, the finish line just ahead. The roar of the engine and the rhythmic pounding of his heart drowned out everything else. At that moment, there was only the race, only the path that had led him to this point. Jacob's truck shot forward, its tires gripping the gravel with unrelenting power. The finish line loomed closer with every heartbeat. His eyes narrowed, his entire focus zeroing in on the flag—the symbol of everything he had fought for.

With a final push, the roar of the engine exploded, and his truck crossed the finish line. Jacob slammed his foot on the brakes, the tires screeching as the vehicle skidded to a stop, the dust swirling in the wake of his victory. He sprinted to the flagpole, his heart hammering in his chest. The white flag flapped in the wind, waiting.

Jacob reached up and grabbed it, his entire body surging with triumph as he raised it high.

Victory: The Acknowledgment

From a distance, Jake's truck came to an abrupt halt. He stopped off to the side of the road, his engine idling, and watched from a distance, his eyes never leaving Jacob. His crew—Adam, Bob, and Lucas—remained silent in the cab, observing, waiting to see what would happen next. The men in the crowd, who had been gathered around the flag, began to whisper amongst themselves, their faces tightening in reaction to Jacob holding the sacred flag.

Jacob, still holding the white flag high, felt an odd shiver run down his spine. It was as if the entire world had shifted.

And then, from the back of the crowd, a sharp whistle pierced the air.

The sound broke the quiet tension like a crack of thunder, cutting through the murmurs and whispers.

Jake, still watching from his truck, narrowed his eyes. Something had changed. His grip on the steering wheel tightened. His gaze flicked back toward the men in the crowd, and in that moment, he knew this wasn't just about a race anymore. There was something more to this flag, something Jacob hadn't understood—something sacred. The white flag had triggered a reaction that felt as if it went far beyond the competition, beyond the moment of victory.

As the tension in the air thickened, Jake shifted the truck into gear. Without another word, he revved the engine and sped off, pulling away from the scene.

CHAPTER 14
AFTER THE DUST SETTLES

The Calm After the Storm

Jacob raised the white flag high, its fabric fluttering in the wind like a symbol of triumph. It felt unreal, as if the victory were too big to be true. For a split second, the world slowed, and he felt the weight of his achievement: he had won. He had overcome Jake, and in doing so, he had proven his worth—to himself, his friends, and anyone who had ever doubted him.

But as the flag waved in the air, a strange sense of unease crept in. The energy in the crowd shifted, and the roar of celebration he had expected was replaced by a hushed murmur. It wasn't joy—it was fear. And somewhere beneath that fear, a deeper feeling stirred: anger.

Jacob scanned the crowd, his heart pounding as he tried to make sense of the sudden shift. What had gone wrong? Why did the faces that had once been eager now look apprehensive, even hostile? There was a palpable tension in the air, and the weight of the eyes on him made his skin prickle. Some men in the crowd exchanged hard looks, and Jacob's stomach tightened with dread.

From the corner of his eye, he noticed a man in a faded denim jacket—tall and broad-shouldered. He locked eyes with Jacob for a brief moment before nudging the person next to him. Without a word, he whistled sharply, cutting through the tense silence.

The effect was immediate. The air thickened with a new, menacing energy. Jacob's pulse quickened. He tightened his grip on the flag's fabric, but his mind raced, trying to figure out what was happening.

Erick's voice cut through the tension, low and urgent. "We need to go. Now."

Jacob hesitated. He didn't fully understand what was going on, but the fear in Erick's eyes made the decision clear. Without a word, he tossed the flag onto the passenger seat and climbed into the truck, his hands shaking as he fumbled to start the engine. The truck roared to life, and with a screech of tires, they tore down the dirt road, the dust kicking up around them. The highway ahead seemed like the only safe option, but something about the chase felt like more than just physical danger. It was a shadow that followed them, heavy with impending doom.

The Chase Begins

"Jacob, they're coming after us!" Nick's voice broke through his thoughts, sharp with panic.

Jacob glanced in the rearview mirror, and his stomach dropped. A few trucks had started to move, their engines growling as they followed. The men in the trucks looked angry, their faces set in grim determination.

"Who are they?" Jacob whispered under his breath.

"They're local," Erick said, his tone grim. "They must be. And that flag... it probably means something to them. Something big."

"Oh my goodness, they're going to kill us," Nick muttered, almost in disbelief.

Jacob slammed his foot on the gas, pushing the truck to its limits. But even as they gained some distance, a sense of inevitability clung to the air. It wasn't just a chase. It felt like they were being hunted—like the flag had unleashed something far more dangerous than they understood.

"Guys, we're not dying here today," Jacob said, his voice tight but resolute. He couldn't let fear control him. Not again.

The Pursuit Escalates

"Take the next road! It's less traveled. We can lose them there!" Erick's voice was urgent.

Without hesitation, Jacob swerved the truck onto a narrow, winding road, the tires skidding as they fought to stay on course. The trees pressed in around them, their branches forming a canopy of shadows overhead. The road felt unfamiliar, yet strangely comforting—like a hidden path leading away from the chaos.

Jacob's pulse raced, and for a brief moment, he let himself hope. Maybe this was the escape they needed.

But then the dogs started barking. The sound was frantic, high-pitched, and distant at first, but it grew louder with each passing second, like a pack of beasts closing in on their prey.

"They're right behind us!" Nick screamed, his voice trembling.

Jacob's heart pounded in his chest, and he stole a glance at the rearview mirror. The trucks were gaining on them. The headlights were growing brighter, the engines louder. Panic clawed at his throat, but there was no time for it. Survival came first.

"Forget it," Jacob muttered. "I'm throwing the flag out. Let them have it."

He grabbed the flag, feeling its weight—its power—pressing against him. With a grim look on his face, he rolled down the window and tossed it onto the dirt road, hoping it would be enough to stop the pursuit. For a moment, one of the trucks slowed, and a man climbed out to retrieve the flag. But instead of stopping, the man gave a signal, and the chase continued.

Jacob cursed under his breath and slammed his foot on the gas again. The truck swerved wildly, the tires screeching as they fought to stay on the road. But just when they thought they had a chance, the road ahead disappeared. There was nowhere to go. Nowhere to hide.

"Everybody out!" Jacob shouted, his voice urgent. "We're running!"

Running for Their Lives

They jumped from the truck, adrenaline pumping through their veins as the sound of the mob's trucks grew closer. Their hearts pounded in their chests, and fear made their breaths ragged. The world around them felt like it was closing in, and Jacob could feel the weight of their desperate situation. But they were in it together, and that gave him strength enough to keep running.

"Where to now?" Nick gasped, looking around in a panic.

"I don't know," Jacob said, scanning the thick brush around them. "We just need to keep moving. We can't stop."

They pushed forward, their feet pounding against the ground as they ran through the underbrush. The sound of an approaching engine pierced the air, sending a fresh wave of panic through Jacob's chest. But then he saw it—a truck. An old one, its engine sputtering. The man inside looked older and weathered, but his eyes held something kind, something that made Jacob hold onto hope.

"You folks lost or something?" the man called out as he pulled up beside them.

"Please," Jacob gasped, his voice hoarse with fear. "We need help. We're being chased. They're going to kill us if you don't take us somewhere safe."

The man eyed them carefully before nodding. "Get in, boy. This ain't a place for folks like you."

Jacob motioned for Erick and Nick to follow. "Let's go."

They climbed into the truck, and the man revved the engine, steering them away from danger. As they drove off, Jacob couldn't shake the feeling that their troubles were far from over. But for now, they were alive. And that, at least, was enough.

CHAPTER 15
THE ROAD TO RECKONING

The Wild Ride

The truck bounced over rough terrain, the tires screeching as the old man drove with a determination that suggested he'd faced far worse than a few angry pursuers. Jacob gripped the seat, trying to ignore the feeling of dread creeping up his spine. He couldn't shake the thought that the mob was still after them, that the danger hadn't passed, and worse, that the flag might still hold some unspoken power over them.

Nick, from the back seat, shot him a glance. "You think they're giving up?" he asked.

Jacob didn't answer immediately. His mind raced, turning over all the things that had happened—the race, the mob, the flag. Something about it felt unfinished, like a story still being written. The flag was more than just a symbol. It felt like a tether, pulling them deeper into something bigger than they could comprehend.

The old man's voice broke the silence. "They won't give up easily," he said grimly. "But that doesn't mean you're out of options. Stay sharp. We've got one more thing to do before we're safe."

Jacob glanced at him, confused. "What do you mean?"

The old man gave him a cryptic look. "I'm talking about the real test. You've been running, but now you've got to show 'em what you're made of. The chase ain't over yet. Not for you, not for that flag."

The truck jolted as it hit a particularly deep hole in the dirt road. Jacob's heart thudded harder, realizing that he'd been in this position before—running, waiting for the right moment. But this time, the old man was right. It wasn't just about escaping anymore. It was about what he'd become, about proving that he wasn't just some outsider running from trouble. He was a cowboy. A Nigerian cowboy.

The Moment of Truth

They continued to weave through the countryside, the engine of the old man's truck humming steadily beneath them. Jacob's thoughts raced as they drew closer to their destination. Where exactly were they headed? What was the old man preparing him for?

And then it hit him—the truck. The one Jacob had left behind when the chase began. His truck. It sat abandoned in the middle of the woods, waiting for him to make a decision. Would he go back for it? Would he leave it behind?

The memory of that truck, once his pride and joy, now felt like an anchor, holding him to the past, to a version of himself that wasn't quite ready to let go. He had fought so hard for everything that had brought him here, and now, with the race, the flag, and the mob chasing them, it felt like there was more at stake than just his survival.

The old man's voice cut through the air again, his tone filled with quiet wisdom. "You don't need the truck to be a cowboy, boy. You need the spirit that drives you. A real cowboy knows when to ride and when to let go."

Jacob let out a breath, the realization settling in his chest. This wasn't just about the truck, or the flag, or even the chase. This was about the kind of man he wanted to become. And right now, he needed to face the truth. The cowboy spirit wasn't something you could just own; it had to be earned, forged in decisions like this one.

Breaking Free

The old man's truck came to a stop. They had reached the place where Jacob had abandoned his vehicle. He climbed out, the cool air biting at his skin as his boots crunched against the dirt. For a long moment, he stood there, staring at his truck.

It had been his pride, his symbol of independence. But now, it felt heavy, like a burden. The weight of every decision he'd made, every loss, every victory, seemed to be tied up in that truck. But the more he looked at it, the more it felt like an anchor, holding him in a past he couldn't return to.

"You ready to let go?" the old man asked, his voice steady.

Jacob nodded slowly, the weight of the decision settling in. This wasn't about the truck. It was about who he was becoming. The courage, the heart—that's what made a cowboy. And right now, the most important thing was to move forward, not to cling to something that had outlived its purpose.

With one last look at the truck, Jacob turned away, walking back to the old man's vehicle. His heart steadied as he climbed in. The road ahead was uncertain, but for the first time, Jacob wasn't afraid to face it. He was a cowboy because of the choices he made.

The Old Man's Help

The old man's truck bounced along the dirt road, the tires kicking up dust behind them. Jacob sat on the edge, still processing what had just happened. The flag, the chase, the mob closing in—it was all too much to make sense of.

Nick, still catching his breath, glanced at Jacob, his brow furrowed in confusion. "But Jacob," Nick said, his voice tight, "you dropped the flag, and their mob leader picked it up. Doesn't that mean they still have it?"

Jacob's heart skipped a beat as Nick's words pierced through him. The realization hit like a cold splash of water. He had dropped the flag, and the mob leader had picked it up. Was this why they were chasing them? Was it about the flag, after all? His gut twisted as the weight of the situation sank in. It wasn't just a race—it was something far more dangerous, and now, they had made themselves enemies of a group willing to kill to protect it.

The old man glanced over at them, his eyes sharp as he steered the truck through the brush. "What's this about a flag?" he asked, his voice steady, though there was a hint of curiosity beneath it.

Jacob hesitated, but with the weight of the truth pressing down on him, he spoke. "It's... It's a sacred flag," he said, his mind still racing. "I grabbed it, but then I dropped it, and the leader of the mob picked it up. Now they're after us. We don't know why, but it seems like they'll stop at nothing to get it back."

The old man nodded solemnly, but there was a strange glimmer in his eyes. "I've seen that flag before. It's not just a symbol of power—it's a relic. There's a story behind it, one that goes back generations. It's a flag of protection, of courage, but also of blood. People have killed for it before, and they'll do it again."

Jacob turned toward him, his heart pounding in his chest. "What does it mean? Why would they want it so badly?"

The old man's grip tightened on the steering wheel as he looked ahead, his face hardening. "That flag is tied to a long-standing tradition in these parts—something that goes back to the old days of the land, before the railroads, before the cattle drives. It's a symbol of leadership, of authority. Only those deemed worthy, those who've proven themselves in the trials, are allowed to carry it. It's a symbol of strength and power."

Jacob's mind was swirling. So much was happening so quickly, and he didn't understand all the pieces yet. Why would a flag carry so much weight? And how had it ended up in his hands, only to be dropped?

But before he could ask more, the truck lurched, and the sound of distant engines reached their ears. Jacob's heart sank. "We're not alone anymore," he muttered, barely able to keep his voice steady.

The old man's eyes darted to the rearview mirror, then forward again. "I figured. They won't give up so easily. Hold on tight."

A New Obstacle

The truck veered off the main road, taking a sharp turn into a narrow, less-traveled path that led through dense trees. Jacob's pulse quickened. The sound of the mob's vehicles was growing louder, and the old man's determination to keep them safe was evident, though his every move seemed calculated as if he knew exactly how to avoid being caught.

"Where are we going?" Erick asked, his voice tense.

The old man didn't answer right away. Instead, he focused on maneuvering the truck around the winding, overgrown path. The truck's headlights barely cut through the thickening woods, and the only sounds were the engine's hum and the faint, erratic beats of their own hearts.

"We're going to my place," the old man finally said. "It's not far. But we'll need to lose them first."

Jacob glanced behind them, barely able to make out the shapes of the pursuing vehicles through the trees. His hand clenched the seat, anxiety gnawing at him. He still couldn't shake the feeling that something bigger was at play here—something much darker than just a simple race.

And the flag... He couldn't forget the flag. It felt like it had bound them to this madness.

Chasing Shadows

The pursuit grew more intense. The sound of engines was now unmistakable—there were more of them. Jacob's heart pounded harder with each passing second. Were they gaining on them? Were they about to be caught?

"We need to pick up the pace," Nick urged.

The old man's eyes darted to the rearview mirror again, then to the path ahead. He nodded once, determined. "Hold on tight. We're going to have to make a run for it."

The truck bounced over a particularly rough patch of ground, and for a moment, it seemed like the mob might be closing in. But the old man didn't falter. His focus was unshakeable. Every twist and turn felt like a calculated escape, one that only someone familiar with the land could pull off.

Finally, after what felt like an eternity of evasive maneuvers, the trucks pursuing them veered off to the left, the sound of their engines fading into the distance. Jacob, Nick, and Erick exhaled in relief. For now, they were safe.

A True Cowboy's Lesson

As the truck slowed to a steady pace, the engine's hum settled into a more rhythmic tone, and the tension that had held the group tight began to dissipate. Jacob looked out through the windshield, his mind still racing, but the adrenaline of the chase had begun to fade. They were no longer running—they were in a strange kind of limbo between safety and uncertainty.

The old man, his knuckles still white on the steering wheel, didn't say a word as he navigated the winding road through the thick woods. He seemed to be waiting for something, his eyes narrowed and focused. Jacob couldn't help but feel like they were being led to a place of reflection, not just a physical location but a point of understanding.

"Are we safe now?" Erick finally asked, breaking the silence. His voice was weary, tinged with exhaustion, but there was a spark of hope in it, too.

The old man nodded slowly, his face still stoic. "For now. But the chase doesn't end just because you lose 'em on the road. It's about what happens inside you—whether you stand up and face the storm or let it knock you down."

Jacob's heart skipped. The old man's words felt like they were aimed directly at him. "What do you mean?" Jacob asked quietly.

The old man took a deep breath, exhaling slowly as the truck continued down the narrow, dusty path. "Being a cowboy... it ain't just about what you wear or the horse you ride. It's about *how* you ride and why you do it. The cowboy spirit is forged in the tough times when you've got nothing left but your grit, your courage, and your belief in something bigger than yourself."

Jacob felt the weight of those words settle deep into his bones. He had always thought of the cowboy spirit as something that came with strength—raw, unyielding strength. But the old man was speaking of something different. Something more elusive yet more vital.

"You have the strength in you," the old man continued, his voice calm but firm. "But strength alone won't carry you far. It's the heart that makes a true cowboy. That heart is the one that keeps fighting, even when the odds are stacked high, even when the world's against you. And the flag? That's just a reminder. It's not the flag that makes the cowboy; it's the cowboy who makes the flag."

Jacob let out a breath he didn't know he had been holding. The old man was right. All this time, he had been fixated on the flag, the symbol, the chase. But in the end, it wasn't the flag that would define him—it was the choices he made, the courage he carried, the spirit of resilience he carried within him.

The Final Stretch

They drove for what felt like an hour, the truck's headlights cutting through the darkness of the forest, when finally, the trees began to thin. A small clearing opened up, revealing a modest cabin nestled among the rolling hills. The old man slowed the truck, turning into a gravel driveway that led to the cabin's front porch.

"We're here," the old man said, cutting the engine. The quiet that followed was heavy, filled with a sense of both arrival and expectation.

Jacob stepped out of the truck, the cool night air hitting his skin like a cleansing wave. He stood there for a moment, taking in the simplicity of the scene—this cabin, tucked away in the woods, away from the chaos and the danger. The stillness felt like peace, and for the first time in a long time, Jacob felt the tension in his body ease.

Nick and Erick, having followed suit, stood next to him, looking around with equal wonder. The old man climbed out of the truck and gave them a slow, thoughtful look.

"This is where you learn what it really means to be a cowboy," he said. "It's not in the fight. It's in how you pick yourself up after the fight and how you carry that strength with you as you face whatever's next. You've already proven you've got the grit. Now it's time to prove you've got the heart."

Jacob nodded slowly, absorbing every word. He knew the old man wasn't just talking about surviving this chase. He was talking about something deeper—about how the journey to becoming a cowboy was never just about surviving the hardships. It was about *how* you moved forward, how you lived, how you stayed true to your values, your honor, and your faith.

As the night deepened around them, the old man led them to the cabin's porch, where a dim light flickered from inside. "Come on in," the old man said, "You'll need rest. Tomorrow, we'll talk more. You'll be ready when the time comes. And believe me, the time will come."

Resting Before the Storm

Inside the cabin, the warmth of a fire crackled in the stone hearth. Jacob and the others sat around the fire, their eyes heavy with exhaustion, but something else—something profound—had settled in their hearts.

Jacob didn't know what the future held. He didn't know if the mob was still hunting them or if they would be safe in the days ahead.

But for the first time, he wasn't afraid. He had learned something tonight—a lesson about courage, resilience, and, most of all, about the heart of a cowboy.

He looked across at Nick and Erick, who were both staring into the fire, lost in their thoughts. He smiled quietly to himself. Whatever came next, he knew he would face it with strength. Not just the strength of his muscles, his knowledge of the land, or his reputation. But the strength of his heart.

A cowboy didn't just survive; a cowboy thrived, not by overcoming the world, but by embracing it. And that was what Jacob was learning—slowly but surely. He was beginning to understand the true essence of what it meant to be a cowboy.

As the night deepened and the fire burned low, Jacob whispered to himself, "I am a cowboy, a Nigerian cowboy."

Nick and Erick exchanged looks, then grinned. Erick clapped Jacob on the back.

"You sure are, my friend," he said, a knowing smile crossing his face.

And for the first time, Jacob believed it.

CHAPTER 16
THE COWBOY'S TRUE TEST

A Quiet Dawn

Before the sun crept over the horizon, the world outside the small cabin held its breath. The air was cool and fresh, with only the soft rustle of wind through the trees breaking the silence. The old man stood by the door, his weathered hands resting on his knees, a silhouette against the first light of dawn. He hadn't slept much, if at all. But something about the stillness made him feel like now was the time to act.

He glanced at Jacob, who was just stirring awake on the couch. His face was drawn with the exhaustion of their long night, but his eyes—those eyes—were sharp despite the weariness. The old man's voice broke the silence, gravelly yet firm, like the gravel roads they'd driven on earlier.

"Best time to go back for your truck is before the sun shows its face," he said, his words clipped but purposeful. "Everything's quieter then. You're out of sight. Less chance of getting noticed. But don't let that fool you, boy—danger doesn't sleep. And neither do I... at least not much."

Jacob blinked, still groggy. "You mean now? Before dawn?"

The old man gave him a sly smile, one that was both knowing and comforting. "Ain't no time like the present. Trust me, you want to get this over with before the world turns really bright. You're still dodging bullets, even if you can't see 'em."

Jacob hesitated, a knot forming in his stomach. Something about the quiet, the calm of the moment, felt strange, like an invitation to make a choice. He glanced at the old man, whose confidence was infectious. The promise of the day ahead—or maybe just the certainty of what needed to be done—stirred something in him.

With a deep breath, he nodded, pushing himself upright. It was time.

The Journey Back

The truck's engine hummed steadily as they sped down the narrow road, the windows cracked to let in the early morning chill. The landscape was almost eerily still, as though nature itself was holding its breath.

Nick, beside Jacob, rubbed his eyes, clearly still struggling to shake off the grogginess.

"Are we really doing this?" he muttered, a yawn following his words. "It's barely light out."

Erick, from the backseat, stretched and yawned loudly.

"We don't have a choice, Nick. The truck's back there. It's just... a little strange."

The old man didn't answer immediately. His eyes were fixed on the road ahead, but there was something in his tone when he spoke that caught Jacob's attention.

"There's a thing about cowboys," he said, his voice steady but contemplative. "They don't cling to their saddles, their boots, or even their horses. Hell, they'll sell their last saddle if they have to. But what they never sell is the spirit inside 'em. That's what makes 'em cowboys, not a truck or a flag." His gaze flicked to Jacob for a brief moment. "So don't go thinking that truck's what makes you. It's the choices you make—just like now."

Jacob swallowed, the weight of his words sinking in. The truck had always been more than just a vehicle to him—it was a symbol of independence, of survival. But the old man's words hit deep. It wasn't the truck that made him a cowboy. It wasn't the flag. It was the choices, the heart inside him.

"I never thought I'd have to leave it behind," Jacob muttered, the idea still hard to grasp.

The old man's chuckle was dry, but it carried a hint of understanding.

"Part of you, huh? Sometimes, the hardest thing to do is walk away from the things that weigh you down. Don't worry about it, boy. We all gotta learn when to let go."

Back to the Past

The journey to Jacob's truck felt long, though the miles seemed to slip away faster than his thoughts. It was as if the road itself was pulling him back, drawing him to this moment. The truck, now abandoned, stood like an old ghost on the side of the road, its worn exterior dimly illuminated by the headlights of the old man's truck.

Jacob stepped out into the chilly air, boots crunching softly on the earth beneath him. The truck was a presence, a thing that had been part of him for so long. But now, standing before it, it felt different—heavier somehow. The pride and stubbornness he had once associated with it now felt more like a burden. The truck had become a metaphor for everything he had fought to prove. But in the harsh light of this moment, it was just a machine, like everything else.

"Well, at least I didn't put a 'Best Cowboy' bumper sticker on it," Jacob muttered, forcing a smile through the tension in his chest.

Nick shot him a half-smile.

"Yeah, but don't worry. It'd be a bestseller if you did."

Jacob managed a weak glare, though the grin that followed was genuine. He appreciated the humor, even if it didn't feel like the time for it. It was all too real now. This wasn't just about a truck—it was about who he was and who he was becoming.

The old man didn't speak, but his steady gaze rested on Jacob as though waiting for him to come to terms with the moment. Jacob took a deep breath, his fingers brushing the cool metal of the truck. It had served him well, but it wasn't him. It wasn't the cowboy spirit he was beginning to understand.

"Let's go," the old man called, breaking the silence. "They're still out there."

Jacob nodded slowly, his heart pounding, and climbed back into the truck. As the engine roared to life, he felt a strange sense of peace settle over him. The road ahead was still uncertain, but he knew that it wasn't about the truck or the chase anymore. It was about the choices he made. And for the first time in a long while, he was ready to face them head-on.

The Ride Home

The truck rumbled back down the road, the rising sun casting a warm glow over the horizon. The tension of the past few hours was still fresh in Jacob's mind, but there was also something else—

something lighter. They were free for the moment, but Jacob knew it wasn't over yet.

Nick yawned again, stretching his arms out.

"You think we've lost 'em?" he asked, glancing nervously behind them.

Erick shrugged.

"We're not in the clear yet. But we will be. Just need to keep going."

Jacob's eyes flicked to his friends. Despite the danger, despite the uncertainty, there was a shared understanding between them now. They had faced this together. They had survived together.

As they neared the main road, Jacob threw his arms up in the air, his voice loud and triumphant.

"I am a Cowboy! A Nigerian Cowboy!"

Nick rolled his eyes but couldn't suppress a grin.

"Oh boy, here we go."

Erick slapped Nick on the back, laughing.

"Hey, at least it's not 'I'm a cowboy, and I'm just passing through.'"

Jacob laughed. The sound was genuine and full of relief.

"Hey, there's no one else here to stop me from shouting it loud!" His eyes sparkled with the thrill of the moment, but deeper still, he felt something else—something that wasn't just about shouting a declaration.
It was about the heart inside him. The courage, the wisdom, and the resilience to stand tall, no matter what.

The old man's truck rolled down the road, the sun rising higher with each passing minute. The past was behind them, the future uncertain, but Jacob didn't feel afraid anymore. For the first time in a long while, he felt like he was exactly where he needed to be.

And maybe, just maybe, he was starting to understand what it meant to be a cowboy.

CHAPTER 17
A COWBOY'S HONOR

The Aftermath of the Rodeo

The rodeo had come and gone, but its impact lingered like the echo of a thunderstorm that hadn't quite passed. Jacob felt an unfamiliar weight on his shoulders—not from the physical exhaustion of the ride, but from the mental fatigue of battling both the competition and the resentment simmering in the hearts of those who thought he didn't belong.

As he walked through the dusty grounds of the rodeo, his boots kicking up clouds of dirt, the clatter of hooves and the fading murmurs of the crowd felt distant, like sounds from a dream already slipping away. The event was over, but its consequences had only just begun to settle in his bones. He could feel eyes on him—not just from the cowboys, but from the town itself. He had made a name for himself that day. But was it enough?

Jake, Adam, Bob, and Lucas had disappeared into the crowd, but their presence loomed over him. The rivalry wasn't over. If anything, it had only just begun. Jacob knew this wasn't going to be an easy ride. But despite the tension in the air, he felt a strange sense of peace. He hadn't just stayed in the game. He had proven something to himself. He had faced his fear, competed with the best, and stood his ground. And maybe, just maybe, he had earned a little respect. Though it was hard to tell, especially when Jake's cold glare still burned in his mind.

Jacob's hand subconsciously went to his chest. He could feel the weight of his cowboy spirit—a fire he'd carried with him all his life. He wasn't just here to prove himself to others. He was here to prove to himself that he was more than just an outsider. More than just the "Nigerian Cowboy" people whispered about.

A Visit to the Saloon

That evening, Jacob found himself in the local saloon, nursing a bottle of dark malt-rich, bitter, and bold enough to match his thoughts. The amber liquid reflected the warm light from the rustic lamps hanging overhead, casting long shadows across the worn wooden floors. The atmosphere felt different now that the rodeo was over. People were relaxed, exchanging stories, laughter, and the occasional joke. Cowboy hats tilted low over eyes, boots clinking against the wood floors, and the sound of soft country music hummed through the air.

Jacob didn't exactly feel like he belonged here—not yet, anyway. He hadn't earned the right to sit at the table with the veterans of the rodeo just yet. But he wasn't alone. Erick and Nick had followed him into the saloon, their faces lit up with a mixture of relief and camaraderie. They had been through the war together on the rodeo grounds, and now they were just three guys sitting down for a drink, trying to forget the grind of the day.

"Hey, man, you did well out there," Erick said, slapping Jacob on the back. "Seriously. You showed 'em all what a real cowboy looks like."

Nick joined in, raising his glass in a small toast. "I mean, I still can't believe you stayed on that bull for as long as you did. You're the real deal."

Jacob smiled but felt a little uncomfortable, like he was still the new guy trying to fit into a world that didn't quite have room for him. "Thanks, but I'm still learning. I'm just trying to be a good cowboy, you know?"

"Good cowboy, huh?" Erick laughed, shaking his head. "You're a damn fine cowboy. Don't let anyone tell you otherwise."

The conversation flowed easily, and for the first time since arriving, Jacob felt a sense of belonging. It wasn't about the competition anymore. It was about the honor, the people, and the community.

Even though the rivalry with Jake and the others still hung in the air, for now, it felt like it was on the back burner. Jacob was beginning to understand that being a cowboy was more than just winning contests—it was about earning respect, standing tall even when everyone else tried to knock you down, and finding that rare moment when everything felt right, even if it was only for a few minutes.

Jacob's gaze wandered across the room, catching the flicker of light that framed a familiar face. Lucas, the quieter of the four rivals, was standing near the door. Jacob had expected nothing more than a passing glance, maybe even a silent challenge, but Lucas surprised him.

Lucas's Unexpected Visit

Lucas, with his glasses slightly askew and his hands nervously fiddling with the brim of his hat, walked over to their table. His eyes flickered between Jacob and the others before he spoke, his voice low but sincere.

"Hey, Jacob," Lucas said quietly. "I just wanted to say… that was a hell of a ride out there. You've got guts, I'll give you that."

Jacob didn't know how to respond at first. The last thing he expected was a compliment from one of his rivals, and Lucas, of all people. "Uh, thanks," Jacob said, unsure whether to trust the sincerity in Lucas's voice. "I'm just doing my best."

Lucas shifted, his gaze briefly dropping to the floor before meeting Jacob's eyes again. "Look, I know the others are hard on you. But don't let them get to you. They're just jealous. You're doing what they can't."

Jacob raised an eyebrow. "Jealous?"

"Yeah, man," Lucas replied, his voice gaining a little more confidence. "They don't want you here. They don't want anyone rocking their world. But I think deep down, they know… you've got something they don't. You're real. And they can't stand that."

Jacob felt a strange warmth in his chest. *Real.* The word lingered, and for the first time, Jacob realized he might belong. "Thanks, Lucas. That means a lot coming from you."

Lucas gave a half-smile, shifting uncomfortably. He wasn't sure whether to keep talking or just leave. "I don't agree with everything they do, but I'm not the kind of guy to stand by and watch. Just… don't let 'em break you down, okay?"

"I won't," Jacob promised, the words tasting new on his tongue. For the first time, he felt like he was earning something beyond his spot in the competition. Maybe Lucas wasn't the enemy after all.

Before Lucas could say anything else, the moment was interrupted.

The Rivalry Escalates

"Hey, Nigerian cowboy!" Jake's mocking tone cut through the air, sharp as a blade. Jacob's heart sank, and he turned to face him, already sensing the confrontation that was about to unfold.

Jake, flanked by Adam and Bob, swaggered up to Jacob's table. His smirk was wide, but there was something about the way his eyes narrowed that told Jacob this wasn't just idle teasing.

"You think you've earned your spot here?" Jake sneered, his voice dripping with disdain. "You're not a cowboy. You'll never be one of us. Go back to wherever you came from."

Jacob stood tall, feeling the sting of Jake's words, but refused to let them break him. Anger simmered just beneath the surface, but he stayed calm, steadfast, like the cowboy spirit that had brought him this far.

"I'm not going anywhere," Jacob said, his voice steady but resolute. "A good cowboy doesn't run away. Good cowboys don't give up. And I'm a damn good cowboy."

Jake took a step forward, his nostrils flaring. "You're not even a real cowboy. You don't know what it means to be a cowboy. You'll never be one of us."

Jacob met Jake's gaze head-on, unwavering. "It's not about where I come from. It's about who I am. A cowboy's heart is in here," Jacob said, tapping his chest. "And I've got a heart full of cowboy spirit."

For a long moment, the words hung in the air, thick and heavy. Jake opened his mouth as if to retort, but he paused—his expression shifting in ways Jacob couldn't quite interpret. Then, with a grunt, Jake turned away, muttering something under his breath.

The tension in the room didn't dissipate immediately, but Jacob felt a sense of quiet victory. It wasn't about winning. It was about standing his ground.

A Glimmer of Hope

Later that evening, Jacob stood outside under the stars, leaning against the fence, gazing out at the vast expanse of land. The air was still, and for the first time in days, Jacob felt a deep sense of peace settle in his chest.

Erick and Nick joined him, both smiling in quiet understanding.

"You did good today, man," Erick said. "You stood your ground, and you didn't let Jake or anyone else push you around."

Jacob chuckled softly; his breath was visible in the cool night air. "Yeah, but it's not just about standing my ground. It's about showing them that no matter what they throw at me, I'm not going to quit. I'm a cowboy. And good cowboys don't give up."

Nick smiled and nodded, clapping Jacob on the back. "And that's why you'll make it, Jacob. You've got what it takes."

Jacob stood in the silence, the stars twinkling above him like a promise. For the first time, the vastness of the open sky didn't feel lonely. It felt *right*.

He took a deep breath, letting the cool air fill his lungs, the weight of the day lifting off his shoulders. The rivalry with Jake, the doubts about whether he truly belonged, the long days spent trying to prove himself—they all seemed distant now. In this moment, there was only him, the stars, and the steady pulse of his cowboy spirit.

"It's funny," Jacob said quietly, more to himself than to the others, "When I first got here, I didn't know if I could do this. If I could really *be* a cowboy. But now, after today... I'm starting to believe I can."

Nick leaned against the fence beside him, his voice low but filled with warmth. "You don't have to prove it to anyone but yourself. You're already a cowboy. You've got the heart for it. And that's all that matters."

Erick nodded, his face more serious now. "What Jake and the others don't get is that a cowboy isn't made in a day. It's a way of life, a state of mind. You've got that. You've always had it."

Jacob looked at both of them, a small smile tugging at the corners of his lips. "Thanks. That means a lot, you know?"

Nick clapped him on the shoulder. "No need to thank us. You've earned it. The rest of the world just needs to catch up."

The three of them stood there for a while, soaking in the calm of the night, the soft sounds of the wind rustling through the tall grasses, and the distant hum of the town behind them. It was a moment of quiet after the storm—a moment of reflection, and of hope.

The Next Day

The morning after the rodeo dawned clear and bright, the sky a brilliant blue that stretched out endlessly. Jacob woke up early, as he always did, drawn to the stillness of the world before anyone else was awake. He slipped out of bed, careful not to wake Erick or Nick, and grabbed his boots and hat. The air was cool, and the sun had just begun to rise, casting long shadows across the earth.

He walked outside, the crunch of gravel beneath his boots the only sound as he made his way toward the stables. His horse, *Thunder*, was waiting for him. Jacob took a moment to simply stand there, looking at the horse—his companion, his partner. Thunder had always been there when he needed him, steady and true.

As Jacob approached the stall, Thunder nickered softly, lifting his head as if greeting his rider. Jacob smiled, a rare feeling of contentment spreading through him. *This is where I belong*, he thought. It wasn't just about the rodeo or the competition. It wasn't about winning or losing. It was about the journey. About the path he'd chosen and the man he was becoming.

He saddled up and led Thunder out of the barn, mounting him with a practiced ease. The early morning air was refreshing, and as he rode out into the open range, Jacob felt the tension in his shoulders finally begin to melt away. It was just him, Thunder, and the endless horizon stretching before them.

There was a sense of freedom in the air, a quiet promise that no matter the obstacles, no matter the challenges that lay ahead, he would face them the same way he always had—head held high, heart steady, and a fierce determination to never back down.

An Unlikely Friendship

Later that day, Jacob found himself face-to-face with Lucas again. This time, it wasn't in the saloon or at the rodeo grounds. They were both standing by the horse pens, each tending to their horses, the quiet sounds of hooves and soft murmurs of the animals filling the space between them.

Jacob had to admit there was something about Lucas that made him different from the others. The way he spoke—carefully, thoughtfully showed a side of him that Jacob hadn't expected. Maybe it was because Lucas didn't have the same bravado as Jake. Maybe it was because Lucas saw something in Jacob that others didn't.

"Nice ride this morning," Lucas said, breaking the silence as he adjusted his horse's saddle. "I saw you out there with Thunder. He's a good horse."

Jacob looked at him, surprised by the compliment. "Thanks. He's been with me a long time."

Lucas nodded, his expression softening. "I can tell. You two make a good team."

There was a long pause before Lucas spoke again. "You know, I don't know what the others have against you. You've earned your place. But some people… they don't like change."

Jacob shrugged, brushing a strand of hair away from his forehead. "I don't think it's just about change. It's about me not fitting into their idea of what a cowboy should be. They see me as an outsider. And to be honest, I can't blame them."

Lucas gave a small laugh, a hint of irony in his voice. "Well, they've got it wrong. You're one of the few real cowboys I've met in a long time. You don't try to be anyone you're not. And that's more than I can say for some of the others."

Jacob met his eyes, studying the sincerity there. For a moment, there was no rivalry between them, no history of competition. Just two men talking, sharing something honest.

"Maybe we're not so different after all," Jacob said.

Lucas gave a slight nod. "Maybe not."

A New Beginning

As the day turned to dusk, Jacob found himself back at the saloon. The atmosphere was different now. The tension of the rodeo was gone, replaced by the soft buzz of conversation and the occasional clink of glasses. Jacob stepped inside, his boots sounding firm on the wooden floor. The room fell a little quieter as he walked in, but it wasn't the same cold reception he had received before. This time, people nodded at him, some even offering a small smile.

Jacob had earned something more than just a place in the rodeo. He had earned respect, not just from the cowboys, but from himself. And that, for the first time, felt like a victory that no one could take away.

He made his way to the bar, where Erick and Nick were already seated, grinning like they knew something Jacob didn't.

"You look like you're in a good mood," Nick remarked with a wink.

Jacob smiled, feeling a deep sense of contentment settle in his chest. "Yeah, I think I finally figured it out. It's not about the fight or the competition. It's about living the life of a cowboy. And I'm ready for whatever comes next."

Erick raised his glass, his smile broad. "To the Nigerian Cowboy. The real deal."

Jacob chuckled, raising his own glass in return. "To the cowboy way. And to never give up."

And as the laughter and conversation swirled around him, Jacob felt a warmth in his heart stronger than any rivalry or challenge he had faced. The road ahead was long, but it no longer seemed so uncertain. He had his place here—among the cowboys, the open skies, and the promise of something greater than himself.

He was a cowboy, and this was only the beginning.

CHAPTER 18
TENSIONS RISE

Jacob's Grit

Jacob stood in the dusty practice pen, muscles aching from hours of grueling preparation. The heat from the afternoon sun pressed down on him, and sweat trickled down his forehead, mixing with the dirt on his skin. He tied the rope around the bull's horns, his fingers trembling slightly. The sound of the arena gates closing echoed in the distance, signaling the start of the day's events. The other cowboys were gearing up, but Jacob was already deep in his thoughts. His focus was unshakeable, but his mind wrestled with doubt.

Today wasn't just another ride. It was something bigger. He had already been through the motions, his body accustomed to the grueling physical demands of rodeo life, but something was off. *This isn't just about riding anymore*, he thought. *This is survival. Proving I belong here.*

His thoughts drifted back to his childhood in Nigeria. He remembered the long hours spent in the fields with his father, learning the value of hard work, patience, and resilience.

His mother's voice echoed in his mind, telling him, "When you fall, you rise again, because our faith is stronger than any obstacle the world throws at us." Those words had carried him through life's toughest challenges. But here, in this rodeo arena, they seemed distant, as though his roots weren't enough to hold him steady.

He gripped the rope tighter, drawing strength from his upbringing. In Nigeria, he'd learned to weather storms—literal and metaphorical. His father, a preacher, had always said, "The Lord's will make a way, but you must walk through the fire first."

Jacob had walked through fire before. Maybe this was just another test, another way for him to prove that his place here wasn't a mistake.

The bull snorted beside him, snapping him out of his thoughts. *I belong here,* Jacob reminded himself. *No one can take that from me.*

The Rivalry Intensifies

Later, Jacob walked into the arena, his hat low over his brow. The weight of a thousand eyes felt like an invisible force pressing against him. He could feel Jake, Adam, and Bob's eyes on him, their judgment as sharp as a blade. They stood near the gate, whispering and laughing, clearly amused by his presence.

Erick and Nick flanked him on either side, offering silent support. Their presence was comforting, and for a moment, Jacob allowed himself to appreciate it. These men weren't just fellow riders; they were his allies, the few people he could trust in this cutthroat world.

"Don't let them get to you," Erick murmured, nudging him with his elbow. "You've been riding better than all of them combined. They know it. That's why they're angry."

Jacob forced a smile, but there was bitterness behind it. "I don't care if they're angry. I care about proving I'm not just some outsider they can toss aside."

Nick, ever the optimist, grinned. "And you're doing it, man. One ride at a time. They're just scared of you, that's all."

The thought caught Jacob off guard. *Scared of me?* He didn't feel intimidated—he felt like a man on the edge of a precipice. But there was something about the idea of fear that resonated with him.

Maybe, just maybe, he had something they didn't. A drive that couldn't be snuffed out. *Maybe they're scared of me*, he thought. *Maybe I've got something worth holding onto.*

As he watched Jake and the others huddle together, Jacob's jaw tightened. This wasn't about revenge. It was about respect. He wasn't going to let anyone take that from him.

A Test of Will

Jacob's next ride was going to be his hardest yet. His nerves were on edge, and the familiar twist of anxiety curled deep in his gut. The crowd murmured in the stands, and for the first time, their words weren't supportive. They were filled with doubt, questioning whether he'd last.

"Let's see how long he lasts this time," Jacob heard Jake's voice cut through the murmurs, his tone dripping with mockery.

Jacob squeezed his eyes shut, willing the noise away. He had to block it all out. It didn't matter what Jake said. It didn't matter what anyone else thought. He was here for one reason—to prove he belonged.

The gate slammed open. The bull exploded into the ring, a wild mass of muscle and fury. Jacob's body tensed, every fiber of his being reacting to the bull's violent bucking. The animal twisted beneath him, throwing itself in a blur of raw power. Jacob's grip tightened on the rope, the fibers biting into his gloves, the pain of holding on an unfamiliar comfort.

He could feel the rush of wind against his face, the heat of the bull beneath him, and the relentless bucking that jarred his bones. Every second felt like an eternity. It was a fight to stay on, to stay present. The crowd's roar was distant, like the sound of waves crashing far off on the shore. Jacob's entire focus was on the rhythm of the ride, the way the bull moved, the strength of his body fighting to stay attached. His legs burned, but he didn't let go. Not after everything he had fought for. Not after every insult. Not after everything Jake had said.

Eight seconds later, the buzzer sounded. Jacob was thrown from the bull's back, landing in a controlled roll. He stood, his body shaking with adrenaline, as the crowd erupted in cheers. He had done it.

But it wasn't the cheers that made Jacob's chest tighten. It was the look on Jake's face. His jaw was clenched, his eyes full of frustration. The satisfaction in Jacob's chest soured. Jake had underestimated him, and now Jacob was the one standing, not him.

The Conversation with Lucas

After the ride, Jacob found himself alone by the stables, his breath coming in ragged gasps. The adrenaline buzzed through his veins, but under it, there was an unexpected calm. He wasn't just proving something to Jake anymore. He was proving it to himself. Before he could head back to the others, he heard footsteps approaching. He turned and saw Lucas, the quiet member of Jake's group, walking toward him.

"Hey," Lucas said, his voice softer than usual. "That was a hell of a ride."

Jacob raised an eyebrow. "Thanks," he replied. "Didn't expect you to be the one to say that."

Lucas shifted awkwardly, glancing over his shoulder at the group of cowboys still talking amongst themselves. "I don't agree with everything they say or do," Lucas admitted, his voice low. "But you earned that ride. You've got guts. I respect that."

Jacob stared at Lucas, surprised. He hadn't expected this—had never thought that Lucas, of all people, would be the one to offer him respect. "I didn't expect that from you," Jacob muttered. "You and your crew... you've made it clear you don't want me here."

Lucas shrugged, his eyes distant. "Yeah, well, I've never really fit in with them either. But I see something in you, Jacob. Something they don't have. You're real. And that scares them."

Jacob was stunned. The quiet man before him had just opened up, revealing something Jacob hadn't expected. Lucas wasn't the enemy—he was just another man caught in this world of competition and expectations.

"Thanks," Jacob said quietly. "That means more than you know."

Lucas gave a half-smile, awkward as ever. "Just don't let them break you. Don't let them make you doubt yourself."

Jacob nodded, the weight of those words settling deep within him. He had to hold onto that. Lucas wasn't the enemy. Maybe, just maybe, he wasn't the only one struggling to find his place.

The Growing Pressure

The days following Jacob's ride were filled with mounting tension. Jake, Adam, and Bob continued their silent treatment—more mocking glares, more taunts under their breath. But Jacob refused to rise to it. The more they mocked, the more Jacob realized it wasn't about him. It was about their fear. They feared he might be good enough to compete with them.

But even Jacob could see how the pressure was starting to take its toll on Erick and Nick. Jacob had raised the bar, and the weight of that responsibility hung over all of them. Nick had joked about it, but Jacob could feel it. Every ride now felt like it might be his last.

In the quiet moments, when the arena was empty and the stars hung heavy in the sky, Jacob began to wonder if the rodeo world was really where he belonged. There was something deeper here—something bigger than the rivalry, bigger than the competition. The nights when his mind drifted to his parents' letters, he found strength in the words his father often said: "The road may be long and hard, my son, but trust in the Lord and in yourself."

He clung to that faith. He wasn't alone, no matter how much the world tried to tell him otherwise. But for now, all he could do was ride. And the next challenge would be even harder. Each ride, each moment in the arena, felt like a battle, a struggle not just to stay on the bull, but to stay true to who he was, and why he'd come this far.

He wasn't just fighting the animals in the ring anymore. He was fighting the whispers, the doubts, and the ghosts of his past that threatened to pull him down. But he couldn't afford to let them win. Not now. Not when he was so close.

The night before his next big ride, Jacob sat alone in the quiet of his trailer. The noise of the competition, the laughter of the other cowboys, all felt miles away. His mind was a storm of thoughts, fears, and hopes. He'd come here to prove himself, not just to the others, but to the man he wanted to be. And he was so close, yet it all felt like it could slip through his fingers at any moment.

As he lay back, staring up at the ceiling, he recalled the faith his mother had always shown. "Your strength comes not from what the world can give you, but from what God has already placed inside you. No matter where you go, remember that." She had spoken those words so often, and now, they came back to him, a lifeline in the swirling sea of doubt.

Jacob's eyes closed, and a sense of peace began to settle over him. Tomorrow was a new day, and he would face it as the man his parents had raised him to be—a man of courage, faith, and resilience.

The Ride of His Life

The next day, Jacob stood in the arena again. The air was thick with anticipation. The gate was about to open, and he could feel the energy vibrating through the ground beneath his boots. He had done this a thousand times before, yet today felt different. The crowd seemed louder, the arena more intimidating, and the bull he was about to face was a force of nature.

The gate swung open with a loud crack, and the bull stormed into the ring with terrifying force. Jacob's heart raced as he mounted the animal, his hands slick with sweat, his body tense. He could hear the crowd's mixed cheers and jeers, the sounds of the other cowboys shouting at him to hold on.

He gritted his teeth and settled into position. This time, there was no space for doubt, no time for hesitation. The bull bucked hard, its hooves pounding against the dirt with a deafening rhythm. Jacob's body jolted with each violent movement, but he stayed grounded, his grip unyielding.

Every muscle screamed in protest, but Jacob refused to let go. *I am here. I am not afraid*, he thought, as the bull twisted and thrashed beneath him.

The seconds felt like hours. The pain was almost unbearable, his body instinctively fighting the wild ride. Yet there was something inside of him that pushed back harder than the bull's fury. He thought of his mother's words. He thought of his father's sermons, his teachings of resilience, faith, and strength. *This isn't just about riding a bull. This is about showing the world who I am.*

The buzzer sounded.

Jacob was thrown from the bull's back, his body flying through the air before landing hard on the dirt. He rolled, instinctively absorbing the impact, but he didn't stay down. His chest heaved as he pushed himself up, his body aching with every movement.

The crowd's roar filled the air, a mixture of awe and disbelief. Jacob had stayed on for the full eight seconds.

As he stood, shaking with adrenaline, his gaze met Jake's. The other cowboy's face was twisted with frustration, his eyes burning with a combination of rage and disbelief. Jacob didn't flinch. He stood tall, shoulders squared, chest rising and falling with the rhythm of his breath.

He'd done it. Not just for the crowd. Not just for the win. But for himself.

A Moment of Clarity

Later, as Jacob walked toward the stables, his body battered from the ride, he spotted Lucas again. The quiet cowboy was leaning against the fence, watching the others from a distance.

"Nice ride," Lucas said quietly, his voice calm but sincere.

Jacob nodded, feeling an unexpected connection with the man. "Thanks," he replied. "I couldn't have done it without the training."

Lucas gave a small nod. "You're not like them," he said after a pause. "The way they push and fight, trying to break you. It's not the same with you. I think that's why they're scared of you."

Jacob glanced at him, surprised. "Scared? By me?"

Lucas met his gaze, his expression serious. "Yeah. You're not here to just prove something. You're here because it's who you are. And they can't handle that." He looked over his shoulder, as if to make sure no one else was listening, then added, "You've got something that they don't—faith. And I think that's what makes them afraid."

Jacob stood there, processing Lucas's words. There was something powerful in that simple statement. He had faith—not just in his abilities, but in the belief that he had been placed here for a reason.

A moment of clarity washed over him. He wasn't just fighting the bulls, the other cowboys, or even the critics. He was fighting to honor everything he had learned, to prove that his roots, his faith, his identity, were powerful forces that no one could break.

"I'm not going anywhere," Jacob said, a firm conviction in his voice.

Lucas smiled. "Good. Then let's see where this goes."

CHAPTER 19
THE BREAKING POINT

A Test of Strength

Jacob stood in the dusty practice pen, his muscles sore from the endless hours of riding, each movement feeling like it came at the cost of his body's endurance. The sun hung low in the sky, casting long shadows over the arena as the air hummed with the sounds of the other cowboys prepping for the evening's competition. Sweat poured down his face, mixing with the dirt that clung to his skin—a reminder of the battle he was waging not just against the bulls but against everything that whispered he didn't belong.

He tied the rope around the bull's horns with hands that were already raw from countless rides. The familiar burn in his arms only pushed him harder. He couldn't stop. Not now. Not when every second felt like a countdown to something bigger than just riding.

The scent of leather, sweat, and dust filled his nostrils, mixing with the faint tang of metal from the gates. Each breath he took felt heavy, like the air itself was thick with the weight of his doubts. He wanted to shake it off. But the voices crept in anyway—the ones that said he wasn't good enough, that he didn't belong here.

Not now, Jacob. Focus.

His horse snorted beside him, pulling him from his thoughts. The bull shifted impatiently, its nostrils flaring with aggression, but Jacob's focus never wavered. He could hear the faint sounds of the arena gates clanging behind him, the distant voices of the crowd growing louder as the other cowboys began lining up for their turns.

Today wasn't just about riding a bull. It was about survival. Proving he had what it took to earn his place in this world.

The doubt crept in like a shadow in the back of his mind—Jake, Adam, Bob—all of them watching, waiting for him to fail. The tension in his chest was as tight as the rope he'd just tied. But this time, the pressure wouldn't break him.

He didn't belong here in their eyes, but he was here anyway.

With a deep breath, Jacob climbed onto the bull, feeling the burn in his legs as he gripped the rope with all his might. His heart hammered against his ribcage. He steadied his breath. The bull snorted again, ready for the release. And Jacob, ready to prove his worth, braced for what was to come.

The Rivalry Intensifies

Later that day, Jacob walked into the arena, his hat pulled low over his brow. The world felt strangely muffled, as though he were in a bubble. His boots kicked up clouds of dust with every step as he made his way toward the waiting gate. The eyes of Jake, Adam, and Bob followed him, their low murmurs cutting through the air like daggers.

Every part of him wanted to respond, to lash out, but he knew that would be exactly what they wanted. They wanted him to snap. They wanted to see him break.

Erick and Nick were standing nearby, talking in low voices, but their presence was a silent form of comfort. The tension between Jacob and the others had been growing for weeks now, but with his friends beside him, Jacob felt like he could weather the storm.

"Don't let them get to you," Erick said, nudging Jacob's shoulder with a grin that was as much a challenge as it was reassurance. "You've been doing better than all of them combined. They know it. That's why they're angry."

Jacob tried to force a smile, but the bitterness in his chest was like a rock he couldn't dislodge. "I don't care if they're angry. I care about proving I'm not just some outsider to be tossed aside."

Nick chimed in from the other side, his grin wide and infectious. "And you're doing it, man. One ride at a time. They're just scared of you, that's all."

The idea that they might be scared of him felt strange, almost laughable, but Jacob allowed himself a fleeting moment of pride. For the first time, he wasn't just trying to stay afloat—he was pushing back.

"Yeah, well," Jacob replied, his tone quieter now, "they'll see that I'm not just some guy who doesn't belong here. I'm here to stay."

He could almost hear Jake's sneer, feel the weight of it on his back. *I'll show them.*

A Test of Will

Jacob's next ride was a test in every sense of the word. As he mounted the bull, a wave of unease rippled through him, his stomach churning with nervous energy. The crowd's whispers filled the air, not with praise but with doubt. It always started like this—doubt, like a seed in his chest that had taken root and grown with every taunt, every look from Jake.

"Let's see how long he lasts this time," Jake's voice rang out from the sidelines, dripping with sarcasm.

Jacob clenched his jaw but refused to let the words sink in. He focused on the bull beneath him—its muscles rippling under his thighs, its body tense with fury, ready to explode. The gate swung open with a crash, and the bull launched forward like a bolt of lightning. The force of it nearly threw Jacob off, but he gripped the rope tightly, his body going rigid.

The bull twisted violently beneath him, bucking with all its might. For a moment, it seemed like Jacob might lose his grip. His heart pounded; his breath ragged as the bull spun again. The ground seemed to shift beneath him, but he held on.

Stay on. Stay on.

The pain in his legs was excruciating, but Jacob ignored it, focusing on the rhythm of the ride. The bull fought like it was possessed, but so did Jacob. He stayed on for eight seconds, barely, but the crowd erupted in a roar. His body felt like it was on fire as he dismounted, landing heavily in the dust.

He could hear Jake's muttered curse from the sidelines and see the venomous glare burning into his back. But Jacob didn't care. He'd done it. He'd proven something to himself, something that had nothing to do with Jake or the others. This time, it was about him.

The Conversation with Lucas

As Jacob caught his breath, wiping the sweat from his brow, he stepped away from the arena and made his way toward the stables.

His legs felt like rubber, the adrenaline still coursing through his veins, but the weariness was creeping in.

Just as he was about to retreat into the quiet space behind the barn, a voice called out from behind him. "Hey."

Jacob turned, surprised to see Lucas standing there. Lucas, the quiet one, the one who never quite fit in with Jake and the others, was watching him intently.

"That was a hell of a ride," Lucas said quietly, his voice almost lost in the sound of the crowd's fading cheers.

Jacob raised an eyebrow. "Thanks. Didn't expect you to be the one to say that."

Lucas shuffled his feet, glancing over at the group of cowboys still watching from the other side of the arena. "I don't agree with everything they say or do, but they don't get it. You've got guts, man. Not many people would've stayed on that bull for as long as you did."

The unexpected compliment took Jacob aback. "I'm just doing my best. I'm still learning."

Lucas nodded, his gaze shifting to the ground for a moment. "I get it. I've seen what it's like to fight for your place, but it's hard when you don't have people on your side, you know? I've had my share of doubts."

Jacob studied him, wondering if Lucas was trying to say something more. "I never thought you'd be the one to get it."

Lucas gave a small smile, his eyes revealing something deeper— something that Jacob couldn't quite place. "I know what it's like to be caught between two worlds. But you don't need to prove anything to them. Just keep doing what you're doing. Don't let them get to you. You've got something they don't."

Jacob felt a warmth in his chest—something he hadn't expected from Lucas. "Thanks, Lucas. I won't forget that."

For the first time, Jacob didn't see Lucas as just another one of Jake's friends. There was more to him, something he couldn't ignore. Maybe, just maybe, Lucas wasn't the enemy after all.

A New Challenge Approaches

As Jacob walked back to the stables, he noticed a figure standing near the gates. Marcus. The man who had been making waves in the rodeo circuit, the one who had a reputation for being ruthless. He'd been eyeing Jacob for a while now, and Jacob knew this wasn't just a casual encounter.

Marcus smiled as Jacob approached, a cold, calculating look in his eyes. "Nice ride," he said, his voice smooth, almost too smooth. "But I think you'll find the real challenge isn't about staying on the bull. It's about staying relevant. Out here, you either make your mark or get left behind."

Jacob met his gaze, feeling an unease stir in his gut. "I'm not here to be anyone's pawn."

Marcus's smile didn't falter. "No one's asking you to be, kid. But if you want to make it, you'll have to face the truth. This is a world for winners. And if you don't make it to the top, the only place you'll be is at the bottom."

Jacob held his ground, his fists clenching at his sides. "I'm not afraid of the competition."

Marcus's laugh was low, almost mocking. "We'll see, won't we?"

As Marcus walked away, Jacob felt the weight of his words press on him. A challenge was coming, and it wasn't just about the rodeo anymore. It was about everything he had fought for—and everything he was willing to risk.

The Moment of Reflection

That night, as Jacob lay in the bunkhouse, staring up at the ceiling, the weight of the day pressed heavily on him. The constant battles, both internal and external, were starting to take their toll. He was exhausted—physically, emotionally, and mentally—but there was something else lurking in the shadows of his mind.

He'd fought so hard to prove himself, to belong. And now, he was starting to wonder if it was enough. He'd made it this far, but the next step was going to be the hardest yet. There were no guarantees in this world, no safety net. Just him, his determination, and the endless road ahead.

Jacob's thoughts drifted to his parents back home—his father's steady encouragement, his mother's unwavering faith. He could almost hear their voices, feel their prayers, a reminder of why he was here. This wasn't just about proving himself to the cowboys around him. This was about living up to the dreams and sacrifices of his family.

And yet, he couldn't shake the feeling that there was more at stake now than just the rodeo. His life was on the line, his sense of identity, his place in this world. It wasn't just about the bulls, the competition, or even the victories. It was about finding the strength to keep going when everything inside him screamed to stop.

As he closed his eyes and let the silence wash over him, he made a vow to himself: no matter what happened, he wasn't going to let anyone take his place—not Marcus, not Jake, not anyone. He was a cowboy, and he was going to fight for that title with everything he had.

The journey was far from over. But Jacob knew one thing for certain he wasn't done yet.

Chapter 20
The Pressure Builds

The Weight of Expectations

Jacob woke early the next morning, his body still aching from the brutal ride the day before. The sun hadn't fully risen, casting a pale, cool light over the vast stretch of land. He stood by the fence, hands resting on the top rail, staring out over the empty arena. The silence was heavy as if the world itself held its breath.

His chest tightened as memories of the ride flooded back. The bull's violent bucking, the roar of the crowd—it all felt like a test. But despite the applause, one question gnawed at him: Was it enough? Would it ever be enough? Could he truly belong, or was he destined to be the outsider, always fighting to prove himself?

He shook his head, trying to shake off the thoughts, but they clung to him like the dust on his skin. The pressure wasn't just in the physical pain of the ride. It was the constant fear that he wasn't living up to expectations—the ones from the other cowboys, from himself, from everyone watching.

His breath hitched as he thought about the inevitable moment when he'd face them again. Would he ever find his place here? Was it enough just to be a cowboy, or did he need their approval?

A Word with Erick

The sound of boots crunching through dirt broke the silence. Jacob turned to see Erick sitting on a bench by the stables, wiping down his saddle. The rhythmic sound of leather against leather was soothing, grounding him in the quiet morning.

Morning," Jacob said, walking over and leaning against the wall beside him. He glanced down at his raw hands, still stinging from the ride.

"Couldn't sleep?" Erick asked, squinting at him with concern.

Jacob exhaled sharply. "Nah. Too much on my mind. Feels like I'm carrying the weight of every single expectation here."

Erick set down the saddle, his gaze steady as he studied Jacob. "Yeah, but you're carrying it for something. You've come so damn far, Jake."

Jacob turned toward him, the frustration rising to the surface. "But it feels like it's never enough. They don't see me as one of them."

Erick let out a dry chuckle. "Who gives a damn about them? You don't owe anyone anything. You've got something they'll never have: grit. And no matter how many times they try to knock you down, you're still standing."

Jacob hesitated, his fingers tracing the grain of the wood next to him. He stared at the dirt, then met Erick's eyes. "You think so?"

Erick shrugged, a grin tugging at the corner of his mouth. "Hell, I know so. Just look at your damn ride yesterday. I couldn't do that if you paid me."

Jacob laughed softly, shaking his head. "Thanks, Erick. I needed to hear that."

The Ride of a Lifetime

Later that day, the arena was alive with energy. Jacob's heart raced as he stood at the gate, waiting for his turn. The crowd murmured, the tension thick in the air. When the bull was led into the chute, Jacob felt the familiar knot in his stomach twist.

The gate swung open. The bull exploded from the chute with terrifying power. Instinct took over as Jacob's hands locked onto the rope and his legs clamped down. The world around him blurred into motion—a whirlwind of dirt, sweat, and muscle. But in the chaos, his mind was strangely clear. Stay on, Jacob. Stay on.

The bull whipped and twisted beneath him, its hooves pounding the earth like thunder. The crowd's energy surged, their encouragement blending into a low hum of anticipation. His grip tightened, his body feeling as though it were being torn apart with each violent movement.

Stay steady, stay focused. Breathe.

His legs burned, his muscles screamed, but the finish line was in sight. Eight seconds. The buzzer rang, and with a final wrench of the bull's body, Jacob flew from its back. His boots hit the dirt hard. The crowd erupted in applause, but Jacob's heart hammered in his chest—part relief, part adrenaline.

He had done it. He had made it.

But as he rose, his gaze locked with Jake's—cold, unyielding. The other cowboys hovered nearby, watching for something to go wrong. But Jacob had proven them wrong. Again.

The Moment with Marcus

After the ride, the weight of eyes upon him felt suffocating. The bull may have been a victory, but Marcus's gaze was a challenge all on its own. It was as if the ride had been nothing more than a prelude to something bigger.

"You did alright out there," Marcus said, his voice dripping with insincerity. "But don't forget—this is just the beginning."

Jacob's spine stiffened, but he forced himself to stay calm. "What's your point?"

Marcus leaned in closer, his breath cold against Jacob's skin. "The road to respect isn't paved with a single win. Don't think you've earned it just because you stayed on that bull." His eyes gleamed with a sharp, knowing look. "It's a long road, Jake. And you better be ready for what comes next."

The words stung—not because they were new, but because Marcus knew exactly where to strike. Jacob swallowed hard, the frustration rising, but he kept his composure. "I'm ready for whatever comes my way."

Marcus smirked, his gaze lingering just a beat too long. "We'll see about that."

A Glimmer of Hope

As the sun dipped below the horizon, painting the sky in shades of orange and pink, Jacob leaned against the fence, catching his breath. The arena was empty now, the noise of the crowd replaced with the quiet rhythm of hooves and the soft rustling of wind through the grass. Only the pulse of the earth beneath him remained steady and grounding.

Erick and Nick stood beside him, their presence a quiet reminder of the bonds he had forged. Erick exhaled a long breath, his voice softer than usual. "You did it, man. You proved them wrong again."

Jacob smiled, but it didn't reach his eyes. "It doesn't feel like enough."

Erick placed a hand on Jacob's shoulder, firm and reassuring. "You don't have to prove anything to them, Jake. You've come further than most would ever dream. I'm proud of you. But this fight? It's for you. It always has been."

Nick clapped him on the back, his usual grin softened by something deeper. "Keep showing up, man. Every day. That's how you win—how we all win." He paused, his eyes reflecting a deeper understanding. "You're one of us, whether they like it or not."

Jacob's gaze wandered out toward the horizon. For the first time, the weight of the world felt a little lighter. Maybe he didn't need anyone's approval. Maybe the only thing that mattered was the man he was becoming. His heart felt a little steadier, his resolve a little firmer.

The journey wasn't over. It had barely begun.

CHAPTER 21
THE RIDE

Jacob's Grit

Jacob stood in the dusty practice pen, the weight of the moment pressing down on his shoulders. His gloved hands tightened around the rope as he secured it to the bull's horns. Sweat stung his eyes, mingling with the dust clinging to his face, gritty and relentless. The sun hung low in the sky, casting long, crooked shadows across the arena, and the distant sounds of cowboys preparing for the evening's event echoed like a steady drumbeat. Jacob had been here for hours, the burn in his muscles a constant reminder of his commitment.

Today wasn't just about riding—it was about proving he belonged here.

Every second spent with the bulls was another step toward earning the respect he'd been chasing for what felt like a lifetime. But as he tightened the rope, the familiar sting of rivalry gnawed at him, the faces of Jake, Adam, and Bob flashing in his mind's eye. Jake's mocking grin, Adam's taunting laugh, Bob's quiet, dismissive gaze—they were there, as always, a constant reminder that the path to respect was never easy.

A low whinny cut through his thoughts, and Jacob glanced over to see his horse pawing at the dirt, restless and uneasy. He took a deep breath, shaking off the fatigue and starting to settle into his bones.

"Not today," he muttered under his breath, forcing the doubt aside. Not today.

The sun glinted off the metal bars of the fence, casting fleeting streaks of golden light across the arena, like moments of hope barely visible against the thickening dust. As Jacob gazed toward the horizon, the air was heavy with the scent of leather, sweat, and the earthy tang of the land. The journey to this point rushed through his mind—the ridicule, the doubts, the fight for a place in a world that never seemed to welcome him.

But now, the fight felt different. It wasn't just about the rivalry or the rodeo anymore. It was about survival, about proving to himself that he could withstand whatever this life threw his way. And as the bull snorted, tossing its head in irritation, Jacob felt his adrenaline surge.

This was his moment.

The Rivalry Intensifies

Later that day, Jacob walked into the arena, his head low, the brim of his hat pulled over his eyes, thoughts locked in focus. The weight of the rivalry hung over him like an oppressive storm cloud, its crackling tension palpable in the air. Jake, Adam, and Bob stood near the gate, their eyes following him as he passed. The low murmur of their conversation was like a ripple in the otherwise still air—occasional bursts of laughter, pointed glances, the unmistakable scent of mockery. Jacob had grown used to it, but it didn't make it easier to shake the feeling of being an outsider.

But today? Something was different. Today, he wasn't going to let them have the satisfaction.

Erick and Nick flanked him, their quiet support a steady, unspoken presence. They didn't need to say much—just standing by him, like anchors in a storm, was enough. Over the past weeks, they had become his brothers in arms, the ones who had stuck around when things got tough.

"Don't let them get to you," Erick said, nudging Jacob's shoulder as they watched Jake and the others whisper to each other, casting occasional sidelong glances. "You've been doing better than all of them combined. They know it. That's why they're pissed."

Jacob forced a tight smile, though bitterness still tugged at the corners of his mouth. But Erick's words had weight.

"I don't care if they're pissed. I care about proving I'm not some outsider to be tossed aside."

Nick, always quick to lighten the mood, added with a wink, "And you're doing it, man. One ride at a time. They're just scared of you, that's all."

The idea that they might be scared of him was strange but oddly empowering. Maybe—just maybe—he had something they didn't. That thought made Jacob stand a little taller, the doubts of earlier fading like a morning mist.

A Test of Will

Jacob's next ride would be his hardest yet. Nerves hummed in his stomach, a tight knot he couldn't shake. But he didn't let it show. As he mounted the bull, the world around him seemed to fall away, swallowed by the sheer concentration required to face what lay ahead. The murmurs of the crowd faded, their doubts rising like ghosts in the background.

"Let's see how long he lasts this time," Jake's voice rang out from the sidelines, dripping with sarcasm.

Jacob ignored him. He had faced worse—much worse—and it wasn't going to stop him now.

The gate slammed open, and the bull shot forward with a violent surge of energy. The force rattled even the most seasoned cowboys, but Jacob fought to stay in control. The bull bucked violently, twisting and spinning in a blur of motion. His body screamed in protest, every muscle on fire, yet he gritted his teeth and held on. The ground shook beneath him as the bull's hooves pounded the earth with a rhythm that seemed to match his own frantic heartbeat.

The arena blurred into a tunnel of sound and movement, his vision narrowing as his grip tightened on the rope. His chest burned with exertion, his legs screamed for release, but his mind echoed one thing: Stay on.

The bull's movements became an unforgiving blur, each second a battle. The thundering hooves, the bucking, the twist of the animal's body—it all pushed him to the edge of his endurance. But Jacob clung to his resolve: You're a cowboy. You don't quit.

When he finally dismounted, the crowd's roar felt like a distant echo, fading into the background as he stumbled, his legs weak from the effort. There was no denying it. He had done it. He had stayed on longer than anyone expected.

Jake's glare was the only thing that remained clear in his vision; his face twisted with frustration. The other cowboys gathered around, their expressions a mix of judgment and something else, something

Jacob couldn't quite place. But it didn't matter anymore. He had proven something today—not to them, but to himself.

The Conversation with Lucas

Jacob walked away from the arena, his body sore but his spirit soaring. He needed a moment to breathe, to process what he'd just done. He made his way to the stables, the quiet offering him a welcome reprieve from the noise of the crowd.

But as he leaned against the wall, a familiar figure appeared in his line of sight. Lucas.

Jacob tensed for a moment, unsure of what to expect. Lucas had always been different—quiet, reserved, never fully part of the others. But today, there was something in his approach, something Jacob couldn't quite place.

"Hey," Lucas said, his voice softer than usual. "That was a hell of a ride."

Jacob raised an eyebrow, taken aback. "Thanks. Didn't expect you to be the one to say that."

Lucas shifted awkwardly on his feet, glancing back toward the group of cowboys watching from the sidelines. "I don't agree with everything they say or do," he admitted quietly. "But that ride? Hell, that was something else."

Jacob wasn't sure what to say at first. He had expected mockery—more jeering, more ridicule. But Lucas wasn't like the others.

"Thanks," Jacob said, his voice sincere. "I didn't expect it. Means a lot."

Lucas paused, his eyes flickering with uncertainty and sincerity. "You're different, Jacob. They're all just afraid of that. They don't want someone like you here. But you've got heart, man. I see it. And I think they see it too."

Jacob's chest tightened. There it was again—the feeling of being an outsider. But maybe, just maybe, he wasn't as alone as he thought.

"I'm not going anywhere," Jacob said, his voice steady. "And they can't make me leave."

Lucas gave him a small, genuine smile, then shrugged. "Good. Just don't let them break you."

Aftermath: Quiet Victory

That evening, Jacob sat in the saloon with Erick and Nick, the weight of the day's events settling into his bones. The saloon was loud, filled with the energy of other cowboys, but for once, Jacob didn't feel out of place. He had earned his spot here, and he knew it.

Erick clapped him on the back. "You did well today, man," he said, his grin wide and genuine. "Hell, you did better than good. You showed 'em all what it means to be a cowboy."

Nick chuckled, raising his mug in salute. "Hell, you showed us all what it means to hang on."

Jacob smiled, but it was a tired one. The adrenaline was fading, leaving behind an exhaustion only earned through hard work and relentless determination. He glanced over at the other cowboys, including Jake, who was still glaring in his direction. For a moment, Jacob wondered if the victory would ever feel complete.

Then he remembered Lucas's words. You've got heart, man.

And for the first time, Jacob truly believed it. He wasn't just surviving anymore—he was living. And maybe that was all that mattered.

CHAPTER 22
THE FINAL RIDE

The Weight of the Moment

Jacob stood at the arena's edge, his heart thundering in his chest. The air was thick with anticipation, dust swirling under the horses' hooves, and the pounding of distant drums echoed through the dry, hot air. It was like a drumroll for his fate. The crowd's energy buzzed, making the air feel charged and electrifying. This was it. The final ride. The one that would decide everything.

His body ached from long days of practice. Each bruise is a badge of his determination. His mind raced, but one thought stood out, sharp and unwavering—this was his moment. He had fought too hard, faced too many obstacles, and proven himself time and again. Everything had led to this.

The sun beat down on him, its heat sinking deep into his bones, while the dust scraped at his throat—an unwelcome reminder of the battles he'd fought. But he hardly noticed. His focus narrowed—just him, the bull, and that final ride.

Yet, as he prepared to mount, the familiar knot in his stomach twisted tighter. Jake. His rival. The man who'd made it clear from the start that Jacob didn't belong here. Jake had always lurked in the background, a constant reminder of how far Jacob had to go to earn respect in this world.

He could almost hear the mocking words Jake had thrown at him over the years—those jabs about never making it past the first round. That old wound flared again, and Jacob hated that Jake still had the power to unsettle him.

Jake's Shadow

Jacob felt Jake's eyes on him now, even from across the arena. There was something different today. Maybe it was because they were both competing for the same title or maybe because, for the first time, there could only be one champion.

Jake's sneer sliced through the moment. "You're not cut out for this, Jacob. This world... it's not for guys like you."

Jacob clenched his jaw, biting back the urge to retort. Jake's words had always stung, but today, they didn't feel like the truth. Today, they felt like a challenge—one he was ready to face head-on. He had spent too long fighting for this moment, and he wasn't about to let Jake steal it from him.

Support from Friends

Erick and Nick stood close by, their expressions a mix of tension and quiet support.

"You've got this," Erick said, his hand firm on Jacob's shoulder. "Don't let him get inside your head. You've earned your spot here, man. You belong."

Nick, ever the optimist, gave Jacob a thumbs-up, his grin infectious. "Just ride like you've been doing. Don't worry about what anyone else thinks."

Jacob nodded, the weight of their support sinking in. But deep down, he knew this wasn't just about the ride. It was about everything that had led him here—his past, his struggles, the moments when he'd almost given up.

He thought back to his first ride, the one that had left him bruised and broken. When quitting had seemed easier than continuing. The days when failure felt like an unbearable weight. But those days were behind him. Today wasn't just about proving something to others—it was about proving something to himself.

Nick's lighthearted gesture still carried weight, though. Jacob realized it wasn't just about proving himself in the arena. It was about proving himself to the people who had believed in him when he hadn't believed in himself.

The Sound of the Announcer

The announcer's voice sliced through the noise, but the crowd's hum seemed to rise in intensity like a storm gathering strength. Everything was coming to a head—this moment, this final ride.

"Last rider of the night, folks. Let's see if he has what it takes to finish strong. Jacob, the Nigerian Cowboy!"

The crowd erupted into applause, and Jacob felt the weight of their eyes on him. It wasn't just the people around him—it was the entirety of his journey, his family's legacy, and the cowboy spirit he had fought to embrace.

Each step toward the gate kicked up a small cloud of dust. The sun's heat pressed down on him, sweat dripping down his neck. But his mind was calm. He was ready. This was the culmination of everything he had fought for.

The Bull's Roar

As he approached the gate, Nick's voice rang out from behind him.

"Hey, at least you're not riding a mechanical bull at some honky-tonk bar. This might be easier," Nick called with a grin.

Jacob shot him a smile, the tension easing for a moment. But it didn't last long. He could still feel Jake's gaze burning into him from across the arena.

He mounted the bull, his grip on the rope steady but tense. The bull snorted beneath him, its muscles twitching with pent-up energy. Jacob settled into position, his legs locked around the animal's barrel. The scent of leather, sweat, and adrenaline filled his lungs, making his heart race faster.

The gate loomed. The bull, a living force of nature, pulsed with energy, waiting to explode. For a moment, everything else faded. He thought of his family, his friends, his mentors—all the sacrifices they'd made. They were counting on him, but more importantly, he was counting on himself.

The Final Ride

The gate swung open.

The bull erupted beneath him, its powerful muscles rippling like a coiled spring. Jacob's body jerked violently, his hands gripping the rope so tightly that his fingers burned. The arena seemed to explode with sound—the roar of the crowd, the snap of the rope, the thundering hooves of the bull.

The ground shook under him, but he refused to let go. His mind flashed back to that first ride when his hands were raw, and his body trembled with fear. He had fallen within seconds. He'd wanted to quit then, but something deeper than pride had kept him going… a need to prove something to himself.

His body felt like a rag doll, tossed by the bull's unpredictable movements. His legs burned, his grip ached, but his determination surged. *Stay on. Stay on.* Every muscle screamed, but his resolve tightened. He wasn't done. Not yet.

The bull bucked again, tossing its head wildly. Jacob's legs strained to stay locked, but he kept his focus. This was it—the final test. Every second stretched like an eternity.

The bull gave one last violent toss. Jacob's world spun for a split second, and for an instant, he thought he might be thrown. But then, everything clicked into place. He wasn't done. Not yet.

Victory In More Ways Than One

Finally, with one last burst of strength, the bull calmed. Its body stilled beneath him, and Jacob held the rope, every muscle in his body on fire. The crowd erupted into deafening cheers, but Jacob couldn't hear them. His heart thudded in his ears.

He had done it. He had conquered the bull. And in doing so, he had conquered himself.

The roar of the crowd drowned out the announcer's voice, but Jacob didn't hear it. He was lost in the flood of emotions crashing over him. The years of hard work, the sacrifices, the struggles—all of it had led to this moment.

As he dismounted and waved to the crowd, his gaze flicked briefly to Jake. His rival's face was twisted in frustration, the sneer still there, but it no longer bothered Jacob. Jake didn't have the power to break him—not today. Not ever again.

This was his time now.

Chapter 23
The Turning Point A Crisis Strikes

Jacob sat on the edge of his bunk, staring at the text from Jake. The words hit him harder than they should have. He remembered when he'd first gotten into this—the rush of adrenaline, the feeling of invincibility. Now, Jake's taunt felt like a reflection of his doubts, sharpening his sense of defeat.

"You think you can win the next one? Let's see how you hold up when the pressure's on."

He reread it twice, just to be sure he wasn't imagining it. His finger hovered over the screen. Should he ignore it? Or should he fire back, strike back with something snarky? Maybe a reply like: I'm still standing, aren't I? That would show him.

But the thought of stooping to Jake's level only made him feel worse. Instead, he deleted the text, but the weight of it still hung in the air like a storm cloud. The quiet of the room felt suffocating, the kind of silence that only amplified the noise in his mind—loud, chaotic, and uncertain.

The Quiet Strain

The room felt too small, too confining. For the first time in a long while, Jacob didn't want to go to the arena. He didn't want to climb back onto a bull to fight for something he wasn't even sure he wanted anymore. The adrenaline rush, the cheers from the crowd—it was starting to feel hollow, like a fleeting echo he couldn't chase down anymore.

And there was the pain. Not just physical, though his body ached from the bumps and bruises of too many rides, but emotional too. He couldn't ignore the gnawing feeling in his gut that told him he wasn't yet accepted for what he truly was. A cowboy, yes, but was he *their* cowboy? The question lingered, unanswered. He wasn't just battling bulls anymore—he was battling himself.

Erick and Nick had been great, always there, always supportive. But lately, Jacob couldn't shake the feeling that their words were just hollow echoes, not resonating the way they used to. The easy camaraderie had faded, replaced by an unspoken tension that neither Erick nor Nick seemed willing to acknowledge. Were they waiting for him to fall? Did they still see him as the same guy who rode bulls with confidence, or were they already counting the days until he cracked under the pressure?

Erick's words echoed in his head: You've got this. We've got your back, no matter what. But did he? Had anyone truly seen how badly he was struggling beneath the surface? What more could he do to prove he wasn't just some novelty act—a Nigerian kid in a cowboy's world?

Nick's optimism had always been a lifeline, but even his encouraging words felt like a flimsy bandage over an open wound. There was no time for small talk anymore. The rodeo wasn't just a game—it was life or death for some of these guys. And Jacob wasn't sure he could keep up anymore. Maybe he didn't want to.

A small voice whispered in his mind: *What does it mean to be a cowboy if you're always on the outside looking in?*

A Moment of Reflection

It was late when Jacob finally spoke to Erick about it. They were sitting by the fire, the crackling of the flames the only sound breaking the stillness. Jacob stared into the flickering embers, unsure of how to say what had been building inside him for days.

"I'm not sure I want to do this anymore," Jacob confessed, his voice low, almost swallowed by the night.

Erick didn't respond immediately. He just took a slow pull from his beer, his face a mask of thoughtfulness. "I figured this was coming," he said quietly, his tone even but understanding. "You've been walking around with that look on your face. Like you're waiting for something that's never gonna come."

Jacob glanced over at him, surprised. "What do you mean?"

Erick shrugged. "You've been trying to prove something to them and yourself. You won the title, but what does it mean?"

Jacob swallowed hard, the weight of his question settling in. "Exactly. What does it mean? All I've done is ride bulls, take risks, and get banged up... for what? To hear Jake taunt me every time I step in the ring?"

A bitter laugh escaped his throat. "And now, I'm questioning if I even belong here. It's like I'm stuck in this loop, and I can't get out."

Erick studied him for a long moment, his gaze steady, understanding. "You're not the first guy to think about quitting. Hell, I've had days when I wanted to walk away from it all. But you know what keeps me going?"

Jacob's gaze sharpened, expecting some profound response.

Erick leaned back, taking another slow drink. "It's the bulls. They're unpredictable. They're wild. And that's the one thing in this whole damn game that's never let me down. Every ride is a test of who we are, of whether we're strong enough to face the chaos. And that's what we're really fighting for."

Jacob leaned back, letting the words sink in. The wind howled around them, but Erick's words settled in Jacob's mind like the calm after a storm. Was that the answer? Was it enough to just ride? To let go of the need to prove something and simply embrace the ride for what it was?

But that wasn't all there was to it, was it? Jacob's inner conflict ran deeper. He wondered, as he stared into the fire: *Would the crowd still cheer for me if they knew I was torn inside? Would they see me as a brother, a friend, or just another face in the crowd?*

The weight of his identity seemed heavier than ever. He wanted to be more than just the guy who entertained them. He wanted to be part of something—something that wasn't just about the bull, the title, or the competition. He wanted to feel like *he belonged.*

The Pain of the Game

The next morning, things seemed just a little clearer. But when Jacob pulled himself out of bed and headed toward the arena, that familiar tightness gripped his chest again. His body ached, every muscle sore from the previous days of training, and his mind was clouded with doubt. He hadn't slept well; his dreams filled with images of bulls, Jake's mocking voice, and endless cycles of failure.

The rodeo grounds loomed ahead, the gates standing like a wall between him and everything he had worked for. The familiar scent of dusty leather, the sharp tang of sweat in the air, and the distant sounds of hooves pounding the earth—everything that used to excite him now felt like a burden.

When he finally reached the gates of the rodeo grounds, the realization hit him. The pressure wasn't just from Jake—it was coming from himself. The weight of his expectations, his father's legacy, and the feeling that the clock was ticking. Every ride was a reminder of what he still had to prove. Was the crowd really seeing me for who I am? Or am I just another act they'll forget once the next cowboy rides in?

"Hey, Jacob!" Nick called, jogging up beside him, his grin wide. "You ready to show them how it's done?"

Jacob forced a grin, shaking his head. "I don't know, Nick. I don't know if I've got it in me anymore."

Nick's eyes widened. "What are you talking about? You're the Nigerian Cowboy, man. You can't quit now. That title's yours."

Jacob shook his head again, a deep sigh escaping his chest. "Yeah, but what if I don't want it anymore?"

Nick laughed, slapping him on the back. "You're just in a funk. Trust me, you'll snap out of it."

Jacob wasn't so sure. But before he could respond, Erick appeared, his expression serious. "Jacob, I think we need to talk," he said, his voice low. "Come on, let's walk for a minute."

As they walked through the dusty path leading toward the practice pens, Erick spoke softly. "I know things have been hard lately. But this is what you've been working for, right? To get to this moment?"

Jacob nodded, but his heart wasn't in it.

"Then don't let Jake's words get to you. Don't let anyone tell you that you can't do this. Because I believe in you, man." Erick's eyes were intense now, searching Jacob's face.

"I'm just tired, Erick," Jacob admitted. "Tired of the fight. The constant proving. It's like every time I get ahead, something else knocks me down."

Erick let out a long breath, his gaze softening. "Yeah, I get that. But sometimes, the thing that gets us through is knowing that we don't have to do it alone. Nick and I—we're here for you. You don't have to carry this by yourself."

Jacob looked at Erick, feeling the weight of his words. For the first time, he realized how much he had been pushing them away, fighting alone, trying to prove he could handle it. Maybe, just maybe, it was time to let someone else in.

A Moment of Clarity

By the time the final ride came, Jacob stood at the edge of the arena, the roar of the crowd deafening as the last competitor mounted his bull. Jacob felt the familiar rush of adrenaline surge through him, but it was different now. There was a certain stillness in his mind—something he hadn't felt in a long while. For the first time in what felt like ages, he wasn't just preparing for the next ride, the next victory, the next challenge. He was simply *present*.

As the final cowboy in the competition dismounted, the crowd cheered, and Jacob's eyes caught the reflection of his own face in the mirror of the arena gates. His eyes were tired, yes, but they were more than that. There was something else there—something deeper. His whole life, he had fought to be seen as a cowboy to prove he belonged. But in this moment, he realized something he'd been blind to before.

Belonging wasn't something you could force. It wasn't about the trophies, the titles, or the cheers. It wasn't about the judges or even the crowd. It was about feeling it deep down in your soul—that undeniable truth that you were part of something, no matter how small or big, that *you* had earned your place. The crowd didn't make him a cowboy; he had already become one the moment he decided to keep riding, even when he wasn't sure he could keep going.

The realization was like a weight lifting off his chest. Jacob wasn't trying to prove something anymore. The only thing he needed to prove was to himself. No one else could define what made him a cowboy.

He turned to Erick and Nick, who had been watching him from a distance, their faces filled with concern but also with patience. He could see they were waiting for him to make up his mind—to choose whether to keep fighting or step away. He smiled at them, a quiet but firm resolution settling in his chest.

"I think I've figured it out," he said softly, more to himself than to anyone else.

Nick raised an eyebrow. "Figured what out?"

Jacob took a deep breath and looked at both of them. "I don't need anyone's approval to be who I am. I've been waiting for that moment, that one thing that would make me feel like I belong, but maybe... maybe it's already here. I'm already part of this. Whether they see me as a cowboy or just some kid from Nigeria—it doesn't matter. What matters is what I know about myself."

Erick nodded, his eyes filled with respect. "That's it, man. That's what we've been waiting for you to realize."

Jacob laughed softly, the tension in his body finally easing. "Guess I'm a little slow to figure it out, huh?"

Nick chuckled, slapping him on the back. "We've all been there. Trust me."

Jacob's heart felt lighter, the weight of expectation, doubt, and fear finally lifting. The doubts that had plagued him for so long, the constant need to prove himself, faded into the background. He was no longer a boy trying to be a cowboy. He was a cowboy—a Nigerian cowboy with all the grit and resilience that came with the title.

The Ride of His Life

When the next competition arrived, Jacob felt something inside him click. He wasn't anxious or scared, not in the way he had been before. He mounted his bull, felt the surge of energy that only came when the gate was about to open, and for the first time in ages, he felt *in control*.

The bull's hooves thundered against the dirt, and the roar of the crowd reached a deafening peak. But Jacob's focus was razor-sharp. He wasn't worried about impressing anyone—not about the opinions of Jake, the crowd, or even the judges. His mind was clear. His body moved with a newfound fluidity. He wasn't just fighting the bull anymore. He was *embracing* the ride, understanding it in a way that was deeper than he ever had before.

When the buzzer sounded, signaling the end of his ride, Jacob didn't need to look at the scoreboard to know what had happened. The crowd's roar filled his ears, but it wasn't for the victory—it was for the journey, the grit, the determination. They weren't cheering for a cowboy from Nigeria or for a man trying to prove himself. They were cheering for someone who had finally figured it out.

He dismounted, his legs a little shaky but his heart steady, and saw Erick and Nick waiting for him by the rail. They didn't need to say anything. Their wide smiles and proud nods spoke volumes. Jacob had earned his place, not just as a cowboy, but as one of them.

As they walked off together, the sun dipping low in the sky, Jacob felt a sense of peace wash over him. The doubts that had clouded his mind were gone. He didn't need to prove anything anymore. He wasn't just part of the world he had entered—he was shaping it. And that, he realized, was the true essence of being a cowboy.

He had finally arrived.

CHAPTER 24
THE CROSSROADS

New Challenges

The sun dipped low over the arena, casting long, dramatic shadows across the dirt. Jacob stood at the edge, arms crossed, eyes narrowed. The familiar buzz of anticipation hummed through the crowd, but today, there was something off. The heat pressed down on him, sinking into his bones, but it wasn't just the oppressive sun. It was a shift inside him—a sense of disconnection from everything he used to chase. The rush of the competition, the pull of the crowd—it all felt distant like a game he wasn't sure he wanted to play anymore. His muscles ached, and exhaustion gnawed at him, but it wasn't the physical strain that bothered him most. It was the weight of his own thoughts, relentless and suffocating.

He let his fingers brush the worn leather of his gloves. The familiar sensation should have brought comfort, but instead, it reminded him of the many battles, of the bulls he'd ridden, and the countless times he'd been thrown to the dirt. He'd come far, but now, the victories felt hollow, and the price was steep. It was no longer about the rush. It was about survival.

Jacob scanned the arena, and his eyes locked on Jake at the opposite end. Jake stood tall, arms crossed that cocky grin etched into his face. His presence was a constant reminder of the rivalry that had fueled Jacob's drive for so long. But today, Jacob didn't feel the usual flare of anger. Instead, there was something different—a quiet resolve, a realization that his fire had burned hotter and longer than he ever intended. Maybe this time, it wasn't about proving anything to Jake.

The Inner Battle

Jacob walked toward the back pens, the weight of his thoughts thickening with every step. This wasn't just another ride. It wasn't about outlasting Jake anymore or trying to earn his respect. It was something deeper. Something about proving his worth to himself, not the world around him. He'd spent so long running the race—chasing after victories, titles, approval—and now? He wasn't sure who he was anymore. Could he rise above the chaos of the competition, the noise of others' expectations? Or was he simply another cowboy lost in the storm, trying to stay afloat in a sea of bruises, blood, and hollow victories?

The realization hit him with startling clarity: the game had changed. The competition had once been about outshining Jake, about making a mark that couldn't be ignored. But now, it wasn't about that at all. The more Jacob fought, the more he felt like he was losing himself in the process. Was this all life had to offer—just endless cycles of pain and fleeting triumphs?

Before he could lose himself further, Nick appeared, his face serious, without the usual grin.

"Hey, man... you need to know something," Nick said, his voice low. "Jake's betting big this round. Way bigger than usual. And word is, he's got something personal on the line."

Jacob frowned. "What do you mean, personal?"

Nick leaned in his voice barely above a whisper. "It's not just about winning anymore. He's got something that could mess with you—something you won't see coming."

Jacob's gut clenched. Something wasn't right. Jake's typical tricks were one thing, but this was different. The stakes were higher, and Jacob's instincts screamed that Jake was playing a darker game. It wasn't just about the ride—it was about power. And Jake knew exactly how to manipulate it.

The Moment of Truth

As the competition began, Jacob stood at the edge of the arena, his heart pounding in his chest. The familiar weight of nerves was there, but it felt distant now, like a faint echo. His mind wasn't focused on the other riders or the crowd. He was alone in this moment, facing the toughest bull he'd ever ridden. This wasn't just another ride—it was a statement. A declaration that he could still do this, for himself.

His heart raced as he stepped up to the gate, his hands gripping the rope with the familiar sense of anticipation. But this time, there was something different. Instead of fear, a deep calm washed over him. The doubts, the racing thoughts—they quieted. All that mattered was the bull, the challenge, and the ride ahead. Everything else faded away. The world narrowed to just him and the chaos of the moment.

The gate swung open.

The bull exploded into the arena, hooves pounding the dirt as it bucked violently beneath Jacob. The force shook him to his core.

The Bull and the Cowboy

The bull was a tempest beneath him, an unstoppable force, twisting and thrashing. But Jacob didn't fight it. Instead, he moved with it— his body aligning with the bull's rhythm. The rope in his hands wasn't a lifeline; it was a part of him, guiding him through the storm. Every bone in his body felt the chaos, but there was no fear now. There was only clarity. His heart beat in a steady rhythm with the wild ride beneath him. He wasn't surviving anymore—he was thriving.

Time stretched. Each second felt like an eternity, and Jacob, in that moment, was free. The bull's chaos became his dance, and the storm became his power. His grip tightened, but it wasn't out of fear. It was out of a quiet, undeniable confidence. This was his moment— not for the crowd, not for Jake—but for himself. To prove that he could face the storm and come out the other side unbroken.

A Shift in Perspective

When the ride ended, Jacob hit the dirt with a heavy thud. Normally, he would've jumped to his feet, fueled by adrenaline. But today, he lay there, feeling the dust settle around him. The roar of the crowd was distant, almost muted. He didn't rush to stand. Instead, he let the moment linger. For the first time in years, the weight of the competition didn't press down on him. He hadn't been thinking of Jake, or the title, or any of the usual distractions. He'd been thinking about the ride. About facing the challenge head-on and doing it for the pure joy of it.

When he finally stood, there was no rush. No need to prove anything. He scanned the crowd, his heart steady, a quiet peace settling inside him. For the first time, he felt like he belonged—not because of the title or the win, but because of who he was becoming.

The Unexpected Decision

As Jacob made his way back to the locker room, still buzzing from the ride, he caught sight of Jake standing in the corner. Jake's arms were crossed, his eyes narrowed, and that familiar cocky grin was nowhere to be found. There was something cold in the way Jake stood, a challenge Jacob had grown all too familiar with. But today, Jacob didn't feel the usual flare of resentment. Instead, he felt... pity for Jake, trapped in a cycle of ego and manipulation. For the first time, Jacob realized it wasn't about winning. It wasn't about Jake. It was about his own life on his terms.

With a final glance at Jake, Jacob made a decision. The competition, the rivalry—it wasn't enough anymore. He wasn't going to keep fighting for something that didn't bring him peace. Maybe it was time to step away, to find something bigger than the rodeo. Something that belonged to him and him alone. For the first time, he felt free. He didn't know what that something was yet, but he knew it was time to find out.

The Final Showdown

The next day, the arena buzzed with electric energy. The final event of the season had arrived, and the stakes had never been higher. Jacob stood at the edge of the arena, his heart steady, his mind clear. He had come this far, but deep down, he knew that no matter what happened here, this wasn't the end of his journey.

He stepped into the ring for the last time that season, his heart calm, his focus unwavering. For the first time, he didn't care about the title, Jake, or any of the things that used to drive him. What mattered was that he was here. And he was doing this for himself. Not for anyone else.

The gate swung open.

The crowd roared.

And Jacob rode.

CHAPTER 25
THE FINAL RIDE – NEW BEGINNINGS

The sun dipped below the horizon, casting long, stretched shadows across the dusty arena. Jacob stood at the edge, his boots scraping the dirt as he shifted his weight, eyes scanning the other cowboys warming up. Their horses kicked up clouds of dust in the cooling evening air, the rhythmic sound of hooves pulsing through the ground like the heartbeat of the earth itself. The sky above had deepened into a dusky purple, streaked with gold, the soft light creeping away as the day turned to night. It should've been another regular night before the competition. But something in the air made it feel different—almost like the calm before a storm. Jacob couldn't quite put his finger on it. Was it the buzz of the crowd gathering? Or maybe it was how his body felt—still sore from the last ride, but this time, it felt less like he was fighting through it and more like he was learning to accept it. He wasn't resisting the pain but embracing it as part of who he was now. The ache in his muscles had become something familiar, even comforting. A reminder of what he'd been through and what he'd survived.

His hands brushed over the leather of his gloves, the scent of oil and sweat mingling in the air. For a moment, he thought about the bulls he'd ridden. Some had tossed him off violently; others had been a silent challenge, like a test. It wasn't just the bruises—it was the constant pressure to prove himself. The endless cycle of pushing harder, faster, better. He'd been a cowboy in the rodeo world for so long, but in this quiet moment, something began to feel... off. The drive to prove something to others, to be better than Jake, didn't matter anymore.

But then his eyes landed on Jake. Of course. Jake stood at the far end of the arena, leaning on the gate, a cocky smirk plastered on his face as usual. He looked the part—always had—like the golden boy of rodeo. Jacob clenched his jaw, watching the way Jake's confident swagger seemed to irk him more than it ever had before. It wasn't just that Jake was still playing his games. It was that Jacob finally didn't care. That realization settled in his chest, heavy but freeing. It wasn't about Jake anymore. It was about Jacob—who he was and what he was doing.

The Inner Battle

Jacob walked towards the back pens, the sounds of the arena fading into a dull hum behind him. This wasn't just about proving he could outlast Jake anymore. It wasn't about holding the trophy or earning the respect of others. It was something deeper—a part of him that needed to know if he could truly make it in this world, not just as a cowboy, but as a person. Could he survive the chaos of this life— and not just survive, but thrive?

The evening air was cooler now, the breeze carrying the scent of the nearby wild grasses tickling his skin. He thought back to Erick's words around the campfire a few nights ago: It's about surviving the chaos. But surviving wasn't enough anymore. He needed more. He needed to know if he could do it on his terms. Without the weight of expectation, without constantly chasing after something or someone else's approval.

Jacob's chest tightened with the weight of his thoughts. Was it too late to change? Had the rodeo become nothing more than a mask for the parts of himself he hadn't wanted to face? There was a deep, quiet longing inside him now, not for another victory or another round of applause but for something real. Something that didn't require him to prove his worth. Something that made the pain and struggle worth it.

Just as the weight of those thoughts settled in, Nick appeared beside him, a grin stretched across his face.

"Hey, you look like you're ready to take on the world tonight," Nick said, nudging him with his elbow. "Feeling better?"

Jacob managed a half-smile. "Yeah, I guess. More or less."

Nick's face lit up, eager to share some gossip. "I overheard some of the guys talking. Jake's been betting big on this round—like, really big. He's planning to take down whoever's left standing."

Jacob raised an eyebrow. "What's that supposed to mean?"

Nick lowered his voice conspiratorially. "He's not just in this for the ride anymore. He's got something personal riding on it. It's about power now. Be careful, man."

Jacob's stomach tightened. A part of him had always known Jake was playing a deeper game, but this confirmed it. It wasn't about respect anymore. It was about control—about proving he could tear others down while building himself up. And Jacob knew better than anyone how that felt. But tonight, Jacob realized he didn't have to play Jake's game anymore.

The Moment of Truth

As the competition started, Jacob stood at the arena's edge, his heart hammering in his chest. The bull waiting for him wasn't just any bull. This one had been notorious, a beast that had tossed some of the best riders off without hesitation. Jacob could feel the sweat forming on his palms as he adjusted his grip on the rope. This wasn't just about surviving another ride. No, if he made it through this, it would mean something more than just a win—it would be a statement. A statement that he didn't need to prove anything to anyone anymore.

The announcer's voice echoed over the crowd, the excitement thickening the air like the heat before a storm. Jacob took a deep breath, the sharpness of the evening air filling his lungs, grounding him. He stepped up to the gate, the world around him quieting into a single point of focus. His body hummed with adrenaline, but his mind was clear. This time, he wasn't just fighting to win. He wasn't fighting to beat Jake. He was fighting for clarity—for the freedom to be himself, for once, without the weight of everyone else's expectations.

The gate swung open, and the bull charged into the arena, its roar shaking the ground beneath it.

The Bull and the Cowboy

The bull tore into the dirt, its hooves thundering as Jacob gripped the rope with everything he had. His body screamed as he held tight, every muscle protesting, but he didn't let go. His hands burned with the strain. Pain radiated through his body, but this time, instead of panicking, he leaned into it. The ropes bit into his hands, the sharp sting sending a jolt through his arms as the bull bucked violently beneath him. The air felt thick with dust and sweat; the crowd's roar muffled in the background like a distant storm. Every muscle in his body screamed, but Jacob focused on the rhythm—there was a strange, wild beauty in the chaos. It wasn't just the pain. It was the fight, the dance with this untamed creature, and in that, he found a strange peace.

Time stretched, the world outside his mind fading away. There was just him and the bull, locked in a silent struggle for dominance. The crowd's roar seemed far away, like a distant storm, barely registering in Jacob's mind. All that mattered was the ride.

His grip tightened as the bull bucked again, and something clicked inside him. The fight, the bruises, the fear—none of it mattered. This was what he had been fighting for all along: the clarity. The joy of simply riding.

A Shift in Perspective

When the ride ended, and Jacob hit the dirt with a hard thud, the air whooshed out of his lungs. He lay there for a moment, his body aching but his mind clear. He wasn't thinking about the win, or Jake, or the crowd. He had been so lost in the challenge itself, so consumed by the ride, that it felt... freeing. He wasn't just surviving. He was thriving. His heart still pounded, but it wasn't from fear anymore. It was from a deep, satisfied knowing that he could face anything without losing himself.

Slowly, Jacob stood and dusted himself off. As he scanned the crowd, his eyes caught the glint of something he hadn't seen before—respect. He wasn't just an outsider anymore. He was part of something. For the first time in years, he felt like he belonged.

The Unexpected Decision

As Jacob made his way back to the locker room, he caught sight of Jake standing in the corner, arms crossed, eyes narrowing. But something was different this time. Jacob didn't feel anger or frustration. Instead, he felt a strange sense of pity. Jake had always defined himself by the title—the image of being the best. But Jacob realized something important. In this world, the only person he needed to be better than was the person he was yesterday. Not Jake. Not anyone else.

Jake's eyes narrowed as Jacob passed by, a flicker of something—resentment, maybe—passing through them. But Jacob didn't feel the usual stir of anger or competition. Instead, there was only a quiet, unshakable certainty. He didn't need Jake's approval. Not anymore.

Jacob offered him a small, almost imperceptible shrug, a half-smile tugging at the corner of his mouth. It wasn't a victory—it was just peace. And with that, he walked on, the weight of all those years of rivalry sliding off him like dust on a warm breeze.

The Final Decision

The next day, Jacob sat in his truck, the engine idling, the open road ahead of him. The final event was over. The applause still rang in his ears, but it was different now. His thoughts weren't on the rodeo or the next ride. They were on something bigger—something more meaningful.

He drove through the outskirts of town, the wind in his hair, the sun dipping low in the sky. Maybe it was time to make a change. Maybe he wasn't going to ride bulls anymore. Maybe he'd found something else to fight for—something he could be proud of, win or lose.

The decision wasn't clear yet. He wasn't sure what would come next. But as he drove through the winding road, the quiet stretch of dirt and grass giving way to the expanse of the plains, Jacob realized he didn't need to have it all figured out. For the first time, he felt that not knowing was okay. It was the beginning of something new, something that didn't need a label to feel real. The open road ahead of him stretched as far as his new journey could take him.

CHAPTER 26
THE DECISION

The Road Ahead

The sun dipped low, a fading orange streak across the sky, stretching long shadows over the rodeo grounds. Jacob leaned against the cool metal of his truck's hood, letting the chill seep into his back, trying to ignore the ache in his muscles. It was the same kind of ache he'd felt for years—the kind that came with long days in the saddle, endless hours of training, and the toll of the rodeo life—but today, it felt different. Today, his body wasn't the issue. His mind was.

He looked across the arena, where the other cowboys were warming up, their horses snorting and pawing at the dirt, the sounds of hooves and the occasional low bellow of bulls mixing in the air. It should've felt like any other day, but something had changed. It was like he was looking at it all through a different lens, one that made the world feel... distant, out of focus.

He wasn't thinking about the ride he'd just completed or the upcoming competition. He wasn't even thinking about the fame or the glory that used to come with each ride. No, Jacob was thinking about something else entirely: **What am I doing here?**

A Moment of Doubt

Jacob's fingers brushed against the worn leather of his gloves—the same gloves his father had handed him all those years ago. He could almost hear his father's gruff voice in his head, the one that had become the soundtrack to his life: "Cowboys don't quit."

That had been his mantra—his guiding star. No matter how many bruises or broken bones, how many failed rides or broken dreams, he'd always pushed through. He'd never considered quitting—until now.

But then, a new thought surfaced. **What if his father had been wrong?**

What if real strength wasn't in never quitting, but in knowing when to walk away? The thought made Jacob's chest tighten. What if walking away wasn't failure?

He rubbed the back of his neck, trying to work the tension out, but it only knotted up tighter. He felt like he was standing at a crossroads, a place where the legacy of the sport, the weight of his father's expectations, and his own growing doubts collided with an almost suffocating force.

Nick's Lightheartedness

"What's the matter, cowboy?" A voice cut through Jacob's thoughts, and he looked up to find Nick standing there, grinning despite the exhaustion etched across his face.

Jacob tried to smile but only managed a half-hearted curve of his lips. "Just thinking. Might be losing it."

Nick let out a loud laugh and slapped him on the shoulder. "Man, if you're losing it, then I'm completely gone. Last time I checked, you were still riding bulls, not running away from 'em."

Jacob rolled his eyes, the faintest chuckle escaping him, though it didn't reach his eyes. "Something like that."

Nick leaned in, his voice dropping to a more serious tone. "You've been looking like someone who just got sucker-punched for weeks. I get it, the rodeo's tough. But you gotta take it easy on yourself, buddy. You're not in a damn race with the world."

Jacob let out a tired sigh. "You might be right... just... I don't know. It's not the same anymore."

Nick raised an eyebrow. "You're not talking about the bulls, are you?"

Jacob chuckled bitterly, the weight of his doubts pressing down even harder. "Hell, I don't know what I'm talking about anymore. Maybe I'm just tired."

Nick's expression turned skeptical. "You're always tired, man. Been wearing that damn chip on your shoulder for months now. No one's gonna be impressed if you can't pull yourself together. So quit the pity party, alright?"

Jacob's grin faded, and for a second, he felt the sting of Nick's blunt honesty. Nick always had a way of shaking him out of his spirals, but sometimes, the truth was hard to swallow.

The Weight of Legacy

The sound of hooves pounding the dirt brought Jacob back to the present, pulling his attention back to the arena. The bulls were being prepped for the next round, and he could hear the familiar tension in the air. The cowboys mounting their bulls were all brimming with the kind of confidence Jacob used to feel—the kind of certainty that made every ride feel like a challenge he was meant to conquer.

But now? Now, it was different. It was all starting to feel... foreign.

"You're up soon," Nick's voice cut through again, nudging him out of his thoughts. Jacob just nodded, barely registering the words. The gate would open soon, and he'd be expected to ride. But as the announcer's voice echoed in the distance, Jacob found himself wondering: **Can I still do this?**

His father's voice still rumbled in his head, a steady backdrop to his thoughts, but now it was fading, replaced by his doubts. Was this the life he wanted to lead? Did it define him, or had he let it consume him?

"Next up, Jacob 'The Nigerian Cowboy!'"

The announcer's voice boomed through the loudspeakers, a familiar call that once used to set his heart racing. Now, it just felt like noise—background static. He stared at the gate, his stomach twisting into knots.

He wasn't sure if he was scared or just... empty.

The Moment of Truth

Before he could question himself further, Nick nudged him again, this time harder. "Hey! Don't you dare zone out on me now. You're about to ride that bull like it's your last shot. You hear me?"

Jacob chuckled, despite the heaviness in his chest. "Don't talk to me like I'm your damn project."

Nick grinned wider. "I'm not. But if you keep acting like a brooding cowboy, I'll drag you to a therapist myself. We're all worried, man. You've got more to prove than just to yourself. Don't forget that."

Jacob rolled his eyes but smiled. He didn't want to admit it, but Nick was right. There was still a part of him that needed to prove something—not just to the world, but to himself.

The Last Ride

Jacob climbed onto the bull, his legs sore, his body drained. The animal beneath him was a beast—nasty, unpredictable, and known for sending even the toughest cowboys flying off within seconds. But Jacob didn't feel the usual fear.

This time, he felt... clarity. A strange calm settled over him as the gate swung open. The familiar rush of adrenaline hit him, but it wasn't panic this time. It was as if he were riding for something more than just the ride. He wasn't fighting to stay on anymore; he was fighting for the kind of peace that only came from letting go.

The bull bucked wildly, throwing its head up and down, its hooves tearing into the dirt. But Jacob's grip tightened on the rope, his body moving with it, a rhythm that felt right. For the first time in years, it wasn't about the competition. It wasn't about surviving. It was about thriving.

The Shift

When Jacob hit the dirt, it wasn't the usual agony that greeted him, but a sense of... freedom. The crowd roared, but it barely registered in his ears. For a moment, he just lay there, breathless—not from the fall, but from the realization that he didn't need to be the best. He didn't need to prove anything to anyone.

When he stood up, the pain of the ride was still there, but it didn't matter. What mattered was that for the first time, Jacob felt like he wasn't living in his father's shadow. He wasn't just a cowboy anymore—he was himself.

And that was enough.

The Decision

As Jacob walked toward the locker room, he couldn't shake the feeling that everything had changed. His gaze wandered across the arena, where Jake stood, arms crossed, eyes trained on him. Jacob didn't feel the usual tension between them—no rivalry, no anger. Just... pity.

Jake had built his life around the title, around being the best. But Jacob was ready to define himself by something more than a label. He wasn't chasing the same thing anymore.

Erick caught up to him, clapping him on the back. "Hell of a ride, Jacob. You looked like you were riding for more than just a bull out there."

Jacob met his gaze, his voice soft. "Maybe I am."

Erick narrowed his eyes, almost like he was seeing right through him. "Just don't forget what you're fighting for, alright? If it's worth it, then fight for it. But don't lose yourself along the way."

Jacob nodded. The words hung in the air, but they didn't weigh him down. This time, he wasn't sure what he was fighting for—but he knew he wasn't going to lose himself trying to find out.

The Road Ahead

As he walked away from the arena, the weight of his decision still hung in the air. But instead of feeling trapped, Jacob felt something else—a quiet sense of peace. The road ahead was wide open, and for the first time, he didn't feel like he was racing toward something. He was just living.

The future was his to shape, and whatever came next, Jacob felt ready.

He climbed into his truck, the engine rumbling to life. The road stretched ahead—unpredictable, full of possibility—and for the first time, Jacob wasn't afraid of the journey.

CHAPTER 27
RIDE ON

The Ride of Reflection

Jacob stood in the shadow of the arena, the cool night air brushing his face. The sounds of the rodeo crowd—cheers, the stomp of boots, the hum of anticipation—filtered in from the distance, but they felt miles away. The final ride had been everything he'd hoped for, yet in some strange way, it had been nothing at all. The title wasn't enough. The crowd's cheers? They rang hollow, fading into the night like the fleeting thrill of a ride that was already over.

He'd left the arena in a daze. The weight of the competition was gone, but in its place was a quieter, heavier feeling. What came next?

Jacob had spent years fighting for respect, for the win, for the title. He'd lived for the cheers, the validation, the rush of being the cowboy everyone admired. But now, after everything, he found himself questioning if that was truly the life he wanted. And if it wasn't, what path would he take? He stared ahead, lost in thought, watching the distant lights of the rodeo grounds flicker. Was he riding for a title—or was he riding for something deeper?

The Past Meets the Present

As Jacob walked toward the back of the arena, two familiar faces caught his attention. They weren't rodeo folk and not the kind of people he'd expect to find hanging around after a ride. But there they were, Freddie and Robert, standing by the gate as if they'd been waiting for him.

Jacob had met them long ago—back when he was still finding his way, still new to the area. They weren't just dance instructors; they were mentors, people who had shown him that there was more to life than just bull riding. They'd taught him to dance, not just to follow the rhythm of the music, but to follow the rhythm of life itself.

Freddie spotted him first and waved, her bright smile instantly making him feel like he'd been welcomed home. Robert, her stoic counterpart, gave a slow nod. There was a kind of wisdom in his gaze, the kind that made Jacob feel like he was being read, not judged.

"Jacob, my boy!" Freddie's voice was as warm as always. "You did well out there today. Really well."

Jacob hesitated before stepping forward, the air around him feeling thicker somehow. He didn't know what to say—didn't know if he wanted to talk about the ride, or anything for that matter. Instead, he let her wrap him in a hug, the scent of lavender and fresh air surrounding him. It was a comfort he hadn't realized he needed.

"Thanks, Freddie," Jacob replied, pulling away with a weak smile. "I guess… I don't know. I'm feeling kinda lost right now."

Freddie's smile softened with understanding, and she exchanged a look with Robert before turning her attention back to him.

"I thought that might be the case," she said gently. "A lot of folks think the ride is the finish line. But it isn't. Not really."

Robert, who'd been quietly listening, spoke up, his gravelly voice grounding Jacob. "You've been chasing that title for years, boy. But you've gotta ask yourself—what's the prize? What's it really for?"

Jacob blinked, startled by the directness of the question. "I… I thought it was to prove I belonged. That I was good enough, you know?"

Freddie shook her head softly, her gaze sharp despite her softness. "Proving you're good enough for someone else? That won't fill the emptiness inside you, Jacob. You've gotta ride for yourself. Not for the crowd, not for the title. For the person you're becoming. That's the real prize."

Jacob's chest tightened, and he couldn't look at her. "But what if it's not enough?"

Freddie took a step closer, placing a hand on his arm. "It's always enough when it's yours. You don't have to prove anything, Jacob. The road you choose may not be the one you thought you'd be on, but that doesn't make it any less important."

Robert nodded, his voice steady. "Sometimes the world doesn't give you answers. You have to ride through the storm, even when you can't see the way. But you won't be riding alone. You've got people who care about you. You've got us."

Jacob stood still, feeling their words sink deep inside. He'd spent so long chasing a title, a recognition from others, that he'd forgotten what the journey had really been about. He'd been chasing his sense of belonging, but maybe—just maybe—belonging wasn't something you could win. It was something you built.

A Moment of Clarity

Freddie reached out and patted his arm. "You've got something most people don't have, son. You've got heart. Don't lose sight of that. Ride on, Jacob. This is your moment."

Her words settled in his chest like the weight of a promise—one he wasn't sure he was ready for, but somehow knew he had to carry. For the first time in ages, Jacob felt something other than confusion. He felt hope. A flicker of possibility.

Robert, always the quiet one, offered a nod of approval. "Now go on, son. The future's waiting."

Jacob took a deep breath, feeling the weight of the night fall away like an old coat. He didn't have all the answers. Hell, he barely had any answers. But for the first time in a long time, he felt like he was looking at the next chapter, not with fear, but with something new: possibility.

The Ride Continues

As he made his way back toward the arena, he felt lighter, freer. The tension he'd carried for months, for years, seemed to dissolve with each step. It wasn't that he was running away from the rodeo; it was more like he was stepping into something new.

He wasn't sure where the road would lead, but for the first time in a long time, he wasn't afraid. Because wherever it took him, he knew one thing for sure—he would be riding for himself.

The gates swung open.

The crowd roared.

And Jacob, with the wisdom of Freddie and Robert echoing in his heart, rode on.

CHAPTER 28
THE ROAD AHEAD

A Long Road to Nowhere

The wind howled across the barren road, rattling the truck's windows, a sound that matched the turbulence inside Jacob. The engine hummed steadily, but it did little to settle the storm brewing in his chest. The flatlands stretched endlessly before him, like an invitation to nowhere—a road leading to a place he wasn't sure he wanted to find. Each mile felt like a step farther away from the roar of the crowd, from the title, from everything he'd once thought mattered.

What am I even running toward? The question clawed at him, gnawing like the wind. His hands gripped the steering wheel just a little too tightly, the leather digging into his palms. *Or is it just what I'm running from?*

The days had blurred into one long, heavy time. The thrill of the ride had faded, leaving behind an emptiness that crept in every time he let his thoughts wander. He was caught between two worlds—the roar of the crowd and the quiet, uncertain road ahead. There was a restlessness in him, like a horse that had been ridden too long, its spirit showing cracks. The horizon in front of him felt just as endless as the emptiness inside.

A brief laugh escaped his lips as his father's voice echoed in his mind. *"Kid, life's a lot simpler if you just ride the bull and stop overthinking it."*

He wished his life could be that simple. But it was never that simple, was it?

The Invitation

Hours later, as the sun began to dip below the horizon, painting the sky in warm hues of orange and pink, Jacob pulled up to a small, rustic farmhouse. The place was tucked away from the world, surrounded by wildflowers and tall grasses that waved lazily in the breeze. An old windmill creaked in the distance, turning slowly against the setting sun.

It was peaceful, quiet in a way that felt like it could drown out every worry in his chest. He could almost breathe again. He turned off the engine, letting the silence settle around him. His hands lingered on the steering wheel, feeling the cool metal beneath his fingers as the uncertainty crept back. Was this the right move? He had no idea. But Ray and Louann had extended the invitation. Maybe they had the answers he needed, or maybe it was just a place to rest for a moment. Either way, he needed something.

He stepped out of the truck, his boots crunching on the gravel as he made his way toward the porch. The screen door creaked as he knocked.

Within seconds, Ray appeared, his wide grin filling the doorway, hands on his hips.

"Well, look who finally showed up," Ray chuckled, his voice warm, his eyes twinkling. "I was starting to think you weren't gonna make it. What, you forgot how to drive, or did you just get lost along the way?"

Jacob smiled, a little of the weight lifting off his shoulders. He needed this—a moment of humor, a moment of lightness.

"Nah, just needed to make sure I wasn't getting in the way," Jacob teased, shrugging. "But I figured I'd take you up on that dinner offer."

Ray laughed heartily, giving Jacob a solid clap on the shoulder. "You've got a good sense of humor, kid. I like that. Come on in. Louann has been cooking up a storm, and you've got a seat at the table whether you like it or not."

Louann's Wisdom

Inside, the warmth hit him immediately, a stark contrast to the cold night air. The crackling fire in the hearth filled the room with a comforting glow, and soft country music hummed in the background, mixing with the smells of herbs, roast meat, and freshly baked bread. For the first time in a while, Jacob felt at peace, as if the world outside had momentarily disappeared.

"Get yourself comfortable, hon," Louann called from the kitchen, her voice rich with experience. "Dinner's almost ready, but you look like you could use something stronger than just food."

Jacob slid into a wooden chair at the table. The old wood creaked under him, its familiarity grounding him in the moment. His eyes scanned the room—family photos on the walls, knick-knacks scattered on shelves, the house full of history, full of love. He could feel it. This was a home.

Louann entered with a steaming dish, setting it down in front of him before pulling out a chair and sitting across from him. Her sharp yet gentle gaze met his as she studied him.

"So," she began, her voice soft but firm, "what brings you all the way out here, Jacob?"

Jacob shrugged, unsure of how to begin. "Just... needed a break. Things have been moving fast. I'm not sure where I'm headed next."

Louann nodded slowly, her eyes never leaving his. "I see. Well, you're always welcome here. I can't promise you'll find all the answers, but sometimes, it's the little things that help you see more clearly."

Jacob sighed, running a hand through his hair. The weight of the conversation—his struggles, his doubts—settled in. "I've been thinking a lot about what I want. What am I really doing all this for? It's like... I've been trying to prove something, but I'm not sure to whom anymore. I don't know what's next for me. I'm starting to feel like maybe I don't fit in this world at all."

Ray walked over from the stove, his gruff voice cutting through the quiet. "Well, son, I'll tell you something I wish I'd known when I was your age. You spend all your time thinking you've gotta be somebody for someone else. But in the end, the only person you need to be somebody for is yourself."

Jacob met Ray's eyes, the weight of his words settling in like a stone dropped in a pond, the ripples lasting long after the moment passed. He'd never quite thought of it that way before.

Finding His Way

The conversation drifted on, Louann occasionally chiming in with her wisdom, Ray offering his down-to-earth advice. At one point, Ray shared a small laugh about how he and Louann nearly tore their marriage apart with their stubbornness when they were younger. Jacob chuckled, surprised by the depth of their story.

"You think this life's hard now, Jacob?" Ray said, a twinkle in his eye. "Just wait until you try it with someone else in your corner. You gotta learn to give a little, and more importantly, learn to let go of things that don't matter."

Jacob smiled, a small weight lifting off his chest. He didn't know why, but the heaviness that had been pressing down on him seemed to fade just a little. Louann reached over, patting his hand gently.

"You've got a big heart, Jacob," she said, her voice soft but strong. "Don't lose it, okay? No matter where this road takes you, don't lose the person you are. And remember—there's always room for a second chance, especially in life."

Jacob nodded, though he wasn't sure he believed it just yet. But there was something in their eyes—something in the way they spoke—that made him feel like he could. For the first time in a long while, he felt like he wasn't so alone.

The Ride, Not the Destination

As the evening wore on, Jacob found himself staying longer than he'd planned. He stayed up talking with Ray and Louann, hearing about their younger days, their triumphs, and their losses. Every story seemed to circle back to one thing—no matter what life throws at you, it's all about sticking with it, about finding what matters.

When Jacob finally stood to leave, Ray gave him a firm handshake. "You know, I've seen a lot of people come and go, but you've got something. Don't waste it. This is your moment, son. Ride on, and never forget to hold onto what moves you."

Jacob paused, looking at Ray and Louann one last time. There was a warmth in their words, a fire that burned inside him now, even as he stepped back out into the cool night. He knew he was still uncertain. He knew the road ahead wasn't clear. But for the first time in a long while, he felt like he had a place. Like he wasn't so alone in this world.

The stars above seemed to shine a little brighter as he started his truck again. The engine purred to life, the familiar hum surrounding him in the quiet night. He had no idea what was next. But for the first time, he wasn't afraid to find out.

A Moment of Clarity

Jacob glanced at the rearview mirror as he drove away, the soft hum of the engine filling the air. Ray's words echoed in his head. *"Ride on, son. This is your moment."* Maybe that was all he needed to hear.

He wasn't running anymore. For the first time, he felt like he was riding for himself, not for the title, not for the expectations, but for the journey.

The road ahead stretched long and uncertain, but now, it felt like it was his road to follow.

218

CHAPTER 29
THE MOMENT BEFORE THE STORM

The Calm Before the Ride

The sun dipped lower, a molten orange stretching across the dusty arena, casting long shadows that seemed to crawl over the earth like they were alive. Time seemed to slow down, as if the world itself was holding its breath. Jacob stood at the edge of the arena, his hands wrapped tightly around his gloves, the worn leather grounding him. The rhythm of hooves pounding the dirt filled the air, each sound a heartbeat of its own. Sweat mixed with the sharp, wild tang of the bulls, restless in their pens, snorting and pawing at the ground, their impatience echoing through the arena.

Jacob exhaled slowly, letting the tension in his chest dissipate with each breath. He watched the other riders preparing for their rides, their movements sharp, focused. The air was thick with anticipation, but there was also a strange stillness, like everything in the world had paused, waiting for something. Waiting for him.

He brushed his gloves together, the leather creaking as if whispering old secrets. Memories flooded back—of bruises, falls, and near defeat. The weight of past rides didn't press down on him the way it used to. The doubts and uncertainties were fading, replaced by something deeper, something more primal. This time, he wasn't riding to simply survive. He was riding for himself—to prove something far beyond holding on to the rope.

Erick's Banter

"Hey, big man," Erick's voice sliced through his thoughts, brimming with mischief. Jacob turned to find his friend, a goofy grin stretched across his face.

Erick slapped him on the back with enough force to nearly knock him off balance. "You good? You're looking like you're about to start quoting Plato out there."

Jacob chuckled, shaking his head. "Just… trying to clear my mind."

Erick leaned in, eyes gleaming with that signature spark. "Well, don't think too much, man. You're not out there to solve world hunger. Just ride. That's it."

Jacob smiled, the tension easing from his chest. Erick's words rang true. No need for grand gestures, no need to overthink it. Just ride. Ride like it was the most natural thing in the world. His body began to sync with the rhythm of the arena, its pulse steadying his nerves. The chaos of the world seemed to quiet just for a moment, leaving only the simplicity of the task at hand.

"Don't go getting all philosophical on me now, big guy," Erick added with a wink, "Just focus on staying on your feet!"

The Older Couple's Wisdom

As Jacob walked toward the pens, a voice—warm and familiar—cut through the clamor. He turned to find the older couple sitting in the stands, their faces worn by years but full of life, their eyes wise and steady. The man leaned on a cane, but his gaze was sharp, unwavering.

"Jacob!" the woman called, waving him over. "You're looking strong, son. So proud of you."

A warmth spread through Jacob's chest as he walked toward them, the weight of their words wrapping around him like a protective cloak. They were more than just figures from his past. They were anchors in his life—always there, always offering advice, encouragement, and the kind of life lessons that stick with you long after you've walked away.

"You've got this," the man said, his voice low but full of quiet strength. "But remember, son, it's not about holding on to the bull. It's about holding on to what moves you. When the storm comes, you've got to trust that there's something deeper inside you. Something no one else can see. That's what you ride on."

Jacob stood still for a moment, letting the words wash over him. They felt different now—more powerful than before. He closed his eyes briefly, letting them sink in. *Ride on,* he thought, the words settling deep in his soul. "Ride on," he whispered to himself, repeating the mantra like a prayer.

The woman, always more direct, leaned in, her smile knowing. "You've been through a storm before, haven't you? Don't let it break you. Let it make you."

Jacob nodded, feeling the weight of her words settle deep in his bones. He could almost hear the storm coming in the distance, but this time, he didn't flinch. He was ready.

The Shift in Perspective

As the crowd's roar grew louder, Jacob's thoughts shifted. This wasn't just about surviving anymore—it was about thriving. He wasn't out here to compete with Jake or anyone else. He was out here to make peace with the chaos, to ride the storm on his own terms.

Nick appeared beside him, clapping him on the shoulder, breaking the tension like a thunderclap. "You ready, man?"

Jacob turned to meet Nick's eyes. There was something different in him now—a fire, a clarity that hadn't been there before. The noise of the crowd faded, swallowed by the focus in his mind. In this moment, it wasn't just about the bull. It was about everything—the people who had stood by him, the lessons learned, the journey ahead.

"I'm ready," Jacob said, the words feeling solid and sure, like the toll of a bell calling him to something greater.

The Ride

The gate flew open with a rush of sound and motion. The bull exploded from the chute, its hooves pounding the earth like a war drum, shaking the ground beneath him. The crowd's roar swelled, a tidal wave of sound, but in the thick of it, Jacob found an unexpected calm. The dust stung his eyes, and his body jerked violently as the bull made its first buck, but Jacob's grip remained steady, unshaken.

The ride was pure chaos. Every muscle screamed in protest as the bull tossed him in every direction, but amidst the madness, something else began to happen. Time slowed. For a moment, it felt like the whole world was holding its breath along with him. The pain, the noise, the chaos—they all faded away. There was only the rhythm of the ride, the bull beneath him, and the clarity that washed over him like a cleansing wave.

With each jolt, Jacob's mind raced, but there was a new stillness at the core of it. He wasn't just trying to stay on; he was in sync with the storm, letting it carry him, not fight it.

In that moment, it wasn't about surviving the storm. It was about dancing with it.

The Clarity After the Ride

When Jacob finally hit the dirt, the world seemed to tremble around him. Dust choked his lungs, his body screamed in protest, but beneath it all, there was something else—a quiet understanding. The storm inside him had calmed, and for the first time, he felt it—a steady, unshakeable force deep within him, just like the old man had spoken of.

He lay there for a moment, letting the realization wash over him. This wasn't about surviving the ride or proving his skill. It wasn't about winning. It was about facing the storm, feeling it, and knowing that, for once, he wasn't just trying to survive. He was thriving.

As he pushed himself to his feet, brushing the dust from his clothes, his eyes scanned the crowd. He found the older couple again, their eyes locked on his. They were smiling, nodding, and in their gaze, he saw it—they saw the shift. They saw it all.

He didn't need to prove anything to Jake or anyone else. What mattered was that, for the first time, he was at peace with himself. And that was all he needed.

The Future Ahead

As Jacob made his way back to the locker room, his body sore but his mind clear, something stirred inside him—something unspoken, undeniable. The future no longer felt like a daunting road ahead. It was wide open, and he was ready for it.

He wasn't bound by the storm anymore. He had ridden it, learned from it, and emerged stronger. It wasn't about fame or titles. It was about the journey—the journey of finding his place in this world—not for anyone else, but for himself.

"Ride on," he thought, the words echoing in his mind as he stepped forward, his hands open, ready for whatever came next.

226

CHAPTER 30
THE TURNING POINT

Advice, Reflection, and the Road Ahead

A Surprising Moment

Jacob sat at the back of the arena, his hand wrapped around a cup of coffee that had long gone lukewarm. The cacophony of boots scraping across the floor, ropes clanking, and Nick's ill-timed attempts to sneak up on the younger riders filled the air. Nick's usual antics brought a brief smile to Jacob's lips, but the usual levity didn't penetrate the thick fog in his chest. The weight of the day felt heavier than it ever had.

His muscles ached, the sting of the bruise from his last ride still pulsing on his ribs. But it wasn't the physical pain that gnawed at him now. It was something deeper, more unsettling than any bruise. The rides had always been about survival. But today… Today felt different. The stakes were higher—higher than just the bulls, higher than the competition. They felt like they were about him and something he had to prove to himself, not just the crowd.

"Man, you look like someone just told you the bulls are on strike," Nick teased, his grin wide, but there was a hint of concern behind his playful tone. He plopped down beside Jacob, his usual mischievous energy still intact. But Jacob's faint smile was all he could muster.

The Older Couple

Jacob's mind drifted back to the older couple. The evening sun stretched across the arena, casting a golden hue over everything, as if urging him to stop and think. It was a rare, quiet moment before the storm of the next ride. And yet, the words of the couple lingered like a tether, pulling at his thoughts.

He couldn't remember exactly when they had come into his life—maybe it was a night at the local bar when a line dance turned into something more—an impromptu cowboy waltz. Their hands were weathered, smiles knowing. They had taught him how to dance, yes, but more importantly, they had taught him how to live.

"I may not know much about bull riding," the old man had said, his voice gravelly but warm with life experience, "but I know a thing or two about surviving the rough rides of life."

The words had settled deep within Jacob, becoming a quiet echo in his mind, their weight growing heavier as the days passed.

Their Wisdom

"Son," the old man had said earlier, his voice steady with that calm strength only time could bring, "you're at a crossroads. Life's gonna try to knock you off your feet. When it does, you better hold on to what moves you—because that's what'll keep you steady when everything else tries to take you down."

The older woman's voice had followed, soft yet direct: "You've got to ride with the heart you don't even know you have. Because, in the end, the biggest ride is the one within. Don't let anyone take that from you."

Jacob had smiled then, grateful for their wisdom. But now, sitting alone in the quiet, their words held a different weight. Could he really tap into something deeper? Could he become the cowboy he'd always dreamed of—not just in the arena, but in life itself?

"Ride on, son. Ride on." The mantra echoed in his mind, settling deeper than he'd expected.

A Moment of Reflection

Jacob's chest tightened as he sat there, the advice wrapping around him like a blanket too warm to ignore. He felt something shifting within him, an uncomfortable change. It wasn't just about surviving the ride anymore. Maybe—just maybe—he could ride for something more. For himself. The thought was both liberating and terrifying.

As the noise of the locker room swirled around him, he felt a weight lifting. Not the weight of the competition, nor the bruises from the ride, but the weight of his own expectations. He didn't have to keep riding just for survival. Maybe this was the moment when he could stop running on autopilot. The feeling wasn't easy to name, but it was there, pressing against him like a call to action.

Nick had been watching from across the room, still joking with the younger riders. Yet even his antics couldn't mask the shift Jacob felt. Something was brewing, something bigger than just bulls or rodeos.

"You all right, man?"

Nick asked, his voice light, but the concern in his eyes was hard to ignore. "You seem like you're a million miles away. You thinking about writing a bull-riding philosophy book or something?"

Jacob snorted softly, his lips twitching into a smile. "Yeah, man. Trying to figure out how to stop bull riding with my fists and start using my brain instead."

Nick raised an eyebrow. "Bull Yoga, huh? I'm in. We'll start a movement. I'll even wear the matching outfits—bull-themed."

Jacob chuckled. "Right. And I'll call it 'The Zen of Bull Riding: How to Survive the Ride and Find Inner Peace.'"

Nick burst out laughing. "Best-seller, man. I'd buy that in a heartbeat."

For a moment, the weight on Jacob's chest lifted, if only briefly. The world of bulls and rodeo didn't feel quite as suffocating, not with his friend there. The familiar banter, Nick's attempt to cheer him up, had softened the heaviness in Jacob's heart.

A Vulnerable Truth

But then, Nick's laughter faded as he saw the shift in Jacob's face. The mask had cracked, and for a brief moment, Nick saw what Jacob was really carrying.

"Look, man," Nick said, his voice softer, more serious now. "I get it. You've been through hell. But don't forget who you are. You've got more strength than anyone here. Hell, you've probably had worse days than any of these guys, and you keep getting back up. You don't have to prove anything to anyone."

Jacob met Nick's gaze, the vulnerability in his eyes raw and unguarded. The words were on the tip of his tongue, but they didn't come easily. It wasn't just fear of failure—it was the fear of the unknown. What came after the ride? What came after the competition? Was there anything beyond the ride?

"I just…" Jacob started, his voice trailing off. "I feel stuck. Like I've been trying so hard to live up to something, prove something to people. But maybe I've been missing the point all along."

Nick gave him a comforting pat on the back, his grin returning, though not quite as wide. "Don't go getting all deep on me now. You've got one job right now—get on that bull and ride. And you know what that old couple would say? They'd tell you it's your moment. Ride on, man. Find what moves you and hold onto it."

A Shift in the Locker Room

Jacob stood up, feeling the weight of Nick's words. Hold on to what moves you. It wasn't about impressing anyone—not Jake, not the crowd, not even himself. It was about finding that raw, unshakable thing inside him. That was what would carry him forward.

As he adjusted his gloves and took a steadying breath, he looked at the locker room door. The world beyond felt different now—less like a battleground and more like a place of connection. He wasn't just preparing for a ride. He was preparing to live.

Taking another deep breath, Jacob gave Nick a nod.

"Now go show them what that 'inner peace' can really do," Nick said with a wink.

Jacob couldn't help but laugh. "Yeah, I'll go show them my zen."

The Ride Ahead

As Jacob stepped into the roar of the crowd, something inside him had shifted. The weight wasn't there anymore. The arena, once a battlefield, now felt like a place of connection. His heart raced, not with fear, but with a deep, thrilling anticipation. He wasn't just riding bulls anymore—he was riding for something more.

The gate swung open. The bull waited.

And Jacob? He was ready to ride on.

CHAPTER 31
THE CROSSROADS

A Quiet Moment

The atmosphere was heavy as Jacob sat on the edge of the wooden fence, staring at the fading horizon. The sun, setting in a blaze of orange and gold, stretched long shadows across the empty arena. The air was cool, and the earthy scent of dust from the rodeo ground mixed with the faint hum of crickets in the distance. Jacob's fingers brushed against the splintered wood of the fence, grounding him in the stillness. The usual rush of adrenaline that used to push him forward was gone, replaced by an odd stillness—a disconnect, like the very essence of who he was had slipped away.

"Hey, cowboy," Nick's voice broke the silence, dragging Jacob's attention back to the present. He turned to see Nick and Erick walking toward him, their figures bathed in the soft glow of the dying day.

"You look like you're in deep thought," Nick added with a smirk, a beer in his hand. "Ready to start writing your memoir or what?"

Jacob managed a small laugh, though it didn't quite reach his eyes. "Feels like it," he said, kicking at a small stone in the dirt. "Maybe I'll call it *Rodeo Life and Other Misadventures*."

Nick chuckled. "I'll buy a copy. But only if it comes with a 'how-to' on avoiding bullhorns to the face."

Jacob smiled, shaking his head. "You'd be surprised how much I could teach you."

The Weight of the Choice

Erick leaned against the fence beside him, crossing his arms. "You've got that look, man. The 'lost cowboy' vibe."

Jacob let out a long breath, shaking his head. "I'm not lost. I'm just... confused. I've spent my whole life chasing this, and now it doesn't feel like it's mine anymore. It's like I'm still running, but for what?"

Nick chuckled, handing Jacob the beer. "Don't overthink it. We're just here to ride bulls and make money, not save the world."

"But there's got to be more to it than that," Jacob muttered, staring down at his boots. "I don't know anymore, Nick."

Before anyone could respond, a soft, familiar voice cut through the air, unmistakable in its warmth.

Unexpected Visitors

"Mind if we join you?"

Jacob's head snapped up, eyes widening in surprise. There, standing at the edge of the fence, was the older couple from the dance club. The man, tall and weathered with silver hair, leaned on his cane while the woman stood beside him, her smile as kind and inviting as he remembered.

"Well, look who it is," Jacob said, a genuine smile pulling at the corners of his mouth. "What brings you out here?"

The woman chuckled softly. "We've been watching you, son. And we think it's about time we had a little chat."

Jacob raised an eyebrow. "About what?"

The older man cleared his throat. "About how a guy like you needs to stop thinking so much. If I had a dime for every time I saw a cowboy sit and brood, I'd have my own rodeo by now."

Jacob laughed, surprised by the lighthearted jab. "Well, that makes two of us."

Words of Wisdom

"The world's got a funny way of pushing people to the edge," the man said, stepping forward with measured steps. His cane tapped gently on the ground as he walked toward Jacob, his movements slow but purposeful. His weathered face was softened by years of shared experiences, and his eyes glinted with the kind of understanding that only comes with time. "We've seen it happen before. People get caught up in the hustle, chasing things they don't need. But sooner or later, they all come to a point where they have to choose."

The woman's eyes twinkled with understanding. "And right now, it looks like you're standing right there, Jacob. The crossroads."

Jacob swallowed hard; his throat was dry. "I don't know what to do anymore."

The woman smiled, soft and knowing. "Of course, you don't. That's the trick, son. Sometimes, you have to let go of the things you think you need and figure out what you really want. The rodeo, the fame, all that—it was never really about that, was it? It was about the freedom. The rush."

Jacob stared at her, feeling something shift deep inside him. *Freedom. The rush.*

The man added with a grin, "And if that freedom includes a little less rodeo and a little more peace and quiet, then I wouldn't complain. Trust me, I'm not missing the noise of bucking bulls at my age."

The woman nudged him gently. "Don't listen to him, Jacob. He'd be back on that bull in a heartbeat if it meant avoiding my nagging him about the lawn."

Jacob chuckled, feeling his shoulders loosen for the first time in days.

A New Perspective

"You've been chasing something, Jacob," the older man added, his voice steady but firm. "But now, it's time to chase what really matters."

Jacob fell silent, the weight of their words pressing down on him. His fingers tightened around the beer can, the cold metal a sharp contrast to the warmth spreading through his chest.

The woman stepped closer, her gaze softening. "When we were younger, we had to make a similar choice. We thought the rodeo was all we could do. But life's bigger than that, Jacob. Don't be afraid to take the leap. Sometimes, you only find yourself when you stop running."

Her words hit him harder than he expected. He had spent so much of his life trying to outrun failure, to prove he was worthy, to silence the doubts. But in that moment, Jacob realized maybe it wasn't about winning anymore. Maybe it was about finding peace within himself.

The Moment of Clarity

The man placed a hand on Jacob's shoulder, grounding him in the moment. "You're at the crossroads now, son. The question is, what will you do with it?"

Jacob met their eyes, their gentle but knowing gazes making him feel less alone in this struggle. He thought back on the years of struggle, the sacrifices, the endless rides. It had all been about survival, about proving he could make it. But now, he saw it: It was more than that. It was about living authentically—something he had long forgotten.

"I don't know," Jacob whispered. "I'm scared. What if I walk away from this and can't find anything else? What if I'm just... not good enough?"

The woman chuckled, nudging her husband gently. "You'll find your way, Jacob. But don't let fear hold you back. Don't let it define you."

The pause stretched between them, heavy with unspoken truths. Jacob took a deep breath, letting their words wash over him. He felt lighter but still uncertain. The choice he had been avoiding was now staring him down.

"You know," Jacob said, breaking the silence, "I used to think I was just one ride away from everything making sense. But maybe... maybe it's not about the ride. Maybe it's about the journey itself."

The older man smiled, his eyes crinkling at the corners. "Now you're getting it."

Jacob stood up, his legs shaky from both the weight of the conversation and the sudden clarity settling in his chest. "Thanks," he said, his voice thick with emotion. "I didn't know I needed to hear that."

The woman winked at him. "Well, we've seen a thing or two in our day. Just don't forget—you're not alone in this. We all face those crossroads. It's how you choose to face them that matters."

As Jacob watched the couple walk away, a sense of calm settled over him. The night air felt different now, lighter—like the world had shifted, giving him more room to breathe. He didn't know where this path would lead, but for the first time in a long while, he felt ready to walk it.

Nick, who had been watching the entire interaction quietly, nudged Jacob in the ribs. "Well, damn. I think you just got a pep talk from the best of 'em."

Jacob smiled—a real, full smile this time. "Yeah. I think I did."

CHAPTER 32
THE RODEO AND JACOB'S REALIZATION

Chasing the Ride, Finding the Pause

The day had arrived. The arena hummed with its usual energy—the kind of electricity that only a final rodeo event could inspire. The crowd's cheers echoed in the air, hooves pounding on the dirt, the heat heavy and palpable, thick with anticipation. The scene was familiar, almost comforting. Yet, as Jacob stood at the edge of the arena, his eyes trained on the bullpens and the cowboys gearing up for their rides, something inside of him had shifted.

It was no longer about proving himself to the world, or even to Jake. That battle, those ghosts, were behind him. Today, it felt different. The weight of the decisions he'd made—the conversations with the older couple, the heart-to-heart talks with his friends—had all led him to this moment. For the first time, Jacob didn't feel the usual fire to outdo everyone else. There was something quieter inside of him now, more deliberate. A steady, sure sense that the ride itself, no matter the outcome, would define him.

He wasn't here just to survive the rodeo anymore. He was here to thrive—for himself, for his future, for the person he was becoming, not the one he had been.

The Bull's Eye

The gate creaked open with a sharp, familiar sound, and Jacob stepped forward. His boots met the dirt, the weight of his body sinking into the earth beneath him. There was no rush, no frantic energy. No more second-guessing. Just the steady rhythm of his breath, the deep inhale of the hot, dry air, and the powerful, shifting body of the bull beneath him. Raw. Primal.

For the first time in a long while, Jacob felt a deep sense of peace. He was here, in this moment, not running or escaping anything. He was present.

The bull reared, snorting and tossing its massive head, muscles coiling, ready to explode. Jacob gripped the rope with all his strength, his knuckles going white, but his mind stayed calm— unwavering. The noise of the crowd, the world outside the arena, faded into a distant hum. It was just him and the bull now.

The ride was wild. The bull bucked hard, its powerful body twisting beneath him, but Jacob found his balance with ease, each movement fluid and instinctive. He could feel the power of the animal, the pulse of life that surged through both him and the beast. It was more than a ride—it was a dance. A challenge. And for the first time in his life, Jacob felt truly free.

The Moment of Truth

The ride came to an end with a jolt, and Jacob was thrown to the ground with a sharp thud. His chest hit the dirt, the wind knocked out of him, his body aching from the impact. But something was different this time.

He didn't lie there cursing his bad luck or wondering what went wrong. Instead, he stayed there for a moment, letting the adrenaline course through him, catching his breath. The world around him seemed to pause, the crowd's cheers blurring into the background. He'd made it through the ride, sure. But it wasn't the ride that mattered anymore.

It was everything that had led him here—the choices, the lessons, the people who had shaped him along the way. This moment, this sense of stillness amidst the chaos, was what defined him now. Not the bull, not the win. The journey. He had chosen to live on his own terms.

And for the first time in years, Jacob realized: This was enough.

Slowly, deliberately, Jacob rose to his feet. The world came rushing back—the cheers, the music blasting through the speakers—but it no longer overwhelmed him. He wasn't just part of the noise anymore. He was part of the journey. His journey. Winning didn't matter the way it once had.

He had already won. He had won himself.

Facing the Future

As Jacob made his way back toward the locker room, he could feel the eyes on him—Jake's in particular. The cocky cowboy stood across the arena, arms crossed, waiting. But Jacob didn't feel the usual rush of competition anymore. He wasn't fighting Jake or anyone else. He was simply… living.

Erick and Nick were waiting for him by the locker room door, grinning like they had already seen it coming.

"You did it, man," Erick said, clapping him on the back. "That was one hell of a ride."

Jacob smiled, feeling a weight lift off his chest. "Yeah. It felt right."

Nick, ever the optimist, grinned ear to ear. "Hell, you didn't just ride that bull. You owned it."

Jacob chuckled, shaking his head. "I think we both did."

A New Path

The locker room was buzzing with celebration, the hum of laughter and congratulations filling the air. Fellow riders slapped Jacob on the back, offering their praise. But amidst all the noise, Jacob felt a profound stillness settle in his heart.

He didn't know what came next, but for the first time in years, he felt ready to find out.

Later, stepping outside for a breath of fresh air, Jacob saw the older couple again. They were standing by the fence, watching the celebration unfold, their faces lined with quiet pride. The woman smiled warmly when she saw him approach.

"Well, son," she said, her voice as kind as ever, "how does it feel?"

Jacob looked out at the crowd, the celebration still going strong. He could feel the thrill of the moment, but deeper than that was something else—a peace that no trophy or title could ever give him.

"It feels like freedom," he said simply.

The man nodded, his eyes gleaming with understanding. "We told you. Ride on."

Jacob smiled back at them, his heart full. "I think I finally understand what you meant."

The Journey Continues

As the evening stretched on, Jacob lingered by the arena, watching as the stars slowly began to twinkle in the sky. He wasn't sure what the future held, but for the first time in a long time, he felt a sense of peace. He wasn't running from it anymore.

For the first time, Jacob didn't need anyone's approval, validation, or a prize to measure his worth. He wasn't defined by the competition, the win, or the struggles he'd faced. He was simply Jacob—a cowboy who had found his way back to the heart of the ride.

The gates would open again. The bulls would buck again. But this time, Jacob wasn't riding for the win. He was riding for himself, for his future, for his heart and soul.

And in that moment, he realized: That was enough.

CHAPTER 33
THE QUIET MORNING

A Moment of Reflection

The soft light of early morning bathed the porch in a gentle, golden glow. Jacob sat in the old wooden chair, a coffee mug cradled in his hands, gazing out over the quiet expanse of the ranch, the fields stretching into the horizon. The world felt still, almost as if it were holding its breath. The dust from the rodeo grounds, the pounding rhythm of hooves, and the roar of the crowd had all faded into the distance, leaving only the sounds of nature: the chirping of birds, the rustle of wind through the trees, and the occasional bleat of a distant sheep.

Jacob closed his eyes briefly, letting the warmth of the sun wash over him. It felt different now. There was a depth to it, a soothing comfort that wrapped around him like a blanket. The rush of adrenaline from the rodeo, the fight for the next title, the next win—he couldn't remember the last time he'd felt so disconnected from all of it.

For a long time, Jacob had believed the next competition, the next win, would bring him peace. It was an endless cycle—pursuing something he couldn't quite define. But now, as the morning stretched before him, he realized the thrill of the chase had left him hollow.

He took a slow sip of his coffee, feeling the heat spread through him. It was strong, bitter, the taste lingering on his tongue as he leaned back in the chair. The simplicity of the moment—the silence of the ranch, the rustling trees, the faint whistle of the wind—felt as much a part of him as the rodeo had. He closed his eyes again, savoring the stillness.

"Is this it?" he asked himself. "Is this all there is to the ride?"

The question hit him harder than expected. The years he'd spent running after victory, after recognition, seemed to evaporate in the morning light. For the first time, he felt what true peace might be like—something quieter, less demanding.

He looked down at his hands, weathered and calloused from years of gripping ropes, saddles, and reins. They trembled slightly, a subtle reminder of the bruises—both physical and mental—that he'd carried with him.

"Man, what have you been chasing?" Jacob muttered, half to himself, feeling the weight of his own question. He closed his eyes again, letting the warmth of the sun soak into his skin. The weight that had settled deep in his chest seemed to lighten just a little, as though the sun itself was slowly absorbing the tension from his body.

The Visit to Grace and Henry

Finding the Right Path

A few hours later, Jacob found himself driving down the familiar dirt road toward the small house that had become a sanctuary of sorts. Grace and Henry—an older couple who had taught him how to dance months ago—had given him more than just rhythm. They had offered him perspective. Wisdom. And it had been a balm to his soul in ways he hadn't even fully understood until now.

As Jacob pulled up to their home, he noticed the small garden, alive with wildflowers in shades of violet and gold. The creak of their porch swing in the wind felt like a gentle greeting. The simplicity of their life—a life of quiet purpose—was something Jacob couldn't quite define but always felt when he was near them.

Grace sat on the porch, knitting needles moving with practiced ease. Henry, never far behind, was tending to a few pots of herbs in the garden. When they saw Jacob, their faces lit up with that quiet, knowing smile that always made him feel welcome.

"Well, look who decided to come by," Grace said, standing up and brushing the dirt off her hands. "Come on over, Jacob. We saved you a seat."

Jacob grinned. It had been a long time since he'd had a real conversation with anyone who wasn't pushing him toward a title, a record, or some form of recognition.

Sitting down beside her on the porch swing, Jacob handed Grace a small bouquet he'd picked from the roadside. She smiled warmly, placing the flowers in a jar beside her as she settled in.

"What's on your mind, son?" Henry asked, wiping his hands on his jeans before sitting down next to Jacob.

Jacob hesitated. There was so much—so much he wanted to say but didn't know where to start.

"I don't know," he said finally, his voice softer than usual. "Just... life, I guess." He sighed. "I've been thinking a lot about the rodeo.

About where I'm headed. All this competition, all the pressure—it's starting to feel like it's not enough anymore."

Grace looked at him with a quiet, knowing expression, then glanced at Henry. They exchanged a silent moment before Grace spoke.

"The thing is, Jacob," she began, her voice calm but firm, "life is a lot like a dance. It's not about how fast you go or how perfectly you follow the steps. It's about finding the rhythm. And when you find it, you'll know. It's not always going to be easy, but when you get it right... Well, there's no feeling quite like it."

Henry nodded, his expression thoughtful. "And sometimes, you've got to step away from the crowd and the noise. You need to find that quiet place where you can hear your heartbeat. That's when you know you're on the right path."

Jacob swallowed hard. There was a truth in their words that settled deep within him. The chaos of the rodeo had consumed him for so long, drowning out everything else—his peace, his future, even his sense of self.

"But what if I'm not sure anymore?" Jacob's voice cracked, his vulnerability breaking through. "What if the future I thought I wanted... isn't the one I need?"

Grace and Henry exchanged a glance, a silent understanding passing between them. Grace leaned forward, placing a gentle hand on Jacob's arm.

"Son," she said softly, "that's the hardest part. Finding the courage to let go of something you thought was your purpose, only to realize it's not. But you won't know what's next until you make that space." She gave a small, knowing smile. "You've already faced down some of the hardest bulls out there, Jacob. But now, the hardest ride is within you."

A Moment of Clarity

The Road Ahead

As Jacob drove away from Grace and Henry's house, the road ahead seemed clearer. Not because he had all the answers but because, for the first time, he felt like he was beginning to understand the question.

What moved him? What made him feel alive beyond the arena, beyond the rush of competition, beyond the crowd's cheers?

He didn't have the answer yet. But for the first time in a long while, that felt okay.

The dirt road stretched before him, winding and uncertain. But as the car moved forward, the path began to straighten, as if it, too, was finding its rhythm. The setting sun cast long shadows across the land, painting the earth with hues of gold and amber. Jacob exhaled slowly, feeling a weight he hadn't even realized he was carrying begin to lift.

He knew the ride wasn't over—not by a long shot. But this time, it wasn't about the next title, the next win. This time, it was for him.

"Ride on, son," he whispered to himself, a small smile tugging at his lips. "Find your rhythm."

CHAPTER 34
THE DECISION

The Long Road to Clarity

The sun dipped low in the sky, casting long shadows across the quiet arena. Jacob stood at the edge, his boots sinking slightly into the dirt, the familiar scent of leather and earth mixing in the air. The ground beneath him felt solid, yet the weight of his thoughts made it seem like the earth itself was shifting beneath him. He looked out at the place where he had once poured his heart and soul, where every bull ride had been a test of endurance, of proving something to himself, to the crowd, and to the world. But now, the cheers, the adrenaline, the rush—it all felt distant. It was as if they had belonged to someone else, someone he used to be.

He traced the rough leather of his gloves, the texture worn smooth from years of use. The feeling was familiar, comforting even, but it carried an echo of something else—something that no longer fit. The memories rushed back: the rush of a good ride, the camaraderie of the riders, the heat of competition, and, perhaps most vividly, one particularly memorable ride when he'd ended up getting thrown from the bull in front of the crowd. He could still hear the gasps and the laughter, still see himself spinning like a ragdoll in mid-air, only to land with a thud on the dirt. But the only thing that didn't spin was his dignity, which had taken quite the beating. He chuckled quietly to himself. The sound was hollow, though, as if it belonged to someone else.

"You'd think after all that, I'd be more graceful," he mused, shaking his head with a small grin.

The rodeo had been his identity, his fire. But now, there was a coldness in his chest, a heavy emptiness that he couldn't ignore. It wasn't fear—not exactly, but something else. A realization, sharp and undeniable.

"Was this it?" he muttered, his voice barely above a whisper. "The cheers, the dust, and all the pain... maybe that's the end of the ride."

The crash from weeks ago replayed in his mind—the way it had shaken his body and rattled his soul. Maybe it was time to listen to the whispers he'd been trying to drown out. Maybe it was time to walk away.

Grace and Henry's Wisdom

The sound of footsteps broke Jacob's reverie. He turned and saw Grace and Henry walking toward him, their steps easy, grounded. Grace smiled knowingly, her eyes twinkling with understanding as she reached his side.

"Figured we'd find you here," Henry said, leaning heavily on his cane. Grace nudged him affectionately with her elbow, a quiet tease as always.

"You look like someone trying to wrestle with his own thoughts," Grace observed, her voice soft and warm. "No bull involved?"

Jacob chuckled, but it sounded like it came from someone who had learned to mask the pain. "Something like that."

Grace gave him a knowing look, her eyes crinkling with empathy, and she exchanged a silent glance with Henry. "You know, Henry had to give up rodeo once, back in the day," she said, her voice light. "He was a natural. But his knees started talking back. And let me tell you, they don't take kindly to being ignored."

Henry snorted softly, his face breaking into a grin. "That's right. My knees were done, but my pride was still in the ring. Sometimes, you've got to quit to win, son."

Jacob raised an eyebrow, not entirely sure he understood. "Quit to win?"

Grace smiled gently. "It's not about quitting, Jacob. It's about knowing when to change course. Sometimes, you've gotta step out of the ring to find something real. And that's when you win."

The Fight Within

Jacob felt a knot tighten in his chest. He had always seen the rodeo as a fight, a test of endurance, a way to prove who was strongest. But now, as he stood in the fading light of the arena, he realized that the real fight wasn't out there in the dirt. It was inside him, buried deep in the hollow of his chest.

"You ever wonder what it'd be like to just... stop?" Jacob's voice was barely a whisper, the words floating into the air and being carried away by the breeze. "To let go of all this? To walk away?"

Henry nodded slowly, his face drawn with the weight of memories. His voice was steady, but his eyes held the depth of years lived. "Oh, I've wondered. More times than I care to admit." He paused, thinking back. "It's tough, son. But it doesn't make you weak. It means you've got the strength to choose a different path."

Grace stepped closer, her presence a quiet strength beside him. Her voice was firm but kind. "It's not easy, Jacob. But you've got to ask yourself what matters more—staying in the ring for the applause or stepping out of it to find something real?"

Jacob stared down at the dirt beneath his boots, feeling its rough texture against the soles. The weight of the arena seemed to settle on his shoulders, the echoes of past victories and defeats swirling in his mind. His body ached, but it was his soul that was exhausted. He'd given everything to this life—his blood, his sweat, his tears. But now, the price felt too steep.

"I don't know if I'm ready to let go," Jacob admitted, his voice barely above a whisper. "It's hard to walk away when you've built your whole life around something."

Grace's hand gently gripped his shoulder, grounding him. Henry gave him a small, knowing smile, the kind only someone who had walked this road before could give. "Son, you'll know when it's time. You've got a fire in you—don't let it burn you out. It'll take you places, but you've gotta let it guide you, not consume you."

A Moment of Clarity

Jacob didn't answer right away. Instead, he stood there, his eyes fixed on the empty arena, the fading sun casting long, golden rays across the dirt. The wind shifted, carrying the faint scent of earth and grass, and for the first time, he didn't feel the pressure to make a decision right then and there. It wasn't a loss. It wasn't a defeat. It was an evolution. He wasn't walking away from who he was; he was walking toward who he could become.

Grace's voice broke through the stillness, calm and steady. "Sometimes you've gotta ride the hardest bulls, Jacob, to find out what really moves you. But when you find it, you hold onto it like your future depends on it. And it does."

Jacob nodded slowly, feeling the weight of her words sink in. The knot in his chest loosened, and for the first time in years, something inside him settled. He didn't need to have all the answers right now. The rodeo had been his everything, but now it was time for something else. Something bigger than the arena.

He glanced at Grace and Henry, a soft smile spreading across his face. "You're right," he said, his voice steady now, the weight of his decision finally lifting. "It's time to move on."

A New Beginning

The next day, Jacob found himself back at the barn, packing up the gear he had used for years. The leather of his boots felt familiar in his hands, but it was no longer a symbol of the fight. It was a symbol of the journey he had taken, the lessons learned, and the man he had become.

He smiled to himself as he slipped the rope into the duffel bag, the years of memories packed into the small space. It was a weight, but it was one he carried with gratitude, not regret. He would always carry those lessons with him, but now, they weren't a burden—they were the foundation upon which he would build something new.

As he closed the barn door for the last time, he realized something else. The arena had been a place where he learned how to fight. But now, the world outside was where he would learn how to live.

Jacob looked back at the barn, then ahead to the open fields stretching before him. The future was uncertain, but for the first time in years, he was excited to step into it.

The sun was rising, casting its warm glow across the horizon. And for Jacob, it was the beginning of something new.

CHAPTER 35
THE DECISION TIME

The Weight of the Guitar

Jacob sat on the edge of the old wooden chair, the guitar awkwardly perched on his lap. The weight of it surprised him—he'd imagined it would be lighter, less cumbersome. But the cold metal felt foreign against his rough, calloused fingertips. He strummed the first chord, the sound grating like an unwelcome guest in a place he thought he belonged. It echoed through the barn, harsh and off-key, a stark contrast to the familiar roar of the crowd he'd once known so well. The sound felt foreign, mocking him, and for a moment, the coldness of the strings seemed to press down on his chest.

"Well, that's... definitely not the sound I was going for," Jacob muttered to himself, his laugh dry and strained. The sound was jagged, almost painful, but he tried again—more cautiously this time. The note was slightly better, but it still felt like the music was a language he hadn't yet learned, like something just out of his grasp.

Grace appeared in the doorway, arms crossed, her presence as familiar as the warm, sunlit air of the barn. She leaned against the frame, a smile tugging at the corner of her lips. "If you were aiming for a cat on a chalkboard, you nailed it."

Jacob shot her a quick glance, the faintest smirk tugging at his lips. "Guess I need to take a few lessons, huh?"

She stepped into the barn with a gentle chuckle, walking over to him with a quiet grace. Her eyes softened as she sat beside him on the old wooden chair, her hands effortlessly cradling the guitar as if it had always been hers. She strummed a simple chord, the sound warm and familiar, melodic, in a way that felt like home.

"Just like riding bulls, huh?" Jacob said, raising an eyebrow.

Grace grinned, strumming another chord with ease. "Exactly. You fall, you get back up, and you try again. But you've gotta be patient with yourself."

Jacob nodded, but his chest tightened, a knot of uncertainty twisting deep inside. He hadn't realized just how much he was second-guessing everything until now. The rodeo had been his identity for so long—his purpose, his drive. Walking away from that to pick up a guitar felt like stepping into an entirely new world. The music, though… the music felt different. It was something else. A lifeline, maybe? Or was it just a distraction from something he couldn't face?

Doubts and Reflections

As Grace continued to play, the soft melody filled the barn, its gentle rhythm soothing in contrast to the whirlwind of thoughts swirling in Jacob's mind. The barn felt warmer now, the light filtering in through the cracks in the wooden walls, but his heart remained heavy. He wasn't just holding the guitar—he was holding a decision that could change everything. A decision that might cost him the one thing he had always known.

Could he really leave behind the world that had shaped him for so long? The adrenaline, the thrill of the ride, the roar of the crowd—it had all been part of him. But now, it was fading into the background, replaced by something quieter, something more personal. Music.

His fingers strummed a few hesitant notes, but the sound was hollow as if the guitar itself was echoing his doubts. It was a voice unsure of its truth, a whisper in a language he wasn't yet fluent in. Every strum felt like a question he wasn't sure how to answer. Was this a mistake? Or was it just a way to run from everything he'd built his life around?

"You look like you're trying to figure something out." Grace's voice was soft and steady, her gaze never leaving him. "What's on your mind?"

Jacob hesitated, his gaze falling to his hands, rough and calloused from years of gripping reins and ropes. His fingers felt unfamiliar with the guitar, clumsy even. He thought of the arena, the sound of hooves pounding the dirt, the weight of the bucking bulls beneath him. His grip had always been certain, decisive. But now, this? This guitar felt like a stranger in his hands.

"I just... I don't know, Grace. What if this is just me running away from what I've known? What if I'm making a mistake?"

Grace set the guitar down gently and turned to face him, her eyes unwavering. Her voice, when it came, was full of quiet strength. "I don't think it's about running away, Jacob. It's about finding a new way forward. You don't have to leave everything behind. You're not erasing the past—you're just adding to it. You're figuring out who you are beyond the rodeo."

Finding the Courage to Move Forward

Jacob stood up, the weight of his decision pressing down on him like the saddle he used to wear for every ride. His boots echoed in the silence, the rhythm of his footsteps mixing with the soft melody that still lingered in the air. His mind raced with doubts, with questions that seemed impossible to answer. Could he live without the rodeo? Would he regret leaving it behind? Would the emptiness that had begun to creep into his chest grow louder, suffocating him?

"I don't know if I'm ready to give up the bulls, Grace," Jacob admitted, his voice tight with emotion. "The roar of the crowd, the thrill of the ride—it's everything I've worked for. It's how people see me, how I see myself. I don't know if I can leave all that behind."

Grace stood and walked over to him, her hand settling gently on his shoulder. Her touch was light but firm, a reminder that she was there, steadfast, unwavering. "But Jacob, that's just one part of who you are. The rodeo doesn't define you, no matter how much you've tied yourself to it. The real you—the one who's standing here with me right now—is the one who's been searching for something more. And you've found it. That's something worth holding onto."

Jacob looked down at the guitar in his hands. For the first time, it didn't feel like a symbol of escape or of running away from his past. It felt like a new kind of freedom—something uncertain but full of possibility. It wasn't perfect, but it didn't need to be. It was just... his.

The Final Decision

Grace smiled, a small but proud glint in her eyes. "That's it, Jacob. You've got it. The ride isn't over—it's just changed direction."

Jacob exhaled slowly, a weight he hadn't even realized he was carrying lifting from his chest. He had been so focused on the adrenaline—the rush of the ride, the titles, the crowds—that he hadn't considered what it might be like to find peace in something else. Something quieter but no less powerful. He could still be the cowboy—the man who had faced down bulls, the man who had weathered storms in the arena. But he didn't have to be defined by it.

Maybe it wasn't about leaving the rodeo behind. Maybe it was about growing beyond it—finding something new that made him feel alive, something that was his to hold, without the roar of the crowd or the pressure to be perfect.

Grace squeezed his shoulder gently. "Ride on, son. This is your moment. Hold onto it like your future depends on it."

Jacob nodded, a weight he hadn't even realized he was carrying lifting from his chest. His heart steadied, not with certainty, but with peace. He didn't need to have all the answers, just the courage to take the next step. And in that moment, with the guitar in his hands and the future ahead of him, he felt something like hope, quiet but real.

As he strummed the guitar once more, the sound filled the barn—a new song, a new direction. The rodeo was behind him, but it had led him here. And at this moment, with the guitar in his hands and the future ahead of him, Jacob finally felt like he was exactly where he needed to be.

CHAPTER 36
A CROSSROADS OF DREAMS

The Quiet of the Land

The late afternoon sun hung low in the sky, casting everything in a warm, honeyed light. Orange and purple streaks painted the horizon, stretching the shadows long across the land. Jacob stood at the edge of the porch, his gaze drifting over the rolling hills and the expanse that seemed to go on forever. The wind had picked up, the scent of earth mingling with the sound of leaves rustling—an intimate whisper of the land.

He gripped the neck of the guitar, the worn wood fitting comfortably in his hands. It felt familiar, yet strangely out of place. The world around him was still and peaceful. But inside, his thoughts churned. The rodeo had been his world for so long, but now that world felt smaller, its hold loosening with every passing day. The bruises, the broken promises, and the pressure of being someone he wasn't sure he was anymore had left their mark.

He strummed a few chords, but the sound didn't feel right. His fingers stumbled, his hands sore from the long hours spent on bulls. "Come on, Jacob, you can do better than that," he muttered to himself, a wry smile tugging at the corners of his lips. He tried again, forcing his fingers into a rhythm, only to wince as the notes warbled out of tune. "Oh, yeah. That's exactly what I wanted to hear," he said, the humor barely hiding the frustration in his voice.

A Call from Jake

The sudden buzz of his phone broke through the moment. He glanced at the screen—Jake's name lit up, and with a sigh, Jacob answered.

"Hey, man, where the hell are you?" Jake's voice crackled through the speaker, charged with that familiar cocky tone. "The rodeo's not the same without your swagger. We've got a new bull, and I'm sure you'd love to get your hands on him. You know the bulls miss you, right?"

Jacob chuckled despite himself. The old familiarity in Jake's voice was like slipping into a worn-in pair of boots. He could almost picture Jake leaning back in his chair, smirking.

"You're calling to rub it in, huh?" Jacob replied, trying to keep his tone light, but something deep within felt different.

"Nah, man. Just checking if you're still alive. Can't let you fade off into the sunset without a proper goodbye." Jake's voice softened, a rare sincerity undercutting the usual bravado.

"I'm not fading anywhere, Jake," Jacob said, though the words didn't carry the conviction they once had. His voice felt hollow, the certainty of his old self slowly slipping away.

Jake went quiet for a beat before speaking again, the edge of seriousness returning. "Oh yeah? Then why the hell are you over there playing guitar instead of getting your hands on a bull?" He paused. "Look, I get it. Things are changing for you, but you're not done yet. The rodeo still has your name on it, and you know it."

The weight of Jake's words settled heavily on Jacob's chest. A part of him still craved the rush—the thundering heartbeat of the bulls, the roar of the crowd, the feeling of every muscle straining against something bigger than himself. But another part of him felt suffocated by it all.

"Maybe it does," Jacob said quietly. "But I think there's something else out there for me. I don't know what that is yet, but I'll figure it out."

Jake didn't reply immediately. When he did, his voice was softer, like the old friend Jacob had always known. "Alright, man. Just don't let this be the last thing you do. Don't let the bulls be the only thing that defines you. You're bigger than that. But whatever you choose… ride on."

There it was again. That simple, powerful truth. "Ride on" wasn't just about bulls. It was about life. About pushing forward, even when you didn't know where you were headed. Jacob swallowed hard. "Yeah… thanks, Jake."

Grace's Voice of Reason

Before Jacob could settle back into the quiet, his phone buzzed again. Grace. He almost smiled. Her name had a warmth to it, like a beacon of light in his swirling thoughts.

"Hey," he answered, his voice lighter now, though still tinged with the weight of the conversation he'd just had.

"I was just thinking about you," Grace said, her voice a comforting presence on the other end. "How's the guitar going? Any better?"

"Yeah, I guess," Jacob replied, laughing a little, though it didn't reach his eyes. "Trying to get the hang of it, but my fingers feel like they've been stomped by a bull."

Grace's laugh was soft and understanding. "Well, you can't expect to become a rock star overnight."

"Yeah, but this thing feels like it's gonna buck me off if I don't get it right," Jacob said, the humor lightening his mood, if only for a moment.

"Don't worry. It's not a bull," Grace teased. "You can't get thrown off, remember?"

"Yeah, but sometimes it feels like I might," Jacob admitted. The weight of his decision pressed down on him harder now; every word felt like an unspoken confession. "I've been thinking a lot lately... about the rodeo, about everything. I don't know if I'm ready to let go yet."

"I know, Jacob," she said gently, her voice full of quiet understanding. "But you have to remember, this is your life. You've given everything to it. But now, you have the chance to give something to yourself."

He sat down on the porch, the guitar resting in his lap. Grace's words sank in, slow but steady. For so long, he had given everything to the rodeo—the thrill, the crowds, the name he'd built. But now, for the first time, he was being asked to give something back to himself.

"I'm scared," Jacob admitted, the words coming out before he could stop them. "I don't know who I'll be if I walk away from it."

"You'll be you, Jacob." Grace's voice was steady, offering him the reassurance he hadn't known he needed. "And you've always been more than just a cowboy. You've got a heart and a future. You're still figuring it out. But I promise you this—you'll find your way. The key is to trust in yourself."

Jacob looked up at the sky, the colors fading into dusk. The clouds drifted lazily across the horizon, and for the first time in a long while, it felt as if the world itself was taking its time. Not rushing him. For the first time, he had the space to breathe, to think. Maybe he didn't have all the answers, but he had something he hadn't had before: a real choice.

"Thanks, Grace," he murmured, his voice thick with gratitude. "You always know what to say."

"I'll always be here, Jacob," she replied softly. "Just remember—whatever you choose, I'm proud of you. Ride on, son. This is your moment."

The Future Beckons

As the call ended, Jacob sat still for a moment, the weight of his decision pressing harder than ever. The quiet around him seemed almost too peaceful now, the breeze carrying the hum of cicadas as the world settled into evening. Inside, his mind raced, thoughts tangled in uncertainty.

He stood slowly, the guitar still resting in his hands, and walked to the edge of the porch. He stood there for a moment, looking out at the open land before him—an expanse where so many of his choices had already been made. His life had led him here. And now, it was time to choose the direction he would go next.

He took a deep breath, letting the wind brush against his skin. The sounds of the world were so familiar now, like an old song he hadn't realized he loved. There was no easy answer. No simple way to walk away from everything that had shaped him. But maybe it wasn't about walking away.

Maybe it was about walking forward. Stepping into something new. The rodeo, the bulls, the crowds—they were part of him. But they didn't define him. He was more than that. He could be more than that.

As the last note of the chord hung in the air, Jacob felt a quiet peace settle within him. It wasn't perfect, but it was a start. And for the first time, he felt ready to walk forward.

He strummed a final chord, the sound ringing out into the quiet evening. It wasn't perfect, but it was his. And for now, that was enough.

CHAPTER 37
THE BREAKTHROUGH

Tired of Chasing

The sun hung low, casting an amber glow over the rodeo arena. Jacob stood at the far edge, his boots sinking slightly into the dirt as he gazed across the expanse. The sounds of the crowd, the stamp of hooves, and the crack of ropes all blended into the background, but to him, they seemed distant, like echoes from another world.

His heart felt heavy; his mind clouded. He'd been here before—torn between the thrill of the ride and the doubts creeping in from all sides. But today, the pressure felt suffocating, more than ever. The bruises on his body weren't the worst of it. It was the weight in his chest, the constant noise in his head telling him he wasn't enough, that no matter how hard he rode, it would never be enough.

Jacob ran a hand over the leather of his gloves, worn from use but still comforting in their familiarity. Each ride, each bull, had left a mark on him—physically and emotionally. The rodeo wasn't just a sport; it was a test of everything he had left. But now, he wasn't even sure what he was riding for anymore.

His mind swirled with doubts. He had once ridden with the hope of proving himself, of gaining respect, of earning a title that would make it all worthwhile. But now, it felt hollow. Was it the fame he was chasing? Or was it simply the thrill of the ride, the danger of it all? Either way, it wasn't enough.

What am I even doing here? Jacob thought, staring at his boots, the dust clinging to the leather. He wasn't sure if he was fighting for a dream or running from something—maybe both.

Erick's Wisdom

A soft voice broke through his thoughts.

"Kid, you look like you're carrying the whole world on your shoulders."

Jacob turned to see Erick, standing with his arms crossed and a knowing smile on his face. Erick had seen his fair share of battles, both in the arena and out. He looked older now, his face lined with the wisdom of experience, but there was a quiet strength in the way he carried himself.

"I'm not sure what I'm doing here, Erick," Jacob admitted, his voice tinged with doubt. "I thought I had it figured out. Thought I was fighting for something. But now... now it feels like I'm just running in circles, holding on to something that's slipping through my fingers."

Erick's smile softened. He stepped closer, placing a hand on Jacob's shoulder, a reassuring weight. His touch was steady, grounded— exactly what Jacob needed.

"You're not the first one to feel that way," Erick said, his voice steady and calm. "Hell, I've been there more times than I can count. The trick is remembering why you started this in the first place. When the pain becomes all you know, it's easy to lose sight of the reason you got on that bull to begin with."

Jacob frowned, glancing down at his boots, the weight of his thoughts pulling him down. "Yeah, but it's hard, man. I don't even know what I'm trying to prove anymore."

Erick chuckled, shaking his head. "It's not about proving anything, son. It never was." He took a deep breath and looked out at the arena, where the horses and riders were warming up, the tension building in the air. "You know, when I was your age, I thought the only thing that mattered was being the best. I chased that title like it was my last breath." He paused, giving Jacob a sidelong glance. "Though, to be honest, at the time, I wasn't sure if I was chasing the title or just trying to outrun my own mistakes."

Jacob couldn't help but snort at the image of Erick, younger and more reckless, with the kind of stubborn pride he understood all too well. "Yeah, well, I think I've been doing that too, except instead of outrunning mistakes, I'm trying to outrun a nervous breakdown."

Erick laughed, his eyes crinkling at the corners. "Same difference, kid. But listen, that's the thing about this rodeo—hell, that's the thing about life. It's a long, dusty ride. Doesn't matter how many bulls you ride or how many trophies you win. If you're just doing it for the 'golden buckle' at the end, then you're already looking at the wrong prize."

A Story From Erick's Past

Erick's voice dropped into a more serious tone, the humor fading as he went on.

"You know, there was one ride I'll never forget. I was young, full of fire, and my eyes were fixed on that championship, just like yours. But after the ride, I could barely stand. My back was shot, and I remember lying there in the dirt, thinking, 'What the hell am I doing?'"

Jacob's curiosity piqued. He looked up. "What happened?"

Erick exhaled, a wistful smile tugging at the corners of his lips. "Well, after I thought about it long enough, I realized something. I was looking for validation from everyone—the crowd, the other riders, hell, even myself. But the real question was: What did I need to validate inside myself? That's when I knew, if I kept pushing for the approval of others, I'd burn myself out. If you only ride for someone else, kid, you're already losing. You need to find what drives you, not to please anyone, but because it matters to you."

Jacob mulled over Erick's words, letting the wisdom sink in. For the first time in a long while, he felt a shift—a quiet understanding beginning to take root. Maybe it was time to stop fighting for a version of himself that was shaped by everyone else's expectations. Maybe it was time to fight for the version of himself he truly wanted to be.

He felt the weight in his chest lessen, the burden of needing to prove himself to the crowd, to the world, slowly lifting. A different kind of strength was growing within him, one that didn't require approval from anyone but himself.

A Moment of Clarity

He stood there for a long moment, the weight of Erick's words settling deep inside. The crowd continued to gather, the tension of the competition rising, but Jacob's focus had shifted. The ride ahead didn't feel like a test of endurance anymore. It felt like an opportunity to face the bull, not as a challenge to conquer, but as a partner in a dance he hadn't fully understood before.

"What do you think?" Erick asked, his voice breaking Jacob's thoughts.

Jacob smiled, a little lighter than before. "I think I'm ready to ride."

Erick chuckled, the sound warm and easy. "Damn right you are. But just remember—ride for yourself, not for the crowd, not for anyone else. This is about you, kid. And that's the only thing that matters."

Jacob nodded, his steps feeling a bit more purposeful now. The weight of his decision felt less heavy. As the arena lights flickered on, he walked toward the gates, feeling a calm he hadn't felt in ages.

The Ride of a Lifetime

The bull was massive, its nostrils flaring as it pawed the dirt beneath it. The crowd roared, and the tension in the air was thick.

"Here we go," Jacob muttered to himself, tightening the rope. He could almost hear Erick's voice in his ear: "Don't worry about impressing anyone. You've been doing that your whole life."

With a deep breath, Jacob looked at the bull again, feeling a familiar smirk tug at his lips. "Well, I guess you're not impressed either, huh?" he whispered to the animal, giving the bull a wink. "Alright, big guy. Let's see who's holding on by the end of this."

As the gate swung open, he was thrust into the chaos. The bull bucked and twisted, its raw power a force of nature. But this time, Jacob wasn't just holding on for dear life. He was moving with the animal, listening to its rhythm, feeling its power. For the first time in ages, he was enjoying it. It wasn't a battle. It was a moment to be present in the ride itself, whatever the outcome.

The Quiet After the Storm

When the ride finally ended, Jacob hit the dirt, but instead of the usual rush of adrenaline and shame, he lay there for a moment, still. He could feel the dust in the air, the sweat on his skin, and the exhaustion in his bones. But there was something else too—peace.

The crowd's roar was distant now. And for the first time, he didn't care. It wasn't about impressing them anymore. It was about him. It was about finally breaking free from the chains of expectation.

As he stood up and dusted himself off, he spotted Erick in the crowd, watching him with a proud smile. And for the first time, Jacob didn't need to prove anything to anyone—not even to himself.

A New Path Forward

Walking toward the exit, Jacob felt lighter, as if the weight had been lifted from his shoulders. Clarity came with the release, and for the first time in a long while, the future didn't seem as uncertain. He wasn't sure what lay ahead, but he knew one thing for sure: he was ready to face it, whatever it might be. And if it didn't lead to another championship or title, that was okay. He wasn't riding for those things anymore. He was riding for himself—for the pure joy of the journey, not the destination.

He looked up at the stars, the open sky reminding him of the possibilities. And with a slight grin, he murmured to himself, "Next time, maybe I'll ride a horse, just for a change of pace."

He imagined Erick's grin and chuckled.

CHAPTER 38
A NEW BEGINNING

The Ride, the Fight, the Moment of Clarity

The gates swung open with a metallic screech, and the roar of the crowd surged like a wave crashing against the shore. The heat of the arena washed over him, and dust swirled in the air as the bull beneath him stamped impatiently. Jacob's heart thudded in his chest, his palms slick with sweat as his fingers tightened around the rope. Beneath him, the bull was a storm—wild and unpredictable, its massive body coiled with raw power, ready to explode into motion. This was it. The moment he had been waiting for—not to prove something to others, but to prove it to himself.

Jacob's boots felt solid in the stirrups, but his legs trembled with anticipation. He wasn't thinking about Jake or the weight of the expectations that had always hung over him like an ominous cloud. He wasn't even thinking about the ride itself. His mind was sharp, clear—nothing but the bull, its rhythm, its movement. He was ready to leave everything behind. The past. The doubts. Even the pain. This was about him and the bull—nothing more, nothing less.

His breath slowed, his body feeling more solid in the saddle as the bull stamped beneath him. He remembered the long nights spent questioning his worth, the days he almost walked away from it all.

He could feel those moments in his muscles—every ounce of that struggle was now here, riding beneath him. But this time, he wasn't afraid of it. He wasn't fighting against it. He was simply... present.

As the bull bucked with ferocity, Jacob's muscles burned, but his grip tightened instinctively. The shock of its force sent him into the air, but he was ready. Before he could even think, he was back in the saddle. The impact of the ride jolted through his body, his ribs aching, his breath coming in ragged bursts, but it didn't matter. He wasn't desperately clinging to the saddle anymore. His grip was a partnership now, not a survival tactic. This wasn't just survival. He was thriving. He was dancing with the chaos.

A grin tugged at Jacob's lips as adrenaline surged through his veins. This is freedom, he thought, the power of the bull beneath him. This is it. The thrill wasn't in the fight anymore, in trying to stay on. It was in the ride itself—in existing with it, in perfect sync, no expectations, just the moment.

A Moment of Reflection

When the ride ended, and Jacob was tossed into the dirt, the world seemed to slow down. For a few seconds, everything was muffled, like the sounds of the crowd were coming from a faraway place. He lay there, chest heaving with each breath, his muscles aching in every direction. Dust settled around him, and for the first time, there was no weight pressing down on him. No expectations. No deadlines. No one to impress.

His eyes drifted to the stands. The crowd was still cheering, but something inside him had shifted. It wasn't about winning anymore. It wasn't about the audience's approval. For the first time in his life, Jacob realized that it wasn't even about the bull.

It was about him—his journey, his struggle, his fight to overcome the expectations and limitations he'd placed on himself.

He pushed himself to his feet, muscles screaming in protest, but it didn't matter. The pain, the bruises, the exhaustion—all irrelevant. He wasn't focused on what he'd lost. He wasn't surviving anymore. He was living. And in this quiet moment, he realized he was finally free from the self-imposed cage that had kept him trapped.

Nick's Subtle Support

As Jacob walked slowly toward the edge of the arena, the realization still buzzing in his mind, Nick appeared beside him. His familiar grin stretched across his face.

"You did it, man," Nick said, clapping Jacob on the back, his voice brimming with pride. "Told you you'd find it."

Jacob managed a tired smile, the exhaustion creeping into his bones. "Yeah, guess I'm still working on it."

Nick leaned in, his voice quieter now, more sincere. "Nah, man. You've got it. That wasn't just a ride. You didn't just ride the bull; you rode yourself."

Jacob paused, letting the words settle. It wasn't about the bull, or the competition, or the crowd. It was about finding peace with himself. It was about facing the man he had always feared confronting—and realizing that man was worthy of the ride.

A Quiet Wisdom from Erick

Later, as Jacob sat in the locker room, the hum of the arena still faint in his ears, his mind replayed the day. The endless rides. The bruises. The victories and failures. But there was a clarity now that had been missing before. It had never been just about the bulls. It was always about proving something to himself. Not to the world but to the person he'd feared confronting for so long.

Erick appeared at the door, leaning casually against the frame. His gaze met Jacob's with that unreadable look, yet there was something deeper in his eyes now, something knowing.

"You did well," Erick said quietly, his voice carrying more weight than usual. "Better than you know."

Jacob turned toward him, surprised by the sincerity in Erick's words. "Thanks," he said, his voice rough, as if the meaning of those words needed time to settle.

Erick didn't move, his gaze steady. "Don't let anyone tell you who you should be," he continued, his voice intense. "What you learned out there—it's not about surviving. It's about embracing every moment, every ride, as part of who you are. You can't outrun it, Jacob. You've got to ride it every time."

Jacob nodded, the impact of Erick's words sinking deep. He didn't need to chase some ideal or live up to someone else's standards. What mattered now was becoming the man who could face his fears and doubts and come out stronger. The perfect image could wait. The real work was in the everyday grind.

A Moment of Humor to Lighten the Mood

Nick reappeared, his teasing grin back in full force. "So, are you gonna quit while you're ahead, or are we gonna see you try to ride another bull into the dirt?"

Jacob chuckled, shaking his head. "Not today, man. I think I'll leave the bull-riding to the real pros for a while."

Nick raised an eyebrow, feigning shock. "You are a pro, my friend."

"Yeah, but I think I've done enough for today," Jacob said with a grin. "I'm good."

They shared a laugh, the lightness of the moment lifting the weight of the day. The simple joy of their camaraderie made everything feel easier for just a moment.

The Beginning of Something New

As the evening settled into twilight, Jacob stood outside the arena, gazing at the horizon. The noise of the crowd had faded, but the quiet inside him remained. It wasn't a silence of emptiness but of fulfillment—of peace at last.

The sun sank lower, casting a warm, golden light over the world. Jacob realized he was no longer trying to outrun the person he had been. He had made peace with his past, his present, and the uncertain future ahead. There were no guarantees. But for the first time, he knew that whatever came next—whether he rode again or walked away—he would do it on his own terms.

At that moment, Jacob knew his journey wasn't over. It had just begun.

CHAPTER 39
THE DECISION

A Moment of Reflection

Jacob sat in the back of the truck, his fingers drumming nervously against the dashboard. The truck's tires kicked up the dry dust, creating a cloud that seemed to hang in the air, clinging to everything—his skin, his thoughts, the silence between him and his friends. The sun had dipped low, casting a warm, golden glow over the horizon. The rodeo arena loomed ahead, a distant giant waiting to devour him. He wasn't sure what the night would bring, and he wasn't sure what he was about to bring to it.

The heat of the day still clung to the truck's metal frame, seeping into his skin as the dry wind ruffled his hair. He glanced out the window, watching the familiar, dust-choked roads of the town blur by. The truck was silent, save for the hum of the engine and the occasional squeak of a window creaking open. Erick sat beside him, eyes fixed on the road, while Nick, lounging in the back, tapped away on his phone, lost in the glow of his screen.

The quiet of the truck seemed to amplify Jacob's internal struggle. This wasn't just another ride. This wasn't about winning, proving himself, or showing up Jake one more time. No, this was different. This was about something deeper—something only he could name.

But the question lingered in his mind: Was he strong enough to answer that question tonight?

A Flash of the Past

His hand tightened around the steering wheel, and his thoughts drifted back to that one summer years ago. His father had been sitting on the porch, the last light of the day casting long shadows on the porch swing. "Don't just ride to survive, son," his father had said, wiping sweat from his brow after a long day's work. "Ride to thrive."

Jacob could still hear those words echoing in his mind. He had spent so much of his life fighting just to survive the ride. But tonight, he wondered if it was time to ride for something more. He thought about the men who had come before him—the legends of the rodeo whose names had been etched into the dirt, their legacies written in every bucking bull and every fallen rider. Were they more than just survivors? Did they thrive?

He felt a shift within him, a realization slowly blooming. The men who thrived didn't cling to fear; they didn't just grit their teeth and endure. They embraced the chaos, the risk, the ride itself. Could he do the same?

Nick's Lighthearted Concern

"You okay, man?" Nick's voice was light and casual, but there was an undercurrent of concern.

Jacob turned, offering a faint smile. "Yeah, I'm good. Just thinking."

"About the ride?" Nick leaned forward, eyebrow raised.

Jacob nodded slowly. "About everything, really. Just… trying to figure out what this all means. What does it mean for me?"

Nick, ever the easygoing one, grinned and leaned back in his seat. "Well, if it helps, I think you're gonna kick ass out there. I've seen you ride some crazy bulls, man. You've got this."

Jacob chuckled softly, but the weight of Nick's words didn't quite reach him. He appreciated his friend's confidence, but deep down, he knew there was more to this than just a ride. There had to be.

Erick's Voice of Wisdom

Erick broke the silence with his usual calm, steady voice. "What Nick's trying to say, in his way, is that you've got more than you think. I've seen you ride better than anyone here. But the question is—are you ready to do it for yourself? Not for anyone else. Just for you."

Jacob glanced at him, the intensity in his gaze flickering. "That's the thing, Erick. I don't even know who I am in this anymore."

Erick nodded slowly, his eyes narrowing slightly. "It's easy to lose yourself in the noise. But that's the thing about this life—it forces you to decide who you really are. When the lights are on and everyone's watching, you've got to ask yourself: Who's riding the bull? You or everyone else?"

Jacob fell silent, the weight of Erick's words settling in. They were right. This wasn't just about the ride; it was about defining himself in a world that had already defined so much for him. He wasn't just riding the bull. He was riding for himself.

Humor in the Truck

Just as the tension began to settle, Nick's voice cut through the air, lightening the mood. "You know, if this whole rodeo thing doesn't work out, I was thinking we could open a memorabilia shop. You'd be great at it—just think about it: 'The Last Ride of the Nigerian

Cowboy,' with all sorts of cowboy hats, boots, and signed photos. I bet we'd make a killing."

Jacob barked a laugh. "Yeah, maybe I'll have a special edition with my picture on the cover. 'How to Survive the Chaos: A Bull Rider's Guide to Living with One Leg.'"

Erick shot Nick a look, half amused, half exasperated. "Nick, you're something else."

"I'm just saying," Nick grinned. "It's an option."

The banter was just what Jacob needed. It was a small but significant distraction from the storm brewing inside him. But as the truck rolled closer to the arena, that lightness began to fade, and the familiar weight of the world returned. The crowd's cheers already seemed to vibrate through the air, and the pressure mounted.

The Moment of Truth

When they reached the arena, Jacob felt the weight of the crowd's anticipation hanging in the air. The roar of the audience drifted through the walls of the locker room, reaching into his bones and vibrating in his chest. It was electric, thick with expectation. The tension was suffocating.

His heart pounded. This was it. This was his moment.

But it wasn't just about the bull anymore. It was about him. It was about finding the truth of who he was beneath the layers of competition, beneath the desire to prove something. For the first time, he didn't feel the need to rise to someone else's expectations. He just wanted to ride for himself.

Erick's voice pulled him from his thoughts. "You've got this, son. Just ride for you. The rest will take care of itself."

Jacob nodded, feeling a rush of gratitude toward Erick. A final breath in, a final breath out. He grabbed his gloves and pulled them on, the familiar feel of the leather against his skin grounding him. He glanced at Nick, then at Erick.

"Thanks, guys," he said quietly, his voice steady.

Nick gave him a thumbs-up. "Kickass, cowboy."

Erick smiled. "Ride on, son."

The Ride

Jacob stepped into the arena, the familiar sounds of hooves pounding against dirt filling his ears. The bull was waiting for him, its massive body shifting restlessly in the pen. He took a deep breath, feeling the heat of the crowd at his back, and walked toward it, his mind sharp and focused. For the first time, the chaos of the world around him seemed to fade into the background. There was only the bull. Only the ride.

The gate swung open, and with it came a flood of adrenaline that surged through his veins. He gripped the rope, his hands sweating but steady. The bull jolted beneath him, its power and fury unleashed in a burst of motion. Dust flew in all directions as it twisted, bucked, and fought against him, but Jacob didn't flinch. He had no room for fear anymore. This wasn't about survival. This was about thriving.

The bull bucked again, its movements unpredictable and raw, but Jacob stayed firm. Each second felt like an eternity, each movement of the bull a challenge that pushed him to his limits. His muscles screamed for release, but he held on—focused, determined. The pain, the power of the bull—it all became one, fusing into the ride.

The crowd's cheers felt distant, like an echo. The arena faded. There was only him and the bull. And in that moment, Jacob realized something—he wasn't just surviving this ride. He was embracing it. He was thriving.

As the ride ended, he felt his legs buckle beneath him as he dismounted, but there was something else there now—something deeper than fatigue. A sense of clarity, a lightness, as if he'd just shed the last weight that had been holding him back.

He didn't just ride the bull. He had embraced it. And for the first time, Jacob was truly free.

CHAPTER 40
THE RIDE AND THE REALIZATION

The Calm Before the Storm

Jacob stood behind the chute, his fingers gripping the rope, eyes fixed on the arena ahead. The roar of the crowd felt distant, like a muffled hum beyond a thick curtain. The noise, the energy, the buzz—they all seemed far away, irrelevant in the face of the pounding rhythm of his own heartbeat.

The air was thick, pregnant with tension, as if the very atmosphere were holding its breath. The ground beneath his boots was solid, unyielding, but it felt too real, too heavy. Every vibration from the arena seeped into his bones. Every cheer, every shout—a constant reminder of the weight pressing down on him. This wasn't just another ride. This was the ride.

He could feel the pressure mounting with every passing second. Whatever happened today, this moment would define everything— his journey, his future. He felt the weight of that truth settle heavily in his chest, suffocating in its finality. Could he carry it? Could he face this?

Back in the early days, rodeo had been about the thrill—the rush of adrenaline, the wild freedom. But now? Now it was a test of more than just his body. It was a test of his very soul. He wasn't just riding for glory. He was riding to find out who he truly was.

A memory surged forward—his father's voice, deep and sure: "Ride to thrive, son, not just to survive." The words hit him like a blow to the gut, making him wince. He hadn't understood them before, but now, their truth resonated deep inside him.

"Just breathe, Jacob," he whispered to himself, but the words felt small, swallowed by the chaos around him. His breath came too fast, too shallow. His chest was tight, his muscles wound like a spring. Fear gnawed at his insides, creeping up from his gut. But this wasn't just the fear of the bull. This was the fear of losing it all.

His gaze found Nick in the distance, leaning casually against the rail at the back of the arena, watching him. Their eyes met, and Nick offered a small, reassuring wave. Jacob's lips twitched, pulling into a tight, strained smile that didn't reach his eyes.

Nick's face radiated encouragement, but Jacob didn't feel it. He wanted to. God, how badly he wanted to feel something other than this suffocating doubt.

"You've got this," Nick mouthed, his voice drowned by the roar of the crowd.

But Jacob's thoughts were racing, relentless. Could he really do this? Could he find a way out of the fear, the self-doubt, the constant need to prove himself? Was he forever trapped in this cycle?

Then the gate swung open, and everything else disappeared.

A Change of Focus

The bull surged beneath him, a raw force of muscle and fury. Adrenaline flooded his veins, and for a moment, his thoughts scattered. His heart pounded in his chest, faster than it should have, but this time, something inside him shifted. The fear didn't grip him like before. Instead, there was calm—a stillness that washed over him like a cool wave.

The crowd, the pressure—they all faded into the background. His mind quieted.

Let go, he thought. Let go of the fear. Ride for the ride itself, not for the prize.

And for the first time, he did. He didn't fight. He didn't worry. He simply was. His body loosened, muscles relaxing, his grip steady but not tight. The bull beneath him moved—a living, breathing chaos—but Jacob didn't fight it. He became part of it.

Each twist of the bull, each sudden shift in motion, felt like a challenge he could face without resistance. The world around him narrowed, focused only on the rhythm of the ride—the pull of the rope, the steady beat of his heart, the pounding hooves beneath him. His body was no longer stiff; it flowed with the bull, in perfect sync with its movements.

He wasn't just surviving the ride. He was living it.

Embracing the Chaos

The bull bucked violently, twisting with a force that made Jacob's muscles strain and scream in protest. But he didn't fight it. Every violent jerk, every twist of the bull's powerful body—he flowed with it, let it carry him. The pain, the burn in his legs, the strain in his arms—all of it faded into the background. None of it mattered.

He wasn't fighting for his life. He wasn't worried about falling off. He was in the moment. He was feeling the power, the raw energy of the ride. The smell of sweat, dust, and leather filled his nostrils, but they didn't distract him. The deafening roar of the crowd became a distant murmur, as if the world outside of this moment no longer existed.

He wasn't thinking about the future, about the score, about what anyone thought. He was there—completely, fully, and entirely in the moment.

And for the first time, the fear wasn't driving him. The ride was.

The Final Throw

Suddenly, with a violent twist, the bull hurled him into the dirt. The world blurred as he hit the ground, the breath knocked out of him. For a moment, he didn't move. Didn't think. He just lay there, letting the adrenaline drain from his body, letting the stillness settle in.

His body ached. Every muscle burned, and his chest was tight. But his mind? It was clear. Sharper than it had been in years. The roar of the crowd was just a hum in the distance. The chaos had ended, and Jacob felt something unfamiliar—something peaceful—settling over him.

Slowly, he pushed himself up, brushing the dirt from his clothes. His heart still raced, but now there was a strange sense of calm. The world hadn't stopped, but for the first time, he felt like he was in control of himself.

The Realization

As Jacob made his way back to the pens, something inside him shifted. The heavy weight that had pressed on his chest for years, that had threatened to crush him, was lighter now. It hadn't disappeared completely, but it was no longer suffocating. He hadn't just survived the ride. He'd embraced it.

For the first time in a long time, he didn't feel like he was just hanging on. He wasn't scrambling to keep everything together. He had found something deeper. Something real. The fear and the doubt—they were still there, but they didn't define him anymore.

When he reached the pens, Erick stood off to the side, watching him with that knowing smile, the one that spoke volumes without a word. Jacob smiled back, and in that moment, the weight in his chest shifted. He had nothing to prove. Not to the bull. Not to the crowd. Not to anyone else.

He had proven it to himself.

And that, finally, felt like enough.

Walking Toward the Future

In the locker room, Nick was waiting, his grin wide and uncontainable.

"You did it, man. That was amazing!" Nick's voice rang with excitement, but there was something deeper in his eyes—something like understanding.

Jacob let out a breathless laugh, but it was weary. "Yeah, it wasn't perfect. But it was enough."

Nick raised an eyebrow, his sharp gaze seeing right through him. "You've finally figured it out, huh?"

Jacob nodded, a quiet peace settling deep inside him. "Yeah. I think I have."

For the first time in years, Jacob didn't feel like he was searching for something. He didn't have all the answers, and the future was still unknown. But he wasn't afraid of it anymore. He was ready.

The ride had shown him something he'd never understood before: he wasn't defined by what others thought, by his failures, or by the competition. The ride itself defined him. And that, for the first time, was enough.

CHAPTER 41
A NEW DIRECTION

A Quiet Morning

The sun, barely brushing the horizon, bathed the world in a soft glow as Jacob stepped outside. The cool morning air bit at his skin like a sharp, refreshing breath—a new start, unexpected yet welcome. Jacob had always been a man of routines: awake before dawn, face the day, no matter how heavy the world felt. But today was different. There was an unspoken pull—something gentler, more natural.

The weight he'd carried for so long, though not entirely gone, had lessened. His shoulders, usually tight with invisible burdens, felt lighter, as if the darkness that had shadowed him was loosening its grip just enough to allow him to breathe fully again.

The ranch lay before him, wide and open, like a canvas waiting for its artist. It was a vast invitation—quiet, empty, but full of potential. For the first time in what felt like forever, Jacob didn't yearn to run or escape. He was present—rooted in the earth beneath him, the dirt cool against his boots. A soft breeze played with his hair, and the silence wrapped around him like a comforting blanket.

His mind wandered, almost involuntarily, to the bull ride—the one that had marked the beginning of his shift. It wasn't merely about staying on that beast or the physical struggle against the raw power of nature. No, it was deeper. It was a spiritual awakening, a crack in the hardened surface of his life that let light pour through. That ride had shown him that life wasn't about chasing fame, applause, or validation. It was about something quieter, something more fulfilling.

For the first time in a long while, Jacob wondered what life might be like if he stopped running after external goals—and started living for himself, for the life he truly wanted.

A Return Home

That morning, Jacob made a decision—one that had been quietly taking root in his heart for months, maybe years. He needed to go home.

Nigeria. It had been far too long since he'd walked the streets of Lagos, breathed the air thick with history, and felt the pulse of life that only Nigeria could give. But now, something deep inside him pulled him back—not out of nostalgia alone, but because it was time to return. It wasn't a longing for the past—it was a call to where everything had begun.

The flight was long, marked by quiet reflection—a sharp contrast to the chaotic life he'd built in the U.S. But when the plane began its descent into Lagos, Jacob's chest tightened with anticipation. Despite all he'd achieved in America, part of him had always remained tethered to Nigeria—the frantic energy of the streets, the scent of grilled meat wafting through the air, the rhythmic blend of Yoruba and Igbo mixing in a thousand conversations.

When the plane's wheels touched down, Jacob felt a flood of memories hit him—the distant drumbeats of his past calling him home.

The Old Neighborhood

The driver who met him at the airport took him to his family's new house, situated in a modern area far removed from his childhood neighborhood. The sleek house was a far cry from the colorful, cramped home he remembered. Yet, there was still a sense of familiarity. It wasn't his old house, but it was home nonetheless.

But even after settling in, Jacob couldn't shake the need to visit his old neighborhood. It was as if a magnet were pulling him back to those streets, to the places where he had grown up.

The air, thick with the scent of street food and dust, was a vivid reminder of the past. The sound of children's laughter, the calls of street vendors—it all felt both foreign and familiar at once. The neighborhood had changed over the years. The houses were older, the roads rougher, but the spirit of the place remained unchanged. It still hummed with life.

When Jacob reached his old house, a wave of bittersweet nostalgia swept over him. The small yellow house with the red roof was no more. In its place stood a tall, modern apartment complex—cold and uninviting. It wasn't home anymore.

Just as the weight of that realization settled in, a familiar voice pierced through his thoughts.

"Jacob? Is that you?"

Turning around, Jacob saw Chuka, his childhood friend, his face lighting up with recognition.

"Chuka! My man! You're looking great!" Jacob exclaimed, grinning wide.

Chuka laughed, pulling him into a bear hug. "Look at you! The big man has come home."

They stood there for a moment, laughing, as if no time had passed. No years, no distance. Just two old friends picking up right where they left off. In that moment, Jacob felt warmth fill him—an old, familiar sense of home.

After catching up, Chuka led him to a small, lively local bar. As they settled into worn wooden chairs, the energy of the place washed over Jacob, and he couldn't help but laugh at the contrast between life here and the one he had known in the States.

"You know, Jacob," Chuka said with a playful grin, "life's simple here. You want food? Just walk down the street. You want music? There's a concert on every corner."

Jacob chuckled. "Guess you don't need a five-star restaurant for good food and music."

Chuka grinned wider. "No, man. You just need good people."

Jacob let the words settle in. Good people. That was something he'd overlooked for far too long. But here, with Chuka, with the people from his past, he was beginning to understand what really mattered.

A Sunday at Church

On Sunday, Jacob attended church with his family. The service was nothing like he had experienced in the U.S. Here, church wasn't just a quiet reflection—it was a place of release, where people shed their burdens in the presence of God.

The air pulsed with Nigerian highlife music, the beat of drums, and an undeniable energy that filled every corner of the space. The congregation didn't just sing—they danced, moving with the music, their bodies losing themselves in the rhythm. There was no quiet reverence here; instead, it was a celebration—raw, alive, and emotional. People weren't just expressing faith; they were living it.

Jacob stood at the back, watching. In the U.S., the church had been more contemplative, heads bowed in quiet prayer. But here, it was different. Here, faith was lived—a vibrant outpouring of joy, a catharsis that shook the walls with its intensity. Every movement seemed to release pain, to open the heart to something greater.

For the first time in his life, Jacob felt something deeper than faith—a release, a connection not just with God, but with the people, with himself. It wasn't about rituals or traditions—it was about the freedom of expression, the act of letting go.

The Return Flight

As Jacob boarded the plane back to Texas, a strange sense of peace settled in his chest. The trip had given him everything he needed—reconnection, closure, a sense of belonging he hadn't known he was searching for.

The hum of the engines and the soft click of the seatbelt sign were oddly soothing. Jacob closed his eyes for a moment, letting the calm wash over him. For the first time in years, he felt whole.

He was a Nigerian cowboy—and that identity meant more to him than any title, any achievement. It wasn't a label—it was a mark of resilience, pride, and joy.

He wasn't running anymore. He was grounded.

As the plane ascended, Jacob glanced out the window. Nigeria shrank beneath him, but instead of sadness or longing, he felt clarity.

He was ready for whatever life had next in store. He wasn't lost anymore.

He was home.

CHAPTER 42
THE REUNION

The Barn and the Return

The sun hung low in the sky, painting the horizon with a soft, golden glow. Jacob stepped out of the barn, feeling the cool evening air brush against his skin. It had been a long time since he'd stood on this land. The scent of hay and earth mixed with the faint musk of cattle, stirring something inside him—something familiar, yet foreign. It was still home, but it didn't feel like home anymore.

He inhaled deeply, the sound of the distant mooing of cows and the creak of old wood filling the air. The land had always spoken to him in ways words never could, wrapping around him with a quiet familiarity. But now, something was tugging at his chest—an ache, a discomfort—as though this place had shifted while he'd been gone. It was still the same, but it wasn't.

His thoughts drifted back to the last time he'd been here—the sound of his father's voice, sharp and bitter, disappointment weighing every syllable. Expectations had felt like chains back then, heavy and unyielding. He'd thought the rodeo would release him from all that, but the truth was, it had only given him more chains to carry.

Shaking his head, he chuckled softly to himself. Maybe it wasn't the land that had changed. Maybe it was him.

The rumble of truck engines interrupted his thoughts. Dust kicked up in the driveway as Erick's old truck came into view, followed by Nick's beaten-up Chevy. Jacob stood still, watching as the two trucks screeched to a halt. The doors flew open, and out tumbled Erick, Nick, and the ever-brooding Lucas.

For a moment, Jacob just stood there, soaking in the sight of them. They were older, more worn—but in the same way, they were unchanged. Erick, his beard speckled with gray, had that same mischievous grin. Nick had filled out a bit, but his easy-going nature was as comforting as ever. And Lucas… well, Lucas still wore that impenetrable expression, the one that never seemed to show a thing.

"Look who's back from the big leagues," Erick called out, a crooked grin spreading across his face. He squinted at Jacob like he couldn't quite believe what he was seeing. "Thought you were too big for us now."

Jacob smiled, rolling his eyes. "You always act like I've been gone for a decade. It's only been a few months, Erick."

"Yeah, but it feels like you're some kind of rodeo royalty now. Getting that VIP treatment yet?" Erick's tone was playful, his cigarette dangling from his lips.

Jacob chuckled, rubbing the back of his neck. "Just here for the ride, Erick. It's always been about the ride."

Nick stepped forward, arms open. "Man, it's good to see you. Things haven't been the same around here without you." He pulled Jacob into a half-hug, slapping him on the back.

Jacob returned the hug, feeling the warmth of their bond flood through him. "I missed you too, Nick." His voice was softer than he'd meant it to be.

But Lucas… Lucas didn't move. He stood a few steps back, his hands shoved deep in his pockets, his eyes fixed on the ground. Jacob could feel the distance, the tension simmering between them, unspoken but undeniable.

"Hey, Lucas. How's it going?" Jacob called out, trying to break the silence.

Lucas lifted his eyes slowly, his gaze flat, unreadable. "Same old, same old." His voice was a low murmur, almost reluctant.

Erick and Nick exchanged a glance, but they wisely kept their distance, letting the moment linger. Jacob took a step toward Lucas, his heart tightening at the sight of his old friend.

"Come on, man," Jacob said, trying to force a smile. "You know I didn't forget about you."

Lucas hesitated, his eyes flicking away briefly before returning to meet Jacob's gaze. A long sigh escaped his lips. "It's not about forgetting. It's just… things change, man. We change."

"I know," Jacob said quietly, his voice gentler than he'd expected. "I've been gone a while. But hell, I'm here now."

For a long moment, neither of them spoke. The air between them crackled with unspoken words, with a thousand things left unsaid. Lucas's eyes were sharp when they finally met Jacob's, something raw in them—a mix of frustration, disappointment, and… something else Jacob couldn't place.

Lucas gave a small, almost imperceptible nod. "Yeah, I know. But I didn't expect you to come back like this."

Jacob's frown deepened. "Like what?"

"You've changed," Lucas said softly, the words hanging heavy between them. "It's like you're not the same guy anymore. You've got this whole 'rodeo king' thing going on. And I don't know if I even know who you are anymore."

Jacob's chest tightened, the sting of Lucas's words hitting harder than he'd anticipated. But before he could respond, Nick cut in, his voice warmer, lighter.

"Alright, enough of this heavy stuff," Nick said with a grin, slapping Lucas on the back. "Let's grab a beer, catch up like old times. Jacob's back, and that's what matters."

But even as Nick's words broke the tension, Jacob could still feel it—like a cloud hanging low, thick and suffocating. Some things couldn't be fixed with a quick drink or a joke. Not yet.

Teasing and Banter

Despite the weight in the air, the old rhythm of their friendship settled back in. Erick grinned at Jacob, his voice full of that teasing, sarcastic edge.

"So, the big rodeo winner, huh? What's next? Gonna buy a ranch and live the cowboy tycoon dream?" Erick's eyes sparkled with mischief.

Jacob rolled his eyes, but the playful glint in his gaze quickly dimmed as he caught Lucas's eye. For a second, it felt like the old jokes just didn't fit anymore.

"Yeah, maybe I'll start charging for autographs while I'm at it."

Nick jumped in, a sly grin on his face. "We figured you'd have your own ranch by now. Maybe next, you'll be marrying some Texas socialite."

Jacob laughed, pushing them all good-naturedly. "Yeah, and that's about as likely as me buying a ranch."

The laughter was brief, though, fading as the conversation shifted back to the rodeos. Bob, who had been lurking nearby, couldn't resist chiming in with his usual sharp edge.

"I can barely hang onto a bull for ten seconds, and you're out there making it look easy, Jacob," Bob said, shaking his head, eyes wide with disbelief. "You're a damn force of nature."

Jacob shrugged, a grin tugging at his lips. "It's all about surviving, Bob. You know that as well as I do."

Building Tension

But underneath the humor, the tension still simmered. Lucas stood off to the side, arms crossed, eyes fixed on Jacob, not saying a word. Jacob could feel it—Lucas's quiet resentment, that unspoken jealousy. It wasn't just about being left behind. It was about trying to find his place in a world that was rapidly changing, with or without him.

The Rodeo Challenge

After a few beers and more lighthearted teasing, the group found their way to the corral, where the horses grazed lazily in the dimming light. Jacob cleared his throat, the weight of the past few months pressing down on him.

"I'm thinking about signing up for the big rodeo next week," Jacob said, his voice steady but edged with something deeper. "The final one."

Bob raised an eyebrow, studying him carefully. "You sure about that? You know it's not like it used to be."

Jacob met his gaze, the corners of his mouth twitching into a wry smile. "It's not about winning anymore, Bob. It's about proving to myself that I belong here."

"Prove it to whom?" Lucas's voice cut through the stillness, sharper than before.

Jacob turned to face him, meeting his gaze head-on. "To myself."

Tension in the Air

The moment hung in the air, heavy with understanding and unspoken truths. Bob exhaled slowly, his face serious. "I can't compete with you, Jacob. You're a beast. But don't let it get to your head. There's always a cost to being too good at something."

Jacob laughed, but it was hollow. "I'm not worried about being good, Bob. I'm worried about what happens when people start believing they can't beat you."

The silence that followed was thick, laden with a quiet, shared understanding.

Closing Thoughts

As the last slivers of daylight slipped away, Jacob stood still, feeling the weight of everything—the memories, the expectations, and the pressure to prove himself. But for the first time in a long while, he felt something different: clarity. He wasn't just a rodeo cowboy. He was 'The Cowboy.' A 'Nigerian Cowboy.' And tomorrow, he would step into that story once more.

314

CHAPTER 43
A DANGEROUS PROPOSITION

The Bar and the Weight of Old Friendships

The bar was steeped in history, the kind of place where time seemed to slow. The worn wooden beams, weathered by decades of use, groaned under the weight of stories—some told, some buried. The air was thick with the sharp scent of whiskey, stale beer, smoke, and worn leather, a mix that clung to the walls like the memory of long-gone laughter. It was a place that felt like it hadn't changed in decades, as if time itself had forgotten to leave. Jacob stepped inside, the weight of years pressing down on his chest.

There was something different in the air—a heavy tension that felt more real than any memory. The room felt small, suffocating, even though it had been a refuge once. Jacob's boots echoed softly on the creaky floorboards as he approached the table where his old friends sat. Their faces, familiar but worn, were framed by the dim light filtering through dusty windows. Bob, Lucas, Jack, and Adam—the faces hadn't changed, but the eyes, the eyes told a different story.

A mixture of strained politeness and something else—guarded hostility, maybe—hung between them. Jacob slid into the empty chair, his back straight, though the weight of the moment pressed down on him like an iron shackle.

"Well, if it ain't the prodigal son," Erick's voice rang out, cutting through the tension with his ever-present smirk. "What's it like up there with the big dogs? Rodeo royalty now, huh?"

Jacob laughed lightly, the sound hollow in his chest. He leaned back in his chair, trying to hide the gravity of it all, but it was there, heavy in the space between them. "I'm just here for the ride, man. It's not as glamorous as you think."

Erick, taking a long drag off his cigarette, flicked the ash absently. "Sure, if you say so. So, what's next for the cowboy? Gonna buy a ranch and start your own empire?"

Jacob chuckled, but the sound barely touched his soul. "Maybe. But I'll probably just settle for a cold beer and some peace for once."

The group chuckled, but it was a hollow sound, lacking warmth. The tension didn't dissipate; it only shifted, like the shifting air before a storm.

Bob spoke next, his voice gravelly, slow. "Hell, I can barely hang onto a bull for more than ten seconds, and you're out there making it look easy, Jacob," he said with a smile, but it didn't quite reach his eyes. "You're a damn force of nature."

Jacob met Bob's gaze, offering a tight smile that didn't feel like a smile at all. "It's all about surviving, Bob. You know that as well as I do."

But Bob's words, sharp where they should've been playful, didn't sit right with him. There was something in his tone—resentment, maybe—that Jacob couldn't ignore.

"Yeah," Bob muttered, his eyes narrowing. "Surviving. You make it look effortless."

The words hung in the air, thick and heavy. Jacob's stomach twisted. He'd expected the undercurrent of bitterness, but hearing it out loud made it feel real, like a crack widening in the foundation beneath them.

Lucas's Quiet Storm

Lucas, who had been silent up until now, shifted in his seat. His gaze stayed fixed on the table, but the tension radiating from him felt like a live wire. His eyes, hard and distant, seemed to hold something Jacob couldn't quite name.

"Lucas," Jacob spoke, the name slipping from his lips like a question, a quiet plea for connection. "How's it going, man?"

Lucas's head snapped up, and for the first time, Jacob saw the cold, distant look in his eyes—something that hadn't been there before. "Same old," Lucas muttered, his voice rough and frayed, like an old rope ready to snap. "Same old."

Jacob winced, the weight of those words settling deep in his chest. This wasn't how it used to be. They'd shared everything once. But now, every word felt like it was being pulled from a stranger.

Erick exchanged a quick glance with Nick, sensing the unease between the two old friends. True to form, Erick was the first to try to smooth things over. He slapped Jacob on the back with a grin, though it was a little too wide, a little too forced. "Man, we thought you might've gone off and started your damn ranch with how big you're getting," Erick said, his voice too light. "Next thing you know, we'll hear you're marrying a Texas socialite."

Jacob snorted, giving Erick a playful shove. "Yeah, right. You know I'd rather ride bulls than wear a tux."

Nick chimed in, "Don't be too modest, man. You're probably too busy for us old folks now. Riding high with the big names, huh?"

Jacob smiled, but it felt thin, stretched tight. The words were lighthearted, but the weight between them felt different now. He could hear Lucas's words in his mind: *You've changed.*

The Proposition

A few rounds of drinks later, the group found their way to the corral. The horses grazed lazily, their breath rising in the cool evening air. The world seemed to slow, everything settling into a heavy silence that held more than just the sound of hooves.

Jacob cleared his throat, his eyes lingering on the horses as his words lingered, heavy and full of intent. "I'm thinking about signing up for the big rodeo next week," he said, though the words felt like they carried the weight of years. "The final one."

Bob glanced at him, his brow furrowing in concern. "You sure about that, Jacob? You know it's not like it used to be."

Jacob leaned forward, his voice firm now, carrying a quiet determination. "I'm sure. It's not just about winning. It's about proving I belong here."

Lucas, who had been silent until now, spoke up, his voice cutting like a blade. "Prove it to whom?"

Jacob met his gaze, unwavering, but the silence between them felt like it was building to something. "To myself."

The air shifted then, thickening. Lucas's gaze didn't falter, but the challenge in his eyes was palpable. Jacob couldn't read it— resentment, fear, or something deeper. But the words were unspoken, hanging heavy between them.

Bob exhaled sharply, a nervous tension in his eyes. "I can't compete with you, Jacob. You're a damn beast out there. But don't let it get to you. There's always a cost to being too good at something."

Jacob's smile was tight, his words cold. "I'm not worried about being good, Bob. I'm worried about what happens when people start believing they can't beat you."

The silence that followed felt like it pulled them all deeper into a place they didn't want to go, yet none of them spoke. The implication was clear.

Foreshadowing the Danger

Lucas shifted again, his posture defensive, arms crossed tightly over his chest. He looked away, his voice low and full of something dangerous. "You don't get it, do you? You've got everyone watching you. You think you can just keep winning, keep pushing us aside? That's the kind of thing that gets people hurt around here."

Jacob's heart skipped a beat, and for a moment, everything seemed to slow. His mind raced, trying to understand what was happening. He knew things had changed, but this? This wasn't what he had expected.

Bob looked down at the ground, his fingers fidgeting nervously. Adam, ever the troublemaker, flashed a smile, but it didn't reach his eyes. "Maybe Lucas is right. Maybe it's time we had a little 'chat' about how things are going to go down. You know... one of those friendly talks between old friends."

A chill ran down Jacob's spine, but he wasn't backing down. Not anymore. The same fire that had driven him in the rodeo now burned in his chest. He wasn't the same kid they once knew. With a devilish grin, Jacob leaned forward, his eyes dark with resolve.

"Maybe you should take your own advice, Adam. Because this cowboy doesn't back down."

The group exchanged uneasy glances, the tension in the air thickening like a storm about to break. No one spoke. The silence was deafening. The game had only just begun.

CHAPTER 44
SABOTAGE AND BETRAYAL

Setting: The rodeo event—Jacob is preparing for a career-defining challenge, unaware of the dark plot unfolding behind the scenes.

The Plot Unfolds

The barn was dim, shadows stretching long and heavy as Jacob's former friends gathered in secret. The only light flickered from a single hanging bulb, casting their faces in sharp, ominous relief. The air was thick with tension and an oppressive quiet that weighed on the chest, making each breath feel like a struggle.

Bob's fingers tapped nervously on the edge of a dusty table, his gaze flicking between Adam, Lucas, and Jake. But his attention was fixed, laser-like, on Lucas—the quietest of the group. Lucas's eyes darted to the floor, his expression tight, wrestling with a storm inside him that he didn't want to face. Adam's grin was cold, calculated— a predator relishing the kill. Jake, usually the calm voice of reason, stood in the corner, fists clenched, his jaw working as though he were fighting to suppress an eruption.

"I don't like this," Lucas finally muttered, his voice rough, as if the words themselves were hard to swallow. His gaze remained fixed on the dirt beneath his boots, unable to meet anyone's eyes. "He's one of us, Bob. We don't need to do this."

Bob's eyes hardened, his voice biting. "He's not 'one of us' anymore, Lucas. He's too far gone. You've seen it. He's got his head in the clouds—acting like he owns the damn rodeo world. Meanwhile, we're still stuck here, scraping by."

Adam scoffed, the sound sharp and bitter. "He's the golden boy, Lucas. Trophies, endorsements, a damn fanbase. What do we have? Nothing. I say we knock him off that high horse."

Jake stepped forward, his voice low but fierce. "I'm in. It's not just the spotlight. It's about respect. He's been taking it all, leaving us behind. He needs to know we were here first, and we won't be ignored anymore."

Lucas stayed silent, his arms folded tightly across his chest, his fingers twitching as though they longed to undo what was unfolding. The man he had once called a friend was slipping through his fingers, and the guilt gnawed at him. How had they come to this?

Bob leaned forward, his voice cold and commanding. "The next event's the perfect opportunity. We mess with his gear—just enough to take him out for good. Make sure he doesn't get past the first ride. This is our last chance."

Adam's grin widened, the gleam in his eyes predatory. "And once he's gone, the spotlights are ours. He'll never come close to us again."

Jake nodded, his face hard as stone. "We do this now. No more waiting."

Lucas stayed silent, his mind in turmoil. Finally, he whispered, his voice barely audible. "Are we doing this?"

Bob's answer was cold and final. "We already are."

The Rodeo: Tension Builds

Jacob stood in the heart of the rodeo, the buzz of the crowd surrounding him like a live wire, the air electric with anticipation. The pounding hooves of the horses reverberated through the ground, syncing with the frantic rhythm of his own heart. Sweat trickled down the back of his neck, the familiar weight of his gear feeling heavier today, almost suffocating.

This wasn't just any rodeo. This was the moment—his chance to prove everything. The challenge ahead wasn't just a test of skill; it was the defining moment of his career. His muscles were taut with the pressure of it all. His chest felt tight, but he breathed through it, familiar with the feeling of preparing for something big. But something was off today. There was a heavier weight in the air, something that made the ground beneath his boots feel uncertain.

He scanned the crowd, a sea of faces both supportive and critical. He had seen them all before—the smiles and the sneers, the whispers and the cheers. But today, something was different. The tension in the air was thick, like the calm before a storm. It wasn't just about the ride anymore. It was about survival.

The Sabotage

As Jacob adjusted his saddle, a small, unsettling shift caught his attention. The straps felt slightly off, like something was... wrong. He tried to dismiss it, blaming his nerves, but the unease settled in his gut like a warning. It was subtle at first—just a slight movement in the straps, an imperfection he couldn't quite place. But it didn't feel right. The air seemed to thicken, as if everything around him was holding its breath.

The announcer's voice crackled over the loudspeakers, the crowd's roar washing over him. It was showtime.

But as Jacob mounted the horse, something felt wrong. The saddle shifted beneath him, a jarring motion that made his breath hitch. His left foot slipped from the stirrup, and his hands gripped the reins tighter, but it was as if the saddle had a mind of its own, pulling him in directions he couldn't control.

The horse surged forward, a sudden burst of speed that threw him off balance. He fought to regain control, his grip tightening, but it was too late. The saddle was too loose, too unsteady. It shifted again, and before Jacob could adjust, the horse bucked with an intensity he hadn't anticipated. He tried to hold on, but his body was already spinning, flying through the air.

The impact came with brutal force—a sickening crack as his body hit the dirt. Pain exploded in his chest, his breath knocked from him. For a split second, everything went dark. When his vision cleared, panic rose in his chest. What had just happened? It didn't make sense. Was it a mistake? Or was someone behind this?

The world spun in a dizzying blur. The crowd's shocked silence only heightened his confusion, and for the first time in his life, Jacob wondered if the rodeo had become something more dangerous than just a competition.

The Aftermath

Jacob's eyes fluttered open in a sterile white room. The lights above him swirled in dizzying patterns, and the smell of antiseptic stung his nose. His chest burned with pain, but his mind raced. Was it a mistake? Or had someone sabotaged him? The question gnawed at him, the feeling of betrayal sinking deep into his bones.

Erick and Nick were there, hovering near his bed. Their faces were tense, reflecting the same doubt Jacob couldn't shake.

"I don't know, Jake," Erick said quietly, suspicion creeping into his voice. "Something's off. The saddle—it wasn't just you riding poorly. There was something wrong with it."

Nick nodded, his face grim. "I saw it. The way you fell—it didn't look like a mistake. Someone messed with your gear."

Jacob clenched his fists, his body aching with pain, but it was the deeper ache—the betrayal—that hurt the most. His mind flashed to his old friends: Bob, Lucas, Adam, Jake. Could one of them have done this? The thought twisted in his gut.

The Betrayal Takes Root

As Jacob lay there, the sterile hospital room closing in around him, he knew this wasn't just about a rodeo anymore. This was personal. They had done more than just trying to take him out—they had aimed to destroy him. But Jacob wasn't done. Not yet.

The doctors spoke softly, their words floating in and out of his consciousness. He reached for his phone, his hand trembling with the weight of the decision he had to make. Should he cancel his upcoming events? Was he even ready to return to the arena? Physically, yes, but emotionally? That was a different battle altogether.

In the silence of the room, a new fire began to burn inside Jacob. He wasn't finished yet. He would find out who was behind this, and when he did, they would regret it. He wouldn't stop until he had answers.

Cliffhanger

The rodeo community rallied behind Jacob, their support flooding in from every direction. It bolstered his spirit, but deep down, he knew this was only the beginning. The road ahead would be long, and the scars—both physical and emotional—would remain.

Bob, Adam, Lucas, and Jake were quietly pleased with their success, but Jacob had other plans. He would find them. He would make them pay for what they had done.

The battle had only just begun, and Jacob knew that the rodeo world wasn't the only thing at stake. Someone had tried to take him down, and he would stop at nothing to make them pay. The game had changed, and the stakes were higher than ever.

BAR

CHAPTER 45
THE POLICE QUESTIONS

Under the Spotlight

The morning sun filtered weakly through the blinds, casting faint stripes of light across the sterile white walls of Jacob's hospital room. His body ached, a steady throb from the side injury where the impact had left its mark. But it wasn't just the pain in his body; it was the gnawing doubt, the betrayal, and the uncertainty that plagued him. He stared at the ceiling, his mind a whirlwind of questions: Who did this to me? Why? Will I ever ride again?

The sound of footsteps broke through his haze. The door creaked open and Officer Hardy entered, his polished shoes clicking on the hard tile as he walked toward Jacob's bed. His tall frame filled the doorway, his uniform neat and crisp, but it was the sharpness in his eyes that Jacob noticed first. Hardy's gaze lingered on Jacob's injury before meeting his eyes.

"Mr. Jacob Obi," the officer's voice was steady, but there was something in it that Jacob couldn't quite place—something that made him uneasy. "I'm here to ask you a few questions about your accident."

Jacob's pulse quickened. The accident—the sabotage—suddenly seemed more real, more terrifying. His heartbeat felt loud, like it might drown out everything else.

"I've already told you what happened, officer," Jacob said, trying to sound calm, though his voice betrayed him. "I fell off that bull. It's nothing more than that."

Officer Hardy paused, eyes narrowing, studying Jacob as if weighing the truth in his words. "Is that so?" he asked, his voice a touch colder now. "Because we've been looking into it. And we think this might not have been an accident after all." He took a step closer, his gaze never leaving Jacob's. "We're investigating it as possible sabotage."

Jacob blinked, stunned. Sabotage? The word hit him like a slap to the face. Could it really be true? Had someone deliberately hurt him? His mind raced, but all he could manage to say was, "I don't understand… Why?"

"Do you know anyone who might've had a reason to hurt you?" Hardy asked, his voice softening just a little. But there was an edge to it, a sense that he wasn't going to let Jacob off the hook that easily. "Anyone who might've tampered with your equipment?"

Jacob shook his head, the confusion twisting in his stomach. "No," he said, but the lie felt thin, like a sheet of ice that could crack at any moment. "I don't know anyone who'd do that."

Hardy's expression softened just a touch, but it still didn't reach his eyes. "Alright, Mr. Jacob Obi. We'll keep digging. But if you remember anything—anything at all—don't hesitate to reach out."

As the door clicked shut behind him, Jacob was left alone, the weight of Hardy's words sinking in. Sabotage. Who would do that to me? The question lingered in his mind, unanswered. The possibility that someone had intentionally hurt him seemed unreal. But there was no denying the gnawing suspicion that Officer Hardy knew more than he was letting on. Was it possible that Hardy had already gathered evidence, and this was just a way of gauging his response? Jacob wasn't sure, but he couldn't escape the feeling that someone was playing a game far more dangerous than he'd realized.

Meanwhile, Across Town...

The next stop for Officer Hardy and his partner was Lucas's house. When the knock came, Lucas's heart skipped a beat. He had been expecting this, but it didn't make it any easier. The officers were standing there, their badges gleaming in the morning light, their faces unreadable.

"Lucas Hill?" Officer Hardy's voice was calm but carried a quiet authority that sent a shiver down Lucas's spine.

"Uh, yeah?" Lucas stammered, his throat dry, his heart pounding in his chest. "What's this about?"

"We'd like to ask you a few questions about the accident involving Jacob Obi," Hardy said, his eyes narrowing as he studied Lucas. His gaze was piercing, like he was looking for something—anything—that didn't quite add up.

Lucas swallowed, trying to keep his composure, but it wasn't easy. The walls felt like they were closing in. He had to keep it together. "I don't know anything about it," he said quickly, the words tumbling out in a rush. "I wasn't there."

Hardy didn't budge; his eyes still locked onto Lucas like he was searching for any sign of a crack in the story. "You were with Jacob before the accident, weren't you?" He leaned in just a little, his voice softening, coaxing. "Do you know if anyone might've wanted to hurt him?"

Lucas felt like he was suffocating. The pressure was unbearable, like the weight of the entire situation was pressing down on him, forcing him to make a choice. I can't keep this up. What if they know?

"I don't know," Lucas muttered, his voice barely above a whisper. "I really don't."

Hardy's gaze never wavered. He wasn't fooled. "Alright, Lucas. But if you remember anything—anything at all—reach out to us."

The officer handed him a business card, his fingers brushing against Lucas's as he did. It was cold, like a warning. As Hardy turned to leave, he paused, glancing back over his shoulder.

"One last thing," he said, his voice dropping to a more serious tone. "This is a serious matter. If you're holding something back, now's the time to speak up. It'll be better for you."

Lucas's stomach churned as the door shut behind the officers. What have I done?

The Call to Action

Lucas sat alone in his room, the weight of the situation pressing down on him harder than ever. His hands trembled, his throat tight as he dialed Bob's number.

"Bob, the cops came to see me," Lucas blurted out when his friend picked up. "They know something's up."

Bob's voice crackled with strain. "We need to stick to the story, Lucas. Don't let them shake you."

But Lucas's voice cracked with fear. "What if they find out? What if this is it?"

There was a long silence on the other end of the line before Bob spoke again, his voice quieter now. "Then we deal with it. But don't back down, Lucas. Not after everything."

Lucas sank into a chair, staring blankly at the phone in his hand. His heart pounded in his chest. What if I tell them? What if I'm the one who ends this?

A Moment of Clarity

That night, Lucas sat across from his Uncle Kade, the older cowboy's gaze steady and unwavering. There was no judgment in his eyes—just quiet understanding.

"You know what you've done, Lucas," Uncle Kade said, his voice low and heavy with experience. "But it's not too late to make it right."

Lucas swallowed, the lump in his throat growing bigger. "I don't know what to do, Uncle Kade. I'm scared."

A soft smile tugged at the corner of Kade's lips. "I was scared too, when I was your age. But I did what was right, even when it was hard. You've got to do the same. A good cowboy doesn't run from his mistakes, Lucas. He faces them."

Lucas's eyes filled with unshed tears, his chest tight with a mixture of guilt and pride. "I don't want to let you down, Uncle."

"You won't." Kade reassured him, his hand landing firmly on Lucas's shoulder. "But you've got to make the right choice. Stop running."

The Decision

Outside, Lucas stood alone, the business card from Officer Hardy weighing heavily in his pocket. He stared at it for a long moment, the decision before him feeling impossibly difficult.

With a deep breath, Lucas pulled the card from his pocket and glanced at it one last time before slipping it away. His heart thudded in his chest as he walked toward the door, his mind made up. It's time to stop hiding. Time to face the truth.

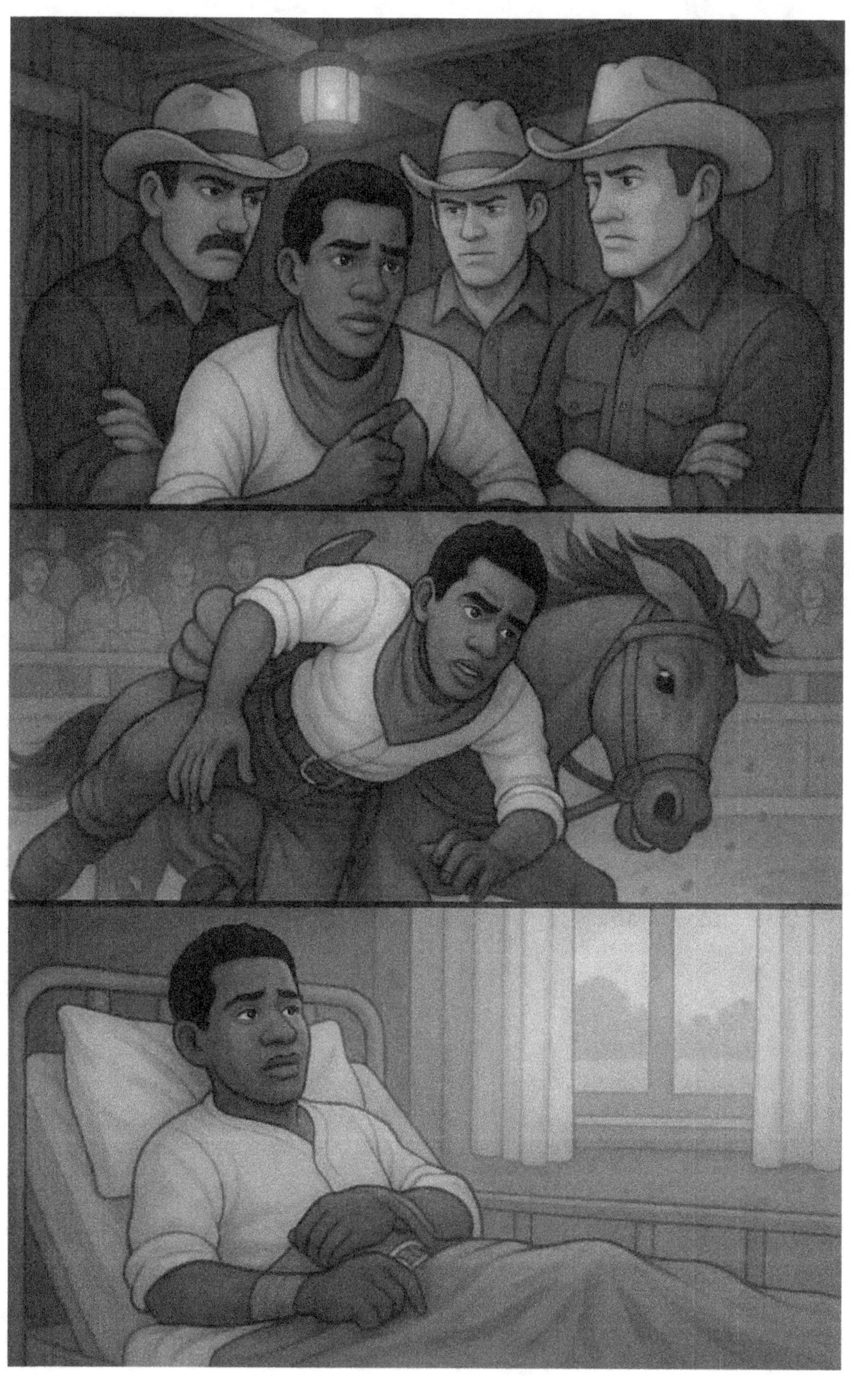

CHAPTER 46
THE ANTAGONISTS' RECKONING

The Tension Mounts

The morning after the police interviews, the air in Lucas's apartment felt heavier, pressing in on him like a wall. The silence was unnerving, filled only with the faint hum of an old fridge and the sound of his breathing. The weight of the day before—the endless questions, the probing looks—clung to him. He paced his living room, the phone in his hand as if it could somehow offer him control. His fingers tightened around it; his knuckles were white.

He thought about calling Bob—needed to. But each time the idea crossed his mind, a knot twisted tighter in his stomach. What if it was worse than they thought? What if it was already over?

Then, his phone buzzed. The screen lit up, and Bob's name flashed across it. A quick breath escaped Lucas's lips.

"Lucas," Bob's voice crackled through the line, almost too tight, like a rubber band stretched to its breaking point. "You good?"

Staying the Course

Lucas dragged a hand through his hair, trying to steady his thoughts. His voice, when it came, was strained. "Yeah, but... what if—"

"No buts, man," Bob snapped, cutting him off with a sharpness that only made Lucas feel more uncertain. "You think you're the only one they're after? Adam's losing it. We're all in this. Stick to the story. We're fine."

Lucas's chest tightened, the lie pressing against his ribs like a weight he couldn't shake off. The story. The lie. It was becoming too much, but what else could they do?

"Alright," Lucas finally muttered, the words tasting bitter on his tongue. "I'll stick to the story."

Bob's voice came through again, quieter now, but still hard-edged. "And Lucas? Don't let them see you sweat."

Cracks in the Façade

Across town, Adam stood in the sterile light of his office, his fingers drumming an anxious rhythm against his desk. His phone, a constant reminder of the mess he was in, vibrated on the table. He couldn't bring himself to read the new messages. Too many. Too much. The pressure was suffocating. What had seemed like control the day before now felt like a mirage, slipping away no matter how tightly he grasped at it.

A knock on the door made him flinch.

"Come in," he barked, his voice far sharper than he intended. He quickly tried to mask the crack in his tone, but it was already out there, hanging in the air.

A Visit from Officer Hardy

The door creaked open, and Adam's associate, Matt, stepped in, his face pale, eyes darting nervously to the phone on Adam's desk. "Mr. Foster, everything's still on track. But... there's a problem. The cops? They're asking about Jacob again. Everyone who was near him... they're asking questions."

Adam clenched his jaw, nodding quickly, but his mind raced. "Yeah, I heard. I just spoke to Bob. Everything's fine." But the words didn't feel true, not anymore. Was it fine?

"Are we really fine, though?" Matt's voice shook with doubt. "They're digging deeper, and—"

"Fine!" Adam snapped, trying to assert control, but his voice was betraying him. "We've been through worse. Stay the course."

Deep inside, Adam knew it wasn't fine. The cracks were widening. And no matter how tightly he tried to hold it together, he wasn't sure how long it would last.

A Sudden Encounter

Bob's footsteps quickened, his thoughts racing faster than his legs could carry him. The cool air nipped at his skin, but it didn't ease the heat curling in his chest. The police had been too calm, too collected during their questioning. Bob couldn't shake the feeling that they were just waiting for him to crack.

As he neared his car, a voice sliced through the haze of his thoughts.

"Mr. Foster."

His body went rigid. His heart skipped a beat. He turned slowly, and there stood Officer Hardy, his stance relaxed but eyes sharp, predatory.

Watching.

Waiting.

The Pressure Builds

Hardy didn't speak right away. He stood there, studying Bob, the silence thick and suffocating. Then, when he did speak, his voice was low, almost conspiratorial. "We just have a couple more questions for you, if you don't mind."

Bob's pulse quickened. He forced a smile, though it felt like a mask. "Of course, Officer. Go ahead."

Hardy's eyes flickered over him. "You're a businessman, Mr. Foster. You know how to keep things running smoothly. But sometimes, in situations like these, things... have a way of falling apart. You understand?"

Bob's throat went dry. His voice cracked slightly when he replied, "I'm not sure what you mean."

"I think you do," Hardy said, his voice dropping to a near-whisper. "We've been talking to people close to Jacob Obi. And a few things aren't adding up. I'd suggest you keep your story straight, Mr. Foster. About the accident."

Bob's hand tightened on the car door; his knuckles were white. "I don't know what you're talking about, Officer," he managed, forcing his words out. "I just want to see Jacob get better."

Hardy's eyes softened, but there was no warmth there—only cold calculation. "Of course. Just remember... We'll be watching."

With that, Hardy turned and walked away, his footsteps slow, deliberate. Bob stood frozen, his breath coming too fast. The chill of the air seemed to creep deeper into his bones.

Lucas's Guilt

Later that night, Lucas sat alone in his dim kitchen, the quiet broken only by the occasional creak of the floorboards. The guilt gnawed at him, heavy and suffocating. Uncle Kade's words had taken root, echoing in his mind. *A true cowboy faces his wrongs, boy.* But what was a cowboy supposed to do when his wrongs were so big?

His phone buzzed again. It was Bob.

"Lucas, we need to talk. Meet at the usual spot. Now."

The Final Confrontation

Later that night, the four men gathered—Lucas, Bob, Adam, and Jake. The place, once a haven, now felt like a trap. The silence that hung between them was thick with unspoken words, with lies too big to ignore.

Jacob spoke first; his voice steady but taut. "The cops are getting closer. They're asking the right questions."

Adam ran a hand through his hair, stress etched across his face. "They came to my office. They're talking to everyone. It's only a matter of time."

Bob crossed his arms, his expression hard. "I'm not worried. We've been through worse. Stick to the story."

But Lucas couldn't stay silent. His heart pounded in his chest. The guilt, the fear, it churned inside him, suffocating him. He couldn't keep lying.

Bob looked at him, his gaze cold. "You're quiet. What's going on with you?"

Lucas swallowed hard, his voice trembling but clear. "I don't know how much longer I can keep this up."

For a long moment, no one spoke. The silence was suffocating.

Bob's eyes narrowed. His voice dropped to a dangerous whisper. "Don't be stupid. We stick to the plan."

But Lucas felt it deep in his gut—the plan was falling apart. And there was no going back.

CHAPTER 47
THE RECKONING

The Weight of Guilt

The night felt heavy, thick with silence, like the world itself was holding its breath. Lucas sat on the edge of his bed, the dim light from the lamp casting long shadows on the walls. The air around him was suffocating, thick with the oppressive weight of his thoughts. He felt it in the tightness of his chest, in the nervous tremor of his hands as they traced the edges of Officer Hardy's business card. It seemed so simple—a plain white card—but in his hands, it felt like both a lifeline and a noose, pulling him closer to something he wasn't sure he could face.

His uncle's words echoed through his thoughts: *"A good cowboy doesn't run from his mistakes, Lucas. He faces them."*

He glanced at the wall across from him, his mind spinning, each thought a tangle of guilt, lies, and betrayal. The weight of it all pressed down on him, like a thousand-pound weight settling on his chest. He couldn't breathe, and he couldn't run any longer.

I can't keep running from this, he thought.

His thumb hovered over Officer Hardy's number again. It was tempting—confession, truth. It all seemed so simple in theory. But then there were Bob and Adam. The lies they'd built together, the mess they'd all created. And now, Lucas was trapped in it. Trapped like a fly in a spider's web. One wrong move, and it all came crashing down.

A knock on the door shattered the silence, and Lucas jumped, his heart racing.

Uncle Kade's Guidance

"Lucas, you okay in there?" His Uncle Kade's voice was calm, steady, like the ground beneath a storm.

"Yeah, just thinking," Lucas called back, trying to keep his voice level. But it cracked at the end, betraying the storm inside.

There was a pause, then the sound of heavy boots crossing the floor. The door creaked open, and Uncle Kade's broad figure filled the doorway, his worn cowboy boots heavy on the floor, a reminder of the grounded strength he carried. He stood there for a moment, his silhouette outlined against the dim light.

"Don't know if I should be worried or impressed," Kade said, his voice teasing, but there was a quiet seriousness underneath. "You've been pretty quiet. Got something on your mind, boy?"

Lucas sat up a little straighter, suddenly feeling the weight of his own skin. He wasn't sure if he could hide from this anymore. "I don't know what to do, Uncle," he said, his voice barely a whisper. "I've messed up. Bad."

Kade leaned against the doorframe, arms crossed, his eyes narrowing slightly, but his face remained unreadable. After a long beat, he asked, "Messed up how?"

Lucas hesitated. His fingers twitched, as though they had a mind of their own. *It's time,* he thought. But the words caught in his throat.

"I... I was part of something. Something that hurt Jacob. And I can't keep pretending I'm not part of it." He swallowed hard, his throat dry. "The cops are getting closer. I'm scared. I don't know what to do. What if I ruin everything? What if I ruin my life?"

Kade didn't rush to answer. Instead, he stepped into the room, his boots thudding softly against the wooden floor. He sat down next to Lucas, the old bed creaking under their combined weight. Kade's presence was solid, unshakable, like a mountain holding steady against a hurricane.

"You think you're the only one who's ever been scared to face the truth?" Kade asked, his voice low but firm, the weight of his words not lost on Lucas. "Hell, we all make mistakes. But running from it? That's the thing that'll kill you."

Lucas's throat constricted, the rawness of his fear swelling up in his chest. "I don't want to disappoint you, Uncle." His voice cracked, raw with guilt. "I don't want to be like them," he added, barely above a whisper.

Kade's gaze softened, and for the first time, Lucas saw the exhaustion behind his uncle's eyes. Kade let out a slow breath, leaning forward, his arms unfolding as he spoke more quietly, almost as if confessing something personal. "Son, no one is perfect. I've been where you are, facing a mess I didn't know how to fix. But that's what makes a man, what makes a cowboy—taking responsibility. Not hiding from it."

Lucas's breath hitched. "But what if they make me pay for it? What if I end up in jail?" The words spilled out in a rush, the anxiety too much to hold in. "What happens to me then?"

Kade placed a heavy hand on his shoulder, the weight of it grounding and comforting all at once. "You take responsibility. You make it right. You walk the hard road with your head held high. The truth is heavy, but it's a hell of a lot lighter than living with the weight of a lie."

Lucas sat in silence for a moment, the enormity of his uncle's words settling into him. His gut clenched. The consequences of facing the truth—real, terrifying consequences—were no longer abstract thoughts. They were as real as the pounding of his heart.

"I don't know if I can do it. I'm scared." But Uncle Kade was right—running wasn't an option anymore.

The True Measure of a Cowboy

"I know," Kade said, his voice full of empathy now, as if he could feel the weight Lucas carried. "But you're stronger than you think. Sometimes, boy, doing the right thing is the hardest thing. You don't have to carry this alone. You've got me. You've got the truth. And the truth... it might sting, but it'll set you free."

Lucas felt something inside him stir. For so long, he'd been running, hiding, pretending everything was fine. But here, with Kade's steady presence beside him, Lucas realized it. Maybe it was time to stop running. Maybe it was time to stop pretending.

"I'll do it," Lucas whispered at last, his voice steadier now, but still raw with emotion. "I'll tell the cops. I'll tell Jacob. I have to make it right."

Kade nodded slowly, a slow smile spreading across his face, but it was a smile full of pride. "Good boy. You're a true cowboy now."

Lucas stood, his legs feeling like jelly. But something in him had shifted. He felt taller, stronger, like he'd shed a layer of guilt that had been suffocating him. His feet weren't quite steady, but his heart was. For the first time in what felt like forever, Lucas felt like he could breathe again.

Uncle Kade's hand landed gently on his back as he rose. "One more thing," Kade added, his voice full of pride. "Don't forget who you are, Lucas. A cowboy's worth is measured by how he faces the toughest days, not by how many he's had."

Lucas looked at his uncle. He had raised him to face the truth, no matter how painful. And for the first time in a long while, Lucas felt ready.

The Call to Action

Outside, the sky was fading, the last slivers of daylight painting the horizon in warm oranges and pinks. The rodeo's big event was drawing near, and Jacob's future—hell, Lucas's own future—was hanging by a thread. But in this moment, Lucas felt something else. Clarity.

His phone buzzed in his pocket, jolting him out of his thoughts. He pulled it out, expecting another ominous message from Bob.

The cops are all over us, man. What are we doing?

Lucas groaned and dropped his face into his hands for a second. *Bob, man, do you ever stop panicking?* He didn't answer right away. But for the first time, he didn't feel like he was running. He wasn't the one avoiding the truth anymore.

He can keep panicking. I'm done with that.

He had a choice to make.

This time, he was going to make the right one.

With a steadying breath, Lucas pressed the call button and waited. The phone rang three times before Officer Hardy picked up.

"Hello?"

"This is Lucas Hill," he said, his voice stronger now, though his heart pounded in his chest. "I need to talk. About Jacob… And what happened."

As he waited for Hardy to respond, Lucas closed his eyes, exhaling slowly. The fear didn't go away, but it wasn't enough to stop him. *This isn't just about facing the consequences of my actions. It's about facing the man I want to become.*

And in that moment, Lucas knew he was ready.

The truth would set him free.

Chapter 48
The Confrontation

The Meeting at the Barn

The barn was dim, its wooden beams groaning under the weight of the past. The smell of hay, sweat, and dust clung to the air, thick like a fog that swallowed them whole. The silence hung heavily between them, a weight that pressed against their chests. The faint creaking of the barn's old frame seemed to echo their anxiety, amplifying the tension.

Jacob, Bob, Adam, and Lucas stood in a loose circle, avoiding eye contact. Each man seemed to shrink into himself, lost in his own thoughts. The space between them felt impossibly wide.

Lucas cleared his throat, but the words stuck. His palms were slick with sweat, his pulse hammering in his ears. He glanced down, his gaze fixed on the worn floorboards, unwilling to meet Jacob's eyes. The truth felt like a stone lodged in his throat, heavy and choking. But there was no turning back now. The truth was coming, and it was going to hurt.

A part of him—just a small part—wished he could step back, pretend this wasn't happening, and make a run for it. But even as that thought flickered, another one came crashing in: What happens to pretty boys like me when we go to jail? He imagined it, grimacing as he clutched his buttocks in mock horror. The image of his own hands held high, as though in surrender, and his backside cradled in both arms, burned through his mind. Not gonna be fun. The self-deprecating humor helped ease the knot in his stomach just a little. He wasn't sure if that was a good thing, but at least it kept him from crumbling under the weight of his guilt.

Jacob was the first to speak, his voice slicing through the air like a hot knife. "What's going on, Lucas? What's this about?"

Lucas swallowed, but his mouth felt dry again. "I... I called the cops," he muttered. The words felt foreign, as if they didn't belong to him. He wanted to take them back as soon as they left his mouth, but he couldn't. It was out now, out in the world, and there was no undoing it.

Bob's eyes went wide, his face draining of color. "You did what?" he barked, taking a step forward, his hands twitching like he was about to do something rash. "Are you out of your mind?"

Lucas nodded, his hands clammy. "I couldn't keep lying, Bob. I couldn't run anymore. I've been hiding from this... from the truth. But I can't do it anymore."

Jacob's face flickered with confusion, then disbelief. "What are you talking about? What's this all about?"

Adam, who had been eerily quiet up until now, finally spoke. His voice was weak, like a man trying to save himself from drowning. "We didn't have anything to do with it, Jake. You know that, right?"

But Lucas just shook his head. "We all had a hand in it. The sabotage... the plan... I started it. I messed everything up."

Bob's eyes were now full of panic, and his hands were balled into fists. "You're really going to throw us all under the bus?" His voice rose, his words sharp, as if the panic was beginning to take control. "After everything we've done for you?"

"I'm not throwing anyone under the bus," Lucas said, his voice steady, though the words felt heavier with each passing second. "I'm just telling the truth. I can't hide it anymore."

The words hung in the air, too big, too raw. Before the tension could suffocate them all, the sound of boots on the wooden floor interrupted the moment. Officer Hardy stepped into the barn, his presence like a stone dropping into a still pond. The room fell silent, all eyes turning toward him.

"I heard someone's been talking," Officer Hardy said, his voice calm but with an undertone that made everyone freeze.

Lucas felt a lump in his throat. He wasn't afraid anymore, though. The truth was out, and it was as if he could finally breathe.

The Interrogation

Officer Hardy's boots struck the barn's floor with rhythmic precision, each step deliberate, like the ticking of a clock winding down to its inevitable end. His gaze, cool and measured, swept across the room, stopping just long enough on each of them to remind them of the weight of his silence. When he spoke, it wasn't with anger—it was the calm before the storm.

"Lucas Hill," Hardy said, his voice sharp but measured, "you've made a bold choice coming forward. You realize this isn't just a little thing, right?"

Lucas swallowed hard; his mouth was dry again. He nodded, though it felt like his neck might snap under the strain. "I know. I'm ready to face whatever comes next."

Hardy turned his gaze to Bob and Adam. "And the rest of you—don't think for a second, you're off the hook just because Lucas decided to spill the beans. The truth is coming out, whether you like it or not."

Bob's face turned an alarming shade of red. His fists were clenched so tightly, his knuckles were white. "This is bullshit!" he spat, his voice shaky with anger. "We haven't done anything wrong. Lucas is just trying to save his skin by throwing us under the bus."

"Save my skin?" Lucas scoffed, the bitter taste of the words in his mouth. "Bob, are you hearing yourself? You think this is about saving me? This is about owning up to what we did. I'm not hiding anymore. I can't live with this lie."

Jacob stepped forward, his eyes wide, as though he was seeing Lucas for the first time. The hurt in his gaze hit Lucas like a punch to the stomach. "Lucas, you... You really had something to do with all of this?" His voice cracked, and it gutted Lucas to hear it.

Lucas lowered his head, unable to face Jacob. He couldn't meet his eyes, couldn't bear the disappointment in them. "Yes, Jacob," he whispered. "I'm sorry. I never meant for any of this to happen. But I'm the one who set it all in motion. And now... now it's time to face the consequences."

Jacob's expression tightened, jaw clenched, but Lucas could see the flicker of something beneath his anger. It was faint, but it was there—something like forgiveness. "You've hurt me, Lucas," Jacob said, his voice steady but cold. "But I never wanted this. I never wanted it to go this far."

"None of us did," Lucas said softly. "But we've all made choices. And now... now we've got to own up to them."

The Tipping Point

Adam's voice broke the silence, trembling with desperation. "This isn't fair. You can't just make us all the bad guys here."

"I'm not making anyone the bad guy," Lucas shot back, his voice sharper than he expected. "I'm just telling the truth. The truth about what happened. About what we did. And the truth is, we all played a part in this mess."

The words settled into the barn like a storm cloud—heavy, inevitable. The silence that followed was suffocating, like the air itself was trying to hold them all in place. The truth was a wrecking ball, and none of them could escape it.

Officer Hardy stepped forward, his voice firm, like a judge about to deliver a sentence. "I suggest the rest of you stop digging yourselves deeper and start talking. Lucas has made his choice, and now it's time for you all to make yours."

Bob's glare could have burned a hole through the floor, but there was a flicker of doubt in his eyes now. The bravado was gone. He knew it was over.

"Fine," Bob muttered, his voice thick with resentment. "I'll talk. But you've got to understand, we never meant for any of this to go the way it did."

"I didn't mean for it to go this far either," Lucas said quietly. "But the longer we waited, the worse it got."

Jacob stepped forward, his gaze hard. "You're really ready to face the consequences?" His voice was low, measured.

Lucas nodded, his resolve firm. "Yes. It's time."

The Final Choice

The barn felt colder now, the shadows stretching long across the dirt floor as the weight of everything settled in. Officer Hardy motioned for them to follow him outside, where the evening sun cast a golden hue on the world. Bob and Adam, despite their protests, knew the game was up. They couldn't outrun this anymore.

Lucas took a deep breath, the weight of his decision heavy on his shoulders. As he stepped outside, the fading light bathed everything in a soft, golden glow, but it didn't quite reach him. The cool evening air brushed his face, carrying with it the scent of earth and grass. It was strange that a sense of peace was creeping in now, like he had just crossed a threshold, leaving everything behind. It wasn't relief. Not yet. But it was something else. Something like freedom.

Chapter 49
The Aftermath

Facing the Consequences

The sheriff's office was cold and sterile, its walls drained of warmth as if every ounce of humanity had been sucked out by the harsh fluorescent lights above. They flickered intermittently, casting an unsettling glow on the faces gathered around the table. The sterile scent of cleaning products clung to the air, mixing with the faint, lingering odor of stale coffee. The room felt small, suffocating, as if the walls themselves were pressing in on them.

Lucas sat across from Officer Hardy, his hands trembling slightly in his lap. Bob and Adam sat beside him, their faces unreadable, yet their silence was thick with guilt. The tension was palpable—each breath felt too heavy, each thought too loud. There was no escaping the reality of the moment. The truth had been laid bare, and now, there was no hiding from it.

Hardy leaned back in his chair, arms crossed, his eyes calculating. He didn't show much emotion, but Lucas could feel the weight of his gaze, like a suffocating pressure. The truth had been told, but that was only the beginning. The consequences were yet to unfold.

"So," Hardy's voice broke the silence, sharp and methodical. "We've got everything we need. Your statements check out. But there's still a lot of work to be done."

Lucas swallowed hard, a lump in his throat making it hard to breathe. His thoughts spun like a whirlwind—guilt, fear, shame. The truth had set him free, but it hadn't brought any relief. It only felt like the ground was slipping out from under him. Every step forward felt like falling deeper into the abyss.

"Lucas," Hardy's voice softened just a touch, a hint of something resembling empathy beneath the professional exterior. "I know this wasn't easy. But it was the right call. You know that, right?"

Lucas nodded, but the words didn't reach him. He wanted to believe Hardy's reassurance, to hold on to the notion that telling the truth could somehow make everything right. But right now, all he felt was the crushing weight of what he'd set in motion. It felt like a nightmare he couldn't escape from.

"So, what happens now?" Adam's voice cracked, raw and tremulous, the bravado that had once been there now replaced by the stark reality of what lay ahead.

Hardy turned his gaze toward Adam, his expression unreadable. "Now we get to the legal part. The investigation is still ongoing, but it's clear there were multiple people involved. Charges will be filed, and you'll all have to face the consequences in court."

The words hit Lucas like a punch to the gut. His stomach churned, and his thoughts turned to Jacob—the friend he had betrayed, the one whose life had been shattered by their actions. No matter what happened in court, it wouldn't change the fact that Jacob had been hurt. That pain would follow Lucas far beyond the courtroom.

"I'm sorry," Lucas whispered, his voice thick with emotion. The words felt so small, so inadequate. He didn't know how else to say it. "I never meant for it to go this far."

Officer Hardy's gaze softened for a moment, and Lucas saw something human flicker in his eyes. But his tone remained steady. "The truth can be a heavy thing to carry," he said quietly. "But it's a start. A good start."

The Ripple Effect

Later that day, Lucas found himself standing at the edge of his uncle's ranch, looking out over the endless stretch of land before him. The sun hung low in the sky, casting a soft golden glow over everything. The fields stretched out before him, their edges blurred by the long shadows of the fading day. A gentle breeze whispered through the trees, rustling the leaves. It should have felt peaceful, but to Lucas, it only felt like the calm before a storm.

Behind him, the ranch house stood in silence, the faint sounds of Uncle Kade moving around inside, probably preparing dinner. But Lucas didn't feel like going in—not now. Not when his mind was racing and his chest felt tight with guilt.

The truth had come out. The investigation was underway. The consequences would unfold soon enough. But where did that leave him? What was supposed to happen next?

His thoughts turned to Jacob—the anger in his friend's eyes, the betrayal that had torn their friendship apart. Lucas had hurt him more than anyone, and that was something he would carry with him forever. For the first time in a long time, Lucas didn't feel like running from his mistakes. He wasn't hiding anymore. The truth had set him free, but it had also made everything harder.

As he stood there, trying to make sense of it all, a thought struck him like a lightning bolt: *What do pretty boys like me do in jail? Hold onto their butts like they're on fire?* He couldn't help but chuckle bitterly at the absurdity of it. There was humor in it, even if it was twisted humor. He was picturing himself, a well-groomed city boy, having to navigate the gritty reality of prison life. Not exactly the life he'd imagined. But there was a dark comfort in the joke—at least it kept his mind from spiraling further.

"Hey, boy."

Lucas turned at the sound of his uncle's voice. Kade stood in the doorway of the ranch house, his large frame filling the space, his eyes warm yet firm. The quiet strength in Kade's presence had always been a comfort to him, but now, it felt like a lifeline in the sea of confusion Lucas was drowning in.

"You doing all right?" Kade asked, his voice low and steady, laced with concern.

"I don't know," Lucas admitted, his shoulders sagging beneath the weight of everything. "I feel like I've ruined everything. I've hurt people. I don't know how to fix it."

Kade stepped outside, the crunch of his boots on the gravel louder than it should have been. He moved to stand beside Lucas, and the two of them stood there in silence, staring out at the land. The quiet stretched between them, not uncomfortable but heavy. No words were needed right now—just being there together was enough.

"Sometimes, boy," Kade's voice broke the silence, slow and deliberate, the kind of wisdom Lucas had always relied on, "you don't fix everything. You can't. But you can choose how to move forward. That's the only thing you can control."

Lucas let out a long breath, the weight of Kade's words sinking in. "I don't know if I can face Jacob. Or anyone. Not after all of this," he murmured, his gaze drifting to his rough hands, now trembling—not from work, but from the emotional weight of everything.

"You'll face them," Kade replied firmly. "But it won't be easy. The hardest thing is running from it. You've made your choice, Lucas. Now you've got to walk through it. Head high."

Lucas lifted his gaze, meeting Kade's steady eyes. His uncle's words weren't comforting in the way he wanted, but they were exactly what he needed to hear. The road ahead would be brutal—there was no avoiding it—but Kade was right. The only way through it was forward.

"Thanks, Uncle Kade," Lucas said quietly, his voice thick with unshed emotion.

Kade's hand clapped firmly on his shoulder, grounding him. "You've got this, boy. You've got this."

An Unexpected Message

Later that night, Lucas sat alone in his room, the weight of everything pressing down on him. He picked up his phone, scrolling aimlessly through messages, searching for a distraction, but his thoughts kept circling back to the same painful places. Then, a new message appeared—Jacob.

Meet me. We need to talk.

Lucas's heart skipped a beat. His hands froze. He had no idea what Jacob wanted or what this conversation would be like. The last time they'd spoken, Jacob's anger had been a raw wound, his trust shattered by the very man sitting here now.

But Lucas knew he couldn't keep running from this. He couldn't hide from the inevitable.

He quickly typed a response.

Okay. Where?

The reply came almost instantly.

The old barn. The one by the edge of the ranch.

Lucas exhaled slowly, the breath he hadn't realized he was holding coming out in a shudder. He wasn't ready for this. Not at all. But there was no turning back now. He had to go.

Stepping outside, the cool night air bit at his skin. The stars above were cold and distant, and the land stretched out before him, empty and quiet. The world seemed to hold its breath as he walked toward the barn—the last place he wanted to be, but the only place left to go. It felt like a confrontation with destiny itself, a moment that could either tear their friendship apart forever or start the long, painful journey toward healing.

One thing was certain: Lucas was ready to face whatever came next.

CHAPTER 50
THE UNRAVELING TENSION

Lucas's Struggle: Guilt and Fear

The days leading up to the final rodeo event were heavy, as if the world itself held its breath in anticipation. There was a quiet intensity in the air—unspoken but undeniably present. Lucas felt it deep in his chest, an oppressive weight that seemed to grow with each passing moment, each second he avoided confronting Jacob.

The guilt had become a constant companion, haunting him at the most inopportune times. It lingered during long days on the ranch, during awkward dinners with Uncle Kade, and in the silence of his bedroom, where the darkness swallowed his restless thoughts. Lucas had confessed the truth, but that didn't make it feel any less painful. The pieces of his life were falling apart, one after another.

He hadn't seen Jacob in days, not since their tense conversation at the sheriff's office. That was the moment Lucas had finally come clean, and the betrayal hung between them like an impenetrable wall. Jacob had said little afterward—only the cold fury in his eyes had been enough to convey everything.

The upcoming rodeo now felt less like a celebration and more like a sentence. The truth had torn everything apart. Lucas kept telling himself that facing the consequences was the only way to make things right, but the reality was messier than he'd imagined. Jacob was hurt. Jacob was angry. And Lucas knew he couldn't undo the damage.

Standing at the edge of the ranch, Lucas rested his hands on the weathered wooden fence, trying to steady his breathing. The air was cool, and the faint scent of hay and earth drifted on the breeze. He tried to gather his thoughts, but no matter how hard he focused, everything circled back to Jacob. His best friend—the one he had betrayed—was about to face the biggest challenge of his life, and Lucas wasn't sure if he could even look him in the eye.

Lucas's Growing Fear

Back at Uncle Kade's house, Lucas paced restlessly in the dimly lit living room. The walls seemed to close in around him, and each step he took on the creaking hardwood floor echoed in the otherwise quiet house. The sound was sharp and deliberate, each click of his boots adding to the suffocating silence.

Cold sweat trickled down his back, his palms slick with anxiety. His chest tightened with dread. What if they come for me? What if they really send me to jail?

There was a time when the thought of jail felt foreign, almost laughable… but not anymore. Now, it felt like an inevitable consequence. In the past, Lucas had always been able to charm and lie his way out of trouble. But this time, that wouldn't be enough. No amount of smooth words could undo the mess he had made. He had crossed a line, and now the consequences were catching up to him.

Jail. The word rattled in his mind like a bitter reminder, cold and unyielding. He could already picture it: the gray walls, the cold clang of iron bars, the bitter taste of fear in his mouth. He swallowed hard, his throat dry, shuddering at the thought.

What would they do to me? He could almost feel the crushing silence of a place where no one cared who you were, only what you could survive. He was scared. Terrified, really. It felt like his body had become a prison, his own bones the bars.

Then the door creaked open, and Uncle Kade stepped inside. His presence was steady, grounded, and for the first time in hours, Lucas felt a flicker of relief. Kade took one look at his nephew and instantly recognized the turmoil written across his face.

"You've been pacing for hours," Kade said, his voice calm, though tinged with concern. "What's going on, Lucas?"

Lucas couldn't meet his uncle's eyes. His throat tightened, words stuck, and he turned away, trying to distance himself from his own panic. When he finally spoke, his fear came rushing out, breathless and raw.

"They're gonna send me to jail," Lucas said, his voice breaking. "I… I can feel it. It's all I can think about."

Uncle Kade watched him for a moment, his face unreadable. Lucas's heart hammered in his chest, his hands trembling. He twisted the hem of his shirt, as though trying to hold himself together.

"Uncle," Lucas whispered, his voice barely audible, "I can't do it. I'll end up in a cell with some big guy named Tiny. I—what if they make me... one of those guys? I can't survive in there. I'm too... too soft. I'll be someone's target. Someone's... friendless." His voice cracked, the weight of his own words almost too much to bear.

Kade was silent for a long moment, processing Lucas's frantic words. Then he blinked, and a soft laugh escaped him. It was a strange sound, laced with both amusement and genuine concern.

"What in the world are you talking about, Lucas?" Kade asked, his voice a mix of disbelief and affection.

But Lucas wasn't laughing. His breath came in short, rapid gasps. His entire body was tense, as if the very act of standing was too much to bear.

"No, I'm serious!" Lucas insisted, his panic rising. "What if they put me in there with hardened criminals? What if they… what if they—"

Kade's chuckle faded. His face softened, and he stepped toward Lucas, placing a hand firmly on his shoulder, grounding him with his steady presence.

"Lucas," Kade began, his voice calm but firm. "You really think that's what's going to happen? That they're going to lock you up with hardened criminals for—what? Some mistake you made?"

Lucas's throat tightened, but Kade's calm, measured tone cut through his panic.

"I've messed up," Lucas murmured, barely audible. "I've done things that could put me away. I can't just run anymore."

Kade's eyes softened. "Listen, kid. You might've gotten yourself into this mess, but you're gonna get yourself out. You're not the guy your fear is telling you you are. You've made mistakes, sure. But they don't have to define you. You're stronger than that."

Lucas hesitated, his gaze searching Kade's face for a flicker of hope. For the first time in a long time, he saw it: reassurance.

"Take a breath," Kade said, his voice steady yet gentle. "Whatever happens, we'll face it. Together."

Lucas stood frozen for a moment, absorbing his uncle's words. Slowly, the knots in his stomach loosened. Maybe it wouldn't be as bad as he feared. Maybe, just maybe, there was a way out.

Jacob's Battle: Internal Struggles and Fear of Failure

Later that evening, Jacob stood at the edge of the rodeo arena, his eyes drawn to the flickering lights in the distance. The preparations were in full swing, but to him, it felt like everything was happening in slow motion. His stomach twisted, a pressure that no physical injury could match. The scars from his past ran deeper than any wound; they were etched into his bones, his mind. The hospital room—those sterile white lights and the helplessness in the doctors' voices—felt like a bad dream. And yet, the weight of it lingered, persistent and unforgiving.

I used to think I was invincible, he thought, a bitter edge to the memory. Now every breath feels like a reminder that I'm not. He clenched his fists, the sharp pain of the old wounds creeping in.

Nick's Support: Encouragement in the Face of Doubt

Jacob was lost in his thoughts when a hand landed on his shoulder, solid and reassuring. He didn't need to look to know who it was.

"Hey, you good?" Nick's voice was soft, but it carried a weight of concern that Jacob couldn't ignore.

Jacob forced a smile, but it didn't reach his eyes. "Yeah, just… just need to clear my head." His voice was raw, betraying the fear gnawing at his insides.

Nick didn't press. He stood by, steady, a quiet strength at Jacob's side. "Jake," he said, his voice firm but gentle, "whatever happens out there, you don't owe anyone anything. This is huge, I know, but you're not alone in this. And you've already fought the hardest battle."

Jacob's throat tightened, the words piercing through the fog of doubt. He shook his head, a bitter laugh escaping. "You don't get it, Nick. It's not about anyone else. It's about me. If I can't do this… If I can't ride again, I'll never be the person I thought I was. I'll be nothing."

Nick's gaze softened, his words never faltering. "You're already more than you were before, Jake. The hardest part is not giving up."

Jacob turned his gaze to the arena, where the sounds of the crowd began to grow louder. The noise was distant, muffled, and yet the pressure was suffocating. The weight of their expectations hung heavy on his shoulders. But Nick was right—perhaps it wasn't about being ready. Maybe it was enough to just take that first step.

Lucas's Realization: Facing His Guilt

In the stands, Lucas watched Jacob. His gaze never left him as Jacob prepared for the ride of his life. But it wasn't just about the bull. It was about everything Jacob had fought for, and everything Lucas hadn't.

The guilt washed over him like a flood. He hadn't been there when it counted. He hadn't stood by his friend when he needed him the most. And now, as Jacob faced the challenge of a lifetime, Lucas couldn't even bring himself to meet his eyes.

Jacob was facing a beast. But Lucas realized, with a pang of sharp clarity, that he had been the one who was broken all along.

He couldn't run anymore. He couldn't keep hiding behind his regrets. Standing up, his breath shallow, his heart racing, Lucas found the courage to do the one thing he'd been avoiding: face the music.

He didn't look away this time. He stood tall, his chest heavy with guilt and a determination he hadn't known he was capable of. The crowd roared, but to Lucas, the noise disappeared. There was only one thing left to do—make things right.

CHAPTER 51
THE FINAL SHOWDOWN

The arena hummed with electricity, a pulse that vibrated through Jacob's bones, carrying the collective anticipation of thousands of eyes on him. The crowd's roar was a constant wave of sound, rising and falling like the tide, reminding him that the stakes here weren't just personal—they were everything. This wasn't just another rodeo. This was "The Rodeo". The one everyone had been talking about for months. The one that would either break him or make him. And Jacob wasn't just fighting to prove he could still ride; he was fighting to prove he hadn't been broken by the pain, the betrayals, the setbacks. This moment was his reckoning.

In the pens, the bulls snorted, their eyes wild with untamed fury. The ground rumbled with the sound of hooves and grunts, the air thick with dust and anticipation. Around him, the other riders moved with practiced precision—tightening ropes, adjusting gear, wearing the faces of men who knew exactly what they were walking into. Jacob stood at the edge of it all, still. The wind stung his skin, and his body—aching, bruised, and exhausted—screamed for relief. He wanted to give in, to collapse and let the pain win. But not today. Not in front of them. Not after everything. Not now. This was his redemption, or his defeat.

Internal Struggle & Flashback to Recovery

Jacob squeezed his eyes shut, the world around him blurring as memories came crashing back. The sterile smell of the hospital, the sharp hum of machines that never stopped. His ribs had been crushed, his future uncertain. The worst part hadn't been the broken bones—it was the hollow fear that maybe, just maybe, he was no longer the man he used to be.

I used to think I was invincible, he thought bitterly, feeling the deep ache in his chest. But now? Every breath is a reminder that I'm not.

The pain never fully went away. His ribs were like old scars—always there, a constant reminder of what could've been. But the real scars ran deeper, where betrayal had cut through the soul. He could still hear their voices—men he had called brothers, men he had trusted. *You're nothing. You'll never be the same.*

But then, like a spark in the dark, something inside him flickered—a defiance, a refusal to let the past swallow him whole. *I'm not done yet.* Standing here, in the face of the crowd, he realized that this was more than just a fight for survival—it was a fight to reclaim himself.

A Moment with Erick

Just then, he felt a hand land on his shoulder. He didn't need to turn around to know who it was. Erick. His closest friend. His rock.

"Look at you," Erick teased, his voice light, but with an underlying warmth. "All geared up like you're ready to take on the apocalypse. You sure you're here to ride, or just to grab some free beer at the afterparty?"

Jacob forced a grin, but it was brief. The pain shot through his chest like an electric shock, and his smile faltered. He sighed, his voice quieter than usual. "I don't know, man," he admitted. "I thought I was ready, but now... It's like every second, I'm walking toward the edge of a cliff."

Erick's expression softened; the playful edge gone. With a firm slap on Jacob's back, Erick spoke low, his words heavy with sincerity. "Jake, you've been through worse. Hell, remember when you broke your arm and still climbed onto that horse the next day? You didn't quit then, did you? Why the hell would you quit now?"

Jacob's gaze drifted toward the arena, where the other bull riders were preparing. The sound of their ropes snapping echoed in the air, and the hooves of the bulls pounded the earth like thunder. But in his mind, Jacob didn't see bulls or riders. He saw everything he'd been through—betrayal, pain, and the endless nights wondering if he'd ever be the same.

"I don't know if I can do this," he whispered to himself. The doubt, the fear—it gripped him tight.

Nick's Support & the Emotional Toll

Then Nick appeared, his usual grin replaced by a quiet seriousness. He placed a hand on Jacob's arm, his touch grounding.

"Jake," he said softly, his voice steady. "Whatever happens today, you don't have to prove anything to anyone."

Jacob looked up at Nick, his heart tightening in his chest. The weight of everything was suffocating. "You don't get it, Nick," he said, his voice tight with frustration. "It's not about proving anything to them. It's about proving something to myself. I need to prove that I'm not done. If I can't do this... if I fail again..." He swallowed hard, the knot in his throat thick. "I'm scared, man. Scared of being nothing."

Nick's grip tightened, his eyes unwavering. "You're not failing, Jake. You're fighting. And that's who you are. That's what you've always been. You never back down."

Jacob's breath shuddered. He wanted to push it all away, to deny it, but the truth was louder than any of his doubts. In that moment, Nick's words were the lifeline Jacob needed. The moment had come. He couldn't walk away now—not after everything he had fought for.

Lucas's Guilt and Conflict

In the stands, Lucas watched, frozen. His heart hammered in his chest. Every part of him screamed for Jacob to fail—not just because of the sabotage, but because of the guilt that now twisted his insides. It was a gnawing, relentless ache.

What have I done?

His fists clenched involuntarily. *I could've stopped this... I should've stopped this.* Watching Jacob now, strong and focused, made the guilt settle deep in his gut.

If I hadn't been so weak, none of this would've happened.

But the pressure from Bob and Adam still lingered in his mind, like a ghost he couldn't shake. He had been swept up in their plan, driven by fear and greed. But now, as he watched Jacob prepare to face the bull, the truth felt undeniable. He wasn't just witnessing a ride; he was witnessing redemption—the one thing he could never have.

The Ride – Climax

Jacob mounted the bull, the steel of the saddle cold beneath his fingers. The crowd's roar surged around him, but it felt distant, muffled. His grip tightened on the reins, his breath shallow. Pain shot through him like a lightning bolt—his ribs, his muscles, every inch of him felt like it was on fire. But this wasn't the time to give in. Not now. Not in front of them.

The buzzer sounded. The bull exploded from the gates with the fury of a thunderstorm, the force nearly ripping Jacob from the saddle. The crowd erupted into a chorus of cheers, but in Jacob's world, everything was chaos. His body was a battlefield, each twist of the bull's body sending shockwaves of agony through his bones. But his mind? His mind was clear, locked onto one thought: *I will not let go.*

Every second felt like an eternity. His body screamed, every muscle in revolt, but he dug deeper. His heels sank into the bull's side. His grip tightened until his fingers went numb. He couldn't let go. Not again. Not after everything.

I am not done, he thought fiercely. I will not quit.

Lucas's Moment of Realization

From the stands, Lucas watched, his breath caught in his throat. Jacob wasn't just battling the bull. He was confronting everything— the pain, the betrayals, the fear. But beyond that, he was fighting for redemption, for everything that had been stripped from him.

He's not just fighting to win, Lucas realized. *He's fighting for everything he's lost... for everything I helped take from him.*

The guilt that had once been a whisper now roared inside him, suffocating him with its weight. The years of selfish choices, of pushing Jacob to the brink, came crashing back. His heart hammered in his chest as the truth cut through him like a knife. But there was nothing he could do. The damage had already been done, the wounds too deep to heal in a single moment. Yet, the understanding was there—guilt had its own purpose now: not to paralyze him, but to drive him to seek redemption. To change. But the question remained—was it too late?

As Jacob fought for his life, for his redemption, Lucas had no choice but to watch. His moment of realization was just the beginning.

Jacob's Final Victory – A Cowboy's Moment of Triumph

The arena was electric, alive with energy, a thundering sea of sound that seemed to pulse through Jacob's very bones. The bull beneath him bucked violently, and Jacob, already battered and bruised from earlier rides, was swept into the whirlwind of it all. Every muscle in his body screamed in protest, the pain from the day's previous rides still fresh. But there was no turning back now. He gripped the reins tighter, determined to hold on, no matter the cost.

His legs, stiff and trembling, threatened to buckle beneath him. The weight of the moment felt suffocating. The crowd's deafening cheers seemed to fade into the background as Jacob focused inward, shutting out the noise. He could feel the raw force of the bull testing every fiber of his being. But deep within his soul, a quiet strength began to rise—something beyond sheer willpower. Something profound. Something divine.

"But they that wait upon the Lord shall renew their strength; they shall mount up with wings as eagles; they shall run, and not be weary; they shall walk, and not faint." (Isaiah 40:31)

The scripture flowed into his mind, not just as words, but as a living truth. In that instant, it wasn't mere faith—it was a reality. His body ached, but the pain no longer mattered. His heart beat in rhythm with the promise in those words, and every breath he took reminded him that he was not alone in this fight.

The bull surged again, twisting violently beneath him, its hooves pounding the earth. Jacob's muscles screamed in protest, but his mind... his mind was calm.

"I can do all things through Christ who strengthens me." (Philippians 4:13)

The words, once just familiar verses, now felt like the lifeline he so desperately needed. They weren't empty anymore. They were the strength that had carried him through everything, that had brought him to this very moment.

With one final, earth-shattering buck, the bull gave one last violent heave. But Jacob held on. His grip wasn't just about survival anymore; it was a defiance of every limitation, every doubt, every expectation that had ever been placed on him. His heart surged as the buzzer rang, signaling the end of the ride. The crowd erupted into thunderous applause, but Jacob stood still, a calm in the storm of noise. His legs shook, his breath came in ragged gasps, but in that moment, he had never felt more alive, not from the victory itself, but from what that victory represented. He had faced his fears—his doubts, his past mistakes, and his own limitations—and conquered them all.

The ride was over, but the true battle had been within himself.

Jacob's Quiet Moment of Reflection

Jacob dismounted slowly, his legs threatening to collapse beneath him. For a moment, he stood there, drenched in sweat, the heat of the sun on his back. The deafening roar of the crowd still rang in his ears, but it felt distant. He pressed a trembling hand to his chest, his heart still racing, and for the first time in as long as he could remember, there was peace. Peace that came from something deeper than just the victory. It was the kind of peace that came when you'd walked through fire and emerged stronger, tested and found faithful.

It was the kind of peace that came when you understood the journey wasn't just about the destination, but about the faith you held onto along the way. Closing his eyes for a brief moment, Jacob's thoughts drifted inward. He thought back to those dark days in the hospital, when the future had seemed uncertain. He remembered the fear, the pain, and the doubt. But standing here, in the light of the arena, with his body battered and his heart full, he understood something he hadn't before. His strength had never come from his own power— it had come from something greater.

"The Lord is my shepherd; I shall not want. He makes me lie down in green pastures. He leads me beside still waters. He restores my soul." (Psalm 23:1-3)

The words spilled from his lips in a quiet whisper. They were no longer just scripture from his childhood—they were his truth. A declaration of who he had become, a statement of the strength now rooted deep within him.

"Even though I walk through the valley of the shadow of death, I will fear no evil, for You are with me. Your rod and Your staff, they comfort me." (Psalm 23:4)

Jacob opened his eyes, and for the first time, he felt the weight of his past—the betrayals, the scars, the mistakes—lift off of him. He had walked through the darkest valleys, and now, standing in the light, he could see it. God had been with him every step of the way. Lifting him. Guiding him. Carrying him when he couldn't carry himself.

"You prepare a table before me in the presence of my enemies. You anoint my head with oil; my cup overflows." (Psalm 23:5)

He could almost see it—the table before him, the overflowing blessings of every trial and triumph. And then, he whispered the final words of the psalm:

"Surely goodness and mercy shall follow me all the days of my life, and I shall dwell in the house of the Lord forever." (Psalm 23:6)

His voice trembled on the last words, breaking as tears welled up in his eyes. But he didn't care. For the first time in his life, he understood what it meant to be at peace with himself. Not because of the victory in the rodeo, but because he had found something deeper. Something unshakable.

With a shaky breath, Jacob lifted his eyes and hand to the sky, the sun blazing down upon him. A single tear traced a path down his cheek. It wasn't sadness—it was release, a letting go of all that had held him captive for so long.

The roar of the crowd swelled around him, but Jacob's voice rang clear, filled with conviction: "I could not have done this without You. Thank You, God."

Jacob shouted, his voice ringing with pride and purpose, "I am a cowboy… A Nigerian Cowboy. And my journey—our journey—is just beginning."

The breeze stirred around him, as though the earth itself agreed. And in that moment, Jacob knew—he wasn't just a cowboy anymore. He was something more. He was a man who had found his place, not just in the rodeo, but in the world. A man rooted in faith, with a heart full of purpose, and a strength that could never be shaken.

CHAPTER 52
THE AWARD CEREMONY

The arena buzzed, but this hum was different—soft, like the calm after a storm, yet underscored by an electric, expectant energy. The crowd, still high from Jacob's victory, settled into a tense silence, as if the air itself was holding its breath. In the VIP section, two figures stood out: Will "The Legend" Harrison and Sarah Foster, icons of the sport, poised to present the most coveted trophy in rodeo.

Jacob's gaze naturally gravitated to Will. A man who had weathered it all. He was tough, weathered, the kind of cowboy whose presence alone commanded respect. Will's worn face and calloused hands spoke of years spent battling the elements, testing his limits, and earning every inch of his success. Jacob could see the respect in Will's eyes, and it filled him with a strange mixture of pride and disbelief. **I've earned this.** The thought settled deep in his chest, unshakeable.

The crowd hushed, and Jacob drew in a steadying breath, bracing himself. This is real, he thought, the gravity of the moment almost too heavy to bear.

The Presenting Speech

Will Harrison stepped forward, his hat removed in one fluid motion. His gaze was steady, unwavering, his voice cutting through the stillness—a gravelly warmth like the sound of a saddle creaking under a cowboy's weight.

"Ladies and gentlemen," he began, his eyes locked on Jacob, "It's an honor to present this award to a man who has made us all proud. Jacob—known far and wide as the 'Nigerian Cowboy'—has shown us what it truly means to ride with heart."

The crowd erupted, but Jacob stood still, his throat tight, overwhelmed by the sound. **This is real.** He was only half-present, the magnitude of Will's words seeming to reverberate in the air. This is the moment I've been waiting for.

Will paused, a smile curling at the edges of his mouth—a look of pride and something more personal. "Jacob's not just any cowboy. He's the kind of cowboy we should all strive to be—fighting through the storm, no matter where you come from. And personally? I think we ought to adopt him. What do you all say?"

The crowd cheered, but Jacob barely heard it. He was lost in Will's gaze, relishing in the unspoken bond between them. Will wasn't just presenting a trophy—he was offering something far more valuable: **validation.**

"This Nigerian Cowboy," Will continued, his voice firm with conviction, "has shown us the true spirit of a cowboy. And for that, Jacob, I give you this trophy. From one cowboy to another—ride on, Jacob. Ride on."

Jacob's Emotional Reaction

For a heartbeat, Jacob didn't move. The world blurred, the faces of the crowd, the rush of sound, fading into the background. This is my moment, he thought, but it felt surreal, as if he were watching someone else. How could it be real? He wasn't sure whether the heat in his chest was pride or the weight of everything he had fought for.

But as Will handed him the trophy, the noise of the crowd faded, leaving him with only the tangible weight in his hands.

His fingers tingled as he took the trophy, and when he spoke, his voice cracked. "Thank you… Thank you all," he whispered, his words barely escaping. "This… this means more than I can put into words."

The crowd cheered again, but Jacob didn't hear it—not really. His heart raced, but it wasn't the rush of victory—it was the overwhelming realization that this moment had been earned through everything he had endured: the struggles, the doubts, the betrayals. It wasn't just a win. This was a quiet victory over everything that had tried to hold him down.

A small, uncertain smile tugged at the corner of his mouth. He thought of the first time he'd stepped onto this ground, unsure of himself, unsure of his place. Now, here he stood—this trophy in his hands was more than a symbol of victory. It was proof of his journey.

Backstage – A Moment of Reflection

Backstage, the trophy sat heavy in Jacob's hands, but the weight felt different now. It wasn't just metal—it was everything he had fought for: the pain, the losses, the moments of self-doubt. He traced the contours of the trophy with his thumb, and his eyes lingered on the scar—a reminder of the first time he had fallen during a competition. That fall had almost broken him, but now the scar felt like a mark of strength, a memory of how far he'd come.

Erick slapped him on the back, his grin wide and knowing. "Hell of a ride, Jacob. Hell of a ride."

Jacob smiled faintly, his heart still racing. "Yeah," he murmured, his gaze meeting Erick's, then Nick's. "It was worth it. All of it."

Looking at the trophy again, he didn't see it as just a prize. This wasn't just a cowboy's victory. It was a man's redemption. **I've earned this.** But this time, it felt different—it felt like the beginning of something new. Something more.

Bar Scene–A Turning Point for Lucas

In the bar, the muted glow of the TV replayed Jacob's victory, a harsh reminder of what they had lost. Bob slammed his glass onto the table, the sound echoing in the quiet tension.

"This was supposed to be our moment," Bob growled, his fist clenched around his glass. He couldn't let it go. Losing stung more than usual.

Lucas sat across from him, silent. His gaze flicked to the screen, but his mind was elsewhere, on Jacob—victorious but carrying the weight of a journey no one truly understood. **He earned it.** The thought twisted something inside Lucas, his chest tightening. He turned his eyes to Bob, watching him seethe, but couldn't bring himself to feel the same anger. He wasn't sure why, but something had shifted.

"Yeah," Lucas muttered quietly, almost to himself. "It was supposed to be."

Bob slammed his fist on the table again, frustration building. "Doesn't matter. We'll find a way. There's always next time."

But Lucas didn't respond. A part of him understood now—maybe being a cowboy wasn't about winning every time, but about getting back up after you've been knocked down. Maybe Jacob had shown him that without even trying.

Final Reflection

Jacob's battle wasn't over. There would be more challenges, more moments that would test him. But for now, he had won. And for the first time in a long time, he felt like he was exactly where he was supposed to be. **This is my moment.** This wasn't the end of a ride; it was the beginning of a new one.

CHAPTER 53
AFTERMATH AND RECKONING

Jacob's Recovery: The Emotional Weight of Victory

The victory had been sweet, but it left Jacob feeling emptier than he'd expected. The cheers from the arena still echoed in his mind, but in the silence of the locker room, the adrenaline quickly faded. His body ached in ways that went beyond the physical—bruises and soreness were the least of his problems. The emotional weight of everything—every injury, every betrayal, every fight—came crashing down on him all at once.

As he sat in front of the mirror, wiping the sweat and dirt from his face, Jacob could barely recognize the man staring back at him. Not just because of the bruises or the exhaustion, but because he had changed. The man who had entered that arena wasn't the same one who left it. His victory wasn't just a triumph over the bull—it was a testament to the survival of his soul. He had fought more than the animal that nearly crushed him; he had fought pieces of himself that had been buried deep.

But even as the trophy sat heavy in his hands, there was still so much left undone. The damage to his relationships, the trust he had lost, the unspoken words lingering in the air—those things weren't as easily healed as a broken bone. He had conquered the ring, but the battles inside were far from over.

Lucas' Guilt: A Decision That Haunts

Lucas had been quiet all evening, retreating into the background, watching from the sidelines. His mind was trapped in a loop of guilt and regret, replaying the moments that had brought him to this point. He had been part of Jacob's downfall—part of the sabotage that nearly destroyed his friend's career.

Standing outside the locker room, Lucas felt the weight of his choices like a physical burden. He had let Jacob down in ways that couldn't be undone. He had been weak. He had been selfish. And now, despite Jacob's victory, the truth still hovered over him like a dark cloud he couldn't escape.

The roar of the crowd outside seemed a million miles away, a distant echo that made everything feel surreal. He wanted to be happy for Jacob—he truly did. But how could he be, when the one person who had earned this victory more than anyone else was the same person he had betrayed?

Jacob and Lucas: Confrontation and Conversation

Later that night, after the dust had settled and the celebration had calmed, Jacob and Lucas found themselves alone in the dimly lit parking lot. Jacob leaned against his truck, his gaze fixed on the ground. His mind was still racing, but this moment felt like a strange reprieve—a chance to breathe, to think, and to confront the past.

"You okay?" Lucas asked, his voice hesitant. He wasn't sure how to approach the man he had wronged so deeply.

Jacob looked up. His eyes were tired but steady, the weight of his thoughts lingering behind them. He didn't answer immediately, taking a long moment to gather his words. The silence between them felt like a weight neither of them knew how to lift—too much had been left unsaid for too long.

Finally, Jacob spoke, his voice low but full of emotions Lucas couldn't quite decipher. "I don't know if I can forgive you, Lucas. I don't know if I even want to. What you did… it almost destroyed everything. And the worst part is… I don't even know if I can get past it. Not now. Not after everything."

Lucas winced, the words cutting through him like a knife. He had known this moment was coming, but that didn't make it any easier. "I know. I deserve whatever you have to say. I should've never—"

"Listen," Jacob interrupted, his voice gaining strength. "I'm not saying I'm okay with what you did, but I know you weren't the only one involved in all this. You got caught up in something you shouldn't have. And that's on me, too. But the thing is, I'm tired, Lucas. I'm tired of carrying this anger around, and I'm tired of pretending like it doesn't hurt."

Lucas swallowed hard, the dryness in his throat making it hard to speak. "I can't make it right, but I want to. I've never wanted anything more than to fix this… but I don't know how."

Jacob's gaze softened, though the flicker of hurt still lingered in his eyes. "Maybe you don't need to fix it all at once. Maybe… maybe we just need to take it one step at a time."

The tension between them slowly began to ease, though neither of them knew what the next step would be. But for the first time in a long while, Lucas felt like there was a way forward—a chance at rebuilding what had been broken.

Uncle Kade's Wisdom: The Price of Redemption

Lucas wandered to a quiet alley behind the arena, his shoulders slumped in defeat. The weight of the world pressed down on him. That's when Uncle Kade found him, standing in the shadows like he always did when Lucas needed him most.

"You're not alone in this, boy," Kade said gently, his voice full of understanding. "I know you think you've failed him. But redemption… that's not something you earn overnight."

Lucas didn't respond. He stood still, letting the weight of his uncle's words settle over him like a heavy blanket. He knew Kade was right, but it didn't make things easier. The guilt gnawed at him, and the apology he longed to offer seemed like it would never be enough.

"I never meant for any of this to happen," Lucas said, his voice cracking with the weight of the confession. "I never meant to hurt him. But I did. And I can't take it back."

Kade placed a hand on Lucas's shoulder, offering him quiet comfort. "You're right. You can't take it back. But you can move forward. You can show him you've learned from this. Show him you're not the same man who made those choices."

Lucas nodded slowly, the words sinking in. The road ahead would be hard, but for the first time in a long while, he felt a spark of hope.

"I'll try," Lucas whispered. "I will. I don't know how… but I will."

The Road Ahead: Unfinished Business

As the night wore on, the celebration continued, but Jacob and Lucas both knew that the real battle had just begun. Jacob's victory had given him a sense of closure, but it hadn't erased the scars of the past. For Lucas, it was the first step toward redemption, but he knew the road ahead would be a long one. The wound was deep, but healing had begun, and it wouldn't be easy.

The next morning, as the sun rose over the quiet ranch, Jacob and Lucas stood side by side, watching the horizon. Neither of them spoke, but the unspoken understanding between them was clear. There would be no easy answers. No quick fixes. No promises of painless recovery.

But there was something else, too. The quiet strength between them, forged in the heat of struggle, was still there. They had both come through the worst of it. And now, the road ahead, though uncertain, felt like something they might be able to walk together.

As the light touched the earth, breaking the long night, the weight of the past began to feel a little less oppressive. The silence between them wasn't filled with bitterness anymore, but with something quieter, something stronger—hope.

There would be no sudden changes, no miraculous transformations. But one thing was clear: they were both ready to rebuild. Together.

CHAPTER 54
A NEW DAWN

Rebuilding Trust

The morning sun spilled over the horizon, painting the sky in soft hues of gold and orange. Jacob stood on the porch, his hands resting against the railing, watching the world wake up. The ranch, bathed in the quiet stillness of early morning, felt miles away from the storm inside him. The victory in the arena, once a triumph, now seemed distant and hollow, overshadowed by the complexity of what was unfolding between him and Lucas.

It had been a long night, filled with difficult conversations and slow revelations. Wounds had been reopened, old scars exposed. But this morning, there was something different in the air—a subtle shift, a soft change in the tension that had gnawed at him for so long. It wasn't a solution, not yet, but it was a beginning.

Lucas stepped out of the house, his eyes still heavy from the weight of the previous day. As he stood there, shoulders squared more firmly than before, Jacob noticed something in his posture—a flicker of resolve, of something deeper that hadn't been there the day before. They didn't speak immediately. The words felt too heavy, too fragile for the moment.

Finally, Jacob broke the silence, his voice low and raw. "I didn't expect this, Lucas," he said, barely above a whisper. "Not after everything."

Lucas hesitated, his gaze not quite meeting Jacob's. He wanted to say the right thing, but what could he say? Was there even a chance to make things right? "I know," he replied, his voice small but filled with regret. "I didn't either. But… I'm here now. Trying to make things right."

The air between them thickened with unspoken truths. Silence stretched like a taut wire, pulling at the seams of their fragile connection. The breeze stirred the leaves in the trees, barely noticeable, a quiet contrast to the heaviness that hung in the air.

Lucas cleared his throat and took a step closer, his voice cracking slightly. "I messed up," he said, each word a painful admission. "And I can't keep running from that. I've run so far, for so long. But I can't anymore."

Jacob's gaze flickered to Lucas's face, his brow furrowing as the weight of Lucas's words settled in. The morning light flickered across his features, but his mind drifted back to all the moments that had led to this—the betrayals, the heartache, the ways they had both failed each other. But there was something different in Lucas now, something more real than what he had seen before. It made Jacob pause.

"Redemption doesn't come easy," Jacob said finally, his voice steady but burdened. "It's not just about saying the right things. It's about action. Day after day. Proving you're ready to change. Trust… it doesn't come in words, Lucas." His gaze sharpened, the weight of his words steady as he met Lucas's eyes. "You've got to prove it."

Lucas looked down at his hands, his fingers fidgeting nervously, as though the words he needed to say were still caught in his throat. He wanted to beg for forgiveness, to throw himself at Jacob's feet and make promises he wasn't sure he could keep. But instead, he just looked up, his eyes meeting Jacob's with raw sincerity. There were no easy fixes. No way to erase the past. But he had to try.

"I want to," Lucas said quietly, his voice thick with emotion. "I'm not asking for forgiveness overnight. I know I have a long road ahead, but I'm ready to walk it. No matter how hard it gets."

Jacob studied him, his expression unreadable. But there was something softer in his eyes now—something that wasn't there before. The weight of the past still pressed heavily on his chest, but he saw something in Lucas's gaze, something vulnerable and determined, that made him pause. It was a crack in the wall Lucas had built, and for the first time, Jacob felt a flicker of hope that this might be real.

"You're not alone in this," Jacob said, his voice firm but carrying an underlying warmth. "But know this—trust takes time. You can't rush it. You've got to earn it."

Lucas swallowed hard, the gravity of Jacob's words sinking in. How long would it take? Weeks? Months? Years? He didn't have the answers. But there was one thing he was sure of: He wasn't going to give up.

"I will," Lucas replied, his voice low but filled with quiet conviction. "I'll earn it. I swear."

Jacob's gaze lingered on him, the silence hanging heavy. There was still so much between them, so much left unsaid. But something had shifted. There was now a small opening, a crack in the wall. For the first time, Jacob believed it could be real. They both had a long way to go, but this moment… it could be the start of something new.

"We'll get there," Jacob said finally, his tone still guarded but lighter than before. "But it's going to take time."

The two men stood side by side, watching as the sun rose higher in the sky. The silence between them no longer felt like a chasm. It was quiet, yes, but now it felt different—less like a gap between them and more like a space they were both willing to step into, one uncertain step at a time. The morning sun illuminated the horizon, casting a golden glow over the world, a promise of a new beginning.

For the first time in a long while, both men felt something shift—a fragile, quiet hope. The road ahead would be long and uncertain, full of challenges, but they were both willing to take the first steps together.

CHAPTER 55
THE RIDE OF A LIFETIME

The Arrests

Jacob stood frozen as the flashing lights of the police cruisers pulsed in rhythm with his heartbeat. The roar of celebration around him—cheers, clapping, shouts of victory—sounded distant, as though muffled underwater.

He wasn't cheering. He couldn't.

Just feet away, Jake, Adam, Bob, and Lucas were being handcuffed, their faces pale and unreadable beneath the harsh glare of the flashing reds and blues. The officers moved with practiced efficiency, leading them toward the squad cars.

Jacob watched silently, arms limp at his sides. He should've felt triumphant. But all he felt was… hollow.

Was this what victory looked like?

His stomach churned with something bitter. The people who'd made his life hell were finally facing justice. And yet… watching them being carted off didn't fill him with satisfaction.

It felt like something was broken—something deeper than bones or rules.

Lucas briefly met Jacob's eyes before ducking into the cruiser, his jaw clenched, his expression unreadable. There was no smugness in that look. Just pain. And maybe something else—regret.

The sound of the doors slamming shut echoed in Jacob's mind long after the squad cars pulled away into the night.

How did it come to this?

The flag. The arena. The brotherhood. It had all felt so real just days ago. Now it felt like it was slipping through his fingers, like dust he couldn't hold onto.

There was no crown in this victory. No throne. Only silence.

The Court Hearing

Morning came like a punch to the gut.

Jacob sat in the passenger seat of Erick's truck, the city yawning awake around them. The streets were busy with honking horns and scattered conversations, but none of it touched him.

His mind was still trapped in the images of the night before.

Nick sat in the back seat, his usual energy muted, his gaze fixed out the window. Erick drove, jaw tight, focused. No one spoke. There was too much weight in the air.

When they arrived at the courthouse, the sterile white building seemed to mock him—unfeeling, indifferent. Inside, the fluorescent lights buzzed overhead, casting pale shadows. The walls smelled like paper, ink, and stale coffee.

At the counter, the clerk handed Jacob a stack of documents.

"Sign here, here, and here," she said, barely glancing up.

Jacob nodded, mechanically obeying. His hand trembled slightly as he signed, the pen dragging across the paper like a lifeline.

Then she asked it.

"You're sure you don't want to press charges?"

The question was casual—too casual.

Jacob froze.

He stared at the paper. His thoughts raced. Press charges? He had the right. They had sabotaged him, hurt him, tried to ruin everything.

But what would that change now?

He lowered the pen and looked her in the eye.

"No," he said softly. "I'm not pressing charges."

The clerk blinked. "Are you sure?"

"I'm sure." He slid the forms back. "This wasn't about revenge."

She gave a slight nod and filed the papers without another word, but Jacob could feel the silent judgment in her glance as he turned away. He didn't care. He hadn't done it for her approval.

He'd done it to let go.

The Meal

Later that afternoon, in a quiet corner of a small restaurant, the clink of silverware and low conversation filled the space. But at Jacob's table, the silence was thick.

He stared down at the salad he hadn't touched. The bright greens seemed to mock his mood, fresh and full of life, while he felt drained, empty.

Nick and Erick made a weak attempt at conversation—weather, headlines, local gossip—but it landed flat.

Across the table sat Bob and Jake. The air between them was charged like a storm about to break. Bob fidgeted with his napkin, jaw clenched. Jake tapped an angry rhythm on the table, his glare fixed in the distance.

Jacob kept replaying the moment in court, the papers, the choice. He hadn't pressed charges, but it hadn't healed anything.

"So…" Nick finally broke the silence, forcing a smile. "You think you'll ride in the next rodeo?"

Jacob hesitated, fork halfway to his mouth. The lights. The crowd. The pressure. Could he go back to all that?

"Why not?" he said after a pause. "Everyone expects me to."

The lie hung in the air.

Jake snapped.

His hand slammed on the table, the sound cutting through the restaurant. Plates rattled. Heads turned.

"Why not?" Jake growled. "You think you can just waltz back in and act like you didn't nearly destroy everything?"

Jacob narrowed his eyes. "What are you talking about? I *won*. I earned this. You tried to sabotage me, Jake."

"You think winning fixes it?" Jake fired back. "You think walking away makes it right?"

Bob stood up, his silence finally giving way to rage. His fists clenched at his sides. Jake followed, his fury palpable.

Without another word, the two of them left the table and walked out, the door swinging behind them.

"Men, can we just—can we get along for once?" Lucas's voice cracked, desperate. But they were gone.

He turned back to Jacob with a nervous chuckle, trying to lighten the mood. "You know, thanks for last night, man. I didn't sleep a wink. I was afraid somebody might… you know…" He trailed off, waving his hand vaguely.

Jacob let out a breath and shook his head. "I should probably charge you for protection."

Lucas smiled faintly. "I guess I owe you a drink."

But Jacob didn't feel like laughing. He nodded, grateful for the gesture, but his chest still felt heavy. The fight wasn't over—it had only changed forms.

The Aftermath

Jacob sat in the booth long after the others had quieted. He stared down at his hands, wondering how he'd ended up here—at the top, and yet somehow at the edge of something deeper than loss.

Erick stared out the window. Nick bounced his leg under the table, anxious. But both of them stayed silent. They could feel the weight pressing down on him.

Finally, Nick spoke. "What now?"

Jacob looked down, his voice a whisper. "I don't know. I guess… I'll figure it out."

Erick turned to him. "It's not over, Jacob. You've still got your fire. You're still standing."

"Barely," Jacob muttered.

"But standing," Nick added. "That counts for something."

Jacob thought about the flag—the symbol of his fight, of redemption. But what had it really cost him?

"I just wanted to be something," he said, his voice cracking. "Something real. But now I feel like I've lost everything."

Erick reached across the table. "You haven't lost who you are."

Jacob shook his head. "And what if that's not enough?"

The silence returned, but it felt less oppressive now, more like a shared moment of honesty.

Then, the door creaked open. Lucas returned. His face was tired, but his eyes had something new in them—resolve.

"You're not alone, Jacob," he said, sliding into the booth. "We all make mistakes. But we don't have to live inside them forever."

Jacob looked up. Lucas's words landed deeper than he expected.

"You've got more ahead than you think," Lucas said softly. "Whatever you decide next—I know you'll make it count."

Jacob blinked back the emotion rising in his throat. Maybe Lucas was right. Maybe there was still time.

"Thanks," Jacob said. "I'm not sure what's next… but maybe I'll try. Maybe I can still make this right."

Nick grinned. "That's the spirit, cowboy."

Jacob smiled—faint, but real.

The future was unclear. The ride wasn't over.

But for the first time in a long while, he was ready to take the reins.

Chapter 56
The Anticipation

The Weight of the Past

The days after their conversation passed in a blur.

Jacob kept his distance from Lucas, but it wasn't silence rooted in resentment anymore. It was something else. An understanding. The kind that forms when two men realize they've both been walking wounded, carrying burdens they were too proud to admit were crushing them.

Lucas was changing. Not dramatically. Not loudly. But with quiet effort. Gone was the cocky smirk, the careless swagger. Now, his hands were calloused from early mornings at the stable. His voice was humbler, his posture less defiant. Every act of service, every moment of restraint—it wasn't redemption yet, but it was the slow crawl toward it.

Jacob saw the struggle in him. He knew it intimately—the way guilt clings to your spine, the way regret creeps into your thoughts when the world goes still.

They weren't rivals anymore.

They were reflections.

The rodeo loomed just days away. The town buzzed with anticipation. For most, it was a spectacle. For Jacob, it had become something more. The arena, once a proving ground, now felt sacred. This wasn't about victory or recognition. It was about closure. About purpose. About facing the ghost of who he once was—and letting it go.

The Mirror and the Morning

On the morning of the rodeo, Jacob stood in front of the mirror.

His hat sat square on his head, shadowing eyes that held no thrill, just quiet fire. He stared at himself, not in vanity but in reckoning. The man staring back wasn't chasing applause anymore. He was also not trying to outrun the shame, the doubt, the pain.

He had already survived them.

Outside, the sun spilled gold over the ranch. The smell of hay clung to the air, and hooves clomped softly in the distance. He stepped out into the morning, boots thudding against packed dirt.

Lucas was already out there, brushing down a mare. Sweat dampened his shirt. Dust lined his sleeves.

"You ready?" Jacob asked, walking up beside him.

Lucas looked up. His face was flushed, but there was a light in his eyes that hadn't been there before. A kind of fragile peace.

"Yeah," he said, simple and sure.

Jacob nodded. "It's not about perfection. It's about the heart."

He clapped Lucas lightly on the back. "And you've got plenty of that."

Lucas smirked, then shrugged. "Let's try not to get blood on the new truck, yeah?"

Jacob chuckled. "No promises."

The Ceremony

By sunset, the arena pulsed with energy.

The bleachers overflowed. Flags waved like prayers. Laughter and cheers rose in waves as the contestants made their way through the dirt.

Jacob stood at the edge of it all, hands at his sides. The lights above weren't just bulbs—they were suns burning down. The roar of the crowd felt distant, like thunder underwater. When his name was called, he walked forward, each step echoing with years of fight, fall, and rise.

At the podium, he paused.

A thousand faces looked back at him. But all he could see was the journey. The voices that had tried to drown him. The quiet moments when quitting seemed like the only sane option. The hands that had lifted him. The prayers he didn't know were being whispered.

He took a breath. And then another.

Not fear. Not anxiety.

Just clarity.

"I stand here today," Jacob began, voice even, "not because of the victories I've earned… but because of the grace I've been given."

The crowd quieted. Not a whisper. Not a cough. Just listening.

"There were days I didn't think I'd make it. Nights when I questioned everything. But the truth is… I didn't walk this alone. The people who stood by me, who prayed for me, fought for me, held me when I couldn't hold myself, they're the real reason I'm standing here."

His gaze drifted toward Lucas, standing near the edge of the arena, hat in hand. Jacob's voice wavered—but didn't break.

"To those learning how to forgive themselves… keep going. The path isn't straight. It's painful. But it's worth it."

Applause swelled slowly, like a wave rolling to shore. And Jacob, standing beneath a sky that had once felt so far away, let the moment settle in his bones.

The Suspenseful End

As the crowd roared and the ceremony closed, Jacob lingered.

The lights dimmed. The arena emptied. But something in the air felt… wrong—Like the hush before a thunderclap.

Across the dirt lot, he saw them.

Jake. Bob. And their crew. Standing just beyond the reach of the spotlight. Faces still. Eyes burning. Their arrest hadn't happened yet. Delays. Technicalities. A window before the law came down.

But this—this presence—wasn't a coincidence.

They weren't here to clap.

Jacob's heartbeat shifted. The noise of the crowd faded into static. His breath slowed, his instincts sharpened. He saw it in their faces—not just resentment.

Something more.

Something calculating.

Then—footsteps behind him.

Slow. Familiar.

Jacob turned.

Lucas stood there, silent, jaw tight. His eyes flicked toward Jake's group. Then back to Jacob.

They didn't speak. They didn't need to.

The past had come to watch the present rise.

The New Ride

Later that night, the lot was nearly empty.

A new, gleaming Ford F-150 sat waiting—clean, full of promise, untouched by blood or mud.

Jacob approached it, his boots kicking up the quiet dust. He paused just before climbing in, looking at his reflection in the truck's window. For a moment, he didn't see himself.

He saw his father.

He saw every failure, every prayer, every mile that brought him here.

Lucas joined him, leaning on the hood. The two stood there, the soft rumble of celebration fading behind them.

"Still think we should've taken that beach trip," Lucas muttered.

Jacob cracked a grin. "Beaches don't have rodeos."

"Yeah, but they've got less mobs."

Jacob looked up at the sky.

The stars were starting to bloom.

The night was warm. But something colder was coming.

"They're not done," Jacob said. "Jake. Bob. Whatever they're planning… it's not over."

Lucas nodded. "Let them come."

Jacob looked at him.

Together, they climbed into the truck.

As the engine rumbled to life and the headlights cut through the night, Jacob whispered, not to Lucas, not even to himself, but to the road ahead:

"I didn't survive just to live. I survived to ride again."

And with that, they drove into the dark.

The stars behind them.

The unknown ahead.

The reckoning unfinished.

422

CHAPTER 57
THE ROAD AHEAD

A New Path

The night after the ceremony, Jacob sat alone in his truck. The stadium lights had dimmed, the cheering crowd had dispersed, and the dust from the rodeo still swirled faintly through the quiet town like a ghost that didn't yet know it was time to rest.

A trophy sat in the passenger seat beside him—solid, gleaming, proud. But its shine did not warm him.

He stared out the windshield, unmoving, his hands resting on the wheel as if the next turn needed divine permission. The road ahead stretched out like a question. His chest rose and fell in a slow rhythm, not from fatigue, but from the weight of everything that had brought him here.

Not just the victory but the voices, the sacrifices, the ones lost, and the ones found.

Jacob leaned over and opened the glovebox. Inside, tucked in the corner, was a red bandana—faded and frayed. Chuka's. The laughter of his friend echoed for a second in his mind. He pulled it out gently, thumb grazing the soft cloth like it was a relic. Right next to it, a crumpled paper wrapper still smelled faintly of jollof—Mama's last snack before the airport.

He smiled—sadly, sweetly.

He could almost hear her voice again:

"Jacob, don't let that hat squeeze your head too tight, Cowboy."

His eyes flicked to the rearview mirror. The town lay still behind him—lights low, like a theater after the final act. He could still see the glint of the arena's roof, now quiet, now done.

But he wasn't done.

Not by a long shot.

He reached for the key, and with a soft twist, the engine roared to life.

Outside, the wind picked up, swirling dust through the headlights, like spirits gathering in ceremony. The truck's cabin filled with the soft hum of motion, and Jacob gripped the wheel like a man about to ride into a storm.

Because, in some way, he was.

The open road welcomed him, not with certainty, but with freedom. Ahead, the blacktop curved into the dark, disappearing into dawn's approaching breath. The early sky was smeared with blues and purples, like a watercolor still wet with wonder. Behind him, the past faded with each turn of the tires.

The horizon was a hush. Not an ending but a call.

He passed the corral and the barn—landmarks that once defined him. And though they stirred something in his chest, they no longer owned him. They were not where he belonged. Not anymore.

Jacob rolled down the window slightly. The wind rushed in, cool and sharp, laced with earth and dawn and promise. And somewhere deep within that breeze, he swore he heard hooves.

Not just memories.

Possibilities.

He glanced at the empty seat beside him and whispered, "Let's ride."

The road stretched endlessly now, neither friend nor foe, but something older, something that judged no one and offered everything. It didn't promise comfort, didn't promise peace. But it whispered one thing:

Keep going.

The hum of the tires was steady, almost holy.

A low rumble stirred far ahead, not from the truck but from the sky. A faint thunderhead loomed on the horizon, distant, pulsing like a heartbeat beneath the clouds. Jacob squinted at it, unconcerned.

Let it come.

The man he had once been would've turned back. But that man was gone, swallowed by fire and forged again.

The road wasn't just a path. It was a crucible. And Jacob Obi was no longer running. He was riding.

As the sun crested the hills, casting long shadows behind him, Jacob looked into the rearview mirror one last time. The town, the rodeo, the ceremony—they were part of his story. But they were no longer *the* story.

His home wasn't behind him. It was wherever his heart could stand tall—unafraid, unbroken, and full of grace.

And so, he drove forward.

Into the wind.

Into the hush of a coming storm.

Into the firelight of a new beginning.

Into the next chapter.

Because the flame still burned.

And the road ahead had only just begun.

CHAPTER 58
THE CROWN OF THE COWBOY

Jacob's Moment

The sun blazed down on the rodeo arena, casting a warm, golden hue over the dusty grounds. The final round was fast approaching. The tension in the air was palpable, buzzing with anticipation as the crowd roared with excitement. The smell of sweat, leather, and freshly turned dirt filled the air, mingling with the rhythmic pounding of hooves on the earth.

Jacob stood at the edge of the arena, his fingers tight around the reins of his horse. The cheers from the crowd felt distant, muffled by the steady thrum of his own heartbeat. His chest tightened, but it wasn't the same nervous energy that had once shaken him before every event. No. This time, it was different. This time, Jacob was no longer just a man fighting for a title. He had transformed. He had faced the demons of his past and emerged stronger, wiser, and more resolute.

He had shed the uncertainty, the self-doubt, the need for validation. The rodeo was no longer about the trophy—it was about showing the world, and himself, who he had become. A Nigerian Cowboy, proud of his heritage, proud of his roots, and proud of the man he had grown into.

Jacob took a deep breath, letting the fresh, warm air fill his lungs. The crowd was here to witness the rodeo, but deep down, he knew there was something far bigger unfolding. He had brought his culture into this world, his story, his spirit. And now, it was his moment to stand tall. He was ready. But before he took the stage, he needed a moment of peace—a quiet moment to himself.

He found an empty chair behind the stalls and collapsed into it with a deep sigh. These moments of solitude, so rare before the storm, were precious. He'd been running on adrenaline for weeks, and now, as he sat, he could feel the weight of it all.

He closed his eyes briefly, allowing the hum of the crowd to wash over him from afar. *Just a moment*, he thought, as though trying to bargain with time. But his moment of peace was short-lived.

The Unexpected Encounter

"Well, well, well," a voice sliced through his thoughts.

Jacob opened his eyes just in time to see Jake, Adam, and Bob swaggering into the area. Jake, ever the menace, had that familiar smug grin plastered on his face. He didn't even bother to acknowledge Jacob, brushing past him like a cockroach with a crown.

And just as Jacob thought the worst was over, Jake did what he did best: make everything worse. Jake spat out a wad of gum, right next to Jacob's chair, as if marking his territory.

Jacob blinked. His first instinct was to roll his eyes. Was this really happening? He looked down at the offending piece of gum, a twinge of irritation sparking in his chest. "This guy," he muttered under his breath.

He stood up, determined to shake it off, but then—he felt it. The sticky, slimy texture beneath him. He froze. He had unknowingly sat on the very same gum Jake had so lovingly discarded. A wave of frustration and embarrassment washed over him. "Perfect. Just what I needed."

Trying to scrape the gum off his pants while maintaining his dignity was no easy task. The absurdity of the situation made him want to laugh, but there was no time for that.

Before he could fully recover, Erick and Nick entered the scene, their eyes narrowing as they noticed Jake's move. Without hesitation, Erick charged forward like a bull, tackling Jake to the ground.

"You've gotta be kidding me," Jacob muttered, fighting the urge to laugh.

Nick, seeing the chaos, shouted, "You guys belong in jail!"

Jacob couldn't help himself. The ridiculousness of it all was almost too much. "I'm about to do the rodeo of my life, and I'm sitting here with gum on my pants. I don't need this drama." He scrubbed at his backside, muttering to himself. The anger still simmered beneath the surface, but it felt lighter now.

Lucas's Intervention

Just as things seemed to escalate, Lucas entered, his calm presence cutting through the chaos. "Jacob," he said, his voice steady and firm, yet filled with the quiet wisdom Jacob had come to rely on. "You're bigger than this."

Jacob lifted his gaze, meeting Lucas's eyes. There it was again—Lucas's unwavering belief in him. It grounded him. "You're right," he muttered, his heart pounding in his chest. But despite himself, a smile tugged at the corners of his lips. "I'm bigger than gum on my pants."

Lucas didn't crack a smile, but there was something in his eyes that Jacob appreciated. "Exactly. You've come too far to let something small like this mess with your head. Focus. The world's watching you."

Jacob took a deep breath. The anger didn't subside right away, but the clarity did. Lucas was right. This was his moment, and no one—not Jake, not the gum, not the petty distractions—was going to take it away.

As the authorities arrived, Jake, Adam, and Bob were escorted out, their time in the arena officially up. The air began to settle, but Jacob could still feel the weight of the moment. This was it.

The Rodeo Event

The final round began. Jacob mounted his horse, his muscles coiled with anticipation, his mind laser-focused. The crowd's energy thrummed through the arena. The music blared, the announcer's voice boomed, and the pulse of the rodeo could be felt in every nerve.

Jacob kicked his horse into action. The first move was smooth. The second was perfect. But then... a moment of hesitation. A small, almost imperceptible misstep. The horse shifted just slightly, throwing off Jacob's rhythm. It wasn't catastrophic, but enough to remind him of his vulnerability—the one he had worked so hard to overcome.

His breath hitched, but then he steadied himself. He wasn't perfect. And in that moment, he remembered something: it wasn't about perfection—it was about heart. And his heart was in this.

With renewed determination, Jacob completed the rest of the round, his confidence building with every stride. By the time the final bell rang, the arena erupted in cheers. But Jacob, for once, didn't hear them. He wasn't chasing applause anymore.

Jacob's Victory

As he dismounted, the roar of the crowd felt distant, as though it were coming from far away. His heart was still racing, but there was something new—a quiet peace, a contentment he had never felt before.

The trophy was just an object, a symbol. The real victory was in the man he had become—the Nigerian Cowboy, who had stayed true to himself. He had learned that this journey was never about proving others wrong. It was about proving to himself that he was enough.

The Reflection

As Jacob walked away from the arena, his thoughts drifted to the people who had helped him get here—his family, his friends, Lucas, Uncle Kade. Without them, this moment wouldn't have been possible.

He looked at the trophy in his hand, not as a symbol of what he had won, but as a reminder of everything he had overcome. He had fought for this moment, but the real victory was in who he had become. The Nigerian Cowboy. Proud. Strong. Unshaken.

He thought back to the long days on the ranch with his family, his mother's words of encouragement echoing in his mind, and the lessons his father had instilled in him. He had worked hard for this, but it wasn't just about the rodeo—it was about the values that had shaped him, the community that had supported him, and the heritage he carried with pride.

And in the quiet aftermath of his victory, Jacob knew this wasn't the end—it was only the beginning.

After Jacob's Victory—Hearts Unbridled: The Night the Arena Loved Back

As Jacob walked away from the arena, the roar of the crowd still ringing in his ears, he felt a strange pull. The adrenaline was wearing off, and the initial rush of victory was fading into something deeper, something richer. The trophy in his hand felt heavier now, not because of the weight, but because of the meaning it carried. It was more than just an object—it was a testament to everything he had overcome, to everything he had become.

But then—something shifted.

Jacob paused.

He turned back.

Without a word, he made his way back to the center of the dusty arena, his boots crunching softly on the earth beneath him. The crowd began to quiet as if sensing the change, the energy gently winding down after the roar of the rodeo.

With a humble yet powerful grace, Jacob dropped into a bow, his head low, as if offering his heart to those watching.

A ripple of applause began—soft at first, tentative—then swelling, growing into a crescendo that resonated throughout the arena.

Voices rose in cheers, claps beating like thunder.

Jacob slowly lifted his head and met the crowd's gaze. His eyes, usually so guarded, were now wide open with emotion. He saw the faces of cowboys, cowgirls, old timers, and young riders—all of them watching him. And in their eyes, he saw something he had never expected: Respect. Acceptance.

He bowed again—deeper this time—and the response was electric. The collective voice of cowboys and cowgirls erupted into a thunderous ovation—shouts, whistles, hats flying off in reverence.

For a third time, Jacob bowed, and the arena seemed to tremble, not just from the noise, but from the force of their admiration. The crowd was no longer just cheering for his victory. They were cheering for him. The man he had become. The Nigerian Cowboy.

Then, standing tall, fist raised high in a champion's salute, Jacob soaked in the love pouring from every corner of the stands.

The cries of the crowd resonated with a shared understanding—a communion of spirit that needed no words. These were no ordinary cheers; they were an embrace. A claim.

Who would have thought a boy from Nigeria could capture the hearts of this rugged, weathered cowboy community?

Yet here they were—every hat lifted, every voice raised in honor of Jacob. This was a moment suspended in time—a beautiful tableau of acceptance and triumph.

They didn't just cheer for his skill; they celebrated the man he was— their brother in the dust and thunder of the rodeo.

And as the crowd stood, so did Jacob—united, victorious, loved.

CHAPTER 59
THE ANTICIPATION – THE WEIGHT OF THE FUTURE

The Quiet After the Storm

The night after the rodeo was too quiet.

Jacob stood at the edge of the now-empty arena, floodlights dimming one by one like stars bowing out from a sky that had seen too much. Victory—his victory—hung in the air like smoke after a wildfire. It should have tasted sweet. Instead, it felt like something unfinished.

Lucas stood beside him, hands in his jacket pockets, eyes tracing the ground where the crowd had roared just hours ago.

"You did it, Jacob," he said, voice hushed but proud. "You really did it."

Jacob offered a faint smile but didn't look away from the arena dirt. "Doesn't feel like I thought it would."

Lucas glanced at him. "How'd you think it'd feel?"

Jacob took a slow breath. "I thought it would be louder. I thought I'd feel… complete. Like I'd finally proven something." He paused, eyes narrowing as if searching for something he couldn't name. "But standing here—it's not the applause I'm thinking about. It's what comes next. What's still out there."

Lucas took a step closer, boots crunching softly on gravel. "You've changed, man. I've seen it. You're not just a cowboy now. You're a survivor. A fighter. You earned every second of this."

Jacob looked at him, grateful, but his heart was somewhere else, somewhere off in the dark.

"Do you know where Nick went?" he asked suddenly, tension creeping into his voice.

Lucas frowned. "Nick? No. He said he'd catch up after the ceremony. He was with Dre and Kalu earlier, I think."

Jacob's brow furrowed. "I haven't seen him. Not since before the ride."

Lucas scanned the quiet stadium. "Maybe he just left early?"

"No," Jacob said softly. "He wouldn't. Not without a word. And it's not just him. Dre's gone too."

The silence grew heavier.

The Vanishing Thread

As they walked toward the truck, the laughter from the nearby parking lot felt like it belonged to another world. Jacob's footsteps slowed, his heart beating faster.

"He was nervous today," Jacob murmured. "Nick. I could see it. He tried to play it off, but something was eating at him."

Lucas gave a slow nod. "You think he got spooked?"

"I think he got watched." Jacob glanced over his shoulder toward the shadows where Jake and his crew had stood earlier, bitter after their loss.

"You think Jake's behind this?" Lucas asked, voice low.

Jacob didn't answer right away. "I think losing didn't sit well with them. And Nick's always been loud. Too loud to ignore."

Lucas shook his head. "I swear, if they laid a finger on him—"

"They'll answer for it," Jacob said, his voice cold.

A moment of silence passed.

"Or maybe…" Lucas added cautiously, "Nick walked off on his own."

Jacob stared at him. "That's what scares me more."

An Uneasy Ride Home

The road back to the ranch stretched long and dark. The truck's headlights carved through the shadows, but Jacob's mind drifted, circling around the same unspoken dread.

"What if he's gone?" he said quietly.

Lucas turned toward him. "Gone where?"

"I don't know," Jacob admitted. "Taken. Hiding. Running. I just know he's not here. And I feel it—like a string pulled too tight. Something's about to snap."

Lucas looked out the window. "Jake and Bob don't go quiet without planning something."

"I know," Jacob muttered. "And tonight feels like the start of something worse."

Lucas leaned back in his seat. "Maybe we need a reset. Some quiet time. No mobs. No fights. Just… a beach. Sun. Peace."

Jacob snorted. "Make sure it's SPF bulletproof."

Lucas laughed. "I'll bring the sunscreen. You bring the therapy."

Jacob let out a real chuckle—his first in hours. But the weight in his chest never left. It sat there, like a storm he could feel but not see.

The Shadow at the Ranch

They pulled into the ranch as the moon slipped behind the clouds, casting long shadows over the fields. As Jacob stepped out of the truck, a cold gust hit him, sending a shiver down his spine.

Then he saw it.

A figure—motionless, just beyond the tree line.

His breath caught.

"Lucas," he whispered. "You see that?"

Lucas turned. "What?"

"There." Jacob pointed. "Someone's standing there. Watching."

Lucas squinted, then shook his head. "I don't see anything."

But Jacob knew what he saw.

The figure was still.

Then, like smoke, it was gone.

He jogged to the edge of the trees, scanning the darkness. Nothing. No movement. No sound. Just the rustle of leaves and the pounding of his heart.

But he had seen him.

Nick.

Or someone who wanted to be seen as Nick.

And that was worse.

The Weight of Tomorrow

Jacob stood on the porch, arms folded across his chest, staring into the dark. His mind raced.

Where was Nick?

Why would he disappear?

Had Jake and the others made their move?

Or… had Nick left of his own will?

Lucas joined him, sipping from a steaming mug of coffee. "Still no word?"

Jacob shook his head.

"We'll find him," Lucas said. "You and me."

Jacob's jaw tightened. "We don't even know what we're looking for."

Lucas put a hand on his shoulder. "Then we start where we are."

Jacob nodded slowly. "This isn't over. Not by a long shot."

And as they stood there, with the night closing in around them, a single truth pressed in like a hand on the chest:

The rodeo was never the end. It was just the opening act.

CHAPTER 60
THE DISAPPEARANCE – A COWBOY'S SEARCH

The Morning After the Storm

The sun broke slowly across the horizon, stretching its amber fingers over the quiet fields of the ranch. Dew still clung to the grass like a memory refusing to let go. The golden haze should've brought peace, a new beginning after the storm of the rodeo.

But Jacob felt none of it.

He stood near the corral, arms folded tightly, boots planted on dry earth that felt far too still. His eyes swept the landscape like a soldier scanning for movement. But it wasn't what he saw—it was what he *didn't* see that clawed at him.

Nick was gone.

And not just Nick. Dre and Kalu, too. Vanished without a word.

They hadn't been seen since the celebration. They hadn't returned to their bunks. Their boots were still there, their gear untouched. No notes. No explanations. Just absence.

Lucas emerged from the barn, rubbing sleep from his eyes and holding a half-eaten biscuit in one hand.

"You know," he said around a mouthful, "I figured maybe Nick was pulling one of his dramatic early-morning meditations. But unless he's trying to find his inner cowboy out in the canyon, I think we've got a problem."

Jacob didn't smile.

"He'd never leave without telling me," he said flatly.

Lucas wiped his hands on his shirt, suddenly alert. "And Dre? Kalu?"

"Same."

Jacob's voice had a steel edge. Beneath it was something more dangerous than anger—**dread**.

The Ride Into Uncertainty

By late morning, the trail had gone cold—except for the feeling. That unshakeable knot in Jacob's gut.

They saddled up without another word, falling into the old rhythm: boots tightening stirrups, leather creaking, reins flicking gently. The sound of hooves hitting dirt echoed through the stillness like a ticking clock.

But this wasn't a rescue mission.

Not yet.

It was a **reckoning** waiting to be defined.

Lucas broke the silence. "Nick's always been loud. You'd hear him before you saw him. He jokes, he talks, he gets under your skin—he doesn't just vanish."

Jacob nodded. "That's what makes it feel wrong."

Lucas turned slightly. "You thinking Jake?"

"I'm thinking Jake doesn't forget a loss. Or forgive one."

Jacob's mind replayed the look on Jake's face after the rodeo—how his eyes didn't just show defeat. They showed **vengeance waiting for its moment**.

The Whisper Beneath the Dust

They rode south, past the edge of the ridge where the land dipped into a quiet gulch. The place felt strange—too silent, as if even the wind had taken cover.

Jacob dismounted first. He dropped to one knee and touched the ground.

"Tracks," he said, more to himself than to Lucas. "Recent. Three sets."

Lucas scanned the area. "Anything else?"

Jacob's fingers hovered over the impressions. "They weren't running. They were circling. Doubtful. Scared."

Lucas crouched beside him. "Reading the dirt again like it's scripture?"

Jacob's eyes narrowed. "The land doesn't lie."

A breeze stirred the dust. Something metallic floated with it, faint, like scorched iron—The scent of danger.

Lucas straightened. "You think they came here on their own?"

"I think they came here because someone led them," Jacob said. "And they didn't leave by choice."

The Voice in the Shadows

Something moved—just beyond two broken-down sheds.

Jacob's breath hitched.

He motioned for Lucas to stay back, then moved slowly, boots silent against the dirt. His hand hovered near his belt.

"Nick?" he called, steady and low. "If you're out here… say something."

A figure stepped out of the shadows.

Dirty. Staggering. Shirt torn. Face pale and drawn. Eyes wild.

It was Nick.

But not the Nick Jacob knew.

His body looked intact, but his spirit had been scraped raw. His eyes darted like he was being watched by ghosts Jacob couldn't see.

"Jacob…" His voice cracked—dry, hollow, laced with something that made the hairs on Jacob's neck stand up. "You shouldn't have come."

Jacob stepped forward, his voice gentler now. "We've been looking for you. What happened?"

Nick shook his head slowly. "They're still out there… Jake, Adam, Bob—they're not done. You think the rodeo changed anything?" He looked around as if the trees might swallow them whole. "They just moved to the shadows."

Jacob clenched his fists. "Where are Dre and Kalu?"

Nick's lip trembled. "I—I don't know. I thought they were with me. Then they weren't. And then… I realized I wasn't even with myself."

His knees buckled, and Jacob caught him—but Nick pulled away, panic overtaking reason.

"You don't get it," he whispered, eyes blazing with fractured fear. "*I was the bait.*"

A Voice That Wasn't Entirely His

Jacob reached for him again. "We're going to get you out of this. You're not alone."

Nick's voice shifted—no longer frantic, but strange… detached.

"You follow me, you lead them right back in. That's what they want. They're watching. Always. And if they can't win the rodeo, they'll win the soul."

Jacob froze. There was something about that last sentence—*"they'll win the soul"*—that didn't sound like Nick at all. Not the words. Not the cadence. It was as if something else had borrowed his tongue, just long enough to leave a scar.

And then, before Jacob could speak again—

Nick turned and ran. He disappeared into the tree line like a shadow swallowed by dusk.

Jacob gave chase, but found nothing.

Just silence, wind, and the ghost of something broken.

The Real Ride Begins

Lucas caught up a minute later, breathing hard. "Was that him?"

Jacob nodded.

"He looked like death warmed over," Lucas muttered. "What the hell happened to him?"

"I don't know," Jacob said. "But I'm going to find out."

Dusk Over Answers

They searched until the sun dipped low, coloring the sky in blood and bronze. Every turn brought more silence, more dust, more weight.

Finally, they stopped at a ridge overlooking the canyon.

Jacob dismounted and stared out, hands resting on the saddle horn.

"He's not just scared," he said. "He's broken. And if they did that to him…"

He didn't finish.

Lucas wiped his brow, shaking his head. "You think we'll find him again?"

Jacob's jaw clenched. "Yes. And when I do, I won't let go. Not this time."

The Glimmer Ahead

As the stars began to prick the sky, Jacob stood tall under their glow. His heart was heavy, but something deeper than fear lit inside him.

This wasn't just about Nick anymore.

It was about *all of them*—the broken, the baited, the brave.

The ones who disappeared because no one looked twice.

The ones who gave everything and still weren't safe.

The ones the mob thought it could silence.

Not today.

Jacob turned to Lucas, fire flickering in his eyes. "You coming?"

Lucas let out a tired grin. "Next time I want an adventure, remind me to pick the one with less ghosts and more hot cocoa."

Jacob cracked a real smile. "Deal."

They mounted up.

And as they rode into the night, Jacob knew one thing for sure:

He wasn't riding for trophies anymore.

He was riding for souls.

And he wouldn't stop until they all came home.

CHAPTER 61
THE CAMPFIRE ENCOUNTER – COWBOYS IN THE CROSSFIRE

The First Night in Unfamiliar Territory

The sun had bled out behind the ridge, staining the sky in streaks of bruised violet and burnt orange. The last warmth of the day vanished with it, replaced by a crisp wind that sliced low across the hills like a silent warning.

Jacob crouched near the fire they'd built—a small, crackling beacon against the vastness of the open range. The flames snapped at the night air, throwing long shadows across the dry grass and hard-packed earth. Beside him, Lucas poked at the embers with a thin branch, his face flickering between light and dark.

Rico and Chuka sat opposite them, flanking the perimeter with quiet vigilance. Both had ridden in from separate directions earlier that day, summoned by Jacob's discreet call for help—two trusted friends of Nick who had once ridden with him across cattle country and crooked borderlands. Now they were here again, not for profit or pride, but for **loyalty**.

This was Jacob's crew. Forged not by blood or title, but by fire, dust, and the kind of friendship that only comes from standing shoulder to shoulder through storms.

And still, Jacob couldn't shake the feeling that something unseen was watching them.

Firelight and Restlessness

Jacob rubbed the heels of his hands against his eyes. The fatigue pressing on him wasn't just from the miles. It was something heavier. A mental weight. The unanswered questions. The unknown fate of Nick. The eyes of the mob he could no longer ignore.

"You're quiet tonight," Lucas said, voice low and calm. "Not like you."

Jacob didn't look up. "I'm thinking."

Lucas nodded, letting the silence stretch. He understood when words had limits.

After a while, Jacob added, "Nick was never supposed to disappear like that. Not without a fight. If he's out there—hurt, trapped—I should've been the one beside him."

"Don't do that," Chuka said from the shadows. "You can't save everyone. But you can find him. That's why we're here."

Rico grunted in agreement. "You called. We came. That's what matters."

Jacob looked up at them—their tired eyes, their weathered hands, their quiet readiness.

"I'm not used to needing help," he said.

Lucas smirked. "Well, tonight you've got it."

And then—**a sound**.

Low. Distant.

A rumble like thunder, but not from the sky.

Jacob shot to his feet. His hand dropped to his holster. The others followed without a word—every muscle tight, every sense honed by instinct.

Hoofbeats.

Strangers in the Smoke

Through the haze of dusk, a group of riders emerged over the ridge.

Silhouettes. Lean. Tall in the saddle.

They approached in formation—too precise to be casual, too familiar with silence to be innocent. There were five of them.

No words were spoken. No greetings were called. Just the horses' slow clop and the weight of arrival.

"Well, well, well…" a gravel-edged voice finally broke the silence. "Looks like the Nigerian Cowboy's got himself a campfire sermon tonight."

Jacob's jaw tightened. "You lost?"

The speaker—a lanky man with a crooked hat and the sun-etched face of a man who'd made peace with violence—smiled without warmth.

"We travel where the wind takes us. And the wind's been whispering your name for days."

The woman beside him dismounted. Her coat flared open just enough to show steel beneath it. Her smile was measured. Calculated.

"Funny thing about wind," she said. "It carries stories. And yours? Let's just say it's getting real popular."

Jacob didn't flinch. "I don't trade in stories. I trade in truth."

She stepped forward, slowly circling the fire like a wolf tasting the air. "That so?"

Rico and Chuka rose behind Jacob. Lucas stayed at his flank. The fire crackled louder, as if sensing what the wind had brought.

The Word That Cuts

"You've been stirring up more than dust," the man said, his gaze unreadable. "The mob's not happy."

The word—**mob**—cut through the night like a knife.

Jacob didn't react on the outside. But inside, a tremor.

Lucas stepped forward. "And what's your interest in their business?"

"We're just messengers," the woman said lightly. "Call it… preventive outreach."

"More like scouting," Chuka muttered.

The woman's grin didn't waver. "Suit yourself."

The flames shifted. A log cracked. The firelight gleamed off the silver at her hip.

"Thing is," she continued, "you've been loud. Too loud. The rodeo. The flag. Your little stand in the dust."

Her voice dipped, almost conspiratorial. "They don't like loud."

Jacob tilted his head slightly. "Then tell them this: they should've shut me up when they had the chance."

The man's expression changed—just slightly. A twitch at the corner of his mouth. "Brave words. But brave men burn too."

The fire flared.

The woman turned to go, then paused. Her voice dropped to something softer… darker.

"Some flames don't die when the fire goes out. They linger. And they consume."

The Stranger's Final Warning

The last of the strangers—an older man, silent until now—stepped forward. His voice came like gravel scraped over stone, but there was something else beneath it. Something **otherworldly**. Not robotic, not ghostly. Just… distant. Timeless.

"Not all fires can be put out, Cowboy. But some were never meant to burn this long.

You keep feeding the wrong ones…and you'll forget what you were trying to light in the first place."

He held Jacob's gaze for a moment longer, then turned and mounted his horse.

The others followed, fading into the dark.

Their hoofbeats left no echo.

Only silence.

The Campfire Standoff

As the strangers disappeared, the fire seemed to dim. The wind slowed.

Jacob stood still, eyes on the place where they had vanished. The crew gathered behind him, expressions tight.

"You believe them?" Rico asked.

"I believe the mob knows exactly where we are," Jacob replied.

Chuka swore under his breath. Lucas checked his blade, re-sheathing it slowly.

"Looks like we're running out of time," he said.

Jacob's gaze returned to the fire. "We've been hunted before," he said. "But this time… we're ready."

The Oath of Dust and Flame

He turned to the crew.

"I won't lie to you. This isn't a trail with a clear end. It's a storm. And we're in the eye."

Nobody moved.

Then Rico nodded. "We've ridden through worse."

Lucas smirked. "Speak for yourself."

Chuka pulled his hat low. "Let's ride the storm."

Jacob looked around the fire—four men, four lives, one cause.

This wasn't just a crew.

This was a stand.

"We ride together," he said. "We protect what's ours."

The fire gave one last crack.

And then the wind picked up again.

458

CHAPTER 62
THE RECKONING

The Stillness Before the Storm

The sky was the color of ash.

No birds sang. No wind stirred the grass. Even the trees seemed to hold their breath.

Jacob stood at the crest of the ridge, one boot anchored in the dry earth, the other resting on a rock like a man preparing to deliver a sermon to the battlefield below. In the distance, the land stretched out in jagged veins—ridges and ravines and the skeletal remains of cattle fences long abandoned.

Behind him, Lucas, Chuka, Rico, and a growing circle of allies saddled their horses, checked their ammo, and tied red and white cloth around their arms. Some were old friends. Others were strangers who had heard the stories, seen the videos, felt something stir in their hearts when they heard the name *"The Nigerian Cowboy."*

Jacob tightened the knot around his wrist. The flag lay folded in his saddlebag—not just a relic, but a responsibility. A covenant.

He turned to face the others. His voice was low, steady. "They're coming."

Lucas gave a small nod. "Then we stand like giants."

A Shadow Returns

Before the sun broke the horizon, a silhouette stumbled out of the canyon mist.

Ragged. Slouched. Limping like a man stitched together with threadbare hope.

Jacob's heart seized in his chest.

"Nick?"

The figure staggered closer, his boots scraping stone. His clothes were torn, dried blood streaked his shirt, and his eyes—once full of mischief and laughter—now held something feral. Haunted.

Lucas ran forward but hesitated. "What happened to you?"

Nick blinked. His voice cracked, more breath than sound.

"They let me go… so I'd lead them to you."

Jacob stepped forward, arms steady, heart thundering. "You're safe now. You're with us."

Nick shook his head. "No one's safe. Not while they're still breathing."

He looked around, panic rising. "Dre… Kalu… they were with me. But then they weren't. It's like the world split. Like we were in two places at once. They told me… they'd spare me. All I had to do was talk."

Jacob's fists clenched. "What did you tell them?"

Nick's eyes filled with tears. "Nothing. I swear. But it didn't matter. They already knew everything. They'd been watching… listening. Since the first ride."

And then—his voice shifted. A deeper tone. Not his, not fully. Something borrowed.

"They're not hunting you to kill you. They want your flame. And if they can't put it out, they'll use it to burn the world."

Jacob staggered back, stunned by the sudden coldness in Nick's words.

Then, just as suddenly, Nick crumpled to the dirt—body intact, but spirit frayed.

And before Jacob could speak, **the first shot rang out.**

The Mob Descends

Dirt exploded near Jacob's feet. Then another shot. And another.

Hoofbeats thundered across the ridge. Over two dozen riders emerged through the low mist—black scarves fluttering like crows' wings, rifles drawn, spurs singing as horses charged.

Jake rode at the front. Adam and Bob at his flanks. Their eyes were hard with pride, fury, and fear of becoming irrelevant.

Lucas pulled his revolver. "They brought hell with them."

Jacob didn't flinch. "So did we."

From behind the trees, from nearby ridges and gullies, Jacob's crew rose—ranchers, rebels, dreamers, and outlaws. A mosaic of believers in freedom. In him.

The air was charged, every heartbeat a drumroll.

Dust and Fire

The clash came like lightning—sudden, merciless.

Horses collided. Bullets tore through the air. Chuka fired two rounds with the precision of a surgeon. Rico tackled a rider to the ground and threw a punch that echoed like thunder. Lucas rolled behind a wagon and picked off attackers one by one.

Jacob charged straight into the fray.

The flag flew behind him, tied to his saddle like a banner of defiance.

He wasn't just fighting back. He was *fighting for everyone and everything*—for Nick, for the silenced, for the kids back home who thought cowboys didn't look like them.

Jake found him.

They collided mid-charge, Jacob dismounting to meet him man to man.

"Still standing, huh?" Jake spat.

Jacob's lip bled, but he smiled. "Still rising."

They fought like two storms clashing—dust rising around them as fists, knees, and old grudges collided.

The Elder's Voice

The battle paused.

A new rider emerged. Not part of either crew. Draped in a long black coat, face obscured beneath a wide-brimmed hat.

He rode slowly, silently, as if the world parted for him.

Nick stirred from where he lay and whispered, "He's not just a man. He's… something else."

The rider stopped beside Jacob. His voice came like rusted wind chimes in a forgotten chapel—cold, lyrical, and ageless.

"You think this is about land? Or rodeos? You think the mob was ever your real enemy?

"This is about *fire*. And fire, once kindled, must choose: Will it warm the world…or consume it?"

Jacob stared at him. "Who are you?"

"A reminder."

And then the rider vanished—dust rising in his place.

The Rescue and the Turn

From the rear, a flare shot into the sky—green and sharp.

Nick had crawled to a rock and launched it.

Jacob looked where it pointed—and saw them, Dre and Kalu, tied to fence posts, barely conscious.

"Lucas—on me!"

Together, they tore through enemy lines, carving a path with grit and fire.

Jacob cut the ropes.

Dre blinked up. "You came."

Jacob smiled, jaw tight. "Always."

Jake Falls

Jake tried to run, spurring his horse toward the far ridge.

But Chuka was faster.

He intercepted him, gun drawn—but didn't fire.

Instead, he dismounted and walked up slowly.

Jake sneered. "What now, Cowboy? Gonna kill me?"

Chuka shook his head.

"No," he said. "You get to live. And you get to watch. Because men like you…the worst thing that can happen is being forgotten."

Legacy Forged in Ash

The mob fled.

Their riders scattered into the hills, names forgotten even before the dust settled.

Jacob dismounted slowly.

Nick leaned on Lucas. Dre and Kalu were being treated.

The wind returned. Not sharp. Not biting. Clean.

A new wind.

Jacob stared out across the horizon, where the sun had finally broken free of the mist.

Lucas stepped beside him. "It's over?"

Jacob shook his head. "No. But something new's begun."

Final Vow

That night, under the stars, Jacob unfolded the flag one last time.

He held it close. Not in victory. But in vow.

"This isn't the end. This is the beginning of the trail.

"For every soul who was broken. For every name they tried to bury. For every kid who was told they weren't enough—I ride."

The fire crackled behind him. And in the dark, something brighter than flame flickered in the hearts of all who watched.

The world wouldn't forget. The *Nigerian Cowboy* had taken his stand.

And the world would never be the same.

CHAPTER 63
THE LAST RIDE

The Silence After the Storm

The morning came soft, like the first breath after a long-held cry. The sky was streaked with gentle peach and indigo hues, brushing the rooftops of the ranch with quiet mercy. The earth was still damp from yesterday's blood and thunder, but the wind felt different now—cleaner, like a confession whispered into the open sky.

Jacob sat alone on the porch steps, the folded flag resting beside him. Not raised. Not waving. Just there—heavy with memory. His elbows rested on his knees, hands clasped loosely. Every breath felt sacred. Every heartbeat carried weight.

Down in the yard, Lucas tightened the last strap on a saddle. Chuka stood near the corral, sharpening a blade with the slow rhythm of a man thinking deeply. Rico adjusted the sling on his shoulder and fed a horse an apple. Nick leaned against the post, wrapped in a worn blanket. His eyes were sunken but alert, like the body hadn't caught up with the soul just yet.

Dre and Kalu remained inside the house, healing.

This morning wasn't about battle or victory. It was about something more rare: **what came after.**

Jacob stood and walked toward Nick.

"You good to ride?" he asked gently.

Nick raised his eyes. They were clearer than the day before, but still held a flicker of the wilderness he'd walked through. "Where to?"

Jacob's gaze lifted toward the distant ridge—toward the memory of the canyon, the ghosts of beginnings, and the burial ground of illusions.

"Back to where it started."

The Ride of Reflection

By mid-morning, five horses cut through the tall grass, hooves stirring up dust in the morning light. They rode slow, not like warriors returning from war, but like pilgrims seeking something sacred in the ruins of memory.

Jacob led, flag secured behind his saddle once more. Not flapping. Just resting. Like a torch in its sheath.

Nick rode beside him in silence. The others followed at a respectful distance.

After a while, Nick spoke, voice barely more than a breath.

"There were nights... when I thought I wasn't coming back. But it wasn't pain that broke me—it was silence. I couldn't hear my own thoughts anymore. Like they'd taken even that."

Jacob didn't speak.

Nick continued. "But then, out of nowhere, I remembered your voice. Not what you said... just the feeling of it. That quiet strength. And suddenly, I knew who I was again."

Jacob glanced at him, heart tightening. "You never left us. You just… took the long way back."

Nick gave a small, cracked smile. "Guess I always had a flair for drama."

Jacob chuckled softly. "Still do."

The Burial of the Hat

By dusk, they reached the canyon ridge. The sun dipped low, painting the horizon in hues of fire and forgiveness. Long shadows stretched across the open land like arms reaching back in time.

They dismounted in silence. Jacob approached the old sycamore tree—the same one that had once marked the edge of battle. He removed a small parcel from his saddlebag and unwrapped it.

Jake's hat.

Singed. Scarred. Bent at the rim. But still unmistakably his.

Jacob knelt and dug a shallow grave with his hands, slowly, methodically. When it was ready, he placed the hat inside.

Lucas stepped forward. "That's it? Just bury it and move on?"

Jacob looked at the earth, then at his friends. "This hat wasn't just his. It was the last piece of the lie we were told—that we had to become *them* to win. That we had to hate to survive. I'm done carrying their shadows."

He buried the hat and pressed the earth flat with his palm.

A prayer, unspoken.

A symbol, laid to rest.

The Promise in the Dust

The group gathered around as the wind stirred gently.

Nick looked out at the horizon. "So what now? Do we go back to the ranch? Back to normal?"

Jacob shook his head. "There is no normal anymore."

He walked to the edge of the cliff, where the world looked endless.

"We ride forward. Not to chase vengeance. Not to prove we're right. But because someone, somewhere, is watching. Maybe it's a kid in Lagos. Maybe it's a girl on a dirt road in Montana. Maybe it's someone who thinks they don't belong anywhere."

He turned to face them.

"And they'll need a story. A fire to follow. They'll need to know… we didn't give up.

That we rode on. For something bigger than ourselves."

He removed the flag from his saddle, unfolded it, and raised it gently to the wind. It fluttered—not with pride, but with quiet resolve.

"I make this vow," he said. "We protect the truth. We defend the forgotten. We carry the light.

And we never—ever—go silent again."

Lucas stepped forward and placed a hand on Jacob's shoulder.

Nick did the same.

Then Chuka.

Then Rico.

No words. Just weight. Just presence.

Five men, one flame.

Return with Fire in the Heart

They rode back under a starlit sky.

No torches. No drums.

Just hoofbeats and breath and the rhythm of a story that wouldn't die.

They were no longer riding to find themselves.

They were riding for **those who still needed to believe**.

CHAPTER 64
A COWBOY'S PROMISE

When the Trail Turns Quiet

A week had passed since the battle in the canyon.

The ranch had grown still again—not with the stillness of fear, but the hush of healing. Of rebuilding. Of beginning again.

Horses grazed beneath an open sky, brushed in watercolor blue. Tools clanked softly in the distance as fences were mended and barns restored. The air smelled of sweat, cedarwood, and something deeper—something sacred.

Inside the barn, Jacob stood quietly, arms folded, watching Dre and Kalu restring the new rope line. Their movements were slower than before, but sure—deliberate. They bore the marks of fire, but carried themselves like men who had walked through it and come out wiser.

Nick sat nearby, wrapped in a blanket, a weathered journal open on his lap. His pen moved slowly now—not for flair or drama, but to remember. To bear witness. Chuka carved something from cedar just beyond him, silent as ever, his blade gliding like water across wood.

Lucas walked over from the well, carrying two mugs of black coffee. He handed one to Jacob with a nod. "I still don't know if this place is a ranch or a revolution," he said with a half-smile.

Jacob took the mug, eyes still fixed on the horizon. "Maybe it's both."

Lucas drank, then said, "We're not famous, you know."

"No," Jacob said, cracking a rare smile. "But we're unforgettable."

The Letters from Home

Before Reading the Letters

After driving for a while, Jacob felt the quiet tension in the air—the kind of silence that presses in on you when you're between two worlds. He pulled over on the side of the road, the truck idling softly as he reached for the envelope he'd found waiting for him earlier. The stamps and the handwriting on the front were unmistakable—this letter was from his family back home in Nigeria.

As Jacob sat in the quiet of his truck, the weight of the envelope felt both heavy and fragile in his hands. It was as though the paper itself carried a multitude of emotions—longing, love, and the weight of his family's expectations. The familiar handwriting on the front, especially that of his father, stirred something deep within him. His father's penmanship was always neat and deliberate, a reflection of the man he was—steady, constant, and full of faith. Jacob found himself hesitating before tearing it open. The thought of hearing from home after so much time away was both a balm and a burden.

Carefully, Jacob opened the envelope and pulled out a letter from his father, Reverend Isaac Obi. He unfolded it slowly, savoring the ritual of it, as though each word was a connection to something deeper than the distance between them. His father's words had always been a source of strength, and in this moment, Jacob yearned for that strength more than ever.

His father's letters had always been filled with wisdom, but they had also been filled with expectation. There was a pressure in those words, a reminder that no matter where he was, his actions were seen through the lens of his family's love and their hopes for his success. Jacob couldn't help but feel the weight of those hopes, like the steady pressure of the cowboy boots he wore, reminding him of where he'd come from, who he was, and where he was expected to go.

As he stared at the envelope, Jacob thought about the distance between him and his family. He had been gone so long, and while the rodeo had brought him fame, the road to redemption still felt uncertain. Was he living up to the person they hoped he'd be? Was he fulfilling his father's expectations? Would he ever truly find his place in the world, balancing the man he was becoming with the son they wanted him to be? These thoughts churned in his mind, but there was also a quiet yearning—a longing to feel tethered to something familiar, to hear the words of his father and mother, even if just for a moment.

He closed his eyes, then opened them again, taking a deep breath before carefully unfolding the letter he had in his hand. He wasn't sure what he was expecting, but he knew that whatever it was, it would be a reminder of home. And perhaps, for the first time in a long while, it might be just what he needed to guide him forward.

Letter from: Reverend Isaac Obi

To: My Beloved Son, Jacob

My Dear Son Jacob,

Greetings to you in the precious name of our Lord and Saviour, Jesus Christ. I trust that this letter finds you well and that you are standing strong in the grace and goodness of our God.

Your mother, your siblings, and I miss you dearly. There is not a day that goes by without someone in the house mentioning your name— either during our evening devotions or just in the small conversations of daily life. Your absence is deeply felt, yet our hearts are full knowing you are walking your journey in the will of God. I promised everyone I would send you their love and warmest greetings, and I must keep my word.

Jacob, I write to you today as a father whose love for his son is deep, constant, and prayerful. I know that life in America may not always be easy. The challenges may sometimes feel overwhelming, and there may be moments you feel alone or misunderstood. But I want you to remember this: you are never alone. God is with you, closer than the breath in your lungs.

You see, life will not always offer smooth paths. Even our Lord Jesus said, "In this world you will have tribulation. But be of good cheer, for I have overcome the world" (John 16:33). God never promised a life without storms, but He promised that the waters will not overflow you, and the fire will not consume you (Isaiah 43:2). And in all things, He remains our refuge and strength.

Be strong in the Lord, Jacob, and in the power of His might (Ephesians 6:10). Let His Word be your compass, and let prayer be your lifeline. I encourage you, my son, to love deeply—love even when it is not returned. Love your friends, love your neighbors, and yes, love even those who may not treat you kindly. For love is the true mark of one who knows God.

Love generously.

Love purposefully.

Love people.

Love your calling.

Love the journey.

Love your life.

Love the little things.

And when you have loved all, love them all over again.

Do not keep records of wrongs. Life is too short to carry bitterness. Show mercy. Be wise. Let your heart be open and your hands ready to serve. Always remember who you are and whose you are.

We are praying for you daily, Jacob. Your mother kneels every morning, calling your name before the Lord. Your siblings look up to you, and I carry you in my heart every time I mount the pulpit.

May the Lord keep you, guide you, and favor you in all your endeavors. You are loved, my son, deeply and unconditionally.

With all my heart,

Your Father,

Reverend Isaac Obi

Jacob paused for a moment after finishing the letter, his heart full. The words from his father were a balm, but there was something else hidden within the folds of the letter—another smaller one, addressed from his mother. Jacob chuckled softly. His mother had always been the one to add a personal touch.

A Note from Your Mother

To my son, Jacob Obi,

Hello Jacob,

How are you, my son? I know your father is writing you a full letter on behalf of all of us, but as your mother, I couldn't let the envelope leave this house without adding my own small note—so you can hear me clearly with your two ears!

Jacob, I've heard that in America, nobody goes hungry. So, I will not worry about food. But what I do think about often is this—don't forget us, O! Don't forget your family, your roots, and the many prayers surrounding you from here in Nigeria. You are far from home, but never far from our hearts.

Now, about this, your cowboy business—ha! I keep hearing you're becoming famous as the "Nigerian Cowboy." Hmm, Jacob! I shake my head and smile. I know your dreams are important to you, and as long as you are following God's plan and staying out of trouble, then ride on! But listen well—if you must be a cowboy, you better be a good one. The kind that makes your mother proud. The kind that shines the light of Christ wherever he goes. Don't let anyone trample on your values. Be bold. Be wise. And above all, be kind.

And now, do you remember that morning when we all dressed up to take you to the airport? Eh-heh! I pulled your ears, remember? And you shouted, "Ouch! Mummy, why now?" I told you, "Now that I have your attention, listen very well." I want to remind you again.

Jacob Obi, your father and I are not getting any younger, O! One day—maybe not today, maybe not tomorrow, but in the future, future, future, I want twelve grandchildren. Yes, twelve! One for each tribe of the Obi family. Let no one come and bamboozle you. Tighten your belt, stand your ground, and don't forget the home that raised you.

Your mother has spoken.

And when a mother speaks, heaven listens.

With love, prayers, and a warm bowl of jollof in my heart for you—

Your Mother,

Mama Jacob (Mrs. Obi)

After Reading the Letters

As Jacob finished the last line of his mother's letter, he leaned back against the truck seat, staring out through the windshield at the open road ahead. His thoughts, heavy with emotion, drifted home to Nigeria. His parents' words wrapped around him like a blanket, comforting him yet reminding him of everything he had left behind.

For a long time, he sat in silence, the letters resting on his lap, the faint sound of the wind outside the truck adding to the stillness inside. His father's wisdom and his mother's humor seemed to reach him across the miles, reminding him of who he was—and of who he was meant to be.

Jacob let out a long, steadying breath. It felt as if the weight of the world had just lifted, even if only for a moment. The letters were like a bridge between his old life and his new one, a gentle pull that reminded him of his roots and the deep love and support waiting for him back home. They weren't just letters—they were reminders of his duty, his identity, and the unyielding love of family.

He folded the letters carefully, putting them back into the envelope. He ran his hand over the worn paper, feeling the edges of the envelope as if it could somehow bring him closer to the family he missed so much. There was a part of him that wanted to jump on a plane and go home immediately. Yet, another part of him knew that his journey here—however difficult—was part of something much bigger than himself.

Jacob started the truck, the engine's low rumble filling the air, and pulled back onto the road. The letters rested beside him, a reminder of the call he had to fulfill, not just for himself, but for the people who had shaped him. They had given him the tools to fight, the courage to stand, and the wisdom to lead.

As the landscape rolled by, Jacob felt the weight of his parents' love steady him. He wasn't sure what the future held, but in that moment, he was certain of one thing: he was not alone. Not now. Not ever.

And as the sun dipped lower in the sky, casting a golden glow across the plains, Jacob spoke aloud to himself, as though he were speaking to his parents back home.

"I will make you proud," he said softly, his voice steady with determination.

One More Ride

Later that night, as the stars emerged above the ridge, Jacob walked into the stable alone.

He saddled his horse—not for battle.

Not for fame.

But for one last ride beneath the heavens.

He rode past the edge of the ranch as the world lay quiet, the moon silvering the trail ahead. The flag—stitched, stained, sacred—rested in his saddlebag like a sealed covenant.

Somewhere far behind him, a child would one day ask, "Did he really exist?"

And someone would answer:

"He did.

And when the world went silent…he rode anyway."

The Final Vow

At the top of the ridge, Jacob stopped and looked out across the sleeping land.

No spotlight. No applause. Just the sky, wide and waiting.

He lowered his head and spoke into the wind—not to be heard, but to be felt.

"I won't ride to be seen.

I'll ride so others know they're not alone.

I'll ride for the voiceless,

the weary,

the brave who never had a banner.

I'll ride until the flame I carry

lights another.

And then another.

And another."

He adjusted his hat. Sat tall in the saddle. The stars blinked above him in reverent silence.

And the Nigerian Cowboy turned toward the horizon—And rode on.

EPILOGUE
THE EMBER NEVER DIES

The Boy and the Stranger

The cantina was nearly empty—just the hush of a desert breeze slipping through wooden shutters and the soft buzz of a forgotten radio whispering a mariachi melody.

A young boy sat cross-legged in a faded booth, his wide eyes locked onto the stranger across from him. The man's boots were worn, dust-caked from long miles. A weathered coat hung from his shoulders, and beneath his wide-brimmed hat, his face was half-hidden in shadow.

The boy clutched a small wooden horse in his hands, smoothed at the edges by worry and wonder.

"Is it true?" he asked, voice hushed. "Did he really fight them? The men in the dark—the ones who stole people away?"

The man didn't answer right away. He stirred his coffee slowly, eyes distant.

"He didn't fight them the way most people do," the man said. "He fought them by not giving in. He fought them by standing when everyone else ran. By riding when the path was lost. By carrying the broken when the world looked away."

The boy leaned in. "But was he real? The Nigerian Cowboy?"

The man smiled, faint and sad. "He was more than real. He was a whisper that turned into a roar. A flame the darkness couldn't swallow."

Outside, a gust of wind rustled the cantina's door, and somewhere in the distance, the faint sound of hooves echoed off canyon walls.

Far Away... In Lagos

In a small village tucked between rusted rooftops and orange soil, a young girl sat beneath a mango tree. The sun dappled the pages of the worn book resting on her lap.

Nigerian Cowboy.

The cover was cracked, but her eyes devoured the words as if they were still burning.

Inside the front flap was a handwritten message:

"To the next one who refuses to be forgotten.

—J.O."

She traced the initials with her finger, lips curling into a knowing smile.

Then she turned the page—and kept reading.

And Elsewhere... The Spark Spreads

In Mumbai, a boy read by lantern light in a quiet alley.

In Seoul, a teenage girl scrolled through Jacob's story beneath her desk.

In Peru, a mountain boy carved a stick into a lasso.

In London, someone whispered, *"He was never caught."*

In corners of classrooms, on ships at sea, in the hearts of those who have been overlooked, the story began to stir something old.

Because when the dust settles, *flames travel.*

Elsewhere… The Riders Stir

At the edge of a forgotten canyon, where the wind always whispered secrets, two cloaked figures dismounted from their horses. The sky above them bled red into indigo, and the earth smelled of ash and ancient memory.

One figure knelt and brushed his fingers across the charred ground. He uncovered a frayed piece of cloth—once white, now scorched at the edges. It fluttered faintly in the wind.

"This is where he disappeared," the first rider murmured.

The second—taller, silent—adjusted his hat, face unreadable.

"But not where he ended."

They stood.

And in the distance, shadows moved. Silent silhouettes. Riders gathering on the ridge.

Not all were pure.

Not all were known.

But all had come. For something they felt deep in their marrow.

"He lit the flame," said the first rider, mounting his horse again. "But the fire is no longer his alone."

"No," the second replied, pulling his scarf over his mouth. "It belongs to the ground now. Sacred ground."

They turned toward the hills, where more waited. Some to redeem. Some to avenge. Some to destroy.

Behind them, the sky darkened.

But ahead…Something was waking.

Not just a legend.

A reckoning.

Teaser for Sequel

Coming Soon: Nigerian Cowboy — Riders of the Sacred Ground

A Novel by Dr. Emmanuel X. Okoro

"When a soul is taken, a storm follows.

When many are taken, the land remembers.

And when one rides to bring them back...

Even heaven listens."

He was never meant to become a leader.

He never asked to carry their hope.

But now, the Nigerian Cowboy rides again—not for victory, but for vengeance, not for applause, but for souls.

The mob has grown darker. The disappearances have become more frequent. And whispers of something unholy rising from the ashes stir the land once more.

As Jacob Obi gathers a new band of riders—each scarred, each chosen—they must journey across sacred soil, unlock a truth hidden in the dust, and face enemies cloaked not in guns…but in prophecy.

Legacy began with the flag.

But the next ride will decide who holds the ground beneath it.

www.ingramcontent.com/pod-product-compliance
Lightning Source LLC
Chambersburg PA
CBHW062102290726
48975CB00001B/74